The Ghost Wagon and Other Great Western Adventures

The Ghost Wagon and Other
Great Western Adventures

Max Brand

*Edited and with a Foreword
and Headnotes by Jon Tuska*

University of Nebraska Press
Lincoln and London

Published by arrangement with the Golden West Literary Agency.
Acknowledgments for previously published material appear on pages 243–44.
© 1996 by Jane Faust Easton and Adriana Faust Bianchi. Introduction and
headnotes © 1996 by Jon Tuska. All rights reserved. Manufactured in the United
States of America. ⊚ The paper in this book meets the minimum requirements of
American National Standard for Information Sciences—Permanence of Paper for
Printed Library Materials, ANSI Z39.48-1984.
Library of Congress Cataloging-in-Publication Data. Brand, Max, 1892–1944. The
ghost wagon, and other great Western adventures / Max Brand : edited and with a
foreword and headnotes by Jon Tuska. p. cm. Contents: The ghost wagon—
Rodeo Ranch—Slip Liddell—A matter of honor. ISBN 0-8032-1265-8 (cl : alk.
paper) 1. West (U.S.)—Social life and customs—Fiction. 2. Adventure stories,
American. 3. Western stories. I. Tuska, Jon.
II. Title. PS3511.A87A6 1996 813'.52—dc20. 95-30631 CIP
The texts of the stories in this work adhere as closely as possible to the original
typescripts by Frederick Faust and are published here for the first time as their author
wrote them.

Contents

Foreword

Max Brand is the best-known pen name of Frederick Faust, creator of Dr. Kildare, Destry, and many other fictional characters popular with readers and viewers worldwide. Faust wrote for a variety of audiences in many genres under numerous pseudonyms. His enormous output, totaling approximately thirty million words or the equivalent of 530 ordinary books, covered nearly every field: crime, fantasy, historical romance, espionage, Westerns, science fiction, adventure, animal stories, love, war, and fashionable society, big business and big medicine. Eighty motion pictures have been based on his work along with many radio and television programs. For good measure he also published four volumes of poetry. Perhaps no other author has reached more people in more different ways.

Born in Seattle in 1892, orphaned early, Faust grew up in the rural San Joaquin Valley of California. At Berkeley he became a student rebel and one-man literary movement, contributing prodigiously to all campus publications. Denied a degree because of unconventional conduct, he embarked on a series of adventures culminating in New York City where, after a period of near starvation, he received simultaneous recognition as a serious poet and successful popular-prose writer. Later, he traveled widely, making his home in New York, then in Florence, and finally in Los Angeles.

Once the United States entered the Second World War, Faust abandoned his lucrative writing career and his work as a screenwriter to serve as a war correspondent with the infantry in Italy, despite his fifty-one years and a bad heart. He was killed during a night attack on a hilltop village held by the German army. New books based on magazine serials or unpublished manuscripts or restored versions continue to appear so that, alive or dead, he has averaged a new book every four months for seventy-five years. In the United States alone nine publishers now issue his work. Beyond this, some work by him is newly reprinted every week of every year in one or another format somewhere in the world. Yet, only recently have the full dimensions of this extraordinarily versatile and prolific writer come to be recognized and his stature as a protean literary figure in the 20th Century acknowledged. His popularity continues to grow throughout the world.

The stories I have collected for this book do not appear in chronological order. The organizing principle, instead, is the expansiveness of Faust's imagination when it comes to the Western story as a form of literary art and the fecundity with which he would vary his themes, examining problems and dilemmas of the human condition from numerous disparate viewpoints. In another sense these stories fit together as episodes in a great saga, very much after the fashion of Homer in the Books of *Odyssey*. No matter how much editors or his agent might tell Faust that he was writing stories that were too character-driven, he could never really change the way he wrote. In order to write, he was fond of saying, I must be able to dream. As early as 1921, writing as George Owen Baxter, Faust had commented about Free Range Lanning in "Iron Dust" that Lanning "had at least picked up that dangerous equipment of fiction which enables a man to dodge reality and live in his dreams."

Brave words! Yet, beyond this, and maybe precisely because of the truth in them, much that happens in a Western story by Frederick Faust depends upon an interplay between dream and reality. There will come a time, probably well into the next century, when a reëvaluation will become necessary of those who contributed most to the eternal relevance of the Western story in this century. In this reëvaluation unquestionably Zane Grey and Frederick Faust will be elevated while popular icons of this century such as Owen Wister, judged solely in terms of their actual artistic contributions to the wealth and treasure of world literature, may find their reputations diminished. In such a reëvaluation Faust, in common with Jack London, may be seen as a purveyor of visceral fiction of great emotional power and profound impact that does not recede with time.

The stories collected here, early or late, have all been restored where necessary by comparing the author's manuscripts with the published versions. They are set in that land Faust called the mountain desert, a place for him as timeless and magical as the plains of Troy in the hexameters of his beloved Homer and as vivid as the worlds Shakespeare's vibrant imagery projected outward from the bare stages of the Globe. Faust was not so much mapping a geographical region in his Western stories as he was exploring the dark and bright corridors of the human soul—that expanse which is without measure, as Heraclitus said. For Faust, as for his reader, this experience is much as he described it in 1926 for Oliver Tay in what became *The Border Bandit* (Harper, 1947): " . . . He was seeing himself for the very first time; and, just as his eye could wander through the unfathomed leagues of the stars which were strewn across the universe at night, so he could turn his glance inward and probe the vastness of new-found self. All new!" In these explorations of the inner world Faust's fiction can be seen to embody a basic principle of the Western story, that quality which makes the Western story so vitally rewarding in world literature, the experience of personal renewal, an affirmation of hope through courage, the potential that exists in each human being for redemption.

The Ghost Wagon and Other Great Western Adventures

The Ghost Wagon

"The Ghost Wagon" under the title "The Cure of Silver Cañon" by John Frederick was the second short novel by Frederick Faust to appear in *Western Story Magazine* (1/15/21). The same year it was published Tom Mix would appear on screen for the second time playing Dan Barry, a truly extraordinary Faust protagonist (although certainly not the way Tom Mix portrayed him). Dan Barry was first introduced in "The Untamed," a six-part serial by Max Brand in *All-Story Weekly* (12/7/18–1/11/19).

I believe Bret Harte's great legacy to the Western story is the "Bret Harte country" of the imagination, a world without boundaries in which the lure of gold will be recognized as a metaphor for an entire nation in search of a way of life that would prove somehow very different from all that had gone before it and in which the struggle for social justice and civil rights is combined uniquely with Harte's totally characteristic plea that the most significant achievement humanity can ever hope to attain is to show more mercy toward human beings. In very much the same way the mountain desert in Faust's Western fiction is a country of the imagination where no man is ever a hero and no man is ever a villain, but a mixture of them both. This certainly proves the case in this story in which both Lew Carney and Jack Doyle love Mary Hamilton and where we, as readers, can never know with certitude for whose soul it is that Mary Hamilton weeps or for whom is that look in her eyes Lew Carney shall never forget even to the day of his death.

1 "Eight Men of Mystery"

This is a story of how Lew Carney made friends with the law. It must not be assumed that Lew was an outcast; neither that he was an underhanded violator of constituted authority. As a matter of fact there was one law which Lew always held in the highest esteem. He never varied from the prescriptions of that law; he never, as far as possible, allowed anyone near him to violate that law. Unfortunately that law was the will of Lew Carney.

He was born with sandy hair which reared up at off angles all over his head; his eyes were a bright blue as pale as fire. Since the beginning of time there has never been a man, with sandy hair and those pale, bright eyes, who has not trodden on the toes of the powers that be. Carney was that type and more than that type. Not that he had a taint of malice in his five-feet-ten of wire-strung muscle; not that he loved trouble; but he was so constituted that what he liked, he coveted with a passion for possession; and what he disliked, he hated with consummate loathing. There was no intermediate state. Consider a man of these parts, equipped in addition with an eye that never was clouded by the most furious of his passions and a hand which never shook in a crisis, and it is easy to understand why Lew Carney was regarded by the pillars of society with suspicion.

In a community where men shoulder one another in crowds, his fiery soul would have started a conflagration before he got well into his teens; but by the grace of the Lord, Lew Carney was placed in the mountain desert, in a region where even the buzzard strains its eyes looking from one town to the next, and where the wary stranger travels like a ship at sea, by compass. Here Lew Carney had plenty of room to circulate without growing heated by friction to the danger point. Even with these advantages, the spark of excitement had snapped into his eyes a good many times. He might have become a refugee long before, had it not chanced that the men whom he crossed were not themselves wholly desirable citizens. Yet the time was sure to come when, hating work and loving action, he would find his hands full. Some day a death would be laid to his door, and then—the end.

He was the gayest rider between the Sierras and the Rockies and one of the most reckless. There was no desert which he would not dare; there was no privation which he had not endured to reach the ends of his own pleasure; but not the most intimate of Lew's best friends could name a single pang which he had undergone for the sake of honest labor. But for that matter, he did not have to work. With a face for poker and hands for the same game, he never lacked the sources of supply.

Lew was about to extinguish his camp fire on this strange night in Silver Cañon. He had finished his cooking and eaten his meal hurriedly and without pleasure, for this was a dry camp. The fire had dwindled to a few black embers and one central heart of red which tossed up a tongue of yellow flame intermittently. At each flash there was illumined only one feature. First, a narrow, fleshless chin. Who is it that speaks of the fighting jaw of the bull terrier? Then a thin-lipped mouth, with the lean cheeks and the deep-set, glowing eyes. And lastly the wild hair, thrusting up askew. It made him look, even on this hushed night, as though a wind were blowing in his face. On the whole it was a rather handsome face, but men would be apt to appreciate its qualities more than women. Lew scooped up a handful of sand and swept it across the fire. The night settled around him.

But the night had its own illumination. The moon, which had been struggling, as a sickly circle through the ground haze, now moved higher and took on its own proper color, an indescribable crystal white; and it was easy to understand why this valley had the singular name of Silver Cañon. In the day it was a burning gulch not more than five miles wide, a hundred miles long, banked in with low, steep-sided mountains in unbroken walls. Under the sun it was pale, sand-yellow, both mountains and valley floor, but the moon changed it, gilded it, and made it a miracle of silver.

The night was coming on crisp and cold, for the elevation was great. But in spite of his long ride Carney postponed his sleep. He wrapped himself in his blankets and sat up to see. Not much for anyone to see except a poet, for both earth and sky were a pale, bright silver, and the moon was the only living thing in heaven or on earth. His horse, a wise old gelding with an ugly head and muscles of leather, seemed to feel the silence. For he came from his wretched hunt after dead grass and stood behind the master. But the master paid no attention. He was squinting into nothingness and seeing. He was harkening to silence and hearing. A sound which the ear of a wolf could hardly catch came to him; he knew that there were rabbits. He listened again, a wavering pulse of noise; far off was a coyote. And yet both those sounds combined did not make up the volume of a hushed whisper. They were unheard rhythms which are felt.

But what Lew Carney saw no man can say, no man who has not been stung with the fever of the desert. Perhaps he guessed at the stars behind the moon haze. Perhaps he thought of the buzzards far off, all-seeing, all-knowing, the dreadful prophets of the mountain desert. But whatever it was that the mind of Lew Carney perceived, his face under the moon was the face of a man who sees God. He had come from the gaming tables of Bogle Camp; tomorrow night he would be at the gaming tables in Cayuse; but here was an interval of silence between, and he gave himself to it as devoutly as he would give himself again to chuck-a-luck or poker.

Some moments went by. The horse stirred and went away, switching his tail. Yet Carney did not move. He was like an Indian in a trance. He was opening himself to that deadly hush with a pleasure more thrilling than cards and red-eye combined. Time at length entirely ceased for him. It might have been five minutes later; it might have been midnight; but he seemed to have drifted on a river into the heart of a new emotion.

And now he heard it for the first time.

Into the unutterable silence of the mountains a pulse of new sound had grown; he was suddenly aware that he had been hearing it ever since he first made camp, but not until it grew into an unmistakable thing did he fully awaken to it. He had not heard it because he did not expect it. He knew the mountain desert as a student knows a book; as a monk knows his cell; as a child knows its mother. It was the one thing on earth which he truly feared, and it was probably the only thing on earth which he really loved. The moment he made out the new thing, he stiffened under his blankets and canted his head down. The next instant he lay prone to catch the ground noise. And after lying there a moment, he started up and walked back and forth across a diameter of a hundred yards.

When he had finished his walk, he was plainly and deeply excited. He stood with his teeth clenched and his eyes working uneasily through the moon haze and piercing down the valley in the direction of Bogle Camp, far away. He even touched the handles of his gun and he found a friendly reassurance in their familiar grip. He went restlessly to the gelding and cursed him in a murmur. The horse pricked his ears at the well-known words.

But here was a strange thing in itself: Lew Carney lowering his voice because of some strange emotion.

The sound of his own voice seeming to trouble him, he started away from the horse and walked again in the hope of catching a different angle of the sound. He heard nothing new; it was always the same.

Now the sound was unmistakable; unquestionably it approached him. And to understand how the sound could approach for so long a time without the cause coming into view, it must be remembered that the air of the mountains at that altitude is very rare, and sound travels a long distance without appreciable diminution.

In itself the noise was far from dreadful. Yet the lone rider eventually retired to his blankets, wrapped himself in them securely, for fear that the chill of the night should numb his fighting muscles, and rested his revolver on his knee for action. He brushed his hand across his forehead, and the tips of his fingers came away wet. Lew Carney was in a cold perspiration of fear! And that was a fact which few men in the mountain desert would have believed.

He sat with his eyes glued through the moon haze down the valley, and his head canted to listen more intently. Once more it stopped; once more it began, a low, chuckling sound with a metallic rattling mixed in. And for a time it rumbled softly on toward him, and then again the sound was snuffed out as though it had turned a corner.

That was the gruesome part of it, the pauses in that noise. The continued sounds which one hears in a lonely house by night are unheeded; but the sounds which are varied by stealthy pauses chill the blood. That is the footstep approaching, pausing, listening, stealing on again.

The strange sound stole toward the waiting man, paused, and stole on again. But there are motives for stealth in a house. What motive was there in the open desert?

It was the very strangeness of it that sent the shudder through Lew. And presently he could feel the terror of that presence which was coming slowly down the valley. It went before, like the eye of a snake, and fascinated life into movelessness. Before he saw the thing that made the sound; while the murmur itself was but an undistinguished whisper; before all the revelations of the future, Lew Carney knew that the thing was evil. Just as he had heard the voices of certain men and hated them before he even saw their faces.

He was not a superstitious fellow. Far from it. His life had made him a canny, practical sort in the affairs of men; but it had also given him a searching alertness. He could smile while he faced a known danger; but an unknown thing unnerved him. Given an equal start, a third-rate gunfighter could have beaten Lew Carney to the draw at this moment and shot him full of holes.

Afterward he was to remember his nervous state and attribute much of what he saw and heard to the condition of his mind. In reality he was not in a state when delusions possess a man, but in a period of superpenetration.

In the meantime the sound approached. It grew from a murmur to a clear rumbling. It continued. It loomed on the ear of Carney as a large object looms on the eye. It possessed and overwhelmed him like a mountain thrust toward him from its base.

But for all his awareness the thing came upon him suddenly. Looking down the valley he saw, above a faint rise of ground, the black outline of a topped wagon between him and the moonlight horizon. He drew a great sobbing breath and then began to laugh with hysterical relief.

A wagon! He stood up to watch its coming. It was rather strange that a freighter should travel by night, however, but in those gold-rush days far stranger things had come within his ken.

The big wagon rocked fully into view; the chuckling was the play of the tall wheels on the hubs; the rattling was the stir of chains. Carney cursed and was suddenly aware of the blood running in old courses and a kindly warmth. But his relief was cut short. The wagon stopped in the very moment of coming over the rise.

Then he remembered the pauses in that sound before. What did it mean, these many stops? To breathe the horses! No horses that ever lived, no matter how exhausted, needed as many rests as this. In fact it would make their labor all the greater to have to start the load after they had drawn it a few steps. Not only that, but by the way the wagon rocked, even over the comparatively smooth sand of the desert, Carney felt assured that the wagon carried only a skeleton load. If it were heavily burdened, it would crunch its wheels deeply into the sand and come smoothly.

But the wagon started on again, not with a lurch, such as that of horses striking the collar and thrusting the load into sudden motion, but slowly, gradually, with pain, as though the motive power of this vehicle were exerting the pressure gradually and slowly increasing the momentum. It was close enough for him to note the pace, and he observed that the wagon crept forward by inches. Give a slow draft horse two tons of burden and he would go faster than that. What on earth was drawing the wagon through this moon haze in Silver Cañon?

If the distant mystery had troubled Lew Carney, the strange thing under his eyes was far more imposing. He sat down again as though he wished to shrink out of view, and once more he had his heavy gun resting its muzzle on his knee. The wagon had stopped again.

And now he saw something that thrust the blood back into his heart and made his head swim. He refused to admit it, He refused to see it. He denied his own senses and sat with his eyes closed tightly. It was a childish thing to do, and perhaps the long expectancy of that waiting had unnerved the man a little.

But there he sat with his eyes stubbornly shut, while the chuckling of the wagon began again, continued, drew near, and finally stopped close to him.

Then at last he looked, and the thing which he guessed before was now an indubitable fact. Plainly silhouetted by the brilliant moon, he saw the tall wagon drawn by eight men, working in teams of two, like horses. And behind the wagon was a pair of heavy horses pulling nothing at all!

No, they were idly tethered to the rear of the vehicle. Weak horses, exhausted by work! No, the moon glinted on the well-rounded sides, and when they stepped the sand quivered under their weight. Moreover they threw their feet as they walked, a sure sign by which the draft horse can always be distinguished. He plants his feet with abandon. He cares not what he strikes as long as he can drive his iron-shod toes down to firm ground and, secure of his purchase, send his vast weight into the collar. Such was the step of these horses, and when the wagon stopped they surged forward until their breasts struck the rear of the schooner. Not the manner of tired horses, which halt the instant the tension on the halter is released! Not the manner of balky horses, either, this eagerness on the rope!

But there before the eyes of Lew Carney stood the impossible. Eight forms. Eight black silhouettes drooping with weariness before the wagon; and eight deformed shadows on the white sand at their feet; and two ponderous draft horses tethered behind.

It is not the very strange which shocks us. We are readily acclimated to the marvelous. But the small variations from the commonplace are what make us incredulous. How the world laughed when it was said that ships would one day travel without sails; that the human voice would carry three thousand miles! Yet those things could be understood. And later on there was little interest when men actually flew. The world was acclimated to the strange. But an unusual handwriting, a queer mark on the wall, a voice-like sound in the wind will startle and shock the most hard-headed. If that wagon had been seen by Lew Carney flying through the air, he probably would have yawned and gone to sleep. But he saw it on the firm ground drawn by eight men, and his heart quaked.

Not a sound had been spoken when they halted. And now they stood without a sound.

Yet Lew's gelding stood plainly in view, and he himself was not fifty feet away. To be sure they stood in their ranks without any head turning, yet beyond a shadow of a doubt they had seen him; they must see him. Still they did not speak.

In the mountain desert when men pass in the road, they pause and exchange greetings. It is not necessary that they be friends or even acquaintances. It is not necessary that they be reputable or respectable. It is not necessary that they have white skins. It suffices that a human being sees a human being in the wilderness and he rejoices in the sight. The sound of another man's voice can be a treasure beyond the price of gold!

But here stood eight men, weary, plainly in need of help, plainly scourged forward by some dreadful necessity, yet they did not send a single hail toward Lew.

No man among them spoke. The silence became terrible. If only one of them would roll a cigarette. At that moment the smell of burning tobacco would have taken a vast load off the shoulders of Lew Carney.

But the eight stirred neither hand nor foot. And each man stood as he had halted, his hands behind him, grasping the long chain.

II "Tossed to the Buzzards"

How long they stood there Lew Carney could not guess. He only knew that a pulse began to thunder in his temple and his ears were filling with a roaring sound. This thing could not be, and yet there it was before his eyes.

It flashed into his mind that this might be some sort of foolish practical jest. Some wild prank of the cattlemen. But a single glance at the figures of the eight robbed him of this last remaining clue. Every line and angle of their bent heads and sagging bodies told of men taxed to the limit of endurance. The pride which keeps chins up was gone; the nerve force which allows a last few springy efforts of muscles was destroyed. Without a spoken signal. Like dumb brute beasts, the eight leaned softly forward, let the weight of their bodies come gently on the chain and remained slanting forward until the wagon stirred, the wheels turned, and the big vehicle started on. The sand was whispering as it curled around the broad rims of the wheels; that was the only sound in Silver Cañon.

Stupefied, Carney watched it go without relief. Another man might have been glad to have the mystery pass on but, after the first chill of fear, Lew began to hunger to get under the surface of this freak. Yet he did not move until there was a sudden darkening of the moonlight. Then he looked up.

As he did so he saw that the moon was obscured by a gray tinge, and he felt a sharp gust of wind in his face. Up the cañon toward Cayuse the air was thick with a dirty mist, and he knew that it was the coming of a sand storm.

That dismal reality brushed the thought of the wagon from his mind for a moment. He found a bit of shrubbery a hundred yards away and entrenched himself behind it to wait until the storm should pass over, and he might snatch some sleep. The horse, warned by these preparations, came close.

They were hardly finished before the blast of the wind had a million edges of flying sand grains. And a moment later the sand storm was raging well over them. Lew Carney, comfortable in his shelter except for the grit that forced itself down his neck, thought of the eight men and the wagon. Even in the storm he knew that they had not stopped, but were trudging wearily on. And if the wagon were halted and dragged back by the weight of the wind, still they would lean against the chain and struggle blindly. The imaginary picture of them became more vivid than the picture as they had stood in the moonlight.

It was not a really heavy blow. In two hours it was over; but it left the air dim, and when Lew peered up the valley the wagon was out of sight. For a time he banished the thought of it, wrapped himself again in the blankets, and was instantly asleep.

The first brightness of morning wakened him, and tumbling automatically out of his blankets, he set about the preparation of breakfast with a mind numbed by sleep. Not until the first swallow of scalding coffee had passed his lips did he remember the wagon, and then he started up and looked again at the valley. He rubbed his eyes, but it was nowhere in sight.

Ordinarily it would not seem strange that a night's travel, even at the slowest pace, should take a wagon out of sight, but Silver Cañon was by no means ordinary. Through the thin, clear air the eye could look from the place where Lew stood clear up the valley to the cleft between the two mountains thirty miles away, where Cayuse stood. There were no depressions to conceal any object of size, but the floor of the valley tilted gradually and smoothly up. To understand the clearness of that mountain air and the level nature of the valley, it may be remarked that men working mines high up of the sides of the mountains toward the base of Silver Cañon could see the camp fires of freighters on four successive nights, dwindling into stars on the fourth night, but plainly discernible through the four days of the journey. And a band of wild horses could be watched every moment of a fifty-mile run to the water holes, easily traced by the cloud of dust.

Bearing these things in mind, it can be understood why Lew Carney gasped as he stared up the valley and saw—nothing!

The big schooner had vanished into thin air or else it had reached Cayuse. This thought comforted him, but after a moment of thought he shook his head again. They could not have covered the thirty miles. Two hours' travel had been impossible against the storm. Deducting that time, there remained well under three hours. Certainly, the eight men pulling the wagon could not have covered a quarter of that distance in three hours or double three hours. And even if they had harnessed in the two big horses, the thing was still impossible. An hour of sharp trotting would have broken down those lumbering hulks of animals. And as for keeping up a rate of ten miles an hour for three hours with a lumbering wagon behind them and through soft sand, why it was something that a team of blooded horses, drawing a light buckboard, could hardly have accomplished.

The rest of Lew's breakfast was tossed away untasted. He packed his tins with a rattle and tumbled into the saddle, and presently the gelding was cantering softly toward Cayuse.

As he expected, the storm had blotted out all traces. There was not a sign of wheels; the sand, perfectly smooth except for long wind riffles, scrawled awkwardly here and there. Little hummocks had been tossed up around shrubs, but otherwise all was plainly in view, and the phantom wagon was nowhere on the horizon.

Of course, one possibility remained. They might have turned out of the main course of the valley and gone to one side, ignorant of the fact that those mountains were inaccessible to wagons. It required a horse with tricky feet, unhampered with any load, to climb those sliding, steep, sand surfaces. For the draft animals to attempt it with a wagon behind them was ludicrous. Yet he kept sweeping the hills on either side for some trace of the schooner, and always there was nothing.

As has been said, Lew was by no means superstitious, and now he had broad daylight to help steady his nerves and sharpen his faculties; yet in spite of broad daylight he began to feel once more the eerie thrill of the unearthly, and he felt that even if he had stepped out to examine the tracks of the wagon as soon as it passed him, he would have found nothing.

At this he smiled to himself and shook his head. A ghost wagon did not make eight men sweat and strain to pull it, and a ghost wagon did not rumble as it traveled and make a whispering of the sand. No, a solid wagon and eight solid human beings, and two heavy horses, somewhere between his last dry camp and Cayuse, had vanished utterly and were gone!

Searching the walls of the valley on either side, he almost neglected the floor of the cañon, and it was only the bright flash of metal that made him halt the gelding and look to his right and behind. He swung the mustang about and reached the spot in half a dozen jumps; a man lay with his arms thrown out crosswise, and a revolver was in his hand.

At first glance Carney thought that the fellow lived, but it was only the coloring effect of the morning sun and the lifting of his long hair in the wind.

He was quite dead. He had been dead for hours and hours it seemed. And here was another mystery added to the disappearance of the wagon. How did this body come here? What vehicle had carried the man here after he was wounded?

For, tearing away the bandages around his breast, Carney saw that he had been literally shot to pieces. The tight-drawn bandages, shutting off the flow of blood, perhaps, had bruised the flesh until it was a dark purple around the black shot holes.

One thing was certain: after those wounds the man had been incapable of travel on horseback. He must have been carried in a wagon. But certainly only one wagon had gone that way before the sand storm, and after the sand storm any vehicle would have left traces.

After all then, there had been some freight in the ghost wagon, and this man, perhaps dead at the time, had been part or all of the burden that passed under Lew's eyes.

But why had the wagon carried a dead body? And if it carried a dead body at all, why was it not taken on to the destination of the wagon itself? Certainly the burden of one man's weight was not enough to make any difference.

Two startling facts confronted him: first, here was a dead man; second, the dead man had been brought this far by the ghost wagon.

Here, also, was the chance of learning not only the identity of the dead man, but of the man who had killed him. Carney searched the pockets and brought out a wallet which contained half a dozen tiny nuggets of pure gold, nearly a hundred dollars in paper money, and a pencil stub. Evidence enough that robbery had not been the motive in this killing.

Besides the wallet, the pockets produced a strong knife, two boxes of matches, a blue handkerchief, a straight pipe, and a sack of tobacco.

There was no scrap of paper bearing a name; there was nothing distinctive about the clothes whereby the man could be identified. He was dressed in a pair of overalls badly frayed at the knees, with a smear of grease and an old stain of red paint, both on the right leg; also, he had on a battered felt hat and a blue shirt several sizes too large for him. In appearance he was simply a middle-aged man of average height and weight, with iron-gray hair, and hands broadened and callused by years of heavy labor. His face was singularly open and pleasant even in death, but it had no striking feature, no scar, no mole.

Carney stripped him to the waist and turned the body to examine the wounds, and then he straightened with a black look. It was not a man-to-man killing; it was murder, for the vital bullet which eventually robbed the man of life had struck him in the center of the back. By the small size of the wound he knew that the bullet had entered here, just as he could tell by the gaping orifice on the breast where the bullet had come out. Yet the man had not given up without a struggle. He had turned and fought his murderer, for there were other scars on the front. In five distinct places he had been struck, and it was only wonderful that he had not been instantly killed.

Had they carried him as far as this and, then discovering that he was indeed dead, flung his body brutally from the wagon for the buzzards to find? No, at the very latest he must have died within two hours of the reception of these wounds. He must have been dead long before he passed the dry camp of Lew Carney. But if they had carried him as far as this, what freak of folly made them throw the dead body, the brutal evidence of crime, in a place where the freighters were sure to find him inside of twelve hours?

It was reasoning in a circle. One thing at least was sure. The murderer and the men of the ghost wagon were confident that their traces could not be followed.

As for the body itself, there was nothing he could do. The freighters would take the man up and carry him to Cayuse where he would receive a decent burial. In the meantime, unless that wagon were indeed a ghost, it must have come by means however mysterious to Cayuse also. And toward that town Carney hurried on.

*

III "Carney's Decision"

The mountains went up on either side of Cayuse, but from each side it was easy of access. It gave out upon Silver Cañon in one direction, and on the other side there was a rambling cattle country. As for the mountains, they were better than either a natural highway or a range, for there was gold in them. Five weeks before it had been found; the rumor had gone roaring abroad on the mountain desert; and now, in lieu of echoes, a wild life was rushing back upon Cayuse.

Its population had been more than doubled, but by far the greater number of the newcomers paused only to outfit and lay in supplies before they pushed on to the gold front. The majority found nothing, but the few who succeeded were sufficient to send a steady stream of the yellow metal trickling back toward civilization. Of that stream a liberal portion never went farther than Cayuse before it changed hands. For one thing supplies were furnished here at doubled and redoubled prices; for another a crew of legal and illegal robbers came to this crossing of the ways, to hold up the miners.

In perfect justice it must be admitted that Lew Carney belonged to the robbers, though he was of the first class rather than the second. His sphere was the game table, and there he worked honestly enough, matching his wits against the wits of all comers, and trying his luck against the best and the worst. It meant a precarious source of livelihood, but in gambling a cold face and a keen eye will be served, and Lew Carney was able to win without cheating.

His first step after he arrived was to look over old places and new. He found that the main street of Cayuse was little changed. There were more people in the street, but the buildings had not been altered. Away from this established center, however, there was a growing crowd of tents that poured up a clamor of voices. Everywhere were the signs of the new prosperity. There stood half a dozen men pitching broad golden coins at a mark and accepting winnings and losses without a murmur. Here was a peddler with his pack between his feet, nearly empty. Everything from shoestrings to pocket mirrors, and hardly a man that passed but stopped to buy, for Cayuse had the buying fever.

Carney left the peddler to enter Bud Lockhart's place. It had been the main gaming hall and bar in the old days and, by attaching a lean-to at the rear of his house, Bud had expanded with the expanding times, and he was still the chief amusement center of Cayuse. In token of his new prosperity he no longer worked behind the counter. Two employees served the thirsty line; and in the room behind, stretching out into the lean-to, were the gaming tables.

As he entered, he saw a roulette wheel flash and wink at him, and then the subdued exclamations of the crowd as they won or lost. For the wheel fascinates a group of chance takers at the same time that it excites them. The eye of Carney shone. He knew well enough that where the wheel is patronized by a group, there is money to spend on every game. One more glance around the room was sufficient to assure him. There was not a vacant table, and there was not a table where the chips were not stacked high. Bud Lockhart came through the crowd straight toward Carney. He was a large man with a tanned face, which in its generous proportions matched his big body. What it lacked in height above the eyes it made up in the shape of a great, fleshy chin.

"Hey, Lew," called the big man, plowing his way among the others and leaving a disarranged but good-natured wake behind him. Carney turned and waited. "I need you, boy," said Bud Lockhart as he shook hands. "You've got to break your rule and work for me. How much?"

The gambler hesitated. "Oh, fifty a day," he murmured.

"Take you at that price," said the proprietor and Lew gasped.

"Is it coming in as fast as that?" he queried.

"Faster. Fast enough to make your head swim. The suckers are running in all day with each hand full of gold and they won't let me alone till they've dumped it into my pockets. I've got a lot of boys working for me but most of the lot are shady. They're double-crossing me and pocketing two-thirds of what they make. I need you here to take a table and watch the boys next to you."

"Fifty is pretty fat," admitted Carney, "but I think I'll do a little gold digging myself."

Bud gasped. "Say, son," he murmured, "have they stuck you up with one of their yarns? Are you going in with some greenhorn and collect some calluses on your hands?"

"No, I'm going to do my digging right in your place, Bud. You dig the coin out of the pockets of the other boys; I'll sit in a few of your games and see if I can't dig some of the same coin out again."

"Nothing in that," protested Bud Lockhart anxiously. "Besides you couldn't play a hand with these boys I have. I've imported 'em and they have the goods. Slick crowd, Lew. You've got a good face for the cards but these fellows read their minds!"

"I see," nodded Carney. "But there's ways of discouraging the shifty ones. Oh, they're raw about it, Bud. I saw that fat fellow who's dealing over there palm a card so slow I thought he was tryin' to amuse the crowd until I saw him take the pot. I think I could clean out that guy, Bud."

"Not when he's going good. You could never see him work when he tries."

"He wouldn't try the crooked stuff with me," remarked Carney. "Not twice, unless he packs along two lives."

"Easy," cautioned Lockhart. "None of that, Lew. I paid too much for my furniture to have you spoil it for me. Look here, you're grouchy today. Come behind the counter and have a drink of my private stock."

"This is my dry day. But what's the news? Who's been sliding into town? You keep track of 'em?"

"I'll tell a man I do! Got two boys out, workin' 'em as fast as they blow, and steerin' 'em down to my joy shop. Not a bad idea, eh?"

"What's come in today?"

The proprietor pulled out a little notebook and turned the pages with a fat forefinger.

"Up from Eastlake there was a gent called Benedict and another called Wayne; cowmen loaded with coin. They're unloading it right now. See that table in the corner? Then there was Hoe. . . ."

"I don't know the lay of the land east of Cayuse," protested Lew Carney. "No friends of mine in that direction."

"Out of the mountains," began Bud, consulting his notebook again. "There was. . . ."

"Cut out the mountains, too. What came out of Silver Cañon?"

"What always comes out of it? Sand." Bud's fat eyes became little slits of light as he grinned at his own jest.

He added: "Looking for somebody?"

"Not particular. Heard somebody down the street talk about a wagon that came off the desert with eight or nine men. What was that?" To conceal his agitation he began to roll a cigarette.

"One wagon?" asked Bud Lockhart.

"Yep."

"What'n thunder would eight men be doin' in one wagon?"

"I dunno."

Carney took out a match, scratched it and then lighted his cigarette hastily. Every nerve in his body was on edge, and he feared lest the trembling of his hand should be noticed.

"Eight men in one wagon," chuckled Bud. "Somebody's been kiddin' you, Lew. If this crowd has started kiddin' Lew Carney for amusement, it's got more nerve than I laid to it. But why's the wagon stuff eatin' on you, Lew?"

"Not a bit," said Carney. "Doesn't mean a thing but, when I heard that the wagon came off Silver Cañon, I thought it might be from my own country, might find a pal in the crowd."

"I'm learning something every day," Bud replied with a grin. "Makes me feel young again. Since when have you started in having pals?"

"Why shouldn't I have 'em?" retorted Carney sharply, for he felt that the conversation was not only unproductive but that he had aroused the suspicion of the big man.

"Because they don't last long enough," replied the other, with perfect good nature. "You wear 'em out too fast. There was young Kemple. You hooked up with him for a partner, and he comes back with a lump on his jaw and a twisted nose. Seems he disagreed with you about the road you two was to take. Then there was Billy Turner that was going to be your partner at poker. Two days later you shot Billy through the hip."

"He tried a bum deal on me, on his pal," said Carney grimly.

"I know. I told you before that Billy was no good. But there was Jud Hampton. Nobody had nothin' ag'in Jud. Fine fellow. Straight, square dealin'. You fell out with Jud and busted his. . . ."

"Lockhart," snapped the smaller man, "you've got a fool way of talkin' sometimes."

"And right now is one of 'em, eh?"

"I've given you the figures," said Carney. "You can add 'em up any way you want to,"

It was impossible to disturb the calm of big Bud. "So you're the gent who is lookin' for some pals?" he chuckled. "Say, Lew, are you pickin' trouble with me? Hunt it up some place else. And the next time you start pumpin' me, take lessons first. You do a pretty rough job of comin' to the wind of me."

A lean hand caught the arm of Bud as he turned away; lean fingers cut into his fat, soft flesh; and he found himself looking down into a face at once fierce and wistful. "Bud, you know something?"

"Not a thing, son, but it's a ten to one bet that you want to know something that's got a wagon and eight men in it. What's the good word?"

The knowledge that he had bungled his first bit of detective work so hopelessly made Lew Carney flush. "I've talked like a fool," he said. "And I'm sorry I've stepped on your toes, Bud."

"That's a pile for you to say," replied Bud. "And half of it was enough. Now what can I do for you?"

"The wagon. . . ."

"Forget the wagon! I tell you, the only thing that's come in out of Silver Cañon is you. Hasn't my spotter been on the job? Why he give me a report on you yourself, the minute you blew in sight. What d'you think he said? 'Gent with windy lookin' hair. Rides slantin'. Kind of careless. Good hoss. Looks like he had a pile of coin and didn't care how he got rid of it.' It sure warmed me up to hear that kind of a description, and then in you come. 'There he is now,' says the spotter. 'Like his looks?' 'Sure,' says I. 'I like his looks so much you're fired.' That's what I said to him. You should've seen his face!"

The fat man burst into generous laughter at his own joke.

The voice of Lew Carney cut his mirth short. "I tell you, Bud, you're wrong. Either you're wrong or I'm crazy!"

"Don't be sayin' hard things about yourself," Lockhart retorted.

"It's gospel, is it?"

"It sure is."

"Then keep what I've said to yourself."

"Not a word out of me, Lew. Now let's get back to business. What you need to get this funny idea out of your head is a game. . . ."

But the head of Lew Carney was whirling. Had he been mad? Had it been an illusion, that vision of the wagon and eight men? He remembered how tightly his nerves had been strung. A terrible fear for his own sanity began to haunt him.

"Blow the game," said Carney. "I'm goin' to get drunk!"

"I thought you said this was your dry. . . ."

But the younger man had already whirled and was gone among the crowd. He went blindly into the thickest portion, and where men stood before him he shouldered them brutally out of the way. He left behind him a wake of black looks and clenched hands.

Bud Lockhart waited to see no more. He hurried to call one of his bartenders to one side.

"You see that gent with the sandy hair?" asked Bud.

"Yep."

"Know him?"

"Nope."

"He's Lew Carney and he's startin' to get drunk. I've known him a long time, and it's the first time I've ever heard of him goin' after the booze hard. Take him aside and give him some of my private stock. Keep a close eye on him, you hear? Pass the word around to all the boys. There's a few that knows him and they'll hunt cover if he starts goin'. But some of the greenhorns may get sore and try a hand with him. You're kind of new to these parts yourself, son. But take it from me straight that Lew Carney has a nervous hand and a straight eye. He starts quick and he shoots straight. Let him down as easy as you can. Put some tea in his whiskey if he's goin' too fast. And see that nobody touches him for his roll. And if he flops, have somebody put him to bed."

IV "Oil upon the Troubled Waters"

All of these things having been accomplished in the order named, with the single exception that the "roll" of Carney was untouched, the gambler awakened the next day with a confused memory and a vague sense that he had been the center of much action. But he had neither a hot throat nor a heavy head. In fact after the long nerve strain which preceded the drunk, the whiskey had served as a sort of counter poison. The brain of Lew Carney, when he wakened, was perfectly clear for the present. It was only a section of the past that was under the veil.

Through the haze, facts and faces began to come out, some dim, some vivid. He remembered, for instance, that there had been a slight commotion when news came that a freighter had brought in the body of a man found dead in Silver Cañon. He remembered that someone had jogged his arm and spilled his whiskey, whereupon he had smote the fellow upon the root of the nose and then waited calmly for the gun play. And how the other had reached for his gun but had been instantly seized by two bystanders who poured whispered words into his ears. The words had turned the face of the stranger pale and made his eyes grow big. He stared at Lew, then had apologized for the accident, and had been forgiven by Lew, and they had had many drinks together.

That was one of the incidents which was most vivid.

Then, somebody had insisted upon singing a solo, in a very deep, rough bass voice. Carney had complimented him and told him he had a voice like Niagara Falls.

A little, wizened man with buried eyes and hatchet face had confided to Carney that he was a Comanche chief and that he was on the warpath hunting white scalps; that he had a war cry which beat thunder a mile, and that when he whooped, people scattered. Whereupon he whooped and kept on whooping and swinging a bottle in lieu of a tomahawk until the bartender reached across the bar and tapped the Comanche chief with a mallet.

A tall, sad-faced man with long mustaches had poured forth the story of a gloomy life between drinks.

Once he had complained that the whiskey was too weak for him. What he wanted was liquid dynamite so he could get warmed up inside.

Later he was telling a story to which everyone listened with much amusement. Roars of laughter had greeted his telling of it. Men had clapped him on the back when he was finished. Only one man in the crowd had seemed serious.

Lew Carney began to smile to himself as he remembered the effect of his tale. The tale itself came back to him. It was about eight men pulling a wagon across the desert, while two horses were tethered behind it.

At this point in the restoration of the day before, Carney sat erect in his bed. He had told the story of the phantom wagon in a saloon full of men. The story would go abroad; the murderer or murderers of that man he had found dead in the desert would be warned in time.

He ground his teeth at the thought, but then settled himself back in the bed and, with a prodigious effort, summoned up other bits of the scene.

He remembered, for instance, that after he told the story, somebody had pressed through the crowd and assured him in a voice tearful that it was the tallest lie that had ever been voiced between the Sierras and the old Rockies. Whereat another man had said that there was one greater lie, and that was the old man Tomkins's story about the team of horses which was so fast that when a snowstorm overtook him in his buckboard, he put the whip on his team and arrived home without a bit of snow on him, though the back of his wagon was full to the top of the boards.

After that half a dozen men had insisted on having Carney drink with them. So he had poured six drinks into one tall glass and had drunk with them all, while the crowd cheered. After this incident he could remember almost nothing except that a strong arm had been beneath his shoulders part of the time, and that a voice at his ear had kept assuring him that it was "all right . . . don't worry . . . lemme take care of you."

Finding that past this point it was hopeless to try to reconstruct the past, he returned to the beginning, to the first telling of the tale of the wagon, and strove to make what had happened clearer. Bit by bit new things came to him. And then he came again in his memories to the man who had looked seriously, for one instant. It had been just a shadow of gloom that had crossed the face of this man. Then he had turned and gone through the crowd.

"By Heaven!" said Lew, to the silent walls of his room. "That gent knew something about the wagon!"

If he could recall the face of the man, he felt that two-thirds of the distance would have been covered toward finding the murderer, the cur who had shot the other man from behind. But the face was gone. It was a vague blur of which he remembered only a brown mustache, rather close-cropped. But there were a hundred such mustaches in Cayuse.

He got up and dressed slowly. He had come to the halting point. Dim and uncertain as this clue would be, even if the stranger actually had some connection with the murder, even if he had not been simply disgusted by the drunken tale, so that he turned and left in contempt. Yet in time his memory might clear, Carney felt, and the veil be lifted from the significant face of the man. It seemed as though the curtain of obscurity dropped just to the top of the mustache, like a mask. There was the strong chin, the contemptuous, stern mouth, and the brown mustache, cropped close. But of eyes and nose and forehead, he could remember nothing.

Downstairs he found that he had been the involuntary guest of Bud Lockhart overnight in the little lodging house; so he went to the big parlor to repay his host. Smiles greeted his entrance. He reduced his pace to the slowest sauntering and deliberately met each eye as he passed; the result was that the smiles died out, and he left a train of sober faces behind him.

With his self-confidence somewhat restored by this running of the gantlet, he found Bud Lockhart and was received with a grin which no amount of staring sufficed to wipe out. He discovered that Bud seemed actually to admire him for the drunken party of the day before.

"I'll tell you why," said Bud, "you get in solid with me. Some's got one test for a gent and some's got another. But for me, let me once get a gent drunk and I'll tell you all about how the insides of his head are put together. If a gent is noisy but keepin' his tongue down to make a bluff, he'll begin to shoutin' as soon as the red-eye is under his belt. And if he's yaller, he'll try to bully a fellow smaller than himself. And if he's a blowhard, he'll start his blowin'. But if he's a gentleman, sir, it's sure to crop out when the whiskey is spinning in his head."

At this Carney looked Bud in the eye with even more particular care.

"And after I knocked a man down and insulted another and told a lot of foolish stories, just where do you place me, Lockhart?"

"Do you remember that far back?" asked Bud with a chuckle. "Son, you put away enough whiskey to float a ship. You just simply got a nacheral ability to blot up the booze!"

"How much tea did you mix with my stuff?"

At this Bud flushed a little, but he replied: "Don't let 'em tell you anything about me. No matter what it was you drank, you put away just twice as much as was enough. Son, you done noble, and I tell it to you! You done noble. Only one fight, and seein' it was you, I'd say that you spent a plumb peaceable day."

"Bud," broke in the other, "I think I chattered some more about that ghost wagon. Did I?"

"Ghost wagon? What? Oh, sure, I remember it now. That funny idea of yours about seein' a wagon with eight men pullin' it? Sure, you told that yarn, but everybody put it down for just a yarn and had a good laugh out of it. I suppose you've got that fool idea out of your head by this time, Lew? Good thing if you have!"

Lew Carney began to feel that there was far more generous manliness in Bud Lockhart than he had ever guessed.

"I'll tell you how it is," he said. "I'd put the thing out of my head if I could, but I can't. Know why? Because it's a fact."

The smile of the big man became somewhat stereotyped.

"Sure," he said. "Sure it's a fact."

"Are you tryin' to humor me?" asked Carney with a growl.

The older man suddenly took his friend by the arm and tapped his breast with a vast, confidential forefinger.

"Listen, son. The first time you pulled that story it was a swell joke, understand? The second time it won't get such a good hand. The third time people are apt to pass the wink when you start talking."

"But I tell you, man, I saw that thing as clearly. . . ."

"Sure, sure you did. I don't doubt you, Lew. Not me. But some of the boys don't know you as well as I do. You'll start explainin' to 'em real serious, and then they'll pass the wink along. Savvy? They'll begin to tap their heads. You know what happened to Harry the Nut? Between you and me, I think he had just as good sense as you and me have. But he done that one queer thing over to Townsend's and when he tried to explain, it didn't do any good. Then pretty soon he was doin' nothin' but explainin' and tryin' to make people take him serious. You remember? And after a while he got to thinkin' about that one thing so much that I guess he did go sort of batty. It's an easy thing to do. I'll tell you what, Lew. If you can't figure out a thing, just start thinkin' about somethin' else. That's the way I do."

There was something at once so hearty and so sane about this advice that the young gambler nodded his head. He had a wild impulse to declare outright that he knew there was a close connection between the ghost wagon and the dead man whom the freighters had brought in the day before. But he checked himself on the verge of speech. For this tale would be even more difficult of explanation than the first.

Instead he took the big man's hand and made his own lean fingers sink into the soft fat ones of Bud Lockhart.

"You got a good head, Bud," he said, "and you got a good heart. I'm all for you and I'm glad you're for me. If you ever hear me talk about the ghost wagon again, you can make me eat the words."

The big man sighed and an expression of relief spread visibly across his face. Oil had been cast upon troubled waters.

"Now the thing for you is a little excitement, son," he advised. "Go over to that table. I'll bring you the stakes; and you start dealin' for the house."

"Whatever you say goes for me today," murmured Carney obediently.

"And as for the coin," said the fat man, "you just split it with the house any way you think is the right way."

V "Two on Horseback"

Only half of the mind of Lew Carney was on the cards, and west of the Rockies it needs very close attention indeed to win at poker. Once he collared a fellow clumsily trying to hold out a card. At the urgent entreaty of Bud Lockhart to do him no serious damage, he merely threw him out of the place. Luck now inclined a little more to his side, when the men who took their chances at his table saw that they could not crook the cards; but still he lost for the house, steadily. He had an assignment of experienced and steady players, and the chances seemed to favor them.

By noon he was far behind. By mid-afternoon Bud Lockhart was seen to be lingering in the offing and biting his lip. Before evening Carney threw down the cards in disgust and went to his employer.

"I'm through," he said. "I can't play for another man. I can't keep my head on the game. I'll square up for what I've lost for you."

"You'll not," said Lockhart. "But if you think the luck ain't with you, well, luck takes her own time comin' around; and if the draw ain't with you, well, knock off for a while."

"I'm doin' it. S'long, Bud."

"Not leavin' the house, old man?"

The proprietor moved back before the door with his enormous arms outspread in protest. "Not goin' to beat it away right now, are you, Lew?"

"Why not? I want a change of air. Gettin' nervous."

"Sit down over there. Wait a minute. I'll get you a drink."

"Not now."

"Bah! You don't know what you need. Besides, I've got something to say to you."

He hurried away, turned.

"Don't move out of that chair," he directed, and Carney sank into it, as though impelled by the wind of the big man's gesture.

Once in it, however, he stirred uneasily. The events of the day before had served to make him a well-known character in the place. Wherever people moved, they often turned and directed a smile at the young gambler, and such glances irritated him. Not that the smiles were exactly offensive. Usually they were accompanied by some reference to the celebrated tale of the evening before, the amazing lie about the ghost wagon. Yet Carney felt his temper rise. He wanted to be away from this place. He did not know how many of these strangers he had drunk with the night before. Perhaps he had drunk with his hand on the shoulder of some. He had seen drunken men do that, and the thought made his flesh crawl. For Lew Carney was not in any respect a good democrat and there was very little society which he preferred to his own. Not that he was a snob, but his was a heart which went out very seldom, and then with a tide of selfless passion. And the faces in this room made him feel unclean himself. He dreaded touching his own cheek with the tips of his fingers for fear that he would feel the stubble left by the hasty shave of that morning.

Above all, at this moment, the thought of the vast flesh and the all-embracing kindliness of his host was irksome to him. He felt under an obligation for the night before, and the manner in which Lockhart had handled the delicate situation of the gambling losses deepened the obligation, made it a thing that a mere payment of cash could not balance. He had to stay there and wait for the return of Bud, and yet he could not stay! With a sudden, overmastering impulse, he started up from his chair and strode swiftly to the door.

His hand was upon the knob when a finger touched his shoulder. He turned; there stood Glory Patrick, the man who kept order in the parlor and gaming hall of Bud Lockhart. Glory was a known man whether with his bare hands or with a knife or gun. And Lew Carney had seen him working all three, at one time or another. He smiled kindly upon the rough man; his eyeteeth showed with his smile.

Glory smiled in turn.

Who has not seen two wolves grin at each other?

"The boss wants you, chief," said Glory. "Ain't you goin' to wait for him?"

"Can't do it. Tell Bud that I'll be back." He looked around rather guiltily. The big man was nowhere in sight. And then he turned abruptly upon Glory: "Did he send you to stop me just now?"

"Nope. But I seen that he was comin' back and would want you ag'in."

It was all said smoothly enough, but when Carney asked his direct question the eyes of the bouncer had flicked away for the briefest of spaces, a glance as swift as the flash of a cat's paw when it makes play with the lightning movements of a mouse.

Yet it told something to Lew Carney. It told him a thing so incredible that for an instant he was stunned by it. He, Lew Carney, battler extraordinary, fighter by preference, trouble seeker by nature, gunman by instinct, boxer by training, bull terrier by grace of the thing that went boiling through his veins, he, Lew Carney, was stopped at the door of this place by a bouncer acting under the order of fat Bud Lockhart.

It shocked Carney; it robbed him of strength and made him an infant. "Don't Bud want me to go?" he asked.

"Nope. Between you and me, I don't think he does."

"Oh," said Carney softly. "Wouldn't you let me go?"

"You got me right," said Glory.

Carney dropped his head back so that he could only look at Glory by glancing far down, with only the rim of his eyes. He began to laugh gently and without a sound.

At length he straightened his head. All he said was: "Oh, is that what it means?" Glory went white about the mouth, and his eyes seemed to sink in under his brows. He was a brave man, as all the world knew; he was a strong man, as Lew Carney perfectly understood. But he had not the exquisite nicety of touch; he lacked the lightning precision of the windy-haired youth who now stood with a devil in either eye. All of these things each of them knew; and each knew that the other understood. Glory was quite willing to take up an insult and die in the fight; but he would infinitely prefer that Lew Carney should withdraw without another syllable. And as for Carney, he balanced the chances; he rolled the temptation under his tongue with the delight of a connoisseur, and then turned on his heel and walked out.

It had all passed within a breathing space; yet the space of five seconds had seen a little drama begin, reach a climax of life and death, and end, all without sound, all without gesture of violence, so that a man rolling a cigarette nearby never knew that he had stood within a yard of a gun play.

The door swung behind Lew Carney and he stepped into the street and confronted the man with the close-cropped brown mustache! All at once he felt some power beyond him had taken him by the shoulder and made him start up from the chair where he had sat to await the coming of Bud Lockhart, had forced him through the door past Glory Patrick, and had thrust him out into the daylight of the street and into the presence of this man.

It was no guess work. The moment he saw the fellow the film of indecision was whipped away, and he distinctly remembered how this man had heard the tale of the ghost wagon begun and had turned with a shadow on his face and gone through the crowd. It might mean nothing; but a small whisper in the heart of Lew Carney told him that it meant everything.

He had not met the eye of the other. The man stood at the heads of two horses, before a store across the street, and his glance was toward the door of the shop; the source of the expectancy soon appeared. She was a dark girl of the mountain desert, but with a fine high color that showed through the tan; so much Lew Carney could see, and though the broad brim of her sombrero obscured the upper part of her face, there was something about her that fitted into the mind of Carney. Who has not thought of music and heard the same tune sung in the distance? So it was with Carney. It was as though he had met her before.

In the meantime she had gone straight to one of the horses, and he of the brown mustache went to hold her stirrup and give her a hand. The moment they stood side by side, Lew felt that they belonged together. There was about them both the same cool air of self-possession, the same atmosphere of good breeding. The old clothes and the ragged felt hat of the man could not cover his distinction of manner. He did not belong in such an outfit. His personality broke through it with a suggestion of far other attire. He should have been in cool whites, Carney felt, and the cigarette between his fingers should have been "tailor-made" instead of brown paper. In fact, just as the girl had fitted into Carney's own mind, so now the man stepping up to her drew her into a second and more perfect setting. And it cost the gambler a pang, an exquisite small pain that kept close to his heart.

Another moment and the pain was gone; another moment and the blood went tingling through the veins of Lew Carney. For the girl had refused the proffered assistance of her companion and she had done it in an unmistakable manner. Another woman in another time might have done twice as much without telling a thing to the eyes of Lew Carney, but now he was watching with a sort of second sight, and he saw her wave away the hand of the other and swing lightly, unaided, into the saddle.

It was a small thing but it had been done with a little shiver of distaste, and now she sat in her saddle looking straight before her, smiling. Once more Carney read her mind, and he knew that it was a forced smile, and that she feared the man who was now climbing into his own place.

VI "At the Gate"

A moment later they were trotting down the street side by side, and the pain darted home to Lew Carney again. A hundred yards more and she would jog around the corner and out of his life forever; she would pass on, and beside her the man who was connected with the ghost wagon and the dead body in Silver Cañon. Yet how small were his clues! He had frowned at a story which made other men laugh; and a girl had shrugged her shoulders very faintly, refusing the assistance to her saddle.

Small things to be sure, but Carney, with his heart on fire, made them everything. To his excited imagination it seemed certain that this brown-faced girl with the big, bright eyes, was riding out of his life side by side with a murderer. She must be stopped. Fifty yards, ten seconds more, and she would be gone beyond recall.

He glanced wildly around him. His own horse was stabled. It would take priceless minutes to put him on the road. And now the inertness of the bystanders struck him in the face. Could they not see? Did not the patent facts shout at them? A man sat on the edge of the plank sidewalk and walled up his eyes, while he played a wailing mouth organ. A youth in his fourteenth year passed the man, sitting

sidewise in his saddle, rolling his cigarette, and sublimely conscious
that all eyes were upon him.

A thought came to Lew. He started to the horse of the boy and
grabbed his arm. "See 'em?" he demanded.

"See what?" said the boy with undue leisure.

"See that gent and the girl turning the corner?"

"What about 'em?"

"Do me a favor, partner." The word thawed the childish pride of
the boy. "Ride after him and tell him that Bud Lockhart wants him in
a deuce of a hurry."

For what man was there near Cayuse who would not answer a
summons from Lockhart? The boy was nodding. He swung his leg
over the pommel of the saddle and, before it struck into place in the
stirrup, he had shot his horse into a full gallop, the brim of his hat
standing straight up.

Carney glanced after him with a faint smile; then he started in pursuit, walking slowly, close to the buildings, mixing in with the crowd
to keep from view. What he would say to the girl when he met her, he
had not the slightest idea; but see her alone, he must and would, if this
simple ruse worked.

And it worked. Presently he saw the man of the brown mustache
riding slowly back down the street, talking earnestly to the boy. In the
midst of that earnest talk, he checked his horse and straightened in the
saddle. Then he sent his mount into a headlong gallop. Carney waited
to see no more but, increasing his pace, he presently turned the corner
and saw the girl with her horse reined to one side of the street.

She had forgotten her smile and was looking wistfully straight before her; behind her eyes there was some sad picture and Carney
would have given the remnants of his small hopes of salvation to see
that picture and talk with her about it. He went straight up to her,
pushed by the fear that the man of the brown mustache might ride
upon them at any moment, and when he had come straight under her
horse, she suddenly became aware of him.

It was to Lew Carney like the flash of a gun. Her glance dropped
upon him. A moment passed during which speech was frozen on his
tongue and thought stopped in his brain. Then he saw a faint smile
twitch at the corners of her lips as the color deepened in her cheeks.
He became aware that he was standing with his hat gripped and
crushed in both hands and his eyes staring fixedly up to her, like any

worshipping boy. He gritted his teeth in the knowledge that he was
playing the fool, and then he heard her voice, speaking gently. Apparently his look had embarrassed her, but she was not altogether dis-
pleased or offended by it.

"You wish to speak to me?" she was saying.

"I don't know your name," said Carney slowly, and as he spoke he
realized more fully how insane this whole meeting was, how little he
had to say. "But I've something to say to you."

He was used to girls who were full of tricky ways, and now her
steady glance, her even voice, shook him more than any play of smiles
and coyness.

"My name is Mary Hamilton. What is it you have to say?"

"I can't say it in this street; if you'll go. . . ."

But her eyes had widened. She was looking at him with more than
interest; it was fear. "Why?" she asked.

"Because I want to talk to you for two minutes, and your friend
will be back in less time than that."

"Do you know?"

The excitement had grown on her with a rush, and one gauntleted
hand was at her breast.

"I sent for him," confessed Carney. "It was a bluff so I could see
you alone."

Momentarily her glance dwelt on him, reading his lean face in an
agony of anxiety; then it flashed up and down the street, and he knew
that she would go with him.

"Down here and just around the corner," he said. "Will you? Yes?"

"Follow me," commanded the girl and sent her horse at a trot out
of the street and down the byway. He hurried after her, and as he
stepped away he saw the man with the brown mustache thundering
down the street. But there were nine chances out of ten that he would
ride straight on to find the girl and never think of turning down this
alley. But there was something guilty about that speed, and when Lew
stood before the girl again he felt more confidence in the vague things
he had to say. All the color was gone from her face now; she was
twisting at the heavy gauntlets.

"What do you know?" she asked, and always her eyes went everywhere about them in fear of some detecting glance.

"I think," said Lew, "that I know a few things that would interest
you."

"Yes?"

"In the first place you're afraid of the gent with the brown mustache."

All at once he found her expression grown hard.

"He sent you here to try me," she said. "Jack Doyle sent you to me!"

What a wealth of scorn was in her voice! It made the cheeks of Carney burn.

"He's the one that's with you?"

"Don't you know it?"

"I'm some glad to have his name," said Lew. Suddenly he decided to make his cast at once. "My story you may want to know has to do with a wagon pulled by eight men, with two horses and. . . ."

But a faint cry stopped him. She had swung from the saddle with the speed of a man and now she caught at his hands.

"If you know, why don't you save us? Why. . . ."

She stopped as quickly as she had begun and pressed a gloved hand over her lips. Above the glove her eyes stared wildly at him.

"What have I said?" she whispered. "Oh, what have I said?"

"You've said enough to start me and something you've got to finish."

She dropped her glove.

"I've said nothing. Absolutely nothing. I. . . ." And unable to finish the sentence, she turned and whipped the reins over the head of her horse, preparatory to mounting.

The gambler pressed in between her and the stirrup.

"Lady," he said quietly, "look me over. Then go back and ask the town about Lew Carney. They'll tell you that I'm a square-shooter. Now say what's wrong. Make it short, because this Jack Doyle is driftin' around lookin' for you."

She winced and drew closer to the horse.

"Say two words," said Lew Carney, the uneasy spark bursting into flame in his eyes and shaking his voice. "Say two words and I'll see that Jack Doyle don't bother you. Lift one finger and I'll fix it so that you ride alone or stay right here."

She shook her head. Fear seemed to have her by the throat, stifling all speech, but the fear was not of Lew Carney.

"Gimme a sign," he pleaded desperately, "and I'll go with you. I'll see you through, so help me God."

And still she shook her head. It was maddening to the man to feel himself at the very gate of the mystery, and then to find that gate locked by the foolish fears of a girl.

"I got a right to know," he said, playing his last card. "Everybody's got a right to know; because they's one dead man mixed up with the ghost wagon, and there may be more!"

She went sick and pale at that, and with the thought that it might be guilt, Lew Carney grew weak at heart. How could he tell? Someone near and dear to her might have fired that coward's shot from behind. Why else this haunted look? More than anything, that mute, white face daunted him. He fell back and gave her freedom to mount by his step. And she at once lifted herself into the saddle.

With her feet in the stirrups fear seemed in a measure to leave her. And she looked with a peculiar wistfulness at Carney.

"Will you take my advice?" she said softly.

"I'll hear it," said Lew.

"Then leave this trail you've started on. It's a blind trail to follow, and a horror at the end of it. But if you should keep on, if you should find it, God bless you!"

And she spurred her horse to a gallop from that standing start.

VII "Moving Silver"

It was as though she had smiled on him before she slammed the door in his face. He must not follow the blind trail to the horror; but if he did persist, if he did go to the end of the trail, then let God bless him!

What head or tail was he to make of such a speech? She wanted him to come and yet she trembled at the thought. And at the very time she denied him her secret, she pleaded bitterly with her eyes that he should learn the truth for himself. When he mentioned the ghost wagon, she had flamed into hope. When he spoke of the dead man, she had gone sick with dread. But above all that her words had meant, fragmentary as they were, the tremor of her voice when she last spoke was more eloquent in the ear of Lew Carney than aught else.

Yet, stepping in the dark, he had come a long way out of the first oblivion. He was still fumbling toward the truth blindly, but he knew at least that the ghost wagon had not been an illusion of the senses. How it had vanished into thin air; what strange reason had placed eight men on the chain drawing it; all this remained as wonderful as ever. But now it had become a fact, not a dream. His first impulse, naturally enough, was to go straight to Lockhart and triumphantly confirm his story.

But two good reasons kept him from such a step. In the first place there was now a new interest equaled with his first desire to learn the truth of the ghost wagon, and the new interest was Mary Hamilton. Until he knew or even guessed how far she was implicated, he could not take the world into his confidence. And beyond this important fact there was really nothing to tell the world except the exclamation of the girl, and the frown of Jack Doyle.

These things he thought over as he hurried toward the stables behind Bud Lockhart's saloon. For on one point he was clear: no matter how blind might be the trail of the ghost wagon, the trail of the girl and her escort should be legible enough to his trained eyes, and he intended to follow that trail to its end, no matter where the lead might take him.

Coming to the stables he had a touch of guilty conscience in the thought that Bud Lockhart must be still waiting for him in the gaming rooms; for no doubt Glory had told the boss that Lew Carney had stepped out for only a moment and would soon return. But there was no sign of Bud in the rear of the saloon, and Lew saddled the gelding in haste and swung into place. He touched the mustang in the flank with his spur and leaned forward in the saddle to meet the lunge of the cow pony's start, but instead of the usual cat-footed spring, he was answered by a hobbling trot.

For a moment he sat the saddle, stunned. Lameness was not in the vocabulary of the gelding, but Lew drew him to a halt and, dismounting, examined the left front hoof. There was no stone lodged in it. Deciding that the lameness must be a passing stiffness of some muscle, Lew leaped into the saddle again and spurred the mustang cruelly forward. The answering and familiar spring was still lacking. The horse struck out with a lunge, but on striking his left foreleg crumpled a little, and he staggered slightly. Lew Carney shot to the ground again. If the trouble was not in the hoof, it must be in the leg. He thumped and kneaded the strong muscles of the upper leg and dug his thumb into the shoulder of the gelding, but there was never a flinch.

He stood back despairing and looked over his mount. Never before had the dusty roan failed him, and to leave him to take another horse was like leaving his tried gun for a new revolver. Besides, it would mean a loss of time, and moments counted heavily, now that the afternoon was waning to the time of yellow light, with evening scarcely an hour away. Unless the two took the way of Silver Cañon—and that was hardly likely—they would be out of sight among the hills if he did not follow immediately.

Looking mournfully over that offending foreleg he noticed a line of hair fanning out just above the knee, as if the horse had rubbed against the stall and pressed on the sharp edge of a plank. He smoothed this ridge away thoughtlessly and then looked wistfully down the street. The lazy life of the town had not changed. Men were going carelessly about their ways, yet there were good men and true passing him continually. Charlie Rogers went by him, Gus Ruel, Sam Tern, a dozen other known men who would have followed him to the moon and back at a word. But what word could he give them? A hundred men would scour the hills at his bidding, yet what reason could he suggest? All that wealth of man power was his if he only had the open sesame which would unlock the least fragment of the secret of the ghost wagon. No, he must play this hand alone.

He looked back with a groan to the lame leg of the horse and again he saw the little ridge of stubborn hair. It was a small thing but he was in a mood when the smallest things are irritating. With an oath he leaned over and smoothed down the hair with a strong pressure of his finger tips, and at once, through the hair, he felt a tiny ridge as hard as bone, but above the bone. Lew Carney set his teeth and dropped to his knees. It was as he thought. A tiny thread of silk had been twisted around the leg of his horse, and drawn taut, and that small pressure, exerted at the right place over the tendons, was laming the gelding. One touch of his jack-knife, and the thread flew apart while there was a snort of relief from the roan. And Lew Carney, lingering only long enough to cast one black look behind him, sprang into the saddle for the third time, and now the gelding went out into his long, rocking lope.

The gambler felt the pace settle to the usual stride but he was not satisfied. What if Doyle had given his horses the rein as soon as he found the girl? What if he had made it a point to get out of Cayuse at full speed? In that case he would be even now deep in the bosom of the hills. And many things assured him that the stranger was forewarned. He must have been given at least a hint by the same agency which had lamed the roan. More than this, if someone knew that Lew Carney was about to take up this trail, and had already taken such a shameful step as this to prevent it, he would go still further. He might send a warning ahead; he might plant an ambush to trap the pursuer.

There is no position so dangerous as the place of the hunter who is being hunted and, at the thought of what might lie ahead of him, Lew Carney drew the horse back to a dogtrot. Even if the odds were on his side, it might be risky work, but he had reason to believe that there were eight men against him, eight men burdened with one crime already, and therefore ready and willing to commit another to cover their traces.

The thought had come to Lew Carney as he broke out of Cayuse and headed west and south, but while the thoughts drifted through his mind, and all those nameless pictures which come to a man in danger, his eye picked up the trail of two horses which had moved side by side. And the trail indicated that both horses were running at close to top speed. For the footprints were about equally spaced, with long gaps to mark the leaps. The trail led, as he had feared, into the broken hills south of Silver Cañon where danger might lie in wait to leap out at him from any of twenty places in every mile he rode.

But Lew Carney at any time was not a man to reckon chances too closely; and Lew Carney, with a trail to lead him on, was close to the primitive hunting animal. He sent the roan gelding back into the lope, and in a moment more the ragged hills were shoving past him, and he was fairly committed to the trail.

It was a different man who rode now. With his hat drawn low to keep the slant sunlight from dazzling him, his glance swept the trail before him and the hills on every side. Men have been known to play a dozen games of chess blindfolded; Lew Carney's problems were even more manifold. For every half mile passed him through a dozen places where men might lie concealed to watch him or to harm him, and each place had to be studied, and all its possibilities reckoned with. He loosened his rifle and saw that it drew easily from the long holster. He tried his revolver and found it in readiness. Now and again he swung sharply in the saddle, and his glance took in half the horizon behind him, for in such a sudden turn a man can often take a pursuer by surprise. But the great danger indubitably lay ahead of him, and here he fixed his attention.

The western light was more and more yellow now, and before long the trail would be dim with sunset, and then obscured by the evening.

When that time came, he must fix a landmark ahead of him, and then strike straight on through the night, trusting that Doyle had cast his course in a straight line. Unless by dint of hard riding he should come upon the two before dark. But this he doubted. Riding at full speed, Doyle and the girl had opened up a gap of miles before Lew was even started. Moreover, for all his leathery qualities of endurance, the roan was not fast on his feet over a comparatively short distance. It needed a two days' journey to bring out his fine points.

Lew preferred to keep to a steady gait well within the powers of the roan, and trust to bulldog persistence to bring him up with the quarry. He kept on with the hills moving by him like waves chopped by a storm wind. When the sunset reds were dying out, and the gloom of early evening beginning to pool in blues and purples along the gulches, he caught the first sign of life near him. It was a glint of silver far to his left, and it moved.

The ravine down which Carney rode was merely a flat plateau out of which mountain tops went up irregularly, and the glint of moving silver which he had caught to his left was not in the same ravine, or even in the same bottom, but far beyond in a similar rough and shallow valley. Between two hills he had caught this glimpse into the next gulch, and he rode thoughtfully for a moment.

Once more he passed a gap through which he could look into the next valley but this time he saw nothing.

It occurred to him then that the flash of silver had been moving at a rate close to that of a horse galloping swiftly and, setting his teeth, Lew Carney spurred the gelding to top speed. Weaving through the boulders furiously, he reached the next gap after a half mile sprint, and here he pulled the gelding, panting heavily, to a halt.

Fast as he had traveled over the past furlongs, he had not long to wait before the silver flashed once more out of the thickening gloom of the early night, and this time he saw clearly that it was a gray horse which was being ridden at full gallop through the hills.

But the color of the animal meant a great deal to Lew. He had seen a tall gray, muscled to bear weight, in the stables behind Bud Lockhart's saloon, and he had been told that this was Bud's horse. Moreover, a long train of thought flashed back upon the mind of Lew, with this as the conclusion: he remembered the manner in which Bud had laughed at the story of the phantom wagon, the eagerness with which he had persuaded Lew to drop the tale, his strangely friendly endeavors to keep Lew inside the saloon when the man of the brown mustache was about to leave the room. Bud Lockhart was in some manner implicated. It was he who had posted Glory to keep the gambler in the saloon; it was he who had lamed the roan; and now, finding that his quarry had escaped in spite of all precautions, it was he who mounted his fine gray horse and rode furiously through the hills to carry warning.

VIII "More than Death"

Lust of murder filled the brain of Lew Carney when he thought of the fat face and its pseudo-amiability, the big, fat hand, and the fat cordiality. And yet he saw a way in which he could use the saloonkeeper. He could cut across to the next valley and, at a distance, follow the gray horse through the night, and so reach his destination. The warning of his coming would go before him but he felt that his gain would be equal to his loss.

He swung the gelding across through the gap and a little later sped into the second cañon. The turning to one side brought him out far behind Bud Lockhart and the speeding gray, but for this he cared little. The fat man had apparently assured himself of reaching his destination in time, and he had brought his horse back to a hard gallop which the slow roan could easily match and, keeping carefully within eye range and out of hearing, Lew wove down the valley, putting an occasional rise of ground between him and his leader, and doing all that was in his power to trail unsuspected. One great advantage remained with him in this game. The roan's color blended easily with the ground tones and the gloom of evening, whereas the gray literally shone through the half light.

But in spite of this handicap in his favor Lew presently discovered that his presence to the rear was known. For the gap between him and the gray suddenly increased. Coming up a rise of ground only a short distance to the rear, when he reached the top he discovered the gray gleaming far off, and he knew with a great falling of the heart that his trailing had been at fault.

One hope remained. One bitter chance to take. He could never catch the gray with the roan in a journey which would probably end before the morning. Only one power could overtake the fugitive and that was lead sped by powder. He counted the chances back and forth through the tenth part of a second. His bullet might strike down Bud Lockhart instead of Bud Lockhart's horse, but Bud had played the part of a sneak, and his life to Lew Carney meant no more than the life of a dog. He jerked his rifle to his shoulder, caught the bull's-eye, and fired. As he watched for the effect of the shot he saw the gray horse pause, stop, and lean slowly to one side.

Before the animal fell, the rider had leaped to the ground, looking huge even at that distance. A gun gleamed in his hand but that was only the rash first impulse. A moment later Bud Lockhart's fat arms were heaved above his head and, with his rifle held ready, Lew cantered down to meet his prisoner.

As he came close so that his face could be more clearly seen, there was a roar of mingled relief and fury from the saloonkeeper.

"Lew Carney! What d'you mean by this?" And he lowered his arms.

"Put 'em up and keep 'em starched. Quick!"

For the saloonkeeper, attempting to smile at the first of this remark, had slipped his hands upon his hips; but the last word sent his arms snapping into the air.

"It ain't possible," stammered Bud Lockhart. Even in the half light it was easy to see that his face was gray. "After what I've done for you, it ain't possible that you've double-crossed me, Lew!" He allowed a nasal complaint to creep into his voice. "Look here, son, when a man's broke he'll do queer things. If you're busted, say the word, and I'll stake you to all that you want. But you come within an inch of killin' me with that shot! And that's the best hoss that I ever sat on!"

For answer, Lew replaced his rifle in its case and drew a revolver as a handier weapon for quick use. Then he spoke.

"Yep," he said, "I figured on trimming you pretty close. But I'm sorry about the horse. The only way I could help you, though."

"There's an unwritten law about gents that kill hosses," said Bud Lockhart, his voice hardening as he noted this apparent weakening on the part of Lew Carney.

"Sure there is," said the younger man. "That's why I'm goin' to remove the witness. Your time's short, Bud, because I'm considerable hurried."

The vast arms of the saloonkeeper wavered.

"You can put your arms down now," said Lew kindly. "I'd rather that you tried a gun play. I'll give you a clean break."

And he restored his own weapon to its holster.

The arms of the other lowered by inches, and all the time his eyes fought against those of Lew. But when finally the hands hung by his sides, he was limp and helpless. He had admitted defeat, and he was clay ready for the molding.

"I won't raise a hand," protested Bud with perverse stubbornness. "It's murder, that's all. You spend your life with guns, and then you go out and murder. And murder'll out, Lew, as sure as there's a God in heaven!"

"Truest thing you ever said. That's why I'm here."

"Eh?"

"I'm here because a murder is comin' out."

"What in thunder d'you mean, Lew? D'you suspect me of something?"

"The man they brought out of Silver Cañon, Bud. That's the one."

There was a start and a gasp. "Lew, you are nutty. A hundred gents will swear I ain't never left Cayuse for ten days."

"You didn't hold the gun. You ain't got nerve enough for that. But you were behind it."

The fat coward was shaking from head to foot. "I swear . . . ," he began.

"Curse you." Lew recoiled with sudden horror. "You're a rotten skunk!"

A silence fell between them.

"You ain't left Cayuse for ten days," said Lew when he could speak again. "Where were you bound for now?"

"For Sliver Hennessey's place."

"Good," he said. "You lie well. But here's the end of your trail. You can see Sliver in hell later on."

The craven fear of the other cast a chill through his own blood. He felt shamed for all men, seeing this shaken sample of it, tried and found wanting.

"Lew," said the other in a horrible whisper. "Lew, you and me . . . friends . . . other night when you was drunk . . . I. . . ." He sank to his knees.

"You got the right attitude," said Lew. "Keep on talking. I'll wait till you say amen!"

"You ain't goin' to do it, Lew . . . partner!"

Lew Carney allowed his voice to weaken.

"I ought to. You're as guilty as Judas, Bud."

"I was dragged into it, I swear I was dragged into it! Lew, name what you want, and I'll give it to you. If I ain't got it, I'll find it for you. Name what you want!"

"Where have Doyle and the girl gone?"

The other stumbled to his feet. His little eyes under their fat lids began to twinkle at Lew with the remaining hope of life, but his face was still ashes.

"They're goin' to Miller's shack over to . . . to the Dry Creek."

"Miller's shack?" echoed Lew, noting the faltering.

"Yes."

"On your honor?"

"So help me, God!"

"One thing more: you told Glory to keep me inside the saloon even if he had to fill me full of lead to anchor me."

"He . . . he lied. He wanted to turn you ag'in me, Lew!"

"You hound!" snarled Lew.

The other fell back a step. "You gave me your promise," he retorted shrilly, "if I told you where they was goin'!"

"I gave you no promise. And you lamed the roan for me, Bud, eh?"

There was a groan from the tortured man.

"Lew, I was made to do it. I tell you straight; you'd've been deader than the gent you found in Silver Cañon if it wasn't for me. I headed 'em off. When they got a hunch you was after Doyle, they wanted to finish you. I saved you, son!"

"Because you thought the job might be a bit tough, eh? I know you, Bud. But who are they?"

The big man blinked as though a powerful light had been cast into his eyes. He began to speak. He stopped. Lew raised the forefinger of his right hand and pointed it like a gun at the breast of the other.

"Out with it," he commanded.

Once more the lips of Bud Lockhart stirred, but no words came. And a chill of surprise ran through Lew. Was it possible that this fellow valued that one secret more than his own life?

"Out with it!" he repeated harshly.

The knees of Bud Lockhart sagged. He closed his eyes; he clenched his hands; but still he did not speak. Lew Carney drew his gun slowly, raised it, leveled it, and then put the spurs to his horse. Swiftly down the cañon he galloped. For he had found the one thing Bud Lockhart feared more than death.

*

IX "A Gold-digger Knight"

It was this thought that made him go back more carefully over the words of the big saloonkeeper. For it was strange that if he would not name the men, he dared confess where they were to be found. Now he remembered how Bud had hesitated in mentioning the place. There had been a pause between "Miller's shack" and "Dry Creek," and the pause was the hesitation of a liar. No doubt it was Miller's shack but there were two such shacks in the hills—one at Dry Creek, and the other at Coyote Springs.

It needed only an instant of reflection to convince Lew Carney that the place he wanted was at Coyote Springs. In former days the spring had run full and free, and there had been a fine scattering of houses, almost a village, around it. But of late years the spring had fallen away to a wretched trickle of water, completely disappearing in certain seasons of the year. A fire had swept the village, and then old Miller had constructed his shanty out of the half-burned fragments. Once before Lew had been at the place, and he knew it and its approaches well.

Yet he did not swing directly toward this destination, but struck out down the valley toward Dry Creek. He kept steadily toward this goal until he was more than past the spring to his left. Having gone so far he turned again, and now rode hard straight upon Miller's place.

It was broad moonlight now and, topping the last ridge, he saw the big basin in which the village of Coyote Springs had once lain. To the west, a drift of narrow evergreens went up the slope, dark and slender points. The basin of the spring water was a spot of shining silver with the shack near it, and on the bank of the pool six men sat around a fire. Sometimes when the fire leaped, the long red tongue licked across the still surface of the water, and the murmur of men's voices went up the slope to Lew Carney.

Under these circumstances it was comparatively a simple matter to approach the shack without attracting the attention of the men about the fire. He took the roan to a point behind the ridge which lay on the line of projection through the fire and the shack, and tethered him to one of the young pines. Then he went again over the ridge and ran swiftly down to the rear of the shack.

There were eight men for whom he wished to account, if not for more; and only six were around the fire. It stood to reason that they must be in the cabin, and in the rear room, for that room alone was lighted. The girl, too, would be where the light was. How he would be able to communicate with her, once he was beside the wall of the house, he had not guessed. That was a bridge to be crossed later on. But he had chosen the lighted end of the shack because the light within would effectively darken the moon-lit night outside.

He was halfway down the slope when the boom of a man's laughter from the shack struck him. Someone of the eight watching him, perhaps, and mocking this futile attack by one man? But once started it was more dangerous to turn back than it was to keep straight on. He stooped closer to the ground and sped on, swerving a little from side to side, so as to disturb aim, if anyone were drawing a bead on him.

But he reached the cover of the side of the shack without either a shot fired or a repetition of any human sound in the little house. But outside, from the fire by the pool, a chorus of mirth had risen.

As though the six had heard of his coming and were in turn mocking his powers! He set his teeth at the mere thought, for now that he was actually under the wall of the house, the advantage, man for man, was really with him, and skirting down the wall, he came to a great crack from which he could reconnoiter. It was indeed one of those generous loopholes which occur where a board has loosened at the base, and bulged out. Through it Lew Carney could see the interior of the rear room of the shack as plainly as though he were looking at his ease through a window.

And the first thing on which his eyes fell was the face of the girl. She had apparently paused in her preparations for sleep. Her hair, formed into a great, loose braid, glided over her shoulder and slipped in a bright line of light down to her lap. She had taken off her boots and sat on the floor with her knees bunched high, one foot crosswise on top of the other. On her knees she supported a tattered magazine and, even as Lew glanced in, she began to read in a voice which was subdued to a murmur. The old, old pain which he had first felt when he looked at her was thrust home again in Lew's heart. For the first time he surmised what he might have guessed long before, that the reason she hoped for his interference, and yet dreaded it, was that one of the crew was her husband. Why not? Some gay young chap with a hidden wildness whom she had married before he went wrong; he knew of stranger things than that in the mountain desert. There is a peculiar satisfaction in some forms of self-torture; Lew Carney crouched outside the house and suffered wretchedly for a time before he decided to lean further to one side, to look at the person to whom she was reading. He saw a middle-aged man lying on a bed of boughs and blankets, a bald-headed man who now hitched himself with painful care a little to one side. It was plain that he was wounded. At the movement the girl turned from her reading and touched his forehead with her hand and murmured a few words of sympathy. What the rest of the words were Lew did not try to understand but he made out plainly the monosyllable, "Dad," and a burden dropped from him.

Besides had she not spoken of "us" when she cried out to him for help in that first impulse which she had regretted? Two of them had needed help but what had kept her from continuing her appeal was a mystery to Lew Carney. Perhaps the gang had contemplated moving away and leaving this wounded member helpless behind them. In that case she would at once want help for her father, and dread the course that the law might take with him after his wound was healed. At any rate Lew must speak with her at once. He stood up and went boldly to the window, and when his eyes fell on her she looked up.

There was a moment when he thought that she would cry out; but she mastered herself and ran swiftly across the room to the window. Two small, strong hands closed on his hand that lay on the edge of the window. "You!" whispered the girl. "You! Dad, he's come after me! He's found us!"

"Thank God!" murmured the wounded man. "How many men?"

"None," said Lew Carney.

There was a faint groan. Then: "Go back again. You're worse than useless. One man ag'in' this crew?"

"We'll talk that over when I'm inside," said Lew Carney, and he was instantly through the window and on the rotten floor of the room.

"Mary!" warned her father. "Get to the front of the shack and keep an eye on 'em. Now you, what's you name?"

"Lew Carney."

"All right, Carney, what's your plan? Where's your men? When are they coming? Are you going to try to four-flush half a dozen gun-fighters? Talk sharp and act quick or they may find you here!"

"I'll tell you the whole thing in a nutshell," said Lew calmly. "I followed a hunch and I'm here. And here I stay until we're all three cut loose of 'em or all three go under. Is that clear?"

"That's sand," said the older man, with a grudging admiration. "But it don't get us very far."

Mary Hamilton appeared at the door. "No fear of them for a long time," she said. "They're busy."

"Whiskey?" asked Hamilton.

She nodded.

Then to Lew Carney: "Oh, why, why, didn't you bring a dozen men?"

"Because I couldn't take 'em on a wild goose chase, and because you wouldn't tell me what I could say. I could have taken fifty men with me but not without a reason to give them."

She admitted the truth of what he said with a miserable gesture. "I couldn't talk," she said. "I'd promised."

"Like a fool girl," groaned her father.

There was a flash of anger in her eyes but she said nothing. And turning to Lew Carney she said: "You've done a fine thing and a clean thing to try to help us but it's no use."

"I can go back and bring help."

"It's too late. They intend to move on in the morning."

His head bent.

"Get clear before they know you're here," she added

Lew Carney smiled, and she looked at him in wonder.

"Don't you see?" she explained. "I'm grateful for what you want to do. And when I first saw you, you brought my heart into my throat with hope." She was so simple as she admitted it, so grave in her quiet despair, that Lew Carney felt like death. "But now there's nothing for you to do," she concluded, "except to leave us and see that you're not drawn into this yourself. Will you go?"

"Do you want me to go?" asked Lew Carney.

"What's all this?" broke in her father. "Carney, get out and ride like the devil. They may make things warm for you yet."

But he repeated, looking steadily into the girl's eyes, "Do you want me to go?"

"I like you," said the girl quietly. "I admire you and I know that you're clean and honest. But you can't help us. There's nothing for you to do. Please go!"

"Then, " said Lew Carney, "that settles it. I stay."

He took off his hat to give point to his words, and hung it on a nail on the wall. Feeling their puzzled glances he stiffened a bit and made his eyes, with trouble, meet the eyes of the girl. "I'll tell you why. I've been a drifter and a waster, Mary Hamilton. I'm not clean particularly, and if you ask a good many people they'll laugh if you say I'm honest. No, I'm not a gambler, I'm a gold digger. When you come right down to it, I don't take many chances. Cards are my business. Other fellows got their hands all hardened up with work and their brains all slowed up with makin' money. And after they've got their stake, they meet up with me. They play poker for fun; I play it for a living. What chance have they got? None. Well, that's what my business is. And all at once I'm most terrible, awful sick of it all. You understand? I'm tired of it. I want something new, and the first job that comes up sort of handy seems to be to do what I can for you and your dad. You want me to go. Well, if I'm good enough to be worth havin' my neck saved, I'm good enough to pull a gun in a pinch for you two." He paused. "Seems like I've made a sort of a speech, and now I feel mostly like a fool. But, there, I see that you're about to say somethin' about gratitude. Don't say it. This is only another kind of a game and I enjoy takin' chances. Here's our first chance and our big chance. If your father can stand it, I'll get him through that window and carry him up the hill to my horse, and. . . ."

"Break off," cut in Hamilton. "Son, you mean well but I can't move a hand. I'm nailed here for a month."

And a second glance at his pain-worn face told Lew Carney that it was the truth. Once more the two pressed him generously to leave them but, when he had refused, they sat beside the bunk of the father and talked of possibilities. But always in the midst of a scheme, the laughter from the men beside the pool where the riot was running high broke in upon them and mocked them. The helplessness of Hamilton was the thing that foiled every hope. No scheme could meet the great necessity.

Silence came over them, that grim silence when people wait together for a calamity. In the morning the band was moving on; they could not take the wounded man with them; they could not leave him behind to die slowly or else to be saved and to deliver an accusation which would imperil all their lives. The term of his life, then, was the dawn; and before the dawn came, John Hamilton told Lew the story of the ghost wagon. He told it swiftly in a monotonous voice. Now and again there was a moment of interruption, when Lew or Mary went to the front of the shack to make sure that the gang was thinking of nothing more than its whiskey; but on the whole the story of the phantom wagon went smoothly and swiftly to its dark conclusion.

*

X "The Tale of the Ghost Wagon"

Three short weeks ago John Hamilton had left his ranch for a prospecting tour. Though he had made far more out of cows than he had ever made out of gold and silver, the old lure of the rocks still held for him. From time to time he was in the habit of making a brief circuit through the hills chipping rocks with an unfailing enthusiasm. Ten days of this each year kept him happy; he filled his house with samples and mining, as far as John Hamilton was concerned, stopped at that point.

On this season he had gone out with his burro to see the world, sighting between those two flapping, cumbersome ears. But it had been long since he had really taken his prospecting seriously, and now he chipped rock with more careless abandon than ever. What sincere and hopeful labor had never brought to him, he found by happy chance, or unhappy chance, as it was to prove. For drilling into a lead he had uncovered a pocket of pure gold!

He had run short of powder by this time and that pocket was a most difficult one to open. It was a deposit strongly guarded in quartzite, the hardest of rocks. Yet with the point of his pick he had dug out five pounds of pure gold!

It was enough to set a more callous heart than that of John Hamilton on fire. When he saw that he could not work the deposit without more powder, he debated whether he should go to Cayuse for supplies and to file his claim or whether he should take the longer trip and return home to bring the supplies from there.

The temptation to convince the mockers in his own family, where his annual prospecting trips were an established joke, was too great.

"Mother was away, so I dumped the gold on the table before Mary and watched her eyes shine. Same light always comes in the eyes when you see gold. Can't help it. I've shown it to a baby, and they grab for it every time. It's in the blood."

Finally he had determined to return to the site of his mine with a heavy wagon and a span of strong horses, taking supplies in abundance, one tested ranch hand, Hugh Delaney, and his daughter Mary to run the domestic part of the camp. At the same time he sent to the nearest telegraph office a message to his son, Bill. Bill, it appeared, was the scapegrace of the family. Three years ago, after a quarrel with his father, he had left home, but the finding of the gold unlocked all of John Hamilton's tenderness; for Bill had gone many a time on those annual trips. He had sent an unlucky telegram informing Bill of the find and inviting him to come to Cayuse and ride down Silver Cañon to the claim.

Without waiting for a reply he started out in his wagon with Mary and Hugh Delaney, and they went straight to the pocket.

It had not been disturbed in the interim, and for five days of tremendous labor Hamilton and Delaney broke away the quartzite bit by bit and finally laid the pocket bare. It was a gloomy disappointment. Instead of proving a vein which opened out into the incredibly rich pocket which John Hamilton expected, it pinched away to nothing at the end of a few feet. In fact he had picked out a full two-thirds of the metal in his first attempt. Nevertheless up to this point the venture had been profitable enough in its small way but, when they were on the verge of abandoning the work, and only waiting for the arrival of Bill Hamilton from Cayuse, they were surprised late one afternoon by eight men who had left their horses at a distance, and crept upon the camp.

John Hamilton had thrown up his hands at the first summons and at the first sight of the odds. But Hugh Delaney, ignorant, stubborn, tenacious fighter that he was, had gone for his gun. Before he could reach it, he was shot down from behind, and then a volley followed that dropped John Hamilton himself, shot through the thigh.

The explanation was simple enough. A friend of Jack Doyle, long rider and bandit of parts, had seen the telegram which Hamilton sent to his son, and the outlaw was immediately informed. The surprise attack followed.

But when the first volley struck down the two men, Doyle himself remained behind to help bandage the wounds with the aid of Mary Hamilton until a cry from his men called him to them. They had found the niche in the quartzite and the gleaming particles of gold shining in it. And at the sight the whole crew had gone mad with the gold fever. They seized drills, picks, hammers, and flew at the hard rock, shouting as they hewed at it. There were practical miners among them but science was forgotten in the first frenzy. Jack·Doyle himself was drawn into the mob. They threw off their belts in the fury of the labor. They discarded their weapons.

What were guns with one dying and one wounded man behind them, and the only sound enemy a young girl? But John Hamilton, lying on the sand, had conceived a plan for reprisal and whispered it to his daughter. She took it up with instant courage.

His scheme was both simple and bold. The girl was to come near the workers, get as many of the guns as she could, and at least all of the weapons which were closest to the frenzied miners, and then fall back to one side. In the meantime John Hamilton was to squirm over to his rifle, train it on the bandits, and at his shout Mary also was to level one of the outlaws' own guns upon them.

It was a sufficiently bold plan to be successful. Rapt in the gold lust she could have picked the pockets of the gang as well as taken their weapons without drawing a word from them and, when the shout of John Hamilton came, the eight bold men and bad whirled, and found themselves helpless, unarmed, and looking down the muzzles of three guns. For the dying Delaney had dragged out a revolver, and now twisted over on one side, trained on a target.

Eight to three, when one of the three was a girl, seemed liberal odds but a repeating rifle in the hands of a good shot will go a long ways toward convincing the largest crowd. The gang might have attempted to rush even the leveled rifle of John Hamilton, to say nothing of the girl and Delaney, but a few terse words from their leader convinced them that they were helpless, and that the wise part was to attempt no resistance.

They obeyed grudgingly. John Hamilton issued curt orders; Delaney lay where he had fallen, his gun clenched in both hands, his dying face grim with determination. And the outlaws obediently stepped forward one by one; obediently turned their backs, kneeled, and folded their hands behind them, and each was bound securely by Mary Hamilton. They threatened wild vengeance during that time of humiliation. Only Jack Doyle himself had remained cool and unperturbed, and had whipped his followers into silence and obedience with his tongue.

Accordingly he was the last to be bound and, before the rope was fastened about his wrists, he was ordered to help Mary with the burden of Delaney. Together, under the gun of Hamilton, they lifted the wounded man into the wagon, Doyle making no attempt to escape to cover. And later under the cover of Mary's revolver Doyle, unaided, carried Hamilton to the wagon and laid him tenderly on a bed of straw.

"For his muscles ain't muscles; they're India rubber," Hamilton said. "He handled me like I was no heavier than a girl. He did that for a fact!"

But the problem was still a knotty one. They could not remain in this camp with Delaney dying, Hamilton wounded and liable to become feverish at any time, and therefore helpless, and one girl to guard and tend ten men. For every reason they had to get to the nearest habitation, and the nearest place was Cayuse.

But here again it was easier to name the thing than to do it. If eight strong men were placed in the wagon, bound, who would guard them, and also drive the team of horses? And if they were placed in the wagon, an additional burden of fifteen hundred pounds and more, would not the two horses be taxed to the limit of their strength?

There was only one young girl to handle eight men, bound indeed, but each of them desperate, and each willing to risk his life for freedom. For if they arrived in Cayuse, the mob would not wait for the law to take its course. It was the dying Delaney who suggested the only possible course which would start them toward Cayuse, and at the same time keep all the eight men under the eye of the girl. It was Delaney who proposed that they harness the eight men to the chain of the wagon and let the horses be led behind.

They discussed the plan urgently and briefly, for whatever they did, they had to do with speed. At length they decided that though the progress toward Cayuse by man power would be slow, yet the labor would serve to wear down the strength of the eight until they would shortly be past the point of offering any dangerous and concerted move. And above all it was necessary to keep them from an outbreak. Besides though they might not pick up anyone during the night, it was more than probable that early the next morning some freighter up Silver Cañon would overtake them, and then their troubles would end.

In this discussion Delaney took the weightiest part, for his words had the force of one about to die, and the selfless, kindly Irishman had the pleasure of seeing his murderers harnessed to the wagon which was to draw him to Cayuse and draw them into the power of the law. Altogether, the plan was not without a neatly ironic side.

The outlaws at least felt that side of it. At first, though they could not refuse the urge of the girl's revolver prodding their ribs, they would not take a step forward. Even the voice of Doyle, trembling with passion but submitting to the inevitable, could not stir them.

Until Mary Hamilton took out the long whip and sent the lash singing and cracking above their heads. She did not touch them with it, but the horror of the lash was sufficient. Under its flying shade they winced and then buckled to their work with a venomous lurch that shot the wagon forward.

The load was light for the broad wheels ate very slightly into the sand, rather packing it like the feet of a camel than cutting it like the feet of a horse, and the eight men found their labor easy enough. For the first hour they expended their spare breath in wild threats and volleys of curses. They cursed the girl who tormented them in the driver's seat of the wagon. They cursed themselves; they cursed their luck; they cursed gold; they cursed even the leader who had brought them to this pass.

Eventually the work grew keener, and the burden, which they had hardly noticed at first, now began to tell on them. They took shorter and shorter steps and began to move with a rhythm, leaning forward and swaying like a team of horses. And the spare breath was now gone; the dragging of the wagon burned out their throats and kept them silent. Once, in a futile outburst of rage, they turned and rushed about the wagon, gibbering at the girl, but their hands were still tied behind them, and the compelling point of the revolver sent them back to their places. They went groaning at their impotence.

Night fell on the wagon moving forward by fits and starts in a dreadful silence far more terrible than the air of blasphemy through which it had moved at first. Sitting on her seat she heard the death rattle of Delaney and ran back to him too late to hear his last words.

And later still, she was horrified by the voice of her father speaking to the dead man beside him. She lighted a lantern and spoke to him, but he turned on her glassy, blank eyes. The fever had reached his head, and he was mad with delirium. So she put out the lantern again and went back to her place. There she crouched, never daring to take her eyes off the swaying line of eight who struggled before her, the dead man behind her, the madman close at her side.

Finally her father no longer spoke aloud, but his voice was an insidious whisper hissing into the darkness. And all over Silver Cañon was the ghostly moon.

In this formation they had passed Lew Carney. The girl did not see him, for she was sitting far back in the wagon. No wonder that the eight harnessed men did not speak to him, for he would have been one more enemy to keep them in hand.

But they plodded on interminably until a haze grew up the valley, and then the sand storm struck them. Against it there was no possibility of pulling the wagon. The eight huddled together were a miserable group whipped by the flying dust.

Here the great calamity happened, for her father, rolling a cigarette in his delirium, managed to light a match in spite of the wind, but only to have the sulfur head fall among the straw that littered and piled the floor of the wagon. The blaze darted up at once, and the wind tossed it the length of the wagon in a breathing space. Her father began laughing wildly at the blaze; through the darkness it lighted the dead face and the living eyes of Delaney, and outside in the storm the eight men yelled with joy for they knew that their time had come.

There was no other way. She could not handle the weight of her father, and therefore she went to Doyle, cut his bonds, and forced him at the point of her revolver to drag out the body of Delaney and the living form of her father. He obeyed without a word, but when he had done his work, in the rush of sand, he took her unguarded and mastered her weapon hand. A moment later all eight were loosed, and the victors were again the vanquished.

In the meantime the wagon burned furiously. Some of the eight were for throwing Hamilton back into the blaze along with Delaney, to burn away all traces of their crimes. But when their leader assured them that there was not nearly enough of a conflagration to consume the bodies, they gave up that vengeance. They would have worked some harm to the girl also. They would have driven her with whips as she had driven them, but here again the leader interfered. He had been singularly gentle with Mary from the first and now he stood staunchly by her.

A can of oil overturned in the body of the wagon and the work of the fire was now quickly completed. Literally under her eyes Mary Hamilton saw the vehicle melt away, while the outlaws piled what loot they had rescued on the two horses.

A sharp altercation followed. For the seven insisted that John Hamilton be left to die in the storm where he lay, but once more the will of the leader prevailed. He made them take the wounded man in an improvised litter between the two animals. He himself rode one, and Mary rode the other, and so this strange procession started away toward the southern hills.

Behind them they left the iron skeleton of the wagon, already covered by the blowing sand; and so the mystery of the ghost wagon was explained. As for the revolver in the hand of Delaney, it had been placed there on impulse by the ironically chivalrous Jack Doyle; a tribute from one fighting man to another, as he had said afterward.

They found the shack by Coyote Springs after a march that brought terrible suffering to John Hamilton. Once there the gang insisted on an immediate return to loot the mine and recover their horses. To secure the horses back at the mine, one of the men was dispatched immediately. Another went to Cayuse to buy a second wagon and mules; and then Jack Doyle, giving way to another of his singularly kindly impulses, agreed to ride into Cayuse with the girl, while she met her brother and warned him away from the useless and dangerous trip into the desert. Doyle had risked his own life and the danger of public recognition to escort her; it was partly for the sake of seeing his financial backer, Bud Lockhart, and partly no doubt for the sake of winning the girl. He had only extracted from her a promise that, while in the town, she would not attempt to enlist any sympathizers, and that she would not speak a word or in any way cast them under a suspicion.

When she met Lew Carney the whole truth had come tumbling up to her lips, only to be driven back again by a remorseless conscience. One word to him, then, and she and her father could have been easily saved, and the outlaw apprehended by force of numbers. But she stayed with her promise and, when Doyle found her after his fruitless trip back to Bud Lockhart, she had felt bound in honor to repeat to him every word of her interview with Lew Carney. But Doyle felt assured that Lockhart would take care of the fellow; though, to make matters safe, he made her run her horse with his for the first few miles to outdistance any pursuit among the hills.

Such was the story of the ghost wagon in all its details as Lew Carney gathered it, partly from the girl, mostly from her father.

"And there," said John Hamilton calmly at the conclusion, "is the end of it!"

He pointed as he spoke, and Lew Carney saw the gray of the dawn overcoming the moonlight and changing the black mountains to blue.

XI "The Last Chance"

The three watched in silence.

"There's one thing I can't understand," said Lew Carney at last, "and that's how a man of the caliber of Jack Doyle can stand by and see a helpless man murdered. Why is it? He's played square the rest of the way."

The answer was both terrible and simple. The father raised his arm and pointed to the girl.

"He was pleasant to her as long as he could be," said John Hamilton. "But on the way back from Cayuse he figured that he'd done enough for her. He asked her then if there was any chance for him to be her friend, as much her friend as she'd let him be. She told him that she could never regard him as anything other than a black murderer. And she threw in a word about Delaney. Since then he's changed. He sees there's no chance with her by fair play, and I think he's ready for foul. And there she stands, free to leave if she will; and there she stays, doin' me no good . . . an anchor around my neck draggin' me down, knowin' that I'll suffer double because she stayed with me to the finish! After they finish me . . . Mary. . . ."

He choked as he looked at her, and she laid her finger warningly upon her white lips. She was wonderfully steady, and there was no quiver in her voice as she said: "It'll never come to that. Never!" And the two men glanced at each other, for they knew what she meant.

The revel outside rose to a yell of laughter and song; Lew Carney, his heart too full for endurance, went to the front door and looked out. There sat the six. Five of them were doing a veritable Indian war dance around the blaze, and their faces were the faces of madmen. But one man sat with a coat drawn like a cloak around his shoulders. He did not move; he did not glance at the others once; he sat with his knees bunched before him and his hands clasped around them, and Lew Carney knew that his position had not changed for hours. He felt, also, that there was a greater distance between that calm man sitting beside the fire and the wild men who danced around it, than there was between himself, Lew Carney, and the outlaws. While Jack Doyle was one of the band he led, at the same time he was apart from it. A touch of understanding and pity came to Lew Carney: the outlaw had sat there through the night looking on at the debauch with a stony face, never touching the liquor, but eating his heart out with the acid thought of the girl. He was not with the rest no matter if they rubbed his shoulders. And in that quiet, sitting figure there was a strength greater than the strength of all the others combined, a controlling strength, no matter how they raved.

It was this last conclusion that gave the idea to Lew Carney. He turned and went hastily back to the room.

"Go to the front of the shack," he said to Mary Hamilton, "and call in Doyle. Don't ask no questions. This is the last chance for all of us, and I'm going to take it."

Instead of immediately obeying, she stood for a moment looking at him, her head held high; and he would have thought that she was smiling if her eyes had not been bright with tears. But that look stayed with him to the day of his death.

Then she went to the front of the house, and they heard her calling.

"What is it?" asked John Hamilton. "Are you going to try to do for Jack Doyle alone? No use, Carney. There's too many of 'em. They'd only have to touch a match to the house, and . . . there's the end!"

They heard the girl coming back and the tread of a man moving with a soft, long step behind her. In a moment she was back in the room, and Jack Doyle, entering with her, was met by a soft call from the side. He did not turn. He seemed to see through the side of his head the leveled gun of Lew Carney, but he kept his glance steadily on the girl, and his face was working. She had turned toward him with a faint cry and now she shrank away, frightened by his expression.

"But now that you have him," said John Hamilton in a disgusted tone, "what you goin' to do with him? Eat him?"

"I'm going to use him," said Lew Carney, "to lick seven skunks into shape for us. That's what I'll do with him."

For the first time the outlaw turned toward Lew Carney, and Lew felt as though a pair of lights had focused on him. Once before he had felt fear. It was when the ghost wagon crawled up Silver Cañon. He felt it again looking straight into the eyes of Jack Doyle. For the fellow escaped classification. One could not say of him "good" or "bad." If the eyes of Lew Carney sometimes flamed with mirth or hate, these eyes of Jack Doyle had a property of phosphorus. They seemed self-luminous. He turned to the girl again.

"Is this your idea?" he asked.

She shook her head.

"Well?" he repeated to Lew Carney.

"Yes," nodded the other, "it's my idea. Now, watch yourself, Doyle. I've an eye on every move you make. I'm readin' your mind. These folks didn't see any way of usin' you, but I do. There's only one way we can get loose from this shack, and that's by havin' you call off your pack of bitin' dogs. And you're goin' to do it, Doyle. Why? Because if you don't, I'll blow your head off. Is that all straight? Yes?"

"You want me to talk to 'em while you keep me covered with a gun?"

"No. Give us your word that you'll do what you can to make your men pull away, and you're free to turn around and leave the room."

The outlaw flushed and paled in quick succession.

"I give you my word," he said without effort.

"Wait," murmured Lew Carney. "Don't give your word to me. Give it to Mary Hamilton. She'll be glad to hear you talk, I think."

"Curse you," whispered the leader through his teeth.

He turned slowly to the girl. Standing back against the far wall of the room, with the shadow across her face, she put her hand behind her to get support. She trembled when the look of Doyle fell on her, and Lew Carney saw her eyes shift and glow in the shadow. He knew then that the outlaw had once inspired something more than fear and horror in her. He could see Doyle standing on tiptoe like a leashed dog, straining with all the force of will and mind toward her, and Carney knew that the fellow had at least had grounds for hope, that he was fighting for the last time to regain that hope, and that he read in the whitening face of the girl the end of his chance.

At last—and it all happened in the gruesome silence—he looked across from her to Lew Carney, and the fingers of Lew Carney shuddered on the handles of his gun. He knew why this one man could tame the seven, wild as they might be.

Doyle looked back to the girl. "I give you my word," he said quietly, and he turned away.

"Wait!" called John Hamilton. "Are you goin' to trust to the bare word of a . . . ?"

But Lew Carney raised his hand and checked the father. He did more; he restored his revolver to its holster. And Doyle stepped close to him. He spoke softly and rapidly in such a guarded voice that no one else could hear the murmured words.

"You win," he said. "You've made a pretty play. You've got her. But as sure as there's a moon in the sky, I'll come back to you. I'll smash you as you've smashed me. You're free now. But count your days, Carney. Drink fast. You pay me the reckoning for everything."

He was gone through the door, and his soft, swift step crossed the outer room. They heard the voices of the seven raised beyond the house. They heard one calm voice giving answer. Before the dawn broke the eight men were gone miraculously and all the danger passed with them.

When the last sounds died away, Lew Carney turned to the girl, and she let him take her hand. But her face was hidden in her other arm, and to the end of his life Lew Carney was never to know whether she wept for sheer relief and happiness or because of Jack Doyle.

And this was how Lew Carney came over to the side of the law and reached the end of the trail of the ghost wagon.

Rodeo Ranch

"Rodeo Ranch" by Max Brand appeared in *Western Story Magazine* (9/1/23) and proved one of the most popular of all Faust's stories that year. Over a decade later, when Street & Smith launched the reprint magazine, *Western Winners*, "Rodeo Ranch" was showcased again early on in the (9/35) issue.

Who was Max Brand? A detailed but wholly fictitious portrait of him by D. C. Hubbard was published (along with a pen and ink sketch of his likeness) in *Western Story Magazine* (6/2/28). Max Brand at the time supposedly owned the Cross B Ranch. He was in Ore City, forty miles away, when Hubbard arrived, so Brand's ranch hands filled him in on the kind of man they had for a boss. "A quick mind usually means a quick temper, and although the boys of the Cross B Ranch would not admit it to us," Hubbard reflected, "Max himself, when he showed up two days later, acknowledged it freely." Brand had worked at writing for four years "in a small Western town which gave [him] all the elbow room he needed . . . ," and now he had achieved well-earned success both as an author and as a rancher. "Born and raised on the range, Max Brand at an early age showed great resourcefulness and courage . . . ," Hubbard concluded, adding that the author "is in the front line of worthwhile men today." Frederick Faust, on the other hand, on a trip to the Southwest in February, 1919, wrote his wife, Dorothy, that "this ranch life is worse than being in the Army. Stinking cowpunchers, rides in all sorts of weather—and all the stuff . . . which in reality is so discouraging." Ah, but in the mountain desert of his imagination, Faust could find magic, and it is surely there to be experienced at "Rodeo Ranch."

I "An Attack in the Dark"

It happened to *Señor* Don Ramon Alvarez in the following manner. He was deep in the first sleep of the night and in the middle of the first happy dream when he wakened suddenly. He heard nothing and saw nothing in the blackness of the room, yet he knew perfectly that he was in the greatest danger. So he lay still, concentrating upon the problem. Reason told him that his house was large, his servants many, and the probability of danger reaching him in his own room remote indeed; but when he struggled the hardest to assure himself of his safety, at that very moment instinct protested that he was wrong and that death was stalking softly toward his bed.

He turned his head toward the wall and the door. He could see nothing except those strange, formless objects which sift about in the darkness for those who stare hard enough and long enough into blank space. He reached up and under his pillow. He found the butt of the revolver and squeezed it with a huge relief. In fact, if there were an actual danger confronting him, he would not perish unavenged. Thus he assured himself as he lay there with the perspiration standing upon his forehead and his heart pounding like the thud of a racer's hoofs.

Then at the very moment when he had almost conquered his terror, he received the indubitable proof. For a hand touched him upon his breast, a soft and gliding touch. Still there was nothing to be seen in the darkness above him, and there was not a sound to be heard, but

Alvarez, with a strong twist of his body, whirled himself out from under the danger, whatever it might be, and rolled by a complete turn nearer the window. The cat which darts up and away as the shadow of the dog slides near moves not more quickly than did Don Ramon. And even so the blow missed him by a scant fraction of an inch. The bedclothes were jarred tight around his body. He heard the hiss of a blade that thrust its length into the mattress. He heard the faint grunt of one who has wasted a mighty effort, and then he fired into nothingness.

There was no shout of pain or protest, not even the patter of feet in flight. Far away in the house rolled the echo of the explosion, but still there was no sound of human voice. Small wonder that an assassin had come with a knife to hunt him, seeing that he was so insecurely guarded. Would it be hours before the dull-wits, the blockheads, had heard that gun and realized what it meant? Would it be hours before they rushed to his rescue? He could have been killed a hundred times before their efforts could have saved him or revenged him.

He fired again, with a wild panic starting in his brain, and the flash of the second shot showed him the work of the first. The body of a man was sprawled upon the foot of the bed, lying inert, limp, lifeless, as he knew by even that fraction of a second's glance.

Alvarez jumped from the bed and snapped on the electric light. And now he turned at last toward his victim and assailant. He went to the bed and leaned over. The dead man lay upon his face, his hands thrown straight above his head, and in the left hand was the knife which had already been thrust into the bedding in the search for the body of Alvarez. It was a tawny, long-fingered hand with a big emerald on the third finger, a flat-faced emerald upon which was incised a delicate design.

When Alvarez saw that design he whimpered softly and turned his head over his shoulder. If anyone had come through the door at that instant, he would have seen a face which was a veritable mask of tragedy and fear. The eyes were starting forth; the lips were drawn tight and were trembling; his nostrils expanded; his cheeks were sagging. He had grown, of a sudden, ten years older.

Such was the face which Alvarez turned toward the door; he ran to it and turned the key in the lock. Then back he raced to the prostrate form in the bed and, seizing it by the shoulder, he turned it over. He found himself looking down into wide, dull eyes, and upon the lips there was a crushed smile of foolish derision. Alvarez, however, had no regard for the smile. He was only interested in the features. It was a long, lean face. A habitual frown made a crease, even in death, between the eyes. The face was as yellow-tan as the hands. There was the smoke of Indian blood in that complexion, and in the yellow-stained pupils of the eyes.

Alvarez looked upon the dead man with a peculiar horror. He went backward at a staggering pace and fell into the arms of a big, over-stuffed chair. He slumped into it so inertly that his head struck against the thick roll at the back of the chair, and he sat there with his eyes riveted upon the wall before him as though he saw the pictures of his fate drawn in the clearest outline before him.

He passed his hand hastily through his hair. It was a dense mass of the thickest silver, and it stood up almost on end after the gesture, giving him an unwonted appearance of wildness and dissipation.

Now came footfalls down the hall. How long had it been since that report from the revolver should have roused the household? It seemed a quarter of an hour to Alvarez, though perhaps excitement had lengthened seconds to minutes for him. He heard a hand turn the knob of the door. Then there was a shout of fear when it failed to open. Others took up the cry, up and down the hall. Perhaps there were a score of tongues in the shout:

"They've murdered the master and locked his door! The *señor* is dead!"

Alvarez grinned at the door mirthlessly and shook his clenched fist at it, like one who suffers so much that he is glad to see anxiety in others. Then he hastened back to the limp figure upon the bed. He tore the ring from the third finger of the left hand, looked down with a shudder to the diagram upon the face of the emerald, and dropped it in his pocket. Then he went in the greatest haste through the pockets of the deceased. There was a wallet stuffed with papers and with plenty of currency. Certainly hunger and pressing poverty could not have impelled the stranger to the crime which he had attempted, for there was something over a thousand dollars in that wallet. And had he been in need, he might have raised several thousand more upon the emerald, for it was a stone as large and splendid as it was strangely cut. And it was odd indeed to find a jewel so precious, cut as a seal!

Alvarez shoved the wallet under his pillow. In the other pockets of the stranger he discovered nothing of importance. There were cigarettes, a few cigars—thick at the fire end after the Mexican style—and a heavy pocketknife mounted in gold, but without any identifying initials. All of these things Alvarez left in the clothes of the stranger. Then he turned to the door of his bedroom against which his servants were thundering. He strode to it and cast it wide open, with the result that he nearly received half a dozen bullets in the face, so convinced were his adherents that he was dead and that only his murderer could be living in the room.

They gave back with lowered guns and with yells of joy when they saw that it was Alvarez himself who stood before them. The cook fell upon his knees and threw up his hands in thanksgiving, so that Alvarez was touched, and it took a great deal indeed to move Alvarez.

Yet he would not allow his gentler feelings to control him. As they stood before him, he scowled heavily and let them have the full advantage of his expression before he uttered a word. Then it was to shout at them: "Traitors! Blockheads! Fools! Have you left me here to be massacred while you slept in your beds? I have fed you and clothed you and treated you like my children! I have squandered my money upon you. I have given you all a home. And now I am left here to be murdered in my bed!"

They drew together in a frightened huddle under his torrent of abuse, which was freely interspersed and sprinkled with oaths. They began to protest that the instant they heard the explosion of the gun in the room of the master they had come at once to his rescue, but he shut them off with more curses.

At length he bade them come in and view the villain who would have destroyed his life, and they trooped in together, whispering and gasping with horror until they found the body upon the bed. Then they were speechless and with that as an object lesson before them, Alvarez read to them a long lecture upon the beauties of honest and faithful service to an overgenerous master, for like some other employers of labor Alvarez appreciated his own virtues to the uttermost.

He drove them out, at length, and sent some of them to find the coroner and others to find the sheriff. He himself went back into the bedroom and spent a few minutes walking up and down, up and down, his face twisted with anxiety. It was not the man lying upon the bed to whom he gave a thought. It was rather the presence of some danger in the outer world which troubled him and which caused him, now and again, to pause at one of the big windows and shake his fist at the possibilities which lay somewhere between him and the misty circle of the horizon.

When the sheriff arrived, he found the rich rancher dressed and in his library. The language of Alvarez was strange for a man who has recently escaped from the hands of a secret and midnight murderer, for he told the sheriff that he was sorry for the thing which he had been compelled to do that night. He was confident that no man would willingly assail the life of another man who had not injured him, and that there must have been some cause of great poverty and pressing need which had caused the stranger to invade his home. The sheriff replied with a grunt.

II "The Rodeo"

As a matter of course, Alvarez received nothing but praise for the adroitness with which he had baffled the murderer. It was surmised that the absence of any papers which might identify the stranger, as well as the removal of the ring from his finger—for the pale band was noted as well as the indentation in the flesh of the finger—indicated that the murderer, in taking his chance to kill the rich rancher, had purposely removed all possible means of identifying himself in case he should be killed in the attempt. As for the purpose of destroying Alvarez, it was instantly apparent, for around his neck Alvarez wore the key which opened the safe in which his money for current expenses was kept. And that money was enough to make a large haul.

But, on the whole, the attempt to destroy Don Ramon was considered lucky for the district for it was the immediate cause of the celebration of a great festival by the rancher. He wished to indicate his joy at his escape, and for that reason he organized a rodeo which quite put in the shade other affairs of the kind.

There was one fault to be found with his plans, and that was that there was only a week's notice given. However, the instant his announcement was made, it was carried in all the newspapers of the range towns, and four days were enough to bring in 'punchers from the distant sections. Furthermore, the prizes were of such a nature that every skillful man along the range was sure to come if he possibly could, for Don Ramon had dipped deeply into his pocket for the sake of the festival. There were handsome cash prizes for every event. And the events ranged from fancy roping to foot racing, from horse-breaking to knife-throwing, from boxing to shooting. There were events in which cowboys were sure to excel, and there were events in which *vaqueros* were certain to excel, and there were others in which Indians would stand forth. Who but an Indian, for instance, could be expected to win a twenty-four-hour race across the desert and the mountains?

On the whole it would be a great spectacle, and people immediately began mustering for it. But, in the meantime, there was a single blot upon the happiness of the occasion, and that was the news that Don Ramon was confined to his bed, and that he might not be able to view the sports of the great day. The nature of his sickness was not known. Some held that it was the result of a nervous breakdown caused by the crisis through which he had just passed and others, again, declared that the poor don was suffering merely from old age.

However that might be, Don Ramon did not leave his bed in the interim before the sports began. Neither did he rise on the morning of the festival, but sent his *majordomo* to distribute the prizes in his name. He stayed in his bed attended by his doctors and surrounded by soft-footed servants. It was not until the late afternoon of the day that he arrived in the field. He came there, indeed, barely in time for the last and the greatest of all the contests. That was the shooting.

Ordinarily, gun play held secondary place in such affairs, if it appeared at all, but on this occasion it was given a great emphasis by the prize which was offered. It was a prize calculated to attract every red-blooded cowpuncher who had ever had any skill with guns in his life. It was the sort of prize which made even the spectators yearn to be in the lists taking part in the trial of skill. In a word, the prize which Don Ramon was offering was his famous chestnut stallion, *El Capitán*. He was a six-year-old king among horses, and had been brought to the West especially to give Don Ramon's ranch an unequaled stock of finest horseflesh. *El Capitán* had cost the don a trip to England and many thousands of dollars. *El Capitán,* as Don Ramon christened the horse, was immediately considered an object of public pride by the entire community. Ever since it had been announced that he was to be the prize for the shooting, people had begun to wonder if Don Ramon had gone mad or whether the stallion was not so wonderful after all. The result was that for weeks crowds had come to watch him in his corral.

El Capitán was not much under seventeen hands in height, but for all his bulk he was built like a picture horse. His gait was as light and mincing as any dancing pony's. His head was all that a horse's head should be, a very poem of beauty, courage, pride and great-heartedness. And that this miracle among horses should be given as the prize in a shooting match was almost too strange to be true. Don Ramon was forced to give an explanation through his *majordomo*. His ranch was stocked with *El Capitán*'s progeny and therefore it was possible for him to part with his favorite. But most of all he was giving the stallion to encourage marksmanship and practice with guns among the cowpunchers of the range, for he declared that the greatest of all frontier accomplishments was falling into disuse in the new century, and it was his ambition to restore it.. Beginning with this year he would offer an annual prize for the best shot in the West. And each prize would be almost as splendid as the one he was offering this season.

This explanation was accepted for what it might be worth, but the cowpunchers were frankly incredulous. *El Capitán* was worth a small fortune. It was still incredible that he should be put up for the prize in a day's sport. However, having been carefully examined, he was pronounced without a single flaw. Altogether he was matchless. In England he had not been fast enough to keep up with the light-footed sprinters on the tracks and so he had not been of use either as a racer or as a sire of racers. But where the course was to last all day and where the track was not a smoothed turf but a wild way over mountains and sandy deserts, *El Capitán* kept going where other horses dropped beside the way.

The very best men in the country came to vie with one another in the contest. It was an unusual struggle, unlike any that had ever been held before. It began with rifle shooting at close and long range. It continued with rifle shooting at moving objects. And it closed with revolver work, and skill with the revolver counted against skill with the rifle as three is to one! For the revolver, said Don Ramon in his announcement, should be the unique weapon of the Western ranges.

All centered, then, upon adroitness with the smaller weapon. In the beginning the contestants were lined up and asked to try their skill upon stationary targets. These targets were large-headed nails driven into boards and placed at such a distance that they were almost invisible! Five men came through this contest. The others were hopelessly distanced. Then the five were required to shoot at bricks thrown into the air at a uniform height and distance and, when that part was over, they were made to mount their horses and ride at a gallop between two rows of posts on each of which a small can was placed. Those cans had to be blown off, and there was only one way in which it could be done. The horse must be controlled with the knees and the voice, and there must be a revolver in each hand.

The five set their teeth and prepared for the crucial tests. They had weathered the brick shooting well enough. Shooting from the firm ground at a moving object was one thing, but shooting from a moving object at a stationary point was another. The difference is that which exists between guns on shore and guns at sea. Everyone knows that a single large caliber gun on land is equal to a whole battleship armed with a dozen such guns afloat in the water.

So, with their horses prepared, their guns ready, the five awaited the signal. It was given and Shorty Galbraith, famous in song and story in spite of his scant forty years, went gallantly down the rows. His horse cantered with the rhythmical precision of a circus animal. It rocked slowly ahead, and from either hand Shorty blazed away at the cans. His bullets flicked off the first three pair. Then he began to miss with his left-hand gun and scored two blanks with his port weapon, a thing which so upset him that with his last two shots he missed on both sides. He had knocked off eight out of twelve cans, however, and that was a score amazingly high. It would be extraordinary if it were much improved upon by any of the remaining four champions. For Shorty was almost ambidextrous and could use his right hand almost as well as his left.

The applause which greeted Shorty's effort had hardly died down when old Chapman, hero of a score of fights in the old days and still as steady of eye and hand as ever, started for the posts. He scored a double miss on the first pair of posts. But the next four pair went off as if by magic, and exultant cheers were beginning from his supporters when he missed as completely on the last pair as he had missed on the first. However, he had tied with Shorty. And he reined his horse to one side, prepared heartily to wish bad luck to the remaining three contestants. Of these the first one to make the attempt failed almost completely. He knocked off one of the first pair, but then his horse started forward too fast, and he succeeded in bringing down only three of the remaining targets. But the marksman who followed called up a hysteria of cheering by actually bringing down nine of the cans. So loud was the yelling that the old fellow had to take off his hat to the thunder and wave it at his admirers. He was a veteran frontiersman, tall, lean, with a head on which flashed many a gray hair when he had removed his sombrero. His name was Sam Calkins and, though he was not as well known as some of his competitors, his figure, his stately bearing, his grave and reserved manner of speech complied with all the traditions of the West. Everyone instantly wished him well, particularly because of the character of his single opponent who remained to rival his score.

The latter had won the disapproval of the crowd earlier in the match. In the first place, instead of the usual cowpuncher's outfit, he was dressed in riding trousers of neat whipcord, and his boots of soft, black leather were polished like two dark mirrors. The very hat upon his head was new, and instead of a wide-brimmed sombrero it was a close-brimmed affair which set jauntily a little upon one side of his head. He was set off with a red bow tie. But, above all, instead of sitting in a true range saddle, he was mounted upon a smooth English affair, with short stirrups. But his manners had given even more offense than his clothes. He had joked and laughed through half of the contests. He was still smiling as he reined his horse toward the beginning of the double row of posts. And the crowd, with a scowl of cordial dislike, held its breath. Not that it actually thought that such a hero as the efficient Sam Calkins could be bested by this stranger who was so obviously not of the range, but because they dreaded even the hundredth chance. Moreover, everyone had to admit that Duds Kobbe, as they had nicknamed the stranger, had shot amazingly well hitherto.

He went to the starting point amidst loud yells of advice.

"Mind your necktie, Duds."

"The girls are all lookin' at you, kid!"

"Your mama'd be proud to see you, Duds!"

To this he responded with another of his laughs, and then started his horse down the gantlet, and with such careless speed that his rate of going was half again as great as that of any of the previous riders. And, seeing his nonchalance, the crowd waited with held breath, dreading, hoping.

Crash went his guns, and the first two cans were blown from the tops of the posts. He fired again and the second pair went down. And the pace of his galloping horse had actually increased. Again he fired, and the third pair went down. Still he was not turning his head from side to side, but he rode with his face straight forward and seemed to be sighting his guns either from the corners of his eyes or by instinct. It was like wizardry!

There was a heavy groan of relief when he missed with his right hand gun on the fourth pair. There was an actual shout when he failed with his left hand gun on the fifth. There remained the final pair. Men noticed in the interim that stanch Sam Calkins had not ceased rolling his cigarette, and that at the very instant of the crisis he was actually reaching for a match. He was upholding the good stoical Western tradition in the time-honored way.

But in the meantime young Kobbe was at the final pair of posts. He shot the left hand can cleanly from its post. He had tied Sam at the worst! And at the best he might yet. . . . The crowd refused to consider the possibility. The groan took an audible sound of a word: "miss!"

And it seemed as if there were a magic in that wish. For when he fired his twelfth shot the can was not flicked from the post top. A loud yell of exultation rose from the crowd. However, that cry stopped in mid-breath, for the can had been grazed by the bullet and was rocking and tottering in its place. It reeled to one side. It staggered to the other and would have settled down in its place in quiet, as many of the bystanders afterward declared, had not a gust of wind of uncanny violence at this instant cuffed the can away and tumbled it to the ground!

III "Duds Kobbe"

There could not have been a stronger proof of the unpopularity of the stranger than the groan with which the crowd witnessed this piece of good fortune. But they were stunned by what followed. For Duds Kobbe, riding back from the conclusion of the trial, approached the judges, who were three old ranchers, now sour-faced with disappointment, and assured them that he would not accept a win which had been given him by the wind and chance rather than his own skill.

The judges could hardly believe their ears and, though in strict justice they should have awarded the prize to him and insisted that there should be no further contest, they were only human, and all three of them, if the truth must be admitted, had placed their money upon the celebrated Sam.

In the meantime, Sam had half-heartedly protested that he could not accept another chance since he had been fairly beaten, but in the middle of his protest he glanced across to the place where *El Capitán* was being held, and the sun at that instant flashed along the silken flanks of the great stallion. It was too much for Sam, and his protest died, half uttered. But the news of what had happened swept in stride through the crowd. It was one of those things that make men shake their heads and then see with new eyes. When they looked across to the shining form of the stallion as he turned and danced in the sunshine and, when they realized that a man had voluntarily given up that king of horses for the sake of some delicate scruple of conscience, they prepared to revise their opinions of the stranger. They looked at him through different eyes, and what they saw was something more than the oddness of his appearance. It had been impossible, up to this time, for the spectators to see anything in Duds Kobbe except his extraordinary clothes. Now they discovered that he was a fine-looking fellow, a shade under twenty-five years, straight, wide-shouldered, big-necked, spare of waist, and with long and sinewy arms. He was the very ideal of the athlete, as a matter of fact, and the closer they looked at him the better they liked him.

If his skill with guns had not proclaimed him a man, his fine rich tan, his clear voice, and the manner in which he sat his saddle would have convinced the discerning that there was real metal in him. And when the two sat their horses at the beginning of the double row of posts, when the cans had been replaced, and when Sam had loaded his guns with infinite care, it would have been hard for the crowd to pick its favorite. Sam was a fine fellow, but he had showed himself a little too eager to accept the proffered generosity of the stranger. Kobbe had shown himself above and beyond all meanness.

Sam rode first, as before. He duplicated his original feat, knocking off nine of the cans, but Kobbe, riding down the line, actually blew eleven of the twelve from their places and was rewarded with a roar of applause from the bystanders. The evening was growing heavy in the west when they brought Duds Kobbe to the chestnut horse. Instantly they were aware of an anachronism. For *El Capitán* carried a heavy Western range saddle, and the winner of the prize was dismounting from an English pad. But they were left in doubt for only an instant. Duds Kobbe bounded down from the one horse and onto the back of the other without pause. He swept off his hat and slapped *El Capitán* across the neck with it and at the same time pricked him with the spurs.

Never before had the great stallion been treated in such fashion. He had been surrounded by tenderness all of his days. Now he was used like a common range pony. He tried first to jump into the center of the sky. Then he strove to knock a hole in the earth with his hoofs and stiffened legs. After that he passed through a frantic maze of bucking, only to come out on the farther side, so to speak, with his rider as gay in the saddle as ever, still slapping him with the annoying hat, still tickling his sides with the spurs. *El Capitán* stopped, shook his head, and looked back to consider this curious puzzle in the saddle upon his back.

So the contest ended and passed into legend. The legend grew until it reached amazing proportions, and on this day they will tell the inquisitive stranger how Duds Kobbe tossed his revolvers into the air and caught them again between every shot. But when Duds was riding off the field, surrounded by laughing, shouting, good-natured men, a dark-faced fellow approached him from the side and rode close.

"*Señor* Alvarez," he said, "is eager to see *Señor* Kobbe," and with that he turned and rode away. Kobbe, as soon as he could be rid of his well-wishers and had shaken hands with Sam, who buried his disappointment behind a smile, turned the head of the chestnut toward the house of Alvarez.

He did not stay for the feast at which all the other participants gathered that night, where the long tables were spread with food enough for all the villagers and all the spectators. They were served with the meat of steers roasted whole, to say nothing of scores of kids, fresh from the pits where they had been faithfully turned by the sons and daughters of the ranch hands on the wide lands of Alvarez. There were chickens and geese stewed in immense pots over open fires. In fact, people were staggered when they thought of the amount of money which the rancher must have expended upon this banquet. But it helped them to understand how he could have offered as the prize for the shooting contest the glorious *El Capitán*.

Duds Kobbe had adapted himself with the most perfect ease to the big range saddle which was on the back of *El Capitán,* and which the generosity of Alvarez made a part of the prize. He passed deeper into the domains of Alvarez. He crossed, in the first place, a long drift of rolling hills, covered with rich grass, and now dotted with fat cattle. Then he went on to a valley which was under close cultivation with the plough. It was soil rich enough for truck farming. Vegetables, berries, fruits were produced in vast bulk from that valley. And this was only a simple unit in the estate. He rode on into an upland district which was a sort of plateau whose level top afforded thousands of acres for the raising of wheat, barley, oats, and hay. From the plateau rose a range of high hills, covered with sturdy pine forests. And these were regularly planted and cut, as he could see in passing through. Beyond this was another huge domain of cow country, all good range. And past the extremity of this district he arrived at the lofty trees, the sweeping lawns where a thousand sprinklers were whirring, and the white walls and the red roofs of the house of Alvarez itself.

But what Duds had seen in his approach had been merely an outer segment, a mere wedge of the whole estate. It swept away on all hands in a great circle. No doubt there were far richer things than he had seen. In the upper hills—or mountains they might be called—he understood that there were rich copper mines. These, too, were part of the property of Alvarez, and with the lumber, the fruits, the cattle, the horses, the minerals, he could understand how a single horse and a single saddle might not seem too rich a prize for a shooting contest. For the wealth of Alvarez was a thing which he himself no doubt did not understand and perhaps he could not have guessed half its extent.

There was something inspiring in the thought of such money, for it made of Alvarez a king among men in wealth and power. Every man who passed through a corner of the estate of the rich Spanish-American could not help but feel his spirit expand at the thought of possibly rivaling Don Ramon.

Kobbe came to the patio and there reined the stallion, for the gates in front of the garden were secured. He looked through the bars at the wide façade and the ponderous overhanging eaves and the great, nobly proportioned windows of the house. It had the simplicity of a true Spanish house of the Southwest, but it had the dignity of an Athenian temple. Duds Kobbe, though he was not easily impressed, gaped like a child at the big building. Presently he found that a dark-skinned servant was grinning at him, nearby. And Kobbe grinned back at him. "Very big," said Kobbe frankly. "Very old?" He asked this in good faith.

The servant shrugged his shoulders. "Five years," he said at last.

"Then *Señor* Alvarez built it?" asked Kobbe with manifest surprise.

"No. It was built by another man."

"Who?"

"I forget. He died afterward. He owed the *señor* money, and so the *señor* took the house."

"Ah," said Duds softly. "I thought it would be something like that. Will you tell him that I am here? He has sent for me."

"What name?" asked the servant.

"Kobbe," said Duds.

And the servant went to execute the order.

IV "The Girl"

The *mozo* returned almost at once and opened the gate, bringing a companion with him who took charge of *El Capitán*. Then he led Duds Kobbe into the house to Alvarez. The latter was seated in a little study whose walls were lined with books—books which were decorative rather than for use. They were all in extensive sets of green and red and yellow leather, decorated with expensive tooling in gold. And Kobbe could tell at a glance that their set and ordered ranks were not broken by the hands of casual readers. As for the volume which lay on the table near the hand of Alvarez, it was placed there for effect to complete the picture. Kobbe knew all this the instant he stepped through the door. And he knew, furthermore, that he was seated facing the window, while the master of the house had his back to it so that the latter could study him more carefully while his own face remained in the shadow.

"You are kind," said Alvarez, "in coming to me so quickly."

"I hoped to see you at the barbecue," said Kobbe.

"I am not well," said Alvarez. "The doctors have me on a short rein, and I cannot follow my own wishes. Otherwise I should be down there now. But I was long enough at the ground to see you shoot, *señor,* and to admire you for your skill."

"My horse gave me an easy seat, that's the answer," answered Kobbe smilingly. "But what is it you need of me, *Señor* Alvarez?"

"My need?"

"You have not organized such a festival for nothing."

"Of course not. I have told everyone that my purpose is to begin a long series of such contests. Cool heads and steady hands and straight eyes are worth a great deal, *señor,* and I hope that my little festival will make men value them every year more and more."

"Of course that is one purpose, and a very generous one," replied Kobbe. "But there is another reason. There is a reason which has to do with you, *Señor* Alvarez."

The latter shrugged his shoulders. "I cannot understand," he said.

"If you had given cash prizes, I should not doubt you, but when you give *El Capitán*. . . ."

"After all, a fine horse is only money in another form."

"You made a long trip to England to buy him. He is of great value to you."

"But here he is hardly used for work. He needs to be on a plain and through the mountains with a good rider like yourself, *señor*. I made him one of the prizes for that reason!"

"I shall believe that if you wish."

"You speak strangely, *señor*."

"And you, *Señor* Alvarez, act very strangely."

The rancher flushed. "In what way?"

"You have placed men to watch me even while I am talking to you."

"Certainly not!"

"A touch of wind moved a branch of that tree outside the window. It showed me a fellow crouched in the forking of the limbs. He can peer through the leaves and watch everything that passes in the room. And he has a short rifle in his hands so that if he sees a game worth bringing down . . . you understand me, *señor*?"

Alvarez bit his lip and grew even a brighter red. He seemed to hesitate for an instant whether to deny or admit that his guest had seen the truth.

"You are very frank," he said at last.

"I must be," answered Duds Kobbe. "If I am to be of use to you and you to me, we must be frank. Must we not?"

"Then tell me your opinion. What do you see that is a mystery? What do you understand my motives to be?"

"In holding the rodeo?"

"Yes."

"The rodeo is a mask. What you wanted was the shooting contest only. But it would seem too strange if you sent out invitations for that alone. So you arranged a whole rodeo of which the shooting was only a single part."

"You are very sure!"

"I am."

"And what could my purpose have been?"

"To find a fast and accurate shot."

"*Señor,* you grow omnipotent!"

"I am sorry if I am wrong."

"Why should I need a fast and accurate shot?"

"To take care of you, *Señor* Alvarez, in place of the doctors."

"What manner of foolish talk is this?"

"Only the truth."

"Do you mean that I wish a gunfighter to cure me of sickness?"

"Of the sort of sickness that troubles you a gunfighter could take much better care than a doctor."

"And what is my ailment, *señor?*"

Duds Kobbe glanced hastily around the room to assure himself they were alone. Then he leaned a little toward his companion so that he could bridge the distance between them with the softest of voices.

"You sickness is called acute fear of sudden death, *Señor* Alvarez!"

The rich man half started from his chair. For a moment he remained with his eyes staring, his lips parted, his face the picture of amazement, and his right hand raised in a singular gesture.

"Do not give the signal," said Kobbe, "for, if you do, that fellow in the tree will start shooting at me. And if he does, I shall have to try my hand at you!"

Alvarez recovered himself with a gasp and sank back. "What under the blue heaven has put this idea into your head?"

"A number of things."

"Name a few, then."

"The first sight of *El Capitán.* A man does not give up such a horse unless he is in fear of something no less than death."

"This is only an opinion you are giving me, not a fact."

"Well, then, for the facts. I come out here and am brought before the master of the house. I find him reported to be an invalid, hardly able to journey to the field of the rodeo. I come to his house and find him a sturdy-looking man with a fine, clear color. . . ."

"There are maladies which do not show in the face, my friend," said Alvarez calmly.

"But if you are not sick, what then is wrong with you? Fear can be like a disease, I have been told. Suppose that fear has kept you in your house, since the attempt was made on your life."

"If I considered myself in danger, there are capable sheriffs in this country. They would take charge of my problem."

"Suppose that the power you fear is something that a sheriff cannot help. As for sheriffs and men with guns, you could fill your house with them. There is the fellow in the tree outside the window, for instance."

"The blockhead!" exclaimed Alvarez. "He is a pig without sense!"

"He had not counted on the wind. That is all."

"But in short, my plan in holding the rodeo was to secure the most capable bodyguard that I could find and, in order to do that, I would spare no expense and would use even my finest horse as a bait . . . a horse which my daughter loves passionately . . . yet I give him up as the bait to draw the best man into my trap?"

"That," said Kobbe, "is exactly my idea. Am I wrong?"

The other hesitated a moment, drumming on the arm of his chair and looking straight before him as though, for a moment, he had forgotten the presence of his guest.

"You are entirely right," he said at last. 'I am living in fear of sudden death. I have been existing through this past week in the fear of a knife in the back or a bullet through the heart. And the law I cannot call into my use. How can I tell that the men of the law themselves will not be bribed?"

"How can you tell that *I* may not be bribed?" asked Kobbe.

"By your face," said Alvarez. "There are certain things which we know by instinct. I think that this is one thing. We know a man as we know a note of music from all other notes. The difference appears to the ear alone and cannot be described. In that way I know that you are an honest man."

"And you know nothing of me except what you have seen?"

"I am not a fool. Do you think that I would put my head into the mouth of a strange lion? I know a great deal more about you than you will imagine. The instant the rodeo began, I started inquiries about every one of the men who were entered for the shooting contest. About you I learned that you were born in Wyoming, were taken East when your uncle with whom you were living . . . because your father had been dead for ten years . . . struck it rich in the mines. That you were educated in the East, but that when your uncle lost his money you returned to the West again."

"Then," said Kobbe, "you know my father's name?"

"Of course. His name was John Turner. And your name is John Kobbe Turner."

Kobbe, or Turner, as he had just been called, sat stiffly in his chair. Some of the color had left his cheeks. And his eyes had grown as grave and as brilliant as the eyes of a great beast of prey. Alvarez winced before that stare, but he maintained a steady smile as well as he could.

"What more," asked Kobbe, "do you know about me?"

"That you are a straight shot," said Alvarez. "And that is all I wish to know."

"What is your proposition?" asked Kobbe.

"A salary which you can name at your own pleasure. You will have a room next to my room. It will be your duty to live night and day with weapons at hand ready to come to my help at my first signal. I shall have other guards working outside the house, but if peril comes from within, then I shall have you to strike for me. What do you say to this, *Señor* Turner?"

"Kobbe, if you please!"

"By all means, *Señor* Kobbe."

"Give me a moment to think it over."

"As long as you wish."

Kobbe, as he preferred to be called, stood up and walked slowly back and forth across the little room and finally stood in front of the window looking out upon the garden and the tree which stood in it, holding the guard. He was seeing nothing but his own thoughts, however, and these brought a black frown to his forehead until, out of a side path, a girl walked into his view, singing. She had pushed a small red rose into her black hair. Her face was tilted up by her song and her olive cheeks were bright. Slowly she crossed that part of the garden which Kobbe could overlook, until the weight of his eyes seemed to warn her. She paused suddenly, glanced across to him, and with an exclamation of alarm fled from his view.

He turned slowly to Alvarez. "I shall stay," he said.

V "Señor Lopez"

The stipulations of Alvarez were strict. Kobbe, so long as he cared to stay on the place and with the work, must never leave the immediate precincts of the house and the gardens. He must be ready at any time to accompany Alvarez on journeys, no matter of what extent, and he must hold himself ready, day and night, to come to the defense of the older man with all his skill and with unfailing courage. In return, he was to receive a handsome salary, a chair at the table of Alvarez, a *mozo* to look after his needs, and every possible liberty of motion within the house and its immediate grounds. It was not necessary that he be constantly near the person of Alvarez. It was, however, vital that he be within calling distance at all times.

And Kobbe accepted, making only one exception—which was that he be allowed to take one hour's freedom with *El Capitán* before his period of service began. And so, a few minutes later, he was galloping across the hills at a round rate, with the big chestnut stretching away with a stride as easy as flowing water and almost as smooth.

Kobbe held straight on until he came to a thicket between two hills. There he paused and raised a sharp whistle. It was answered almost at once, and after a moment a second horseman broke out from a covert and rode hastily down to meet him.

The newcomer was a stately fellow, well past middle age, arrow straight in the saddle, with a dark skin and a black eye and a sort of foreign gentility which was as easily distinguishable as the color of his eyes, but which was difficult to describe. He greeted Kobbe by raising his hand in salutation.

"Something has gone wrong, my son," he said as he drew close and reined his horse to a halt.

"It has," said Kobbe.

"What is it?"

"I can't raise a hand against him."

"You?"

"I've made up my mind. I cannot attempt to injure him."

A flush of hot anger settled in the face of the older man but, like a person of experience, he did not speak for an instant, allowing the flush to subside a little and some of the sparkles to pass out of his eyes.

"What has happened?" he asked at length.

"In the first place, he trusted me."

"And so, in the old days, did we trust him."

"*Señor* Lopez, his crime was committed a long time ago."

"But it has never been forgotten."

"Perhaps you are wrong to keep it so close to your heart all these years."

"Your father would not have been of that opinion."

"You cannot judge. My father was a man who often changed his mind. I remember it very well."

"He could change his mind, but he could never change it about his murderer."

"Murderer? I cannot help thinking that that word is too strong."

"Dastardly murder, John, of a man who trusted him and to whom he owed a great deal."

"Nothing has ever been known for certain."

"We have evidence which only a fool could doubt."

"I shall be sorry to have you write me down a fool."

The older man shrugged his shoulders.

"I shall try to be very temperate," he said. "I have no desire to anger you, my boy. I know that whatever conclusion you have come to has the gravest reasons behind it. For you are your father's son, after all, and being his son you must have the strongest desire in your heart to revenge him."

"If I were sure that Don Ramon were guilty. . . ."

"Call him by his true name."

"Why not by the new name? Under the old name I hate him. Under the new name I have found him gentle, courteous, and willing to trust me."

"So did we all find him until the time for the test came."

"But consider that for ten years he has been living in this country, and he has taught his servants and his neighbors to love him. They all swear by Don Ramon."

"So they might have sworn by your father, if he had been alive. But this treacherous hound removed him from the earth."

"It is not proved. Besides . . . it is possible for men to change, *señor*."

"Some men can change from good to better, or from bad to worse. But no man can change his essential nature."

"I cannot help doubting the truth of that."

"Other people have doubted it, but it is always proved."

"If there were not such a thing as repentance, why should people be punished and not destroyed? But society believes that men who have committed one fault may not necessarily be all bad. They may change and learn better ways."

"The spots on the leopard will not change, my son."

"What evil has he done for ten years?"

"He has grown fat with money which is not his. It is easy to be a giver of charity when one is passing on stolen money."

"He has a straight, clear eye, and he talks like a man."

"But he has the heart of a devil under that eye, my young friend. What will the ghost of your murdered father think when he looks down and sees that you are reconciled to his murderer?"

"He will think that I am doing only what my conscience tells me to do."

"Conscience, John?"

"What else?"

"Has the money of Ramon, as you call him, nothing to do with it?"

"Sir?" said Kobbe coldly.

"I am not accusing you. I am only asking you to open your eyes to motives which you yourself may not be aware of."

"His money has no weight with me."

"You are a remarkable young man, then."

"Your tongue is sharp today, *señor.*"

"What has happened? This morning you called him a snake that should be treated as a snake is treated. How has he changed in the meantime?"

"He has changed by being known."

"John, you are talking lightly to me. Do I deserve no better than this from you?"

"I am talking to you as honestly as I know how."

"Tell me this, then. What do you intend to do?"

"I have taken a new position." He raised his head and looked Lopez firmly in the eye, and yet he flushed in spite of himself, in shame for the thoughts which he knew would spring into the mind of his companion when what he had done was known.

"And that position?" asked Lopez, turning pale.

"You have already guessed it."

"I pray to heaven that I have not guessed correctly."

"Very well, then. I'll tell you in so many words. I already know the way in which you will judge me. I only ask you to keep the spoken words to yourself. Yes, I have taken a position as the bodyguard of Don Ramon!"

There was a groan from Lopez. "Treason!" he cried at last.

"No," said Kobbe, "but a love of fair play."

"Is it fair play to leave us and be bought up by the money which our enemy has stolen from us?"

"I know this much," said Kobbe slowly, making a great effort to control himself, "that Don Ramon was always accused by you of having committed a crime which is too detestable to name. Perhaps he is guilty. But my personal feeling after meeting him face to face and talking with him in his own house is that he cannot be guilty of such a crime. If I am wrong, I am very sorry."

"You have not only made up your mind that he is innocent, but you have determined to fight for him?"

"There is no one else in the world who *could* fight on his side. There is no one else who knows the names and the faces of the men who are against him. There is no one else who can tell that he is being hounded down by a conspiracy."

"Conspiracy?"

"There is hardly a better word for it. You have tried him according to your own prejudices and not according to the law. You are going to butcher him like a dog if you can. I tell you *Señor* Lopez, it is going to be my work to keep you from it!"

The eyes of the other flashed fire, and his lips worked for a moment before he could speak in answer.

"Go back to him, then," he said at last. "Tell him the names, describe our faces, tell our purpose. He will have the hills combed with posses before midnight has come. He will hunt us down, perhaps. And rather than be caught, we will die fighting, be assured! Our blood will be upon your head! Farewell!"

"Wait," said Kobbe, greatly moved. "You have misunderstood me. I shall not whisper a word that will identify or accuse a single one of you. He already knows something. He knows that there is a conspiracy against him. He knows that I am my father's son. And yet he seems to feel that I cannot be one of the plot to stab him in the darkness. It is going to be my purpose to make him know that he has not been wrong in trusting me; but at the same time, I had rather have my hands cut off than to speak a word against you. Will you try to believe that?"

"How can I believe that you are able to feel for both sides in a fight?"

"You must believe me, nevertheless."

"Yet you will be with him in his house and you have sworn that if he is attacked you will defend him."

"I have."

"Do you see what that means, John?"

"In what way?"

"It means that you, being our enemy, we must protect ourselves from your interference."

"And that?"

"John, we have sworn to stay together until we have destroyed our enemy. If we find an obstacle in our path, even if it is the son of the man we loved most in the world, do you think that we can afford to hesitate, knowing that we will be truer to his memory and to his wishes than you?"

"You will try to get rid of me, then?"

"If you stay with him, we must. John, if you feel that we are wrong, stand aside and take no part on either side. I tell you, you cannot save him except by betraying us to the law. And if you try to foil us with your single hand, you only bring destruction on your own head as well as upon his. Do you understand me?"

"I wish that I had never heard you speak as you have just done."

"It is the truth."

"Then go back and tell the others that I have made up my mind."

"What shall I tell them?"

"That I am staying with Don Ramon, and that if he is attacked I shall shoot to kill in his defense."

"God forgive you, John."

"And may God forgive you, *Señor* Lopez. But I swear to you that if you yourself come near Don Ramon, I shall shoot you through the body if my gun is out before yours."

"And I swear to you, John, that your death is not twenty-four hours away!"

They reined back their horses until a considerable distance lay between them. Then Kobbe twisted his mount around and sent the chestnut flying down the hollow.

*

But the words of Lopez were working most effectually when Kobbe was far out of his sight, for he turned back and forth through his mind what his late companion had said and he began to confess to himself that it was not a true faith in the honesty of Alvarez which kept him with the latter. It was because he had caught one glimpse of the girl who walked through the garden, and he knew that if he left the service of Don Ramon he was also leaving behind him all hope of ever seeing her again. And see her again he must, for in that instant she had been stamped into his soul. She had added something to his life. She had changed him so utterly that it seemed to Kobbe that he was no longer the man he had been before that vision in the garden. He was happier; he was far stronger. How else could he have faced Lopez without being overawed by that solemn gentleman?

Yet, knowing guiltily that it was for the sake of the girl that he had denied the arguments of Lopez, he could not feel any great repentance. All shadows disappeared in the glorious thought that he was soon to meet her at the dinner table.

He was back at the house so late that he had barely time to get ready for the evening meal, and when he went into the library he found the girl and Don Ramon already there and waiting.

She was presented to him as *Señorita* Mantiez. It was a great surprise to Kobbe, but he made up his mind that she must be a protégée of the rich man—perhaps his niece, perhaps the daughter of some unfortunate friend who had died. But he had no energy left for the determination of her place in the household. All his wits were occupied in the task of watching her with consummate attention and at the same time screening that examination from the eyes of Don Ramon.

The *señorita* wore a dress of yellow lace—indeed, it was closer to ivory than to yellow. And she wore no ornament whatever, saving a single ring with a single ruby set in it. It was a marvelous stone, and Kobbe wondered why women ever wore more than one jewel, and that a ruby. Sometimes it sent an arrow of crimson through the water glass. Sometimes it flashed near the face of the girl and made her seem pale and her eyes great and dark and tragically dull. And again its flash sparkled with the chime of her laughter. And again, it was a bright touch of fire that gave brilliance to her gesture.

And she made so lovely a picture as she chatted with them that Kobbe could hardly answer her when she spoke to him. He could only pray that his silence would be taken as absent-mindedness or as dullness of wit. Anything was preferable to their knowledge that he was lost in the worship of her beauty.

Her first name was Miriam, and the mere turning of that name through his mind enchanted Kobbe. Miriam Mantiez! It seemed to him that there was soft mystery and exquisite charm in that phrase. And he repeated it gently to himself.

But in the meantime the rancher had said: "You must not trouble *Señor* Kobbe with talk, Miriam. He is busy with his thoughts. And one of those thoughts may be worth a very great deal to me. Who knows what he has discovered or what he has seen or where he has been in that ride which he took just before dinner?"

There was a very patent query behind this placid question. But Kobbe returned no answer.

"Unless," continued Alvarez, chuckling, "he was considering the question of the man in the tree. You see," he added, "that Miriam knows all my thoughts, all my plans, all my past, all my future, all my hopes. And you may talk with perfect freedom before her."

Kobbe murmured that this was interesting, but that his ride had showed him nothing of importance.

"Except a look at the landscape?" queried the rancher.

"Yes," said Kobbe.

"And nothing else?"

It was a very sharp touch and Kobbe straightened a little under the prick of it.

"What do you mean, *Señor* Alvarez?"

"Nothing," said the rancher, smiling broadly. "But there are people as well as trees growing on my estate, you know."

It was plain that he had been informed of the interview between Kobbe and Lopez. No doubt he had been told the name of the other, that one of his men had watched the meeting from a distance. And the connotation of this was that Alvarez was keeping spies upon the trail of Kobbe every moment of his stay on the place. Yet when Kobbe met the eyes of Alvarez steadily, the latter turned his glance away, and it was plain that he was not suspicious about the results of the conversation. It was almost as though his spy had heard the exact words of the talk between him and Lopez. And Kobbe could not keep a slight flush from his face. At the same time he felt two things about Alvarez. The one was that the rich don was as full of craft as a serpent. The other was that the complacent laughter of Alvarez showed that he was certain that Kobbe was entirely pledged to his service. And one conclusion was as disagreeable as the other to Kobbe.

Dinner ended. They settled down in a high-vaulted music room and Miriam played for them at a piano and then sang. In the pauses the beat and faint humming of a distant banjo kept breaking in from far away by the servants' quarters beyond the house. Kobbe moved closer to the window until he could look out, and he saw two men pacing ceaselessly up and down on the inside of the wall of hewn rock. They carried rifles, and their whole manner was that of soldiers. No doubt there were other men armed in this fashion and in this fashion mounting guard over the house of the rich man. Was it not strange, then, that Alvarez should pay so much money and so much attention in order to secure one more guard on the inside of the house? He resolved to put that question to the master of the house at the first opportunity. Or was it not better to leave well enough alone? What he desired was to stay near this charming girl until—he hardly knew what.

A servant entered with a whispered message for Alvarez. He rose at once and left the room after an apology to *Señorita* Mantiez, and a wave to Kobbe. Kobbe half expected that she would turn to him and begin a conversation of some sort. And in fact, as her fingers trailed carelessly through some meaningless chords, he thought that she was about to end and was merely hunting for an opening word to begin to talk. He decided to help her.

"May I take that chair at your right?" asked Kobbe.

"Stay where you are!" she said.

He could hardly believe his ears. "I didn't quite hear you," said Kobbe.

"Stay where you are," she said, and began to play something which he did not recognize, just loud enough, as it seemed to him, to enable her to speak to him without fearing that the sound of her voice would carry any farther than his ear. And the heart of Kobbe began to race.

"Do you mean . . . ?"

"That he is still watching, of course."

Kobbe flushed and set his teeth.

"You must smoke and look happy," she said.

Automatically he produced a cigarette. "Because of what? Of *Señor* Alvarez?"

"Yes. He is very suspicious, and he can almost read minds, *Señor* Kobbe, when he is excited."

"That's not very amiable."

"Not at all."

"Why does he do it?"

"He is jealous."

"Jealous?" Kobbe stared at her.

"That is it. He is afraid of other men . . . because he is older than I, you see?"

He would have paid a year of life for the sake of seeing her face as she talked. "Do you mean to say . . . I cannot understand you, *señorita*."

"We are betrothed, *señor*. I am surprised that he did not tell you."

"Not a word! But . . . but you will be a very great lady as the wife of *Señor* Alvarez. I wish you great happiness, also."

"I shall be happy enough, thank you. But people do not marry for romance in these times, of course."

"They do not?"

"No. Girls must realize that life is a hard proposition."

"Ah?"

"And so they are raised to look for contentment in marriage . . . not great happiness. *Señor* Alvarez has explained it all to me many times."

Kobbe could not speak. He puffed at the cigarette until he had regained his composure. He managed to say at last: "It is all a new theory to me."

"Oh, it is not a theory. It is a fact."

"He is very sure."

"He knows the facts."

"What are they, please?"

"When people are driven along by a great, wild love, they are wildly happy for a month, and then they begin to be discontented. Then they grow unhappy. Then they regret. Then they begin to hate each other."

"You speak like a professor of love, *señorita.*"

"Oh, no. Only what he has taught me. But the reason is that love is blind, you know."

"I have read that in a book, I think."

"It simply means that when people are in love, they are not seeing one another, for they are merely seeing their love. But when the love grows just a little cold, then they begin to see the truth. And it is always such a great ways below the thing they saw in their blindness that they can hardly stand the shock of the truth."

"Do none stand it successfully?"

"Almost none," she said.

"Except one's own parents," he said.

"My mother died when I was only a baby," she said. "And yours?"

"They worshipped each other."

"And did they begin with true love?"

"Like music," he said. "He was coming down from a mine where he had been working. His hands were sore; his legs were tired; his pockets were empty. His winter's work had been for nothing, and he had his jaw set for fighting. Then he saw my mother galloping her horse across the trail, with a white feather in her hat, and the wind rippling in her hair. He saw her, and he loved her. They were married in a week. And they loved each other to the day of their deaths."

"Is it true?" she said. And her fingers ceased upon the piano.

"Perfectly true!"

Then she began to play very softly on the piano, drawling the phrases of the music, and all of them were filled with a speaking sadness.

"I wish," she said at last, "that you had not told me that."

"Why?"

"Because I think that I should have been happier without knowing."

And Kobbe knew that his words had taken hold upon her and were working deep and deeper into her mind.

VII "Over the Wall"

She was thrumming at the piano again, but the music was so soft that he knew it could not interrupt her thoughts.

"Oh, of course," she said at last, "I understand that there are these romances. But most of them are in books. However, *Señor* Alvarez and I have decided that the other way is the safer way."

"You and *Señor* Alvarez?" he echoed as the picture grew bright in his mind.

"I'm surprised that he hasn't told you, since he knows that you're to be with us for such a long time."

Still she played the piano. Still her head was turned from him.

He came to his feet, and at the noise she turned toward him. It was only for a glance, but he could tell in that instant that at the least she was not happy. And he forgot that he was showing her the misery of his own face. This child, with all the beauty of her life before her, to be wedded to a man past the middle of his life, gray, already half-prepared for the grave.

He murmured something as an excuse and stumbled out of the room, out of the house. In the garden he dropped on a bench and turned his face up to the stars and the cool of the wind. But when he was motionless, his torment grew too much for him to bear. He started up and began to pace back and forth, for when he was in motion he could struggle better toward a solution of his problem.

She was to marry Alvarez! For that purpose doubtless he had raised her, reveling in the prospect of her beauty one day becoming his. She had passed from his protégée to his fiancée, and in the end she was to be his wife. That certainly must be the story. He saw the tall form of a guard stalking near the wall, and accosted him, for the fellow might be able to tell him something worth knowing.

He had expected a Spanish accent, for in New Mexico Spanish is far more familiar than English, and particularly on the estate of a Spanish-American.

"Maybe you're Kobbe?" he said.

"That's my name."

"Well," said the guard, "darned if I ain't glad to see you. I guess you're here on the same business that keeps me."

"Perhaps. What's your work?"

"Chasing around, hunting ghosts."

"Ghosts?"

"Ever since that gent shoved a knife at Alvarez, he's been scared green. I'm to keep guard here like a soldier. If I see anybody sneaking around, I'm to holler to 'em once, and then start shooting."

"Maybe the fellow Alvarez shot is one of a gang. Maybe Alvarez is waiting for the next one of the gang to show up?"

"Did he tell you that?" murmured the guard. "He's dreaming, partner. I've lived around these parts a mighty long time before Alvarez come, and I've been here all the time Alvarez has been here. He ain't made no enemies. He's a sure enough quiet one. Besides, the folks in this neighborhood ain't the kind that gang together to get a man. They do their hunting one by one."

"Perhaps it's all in the imagination of *Señor* Alvarez."

"It sure is. By the way, I was over to see the shooting today. That was neat work you done. When I see you knock them cans over, I says to myself: 'Alvarez will want Kobbe to help on this job.' And by Jiminy, here you are!"

He laughed softly, rocking back and forth. "You'll get easy work and fat pay," he said. "I guess me and Harry, yonder, and the others do the outside work, and you work on the inside. All I got to say is that if anybody tries to do anything to Alvarez, he's going to get filled with lead."

"What does Miss Mantiez think?" asked Kobbe.

"She don't do no thinking except what Alvarez tells her to do," said the cowpuncher sourly.

"How can that be?"

"Why, since her dad died. . . ."

"Who was he?"

"I see you're a sure enough stranger around here."

"I am."

"Well, Mantiez used to own this here ranch. He was a fine old gent. He was always giving a show of some kind or other. Gave so many that everybody called this Rodeo Ranch. Gave so many that he got plumb in debt. He was a sort of 'everybody's friend.' Couldn't say no to a stranger, even. If a miner was broke, he'd come in to *Señor* Mantiez. If a cowpuncher was down on his luck, he could get a job or a stake or leave to lie around and get chuck with the other boys until he was fed up fat or landed a job somewheres. That was the sort that Mantiez was.

"Of course he'd run over his head in debt. Everybody owed him and he owed the bank. Finally along comes Alvarez, buys in on the bank, and decides that he wants the ranch. He closes in on the ranch; Mantiez has to lay down, and inside of a month the ranch belonged to

Alvarez and Mantiez had died of something or other . . . I dunno what. Everybody said it was a busted heart that really killed him. He had to trust everybody, of course. The last person he trusted was Alvarez. He turned over his girl to him. And dog-gone me if he didn't do a good job of it!"

"Made Alvarez guardian of the girl?"

"Right. And Alvarez has been working ever since for her. Gave her a damned fine education. Had all kinds of teachers here for her and. . . ."

"But never sent her away to school."

"Sure, he didn't. He kept her here and spent five times as much as it would cost if she'd gone to a school, everybody says. And now, what do you think?"

"Well?"

"As if he hadn't done enough for her already, Alvarez is going to up and marry her!" He shook his head in wonder at such greatness of heart.

"He's a lucky man," said Kobbe.

"Lucky? Giving her this here whole ranch? Why, he ain't got any other heir. It'll all go to that girl!"

"Do you think that had any weight with her?"

"She's human, I guess," said the other. "But the main thing was that she don't know how to think anything different from what Alvarez tells her. However, everybody agrees that it's pretty fine of Alvarez to turn this here ranch back to the Mantiez family. But about that *El Capitán* horse. . . ."

Kobbe hardly heard the question. He returned a vague answer and strolled off through the garden. He passed down the side of the house and to the rear, out of sight of the guard, and it was when he approached the broad shining face of a pool into which the fountain had ceased playing that the shot was fired. The wasp hum darted past his forehead, but he was already in mid-air, leaping back into the shrubbery near the pool.

Another bullet followed him and clipped a slender branch above his head and sent it rustling down. Then Kobbe went into action. He had seemed formidable enough in the broad light of the day at the rodeo. But here under the starlight he was turned into a great lurking cat. Behind him he could hear the distant shout of the guard. But he did not wait for assistance. He raced through the shrubbery and darted straight at the wall of the garden.

From behind it he saw the head and shoulders of a man and a gun raised. At the flash of metal he fired, heard a muffled cry, and the figure disappeared. In another instant he was on top of the wall. He saw just beneath him—for a declivity of the ground beyond the wall made it considerably lower than the garden side—a horse with an empty saddle and, on the ground beside the horse, a motionless form.

He dropped down, kicked the revolver away from the hand of the fallen man, and jerked the limp figure to its knees. Then he found that he was looking into the face of Lopez! He swore softly beneath his breath, and Lopez groaned a response.

Kobbe released his grip and the other staggered to his feet. For a second he groped idly around him as though to make sure of his surroundings or to reach his fallen weapon. Then his senses seemed to return. He drew himself up and glared at Kobbe.

"In the name of heaven, Lopez," said Kobbe, "have you descended to this? Are you hunting me as if I were a rat?"

Lopez supported his right arm with his left. It was plain that the bullet had struck the gun, cast it into the face of Lopez with stunning force, and had then ripped up the arm of Lopez.

"I hunted you like a rat," said Lopez, "because whatever you may be to other men, to us you are only a traitor."

"Get on your horse," answered Kobbe. "And thank heaven that your traitor does not treat you according to your own fashion."

"You let me go at your own peril," answered Lopez. "For if I escape now, I shall come again, John, until we have wiped you out of the way. Alvarez is doomed!"

"I take the peril," answered Kobbe hastily. "Now get into the saddle. They're coming. If they see us together, I'll be compelled to take you in spite of myself!"

Lopez hesitated. But whatever was in his mind remained unspoken. He turned, caught the horn of the saddle with his unwounded hand, and dragged himself up. A touch of his spurs sent him flying over the slope, while a shout from the wall warned Kobbe that the guard had come up at last.

Kobbe jerked up his revolver and opened a fire which was intentionally wild. From the wall the guard was alternately shooting and cursing, but Lopez, leaning low over the neck of a fast horse, was almost instantly screened by a veil of mist.

*

VIII "An Interview"

There was a wild pursuit. Kobbe himself was in the van on the chestnut, but in spite of the speed of the stallion, Lopez had gained a lead which could not be overcome, nor could his trail be followed. They came back late in the night and Kobbe found that a message was waiting for him to come at once to Alvarez. He found the rancher walking in deep thought up and down the library. It was not hard to see that he was very excited and very angry.

When Kobbe entered, he was given hardly a glance by his employer, who strode over to the fireplace and, with his hands clasped behind his back, and his back turned to Kobbe, puffed viciously at a cigar and snapped his words over his shoulder.

"What luck this evening, Kobbe?"

"He had too long a start," said Kobbe. "We had no luck at all."

"Your horse was not fast enough?"

"I had to keep back with the others. My speed was their speed."

"What made you stay with them?"

"I might have run into a trap if I had gone on by myself."

"You are paid to take chances, Kobbe."

"I am not paid to throw my life away."

"Good!" But the snarl with which he spoke meant quite the opposite of the word. "When Jenkins found you, what were you doing?"

"Trying to drop him with a chance shot."

"But again you had no luck?"

"None."

"Today, when your horse was galloping, you shot tin cans from the top of posts a dozen or twenty feet away."

"Well?"

"This evening, when you were not in the saddle, you miss shots at a man and a horse not five paces off?"

"There is a difference between day and night."

"Very true. But the stars are bright!"

"Besides, there is a difference between shooting at a target, even at a very small one, and at a man, even a big one. If that were not true, in the old days the good shots would always have won the duels."

"Kobbe, who was the man?"

"The man? I have not the slightest idea."

"What had happened before?"

"He shot at me from behind the garden wall, while I was walking down by the pool. I jumped over the fence and. . . ."

"You ran straight at him?"

"Through the brush and then at the wall from the side so that I took him by surprise. He shot at me and I at him. He fell and I jumped over the fence after him."

"Ah?"

"I saw him lying flat. I called out to him to surrender. Instead, he caught up his revolver and threw it at me. It was a lucky aim. The gun hit my arm and made me drop my revolver which fell several steps away. I ran to scoop it up, but by that time he was in the saddle and riding away and Jenkins was shooting at him over the wall."

"You let a wounded man get away from you?" Alvarez whirled upon him. "Do you think I would be wise to allow such an unlucky man to work for me?"

The first answer which jumped to the lips of Kobbe was a careless and impertinent reply, but he knew that if he angered Alvarez, it meant that he had seen the girl for the last time. And that would be a disaster. He could not get out of his head the picture of her as she had turned toward him from the piano, curious, sad, searching eyes. He must see her at least once more and determine if she were indeed happy in the thought of her approaching marriage.

"You have been guarded by a number of men for a whole week," he said.

"What has that to do with it?"

"How many men have they even touched with a bullet?" asked Kobbe.

"But perhaps they have no enemies?"

"Do you think it was my enemy who fired at me when I was in the garden?"

"Why not? They could never mistake you for me."

"They may wish to get me out of the way before they attempt to get at you."

Talk had relieved the anger of Alvarez somewhat. Now he broke suddenly into laughter. "Well," he said, "the main thing is that you made the rascal run, and that you nipped him with a bullet . . . a rather bad wound, too, for I myself searched the place and saw the stains in the grass. But, Kobbe, I'm very curious to know what it was that you talked about with him."

"Talked about? Nothing!"

The rancher began to nod, looking half in anger and half in whimsical amusement at Kobbe.

"Jenkins saw you jump over the fence whole seconds before he came up. But when he arrived, you still had not had time to finish your enemy. Kobbe. Be frank with me!"

"I am frank as I can be."

"You will not tell me who he was?"

"I do not know."

"Suppose what he said to you was: 'Alvarez can only be willing to pay you a few hundreds for his life. But we will pay you as many thousands for his death!' Suppose that he said only those few words to you!"

Kobbe shrugged his shoulders and allowed the other to study him at leisure.

"Come," said Alvarez suddenly. "I have this to show you."

He led his companion to a small desk at the corner of the room. From the upper part of it he jerked out a little drawer which was tightly packed with a whole stack of greenbacks.

"Today," he said, "I was paid an old debt, and I was paid in cash. Count it, Kobbe!"

Kobbe flicked over a few bills to catch the denominations. "There are several thousands here," he said.

"There are as many thousands as there are days remaining in this month," he said. "And if I am still alive at the end of this month, the money is yours, Kobbe. Do you understand?"

"That is too generous."

"My friend, if I could be sure that you will put all your heart and your brain into this work of defending me, I'd double and treble that sum. My life is in your hands. I am a fool if I do not treat my life with caution."

"Why," said Kobbe suddenly, "do you trust so much in me?"

The rancher made a vague gesture. "If *you* cannot save me," he said, "no one can save me. That much I know!"

He changed the subject suddenly.

"You did not stay long with Miss Mantiez?"

"I did not," admitted Kobbe.

"She thought your leaving was rather strange."

"I am sorry."

"I fear that you are not a great man with the ladies, Kobbe."

"I fear I am not," said Kobbe. "If you have depended upon me to entertain Miss Mantiez, I shall disappoint you again."

And it was plain that the rancher was delighted.

"If we must get along without your talk," he said, "we must do as best we may do. And if. . . ."

Here there was the long and almost human sighing of a draft across the room, and Alvarez whirled as though his name had been called. He saw only a yawning door and the black hall beyond it, yet the sight seemed to steal all his manhood away. He sank into a chair, gasping: "Kobbe . . . for heaven's sake . . . see . . . what it is! Help!"

Kobbe ran to the door and looked down the hall. There was nothing there. He closed the door and turned back with that report.

"It was only the work of the wind," he said.

"Do you think so?" sneeringly replied Alvarez, some of his courage returning. "Do you think it is only the wind? I tell you they have surrounded my house and they are *in* my house. Perhaps *you* are one of them. Perhaps they have poisoned the mind of Miriam against me. Perhaps her hand will tomorrow pour a few drops in the wine which will. . . ."

He broke off with a shudder. And then he added solemnly: "Never think that I am a foolish neurasthenic. I tell you, Kobbe, that there are men in this world who would give their own lives for the sake of taking mine. They have hunted me for years. They have found me at last. The first of them I have killed with my own hand. But the second . . . heaven knows what will happen when the second sneaks inside my house, unless a brave man like you protects me. Good night. And remember, that when I call from my room after dark . . . if it is only so much as a whisper . . . if it is only a sound which you imagine . . . if it sounds only like the beating of the feet or the hands of a man who is being strangled so that he cannot cry out before his death . . . or if in the middle of the night a mere suspicion stirs in you . . . then, for heaven's sake jump from your bed, seize your guns, and dash into my room. Do you hear me, Kobbe?"

And he clutched the arm of his companion with shaking hands. Kobbe turned his head a little away from that yellowed face of fear.

"I shall do my best," he said.

*

IX "On Watch!"

There was no sleep for Kobbe that night. He undressed, went to bed, and made desperate efforts to concentrate on lines of passing sheep, and on columns of figures, but all sleep-inducing devices were of no avail. Finally he dressed again, replaced his guns on his person, and went into the hall. He paced up and down for some time when the door of the room of Alvarez was snatched open and Alvarez himself looked wildly out upon him with a revolver clutched in his hand.

"Praise heaven it is you, Kobbe," Alvarez said. "I listened to that cursed pacing up and down the hall . . . just a whisper and a creak, now and then . . . until it seemed to me that I could count my murderers gathering. I tried to push open the door into your room. I had forgotten that it can only be opened from your side. Finally I determined to rush out and fight for my life. And then I see it is only you . . . walking here deliberately back and forth . . . keeping on the watch to save me . . . oh, Kobbe, God bless you for it!"

And Kobbe saw tears glinting on his cheeks. He felt a touch of shame. Certainly it had not been on account of Alvarez that he had conducted that midnight promenade.

"Go down to the main hall," said Alvarez. "If you will stay up this night for my sake, go down to the main hall and watch there. I have dreamed of them for a week slipping in from the rear garden and coming through the hall and up the steps, softly and silently . . . go quickly, Kobbe! That is the place to watch tonight. Let the hall be. They will beat down Jenkins and the other guards. They will come in a silent wave through the garden and enter the house."

Of course, to Kobbe, it seemed madness. But he could do nothing but obey. He saw the rancher turn, a bowed, slow-moving figure, into his room; then Kobbe went to the great hall.

The approach to it was down a short range of steps, for though the building was of one story, it was constructed upon several levels, according to the original disposition of the ground, and the wing of the bedchambers was at a considerable elevation above the great hall and the living rooms. The hall itself extended through the entire breadth of the house, with great French doors opening on the garden behind the house. Into it he passed, and finding a corner chair he looked over the apartment.

With its lofty ceiling and spacious floor it was worthy in dimensions of some old baronial hall. At parts of it he could only guess, for there was not a light burning. But the moon had lately risen and was pouring its slant light through the tall eastern windows, and that light was dimly caught up by the big mirrors which were built into the walls on all sides, so that the hall was half light and half shadow and even the light parts were little more than starlight darkness.

His mind was still far from his task as guard and deep in the problem of Alvarez and his strange prepossessions when he heard a light whispering sound on the steps which led down from the upper level and into the big room. He had barely time to shrink out of his chair and kneel behind it when a glimmering figure in white stole into view, paused, and then went slowly on, in ghostly silence so far as any footfall was concerned, but with the same light whispering of silk against silk.

It crossed the hall and was swallowed in the blackness of an opposite doorway. Kobbe was instantly after her. When he reached the doorway, the figure was gone, but when he hurried on to the next chamber he saw it again, a pale form disappearing into the music room. And from the doorway, he listened to faint music beginning on the piano, touched so very softly that it was like a ghost of sound. And as he listened, it seemed to Kobbe that he recognized some of the same strains which Miriam Mantiez had played that evening while he sat in the room and while they talked cautiously, just above the sound of the hammers on the strings.

He glided into the room. A great block of moonshine, white as marble, lay upon the floor just beyond the piano. And the room beyond the shaft of light was black with dull outlines—all dull saving for that one form at the piano which seemed to shine by a faint radiance of its own. And he knew that it was Miriam.

The ghostly coldness which had possessed his blood was dissipated. He could suddenly breathe freely. His heart leaped. And when he spoke, he knew what answer he would receive. For she had come down here at midnight to play over again the music which she had played for him that evening. Yes, surely his words to her had sunk far deeper than he had dreamed.

He called softly, and she swerved away from the piano and the moonlight cascaded over her and made her an exquisite creature of light. She recognized him in the next instant and managed a shaky laugh when he came forward.

"I thought . . . a ghost," she said.

"And I thought the same thing," he said.

"But why are you here?"

"And you," he said, "why are you here?"

"I could not sleep," she said.

"Nor I," said Kobbe. "What kept you awake?"

"Oh, I have insomnia now and then."

"I was awake, thinking," said Kobbe.

"Unhappy thoughts, then?"

"Yes, partly. And some very happy ones. I was thinking over all the things that I might have said to you this evening, and which I forgot to say."

"Ah? Then I am glad that I have come down here."

"But I shall never be able to tell them to you."

"And why?"

"They are the sort of things that one tells only to oneself."

"I am a kind critic," said Miriam.

And she said it in such a way that he found himself stealing close and closer to her without his own volition. He came so close that he could see her smile.

"If you tempt me to speak, we may both regret it."

There, certainly, was warning enough. But she did not draw back.

"I know," she said. "All the time I have been in my room I have been trying to guess at the things which were behind the words you were speaking. I have tried to guess. But I cannot guess. That's why I want to hear them now."

"And whatever they are, you'll forgive them?"

"I promise. Because they will be the truth."

"They will be the truth, I think. But do you know the old story of what happened to people on the night of midsummer?"

"Well? They were enchanted with a happy madness."

"That's it, exactly. I am enchanted with a happy madness which makes me say things that I should not say otherwise. But it makes me say that when I met you I became eager for your happiness. You seemed to me so lovely and so good that I made myself happy imagining the sort of life you were to lead after I saw no more of you. And when I learned afterwards that your life was to be spent as the wife of *Señor* Alvarez. . . ."

"Hush!" she whispered.

"No one can hear me."

"I tell you that the stones of the house have ears for that name."

"I know one thing: that you don't worship him blindly, as other people think you do. That he is no oracle to you, as others think."

"How do you know that?"

"I have myself heard you say that he eavesdrops upon you. And in the whole world there's nothing more cowardly and small-souled than that."

"Please . . . please! If you say such things. . . ."

"The floor will gape under us and swallow us both. Is that it?"

"I only warn you that we must not think of such things. How I could have said what I did to you I don't know. But when he left us alone this evening, it seemed to me a trap. Because he knows what is going on in my mind every instant!"

"Nonsense! That's just hysteria."

"And yet if you knew all the things I could tell you . . . but when you were in the room and when I was playing for you, I was afraid of what would happen if he read my thoughts."

"And why?"

"Because all at once it came over me . . . choked me . . . a wave of knowledge that I had been hideously lonely all my life and that I should be lonely all my days to come. And that I had missed and would always miss something that you have and that all sunlit people have!"

"What can you mean by that?"

"I don't know, except that the life I have led here seems made up of shadows and no substance. Can you understand? I feel as if every day was like the day that went before, and that other days would follow exactly like it. I feel as if I were not real, but just a mirror reflecting a pale image of something that I might be."

"And it was this evening you felt it?"

"Yes."

"Then," he said, "it *is* magic, but white magic, you know. For I felt the same thing. As if to take you out of this house would be to lead you out of a darkness into the sun."

"Ah, that is it!"

"But instead you are to stay here as the wife of an old man."

"Hush!"

"But why under heaven do you do it? This is a free country!"

"Nothing that comes near him remains free very long. Everything, sooner or later, becomes afraid of him."

"Do you mean to say . . . ?"

"Oh, yes! Don't you see that what other people think is worship of him . . . is simply terror that freezes my mind and soul? I dread him more than I dread death!"

X "Danger Threatens"

The shock of it numbed Kobbe's very brain. She slipped closer to him, her eyes going wildly over his shoulder on either side, as if searching out an invisible danger which must be gliding upon them. Now she was clinging to him, and her great eyes were fixed upon his.

"Do you know that I have not had the courage to tell you that there is danger threatening you here in this house? Do you know that?"

"Threatening me here? Yes, I think many people know that. From the outside there are. . . ."

"Not the outside . . . not the outside. That's not it! I lay awake on my bed trying to puzzle it out. That was after he told me this evening. For he tells me everything, you know. He feels that I am such a part of him that he can tell me everything. He cannot see that I hate and loathe him and all his thoughts! Oh, with all of his brains and his devilishness he cannot see that I know him and hate what I know! But tonight . . . ah, what is that?"

She swayed to one side, but he caught her and supported her, and at the same time swinging her around, he surveyed the doorway with the muzzle of his revolver. It was only an instant, but in that instant she depended upon him for protection, and in that instant joy almost burst his heart. He could have faced lions with his bared hands.

"Praise heaven! But we must not stay here. If he is not here, he is coming."

"We cannot stir until you've told me what the danger is that threatens me."

"Haven't you guessed?"

"No."

"It is he . . . it is Alvarez!"

"He?"

"When you came, he told me about it. You are one of his enemies."

"Did he know that? I knew that he might have guessed it because
his spies had told him my real name."

"Not his spies. He could recognize you by your face. You are much
like your father, he says, and your father was a man who once injured
Alvarez."

"Injured him? The lying hypocrite!"

"He is worse than that. Only I know what he truly is! But about
you . . . he told you that he knew your name. But it was only so that
by telling you part of the truth he could keep you from guessing that
he understood everything."

"And what is that 'everything?'"

"If he knew that I were telling you, he would have me burned inch
by inch!"

"He shall never touch you with the weight of a finger!"

"Then this is it! He says that you are one of a whole gang. The first
man to attack him was a member. And others were to follow, he told
me. He was in constant peril of his life. So he determined to get an expert fighter's protection, and he started the rodeo. He said that he
knew someone of his enemies would appear at that rodeo in the hope
that they could get into the house and there murder him. He expected
that some enemy whose face was unknown to him. . . ."

"And that was I?"

"That was you. When he brought you home, he told me that he
had the prize he wanted. He had one of the enemy's camp, and he
would buy you. And having bought you, he would have a protector
who knew the faces and all the plans of all his enemies. No one else
could be so valuable. Everything was prepared for your coming as if
it were a stage."

"He was so sure I would answer his invitation?"

"Yes. He was sure of that. And once you came here he depended
on his money to buy you. But even his money would not do entirely.
He said that money was strong, but sometimes romance was stronger,
and so he planned it that I should walk in the garden outside the window while he was talking with you. He even told me what dress I
should wear so as to make the best possible picture."

"He was right," murmured Kobbe. "It was you who kept me here.
But what a dog he is to make you a bait!"

"I was more ashamed than by anything else he has ever made me
do. And when I looked through the window and saw your face and

your honest eyes looking out at me . . . I could not stand it. I turned
and ran."

"God bless you!"

"But now you understand only part. When he has finished using
you, he is going to destroy you. He has told me that. And he has no
shame or remorse about it. He says that you started to threaten his life
and therefore it is only logical and just that he should threaten your
life. When you are no longer of advantage to him, he'll wipe you out
of his way. He says it is the rule of war. And if he knew now what I
have told you, he'd destroy us both, and. . . ."

Again fear choked her. He took both her hands.

"Listen to me. He'll do neither of us harm. We're leaving this
house. And we leave together. God help him if he tries to stop us."

"But he has armed men. . . ."

"I know his armed men. If I have to shoot my way through them,
I'll do it. But it won't come to that. Tell me one thing first: why is he
so afraid if he knows so much about what is going on among his enemies?"

"Because though he trusts that you will be enough to save him, you
expect to become rich from the work, and because you know the
plans of your other friends. Because he is as cowardly as he is cruel."

"I believe in the cowardice. I've seen it. Yet tell me, if you fear and
hate him so, why have you stayed here?"

"Because I didn't know where to go if I left this place. And I had no
one I could trust to go with me."

"And that was all?"

"A hundred times it has been all that kept me from leaving. A hundred times I have lain awake at night and wondered how God could
let me keep living in such unhappiness!"

"Does it mean that you will leave this house with me . . . at once
. . . tonight?"

"The moment I can get a cloak."

"Do not wait even for that!"

"I must."

"And you have thought that if you leave you will become poor at a
step?"

"I have thought of that. That is less than nothing."

"Before you go to your room, shall I tell you the true story of how
I happened to come hunting Alvarez?"

"I know that there was a good reason."

"It was like this: ten years ago my father was in South America. He was rich in coffee plantations, and he had a wide circle of friends who were also great growers. And they, again, were affiliated with other people, and the whole made a large and powerful party in politics. They grew discontented with the harsh treatment which they received from the party which was in power. Finally they were so badly treated that there were imprisonments. And then they decided on a rebellion. In the party which had decided to rebel was my father, and of the others the most prominent was a man named Quinnado. It was Quinnado who first had become discontented with the government. It was Quinnado who first schemed to rebel. It was Quinnado who was the backbone of the whole affair.

"But at the last moment Quinnado disappeared from the country, and at the same moment the chief heads of the proposed rebellion were arrested, given sham trials, and immediately executed. My father was one of those who paid the penalty.

"Of course the reasoning of the other leaders was perfectly simple. It was known that Quinnado had sold his entire estates at a handsome figure, and he had vowed that he would use the entire sum to forward the revolution. This seemed so extremely generous that the other members of the revolutionary party immediately made him treasurer of the scheme and turned into his hands immense sums of money which they had raised for the war which was to come. The size of the sum was too much for Quinnado. He must have sold the secrets of the party to the government for a bonus of hard cash plus liberty to leave the country and go abroad where he could settle down in a new place with a new name, since it was certain that he could never live in his native land where so many hundreds of orphans and infuriated relatives would be willing to sell their own lives if they might take his in exchange.

"That was the general theory. But there were some who felt that Quinnado had been done away with and that his body had been lost as well as the names of those who murdered him. Nevertheless, among those of the revolutionists who survived there were some who escaped the proscription and who organized themselves for the purpose of hunting down Quinnado and pinning the result of his crimes upon him, if he were actually living.

"Finally, after searching for ten years, they found him here in the American West. This was the last place they looked for him because he had always hated America and things American. But they located him here and they organized to get him out of the way. It was about the same time that they found me and brought me into the work. I hardly liked an assassination scheme and told them so, but they swore that they would use me in some such way that I should not at least have to fire any bullet at a man whose back was turned to me.

"I joined in on that presumption. I entered the rodeo and when Quinnado, or Alvarez as he calls himself, sent for me, I came. You know what followed. He called me by my real name, which is John Kobbe Turner. He made me the proposition you know of, and he bought me by letting me see your face.

"There is my whole story. And there is only one thing that I want to write at the end of it: which is that I have succeeded in taking you away to freedom. And yet I've been half-baffled, Miriam, by Quinnado, when I see what he has done. And when I saw how he has made himself respected and liked in this community, I began to doubt what my other friends had told me of him. I began to think that he *must* be an honest man, or if he was crooked before, he must have reformed!"

"But you could not expect to know him as I know him. He has never done anything except what he has figured out to be of benefit to himself. He has raised me for years, but it was because from the very first he had decided that some day he would marry me. And to effect that, he has kept me away from all young people, all. . . ." Her voice broke with her anger. "Then we must go quickly, if we go at all."

He nodded. "I'll take you to the door of your room and wait for you there."

So they hurried out of the room and across the great hall where the weird moonlight had grown brighter, and up the steps and down the corridor to the door of her room. There they paused.

"Do you know," she whispered, "just now when I'm about to leave this house forever, I feel more deeply in his power than ever before? And just now I feel that he knows everything in my mind as clearly as if it were written out for him in black and white."

"Let him know what he pleases about you once we're outside this house."

"But how can we get through his guards?"

"They're posted to keep people out, not to keep them in."

She hesitated with her hand on the door. Then, with a lift of her head so that he almost saw her smiling up to him through the darkness, she opened the door quickly and stepped inside.

The door closed. He heard the faint falling of her steps as she crossed the room, and then—a sharp click and he knew that the door had been locked on the inside, and yet he had distinctly heard her walk away from it! Some other person was in that room.

XI "Quinnado!"

The first thought of Kobbe was that Alvarez had sent Jenkins or some other guard to the room of the girl to take charge of her and see that she did not escape from the house. This indicated that he had knowledge of the interview which had just passed between Kobbe and the girl. Miriam had been so confident that the rancher could not fail to read what was happening in her mind that she had almost persuaded Kobbe as well.

Yet he knew on second thought that there was no man he had seen on the place who would stand guard over the girl against her wish. Certainly Jenkins was not of that ilk.

There was a sound as of someone stumbling and then recovering himself as softly as possible. It came from the short flight of steps leading into the upper hall. Something else stirred at the opposite end of the hall, and the full meaning came to him instantly. They were blocking each end of the hall and were closing in on him. Alvarez had learned the purport of his talk with the girl and was more eager to destroy than to use him for his own protection against his old enemies.

He looked eagerly and vainly around him for an escape, but the trap was nearly shut. There was only one possibility, and that was through the door into the room of the girl.

The stealthy sounds drew closer on either hand. When they came within arm's reach, he would die. He looked anxiously around him. Like all men in desperation, he began to feel about with his hands, as though the eyes were not enough. And, so doing, his fingertips touched the molding beside the door. The post was so massive that it thrust out a couple of inches from the main line of the wall. If it were so thick at the side, above the door lintel might be still deeper. He reached up and tested it. To his amazement he found that there was a ledge a full six inches deep.

After that he was in temporary safety for an instant, at the least. He caught hold on the ledge, swung himself sidewise and up like a pendulum, and managed to plant one foot on the ledge. Then he struggled up above the ledge. He would have fallen back, of course, from such a meager foothold, but he found that there were other projections to which he could cling, and he was able to turn around and finally to squat upon his heels and stare down into the darkness.

The stealthy sounds were gradually approaching down the hall on either side. But in the meantime, what was happening in the room of the girl? There was not a sound, not a whisper. And yet the walls were not at all sound-proof. He had even been able to hear, from the hall, the light tapping of her feet as she had crossed the floor. And that was not all. He had heard the turning of the key within the lock. He knew that another person beside the girl was there, and yet not a whisper to tell him of what was happening came to his ears. It was a maddening suspense.

What happened in the room of Miriam had been sufficiently horrible. She had crossed the room in the thick darkness and already had her hand upon the switch which would flood the room with electric light when she heard the click of the turning lock in the hall door. Yet it gave her only a momentary start. She attributed it, at once, to the touching of the outer knob of the door by Kobbe, who must be waiting there impatiently for her return. And when she returned to him there would be an end to the long shadow of unhappiness in which she had lived. So she pulled the switch, and the lights poured through the room.

When she turned, she saw Alvarez with his back to the door and a smile on his pale face! It was the swift ending of her dream of success. She braced her hand against the table behind her and faced him with her teeth set.

He darkened, at that, and the smile faded from his face. It was the first time she had let him even have a hint of her true emotions concerning him. He recovered almost at once, however, and gestured toward the door to a little study which was a part of her suite. There was nothing to do but obey him. He could make her go by force, if he chose. And the silence of his movements, his use of gestures in the place of words, showed that he knew Kobbe was waiting for her outside the hall door. Waiting for her, at least, unless he had been alarmed by the noise of that turning lock. But in that case, what could he do?

She went into the study. Alvarez, still in silence, followed her and locked that door as well behind them.

"Now," he said, and his voice was as oily smooth as ever, "we can talk here quietly together. There are two doors and two walls between us and any disturbance."

"It is our last talk," she said, "and it will have to be a brief one."

He smiled, showing two perfectly even lines of white teeth, and for the first time she began to guess at what might happen, not to herself, but to Kobbe, who waited outside in the hall.

"I have been listening to you and my friend, Kobbe," he said.

"Eavesdropping?" Miriam asked scornfully.

"An old habit of mine and a very useful one. A proud man does not do it. But I am not proud. If I had been proud, I should have died long ago."

"And now?" she asked.

"I am deciding this moment what to do with him."

"With *Señor* Kobbe?"

"Use his right name!" snapped out Alvarez. "You know it as well as I do."

"Very good, *Señor* Quinnado."

He shrank as though she had struck him. And she instantly regretted that she had gone so far.

"I'm sorry," she said. "But . . . I want to know what you intend doing about him."

"About Kobbe . . . or Turner, to give him his right name? I have this moment made up my mind. He is to be removed, Miriam. He is to make an unfortunate attempt to escape. And he is to be unfortunately shot down by my overzealous guards. A regrettable affair, eh?"

Her lips stirred without making a sound.

"You are white, Miriam," he said. "This evidently cuts rather deep."

"If you do that. . . ."

"I am a devil, eh?"

"There is no word for you if you do that!"

He had been walking back and forth, but now he whirled around on her.

"Miriam, you love him!"

"Love him? I have never seen him before today."

"I say that you love him!"

"He is the finest man I have ever seen. He is the most honest and the most fearless. If I do not love him, at least I honor him!"

"And the word that you have given me that we shall be married?"

"You have dragged that promise out of me. Besides, I promised to marry *Señor* Alvarez and not *Señor* Quinnado."

"That name again? And yet suppose, Miriam, that we make a bargain and that I marry you, after all?"

"I had rather die."

"Because you care so much for this Turner? This Kobbe?"

"Yes, yes! Because I care so much for him!"

"But he is mine, now."

"He will not be taken. There is something about him which cannot be beaten."

Miriam's eyes shone.

"You will see. He is mine, Miriam. I'll offer you his life for the sake of your hand."

"You will marry me, knowing that I detest you?"

"Possession is the main thing. Everything else is an incident. You will understand better later on."

"What a hypocrite and liar you have been for these ten years!"

"I have acted a part with the most consummate difficulty, and I have acted it better than it ever could have been acted upon the stage. That is the point of distinction. I am waiting for your answer, Miriam!"

They were interrupted by a sound of scuffling and then voices loud enough to drift through the two walls to their ears from the inner hall of the house.

"Do you hear?" asked Alvarez, alias Quinnado. "They have taken him now, I believe!"

He threw open the door. At once the noises were more audible. He ran across her bedroom and opened the door into the outer hall. Instantly a group of men struggled in, bringing Kobbe in their center. And there was a faint cry of grief and of terror from Miriam. Kobbe himself was furious rather than frightened. He was busy marking the faces of each of his captors. If he lived out the peril and met them again in freedom, it would go hard with all of them. That much was sure, and the grim expressions of his captors showed that they realized what they had done.

He could hardly hope for mercy.

"We've got him, Alvarez," said Jenkins. "And now that we have him, we're going to get rid of him if you'll say the word. It can show up that we found him prowling around the house. They can never lay a hand on us for getting rid of him in that way. But if he's left alive he's going to make these parts too hot to hold him and us too. Understand?"

"Listen," pleaded Miriam at the shoulder of Alvarez. "Have him freed and I swear that I shall never see him again."

"And become the loving wife of Alvarez?"

She shuddered, but nodded.

"Very well, then, but it will require tact and patience. Let me talk with them first."

He turned toward the others and was about to speak when a window was thrown violently up from the side of the garden and a loud voice shouted into the room: "Quinnado!"

Alvarez whirled with a cry of terror so sharp that it was like the scream of a man in torture. The others saw only a pale blur and the glint of a gun in the darkness beyond the window. But what Alvarez saw made him scream: "Orñate!"

Then the gun spoke, and Quinnado pitched heavily upon his face.

That was the touch that freed the arms of Kobbe. He was instantly left to himself. Half of the men who had recently been busied in the care of him lunged for the garden window through which the avenger had fired. The other half stormed through the door and into the hall of the house. It left the two of them alone, and the instant they were free they fell into one another's arms.

But there was only an instant of that close embrace. The house was still filled with Alvarez's men, and what might happen when they returned from what would be doubtless a futile chase of the slayer could not be guessed.

Kobbe led Miriam swiftly from her room. They hurried down the hall, out through the flowers in the patio, and through the gate and on to the hilltop beyond. There was no time and no courage for them to go to the stables for a horse. They had, above all, to make sure of their safety. *El Capitán* was left behind them, and they ran stumbling on through the night.

They ran blindly, as well, and yet it seemed to both of them that they had found the very road of happiness.

Slip Liddell

"Slip Liddell" first appeared under the title "Señor Coyote" by Max Brand in two installments in *Argosy* (6/18/38–6/25/38). It is the last Western short novel Frederick Faust was to write and *Argosy* was a fitting place for it to have been published. Faust's earliest Western fiction had been sold to *All-Story Weekly* and *The Argosy* owned by The Frank A. Munsey Company. With the issue dated 7/24/20 these two magazines were merged to form *Argosy/All-Story Weekly*. Finally with the issue dated 10/5/29, any reference to *All-Story Weekly* was dropped.

As the bleakness of the Great Depression seemed like it would never end, irate readers of *Western Story Magazine* began to complain about "fairy tale" stories by George Owen Baxter and Max Brand. Faust did often seem to write fairy tales, yet few could know the exhaustive research notes he had compiled on every aspect of Western life from animal husbandry to mining, from transportation to the culture and history of many Indian nations. Perhaps no one except his wife, Dorothy, knew how acutely Faust had suffered during his early years as a farm and ranch laborer; she forbade the children to mention those years in his presence. But it was from this well of early sorrow that Faust created so many of the subtexts in his Western stories, as in his fiction generally. "*In animi doloribus solitudines captare,*" Cicero once wrote, "in anguished souls solitudes are captured." In Faust's stories it is often only a glance, a gesture, a brief and fleeting glimpse that reveals the depth of personal suffering residing behind the surface of even the brightest fairy tale.

1 "They Call Him Slip"

At noon Pollard owed the bank of Henry P. Foster five hundred dollars, but he owed it with a smile. That night Pollard had lost his smile; the bank had lost a lot of money; and Henry P. Foster had lost his life.

In the beginning, it was that confident smile of Pollard's that surprised his friends. They sat in with him at the Royal Saloon and drank the beers he bought for them with his last dollars. The Royal is a comfortable place with ponderous old 'dobe walls that shut out the heat. The shadows that gather inside it are so thick that even the swing-door cannot let in shafts of light that penetrate to the heart of the place.

It is one huge room, with a bar that runs most of the length of one wall. To the rear are tables covered with green baize for the poker games. Other, smaller tables string along through the room, leaving plenty of open space for the standees at the bar; behind the bar stands Chuck Sladin, with a signed photograph of Robert Fitzimmons hanging above the mirror, and his revolver, as everyone knows, lying on the shelf before him.

Age has turned Sladin the color of stone and gathered the sunburn of his youth into a few blotchy freckles; but he still looks alert and aloof. He gave most of his attention now to the table where Pollard sat with Soapy Jones, Mark Heath, and Pudge McArthur. Soapy and Pudge had blunt, rubbery faces that would have been useful in a prize ring; but Mark Heath was young and straight and big and handsome enough to be any girl's hero.

Pudge McArthur kept saying, between drinks: "What's the main idea? Five hundred isn't much, but it's enough to let old Foster squeeze you out of your place. It's not the biggest place in the world, but you'll be damned lonely without that corral to stir up dust in. So what's the idea of that big grin?"

"I told old Foster to come up here and get his money at noon," said Pollard. He stopped smiling and laughed a little. "The money'll be here, all right. Listen to that banjo going by. I'll bet that's Tom Patchen. He's the banjo-pingingest feller I ever heard. Push the door open and see is it Tom?"

Somebody pushed the door open, but the banjo player was out of sight. All they could see were the colored streamers that fluttered across the street, because San Jacinto was having a fiesta and when San Jacinto has a fiesta it dolls up right to the guards, because the people down there are fond of their town and they like to dress it up. Any other town that far west would have called the show a rodeo, but San Jacinto called it a fiesta.

That town felt different and it acted different because it felt that it *was* different. As a matter of fact the water-lily pads down there in the San Jacinto river are as big as the top of your table, and the flowers are bigger than your head, and the cypresses along the banks go slamming up into the air like thunderheads in the sky. San Jacinto is mostly 'dobe, weakening at the knees but looking patient enough to stand there a couple more centuries; it has a big plaza with palm trees in the center and a white-faced church with a bell tower, and you can't tell whether you're in Old Mexico or New. There are eight and a half Mexicans for every American and eight of the Mexicans go around in sandals and home-made straw hats unraveling at the brim, with corn husks stuck inside the band for cigarette papers and a twist of tobacco for the makings.

San Jacinto *is* different, and the men inside the saloon enjoyed that difference while the door was open because, although the fiesta did not open up for a day or two, the people of the town already were tuning up for the show and you could hear guitars and banjoes *thwanging* and mandolins trembling all over the place.

When the door closed, Soapy Jones, who was helping to spend Pollard's last dollars, said: "Loosen up, Frank, and tell us where that money is going to walk in from?"

Mark Heath said: "*We* ought to find that money for Frank."

"Easy, easy!" cautioned Pollard. "No good guy ever has any money in his pocket."

This Pollard had a funny, good-natured face with a big Adam's apple pushed out in front of his throat and a kink in the back of his neck to match it. You could trail him for a year and never see him take a quick step—or hear him speak a quick word, or a mean one.

"The whole of San Jacinto is gonna feel sick if you get frozen out o' your place," Heath went on. "How much would I get for that Jasper of mine, that old cutting horse? How much you think, Pudge?"

"That Jasper looks kind of bad in the knees," answered Pudge.

"He can stand up to it all the whole branding season with any man's bronco."

"Yeah, but looks is looks."

"There ain't anybody going to sell his horse for me," put in Pollard, "because there ain't nobody needs to."

The others looked at him with affectionate concern. He took a drink and licked the beer froth off the edge of his lip. Then he said: "Is Slip Liddell good for five hundred bucks?"

"Hey! You know Slip Liddell?" exclaimed Heath. Because he was younger than the others this news was more exciting to him.

"Kind of," said Pollard. He rubbed his red chin-stubble with the back of his hand and chuckled, a bit self-consciously. "I kind of know him, all right," he admitted.

"Is Slip Liddell coming here?" asked Heath.

"Right at noon, *pronto*," answered Pollard.

"That'll raise a crowd," remarked Heath, and pushed back his chair.

"You sit right still and keep it to yourself," cautioned Pollard. "Liddell sure hates a crowd."

"That's how he got his name, the way he can slip through a crowd," suggested Soapy Jones.

"No, no. He got that name from the way he can slip the cards when he's dealing blackjack," objected Pudge McArthur.

"That's wrong," said Mark Heath. "When he was a kid, he wasn't as big as he grew afterward and they called him a slip of a kid."

"A slip of dynamite, you mean," commented Soapy, and with his fat lips he sneered enormously and pushed his sombrero back on his head and scratched his bald spot.

"How come you and Slip are such friends?" asked Heath.

"Well, it was back there when he wasn't known so good, when he was doing a tramp royal around the world and driving the shacks crazy on every railroad from Mexico City to Juneau. He'd just begun to play cards and work out systems for roulette and faro and all that, and I saw him in that joint over there in Tucson . . . Matty White's place. This kid Slip . . . he wasn't any more than a kid, then . . . he steps up and cracks the roulette and he gets rolled for about fifteen hundred bucks and looks sort of bewildered. Then he kicks the croupier in the shins and turns over a couple of tables and breaks off the roulette wheel right at the floor. When he did that, you could see the apparatus under the boards. There was a brake, all right.

"A ruction started. Slip Liddell reached into the cash box and took a handful of money, but when he started to leave there was a lot of trouble. Some of the *hombres* hanging around Matty's place were hot stuff in those days. So I made a noise and a bit of trouble by the front entrance and I drew a bit of attention from the strong-arm boys, and the result was that Slip and me both got away. Without more than a few bumps we got away."

"I know Matty's place," observed Soapy Jones. "Lucky you both didn't die young."

"If I knew Slip that good," said Pudge, dreamily, "I wouldn't trade it for five thousand in spot cash!"

"Sure," agreed Pollard, "and I've never touched him before today."

"Here's your banker," said Soapy.

Banker Henry P. Foster walked through the swing-door and stood at the bar, resting an important hand on the edge of it. He filled a whiskey glass right to the brim, raised it with a sure hand, tasted it to make sure what he was getting, and poured it down his throat. After that he lighted a cigar, gathered it back in a big pucker in the corner of his mouth, and looked around the room. When he saw the men at the table, he gave one nod to all of them. He said in his sharp, clear voice: "Well, Pollard?"

"It ain't noon yet," said Pollard. He added, under his breath: "The old beagle!"

He had no particular hatred for beagles. He hardly knew what they were. The word simply came to him.

"Suppose that Slip Liddell didn't come?" suggested Pudge McArthur.

"He never disappoints you," answered Pollard, growing nervous.

"Suppose he comes but don't have that much money?" said Mark Heath.

"Yeah, and whoever heard of him not having that much?" asked Pollard.

"There was the time he was down in Mexico and they slammed him into the hoosegow," began young Mark Heath.

"Yeah, that was a lot of baloney," said Soapy Jones.

Then a tall young man pushed open the door with his left hand and stepped inside. He stepped quickly out of the brilliance of the door-way and into the shadow of the wall.

"By Satan . . . it *is* Slip!" whispered Mark Heath.

II "Hold-Up Man"

The cut of him was like the cut of fifty thousand other cowhands and yet there was a difference that stopped the eye. Mark Heath put it in a second whisper as he stared, saying: "Look at how he's set up like nobody's business!"

He was not as big and as strong as he appeared to the excited eye of young Mark Heath, but there was plenty of him at that. You've seen his like in the picture of a football team. He was what is called "a good-looking mug." There was nothing beautiful about him. He was just a mug. But if he came into your house, your wife and daughter would begin being foolish right away. He always wore a faint smile as though he had seen something pleasant and was still enjoying it.

As he came on across the room, it was plain that he had ridden those chaps through a lot of scratchy brush but somehow he didn't look as though he had wrangled many horses or roped many cows, re-cently. And as a matter of fact he had not. Except when he changed location, the toughest work he did was wrangling a pack of cards. The reason he wore that single mark of deep thought between the eyes was that he never played suckers. He preferred professionals, perhaps be-cause he had scruples about taking the money of the innocents, but even more because the professionals carried more hard cash in their wallets and would put it on the line.

Pollard was so glad to see him that he strode across the room and grasped his hand and started steering him toward the bar. Jimmy Lid-dell would not have that. He said: "But I want to meet your friends,

Frank." That pleased the men at the table. It pleased Mark Heath particularly.

He gave Liddell's hand a tremendous grasp when it came his turn. Afterward, Liddell moved the fingers of his right hand one by one and made a pretended face of pain. "Your friends are too strong, Frank," he said, but he smiled at Heath and wrinkled his nose in a most friendly way. Then he ordered drinks. He was not loud about it, but suddenly it became almost rude for anyone else to order a drink.

Pollard could hold in no longer. He broke out: "Slip, I've got to have five hundred dollars!"

"Now?" asked Jimmy Liddell.

"Yeah. Right this minute," said Pollard.

"All right," nodded Liddell, and reached into the inside pocket of his coat. Pollard lay back in his chair and looked around him, triumphantly. The other men wore constrained smiles. They were wishing that they could have a chance to do a thing like that but they were wondering if they could be so free.

Pollard stood up as Liddell, under the shelter of his expert hands, counted out bills.

"I'm gonna lay it on the bar right under his nose and then I'm gonna tell him to go to blazes and how to get there," said Pollard. "The blasted old shark-skin, I'm gonna tell him what I think!"

"Tell who?" asked Liddell, lifting his head.

"That square-faced old son-of-a-bitch at the bar. Look at him!" said Pollard.

"I saw him when I came in," answered Liddell, without turning, and put the money back in his billfold, and the leather fold back in his pocket.

"What's the matter?" asked Pollard.

"I have five hundred for you, not for your chum over there," answered Liddell.

"Yeah, but listen . . . Slip, I owe him the money . . . he'll foreclose on me," explained Pollard.

He was a big, bony man as he bent over, arguing with both hands; making everything clear with the flat of his palms, he seemed to have an extra joint in the middle of his back. Liddell studied him with clear, undisturbed eyes.

Pollard broke out into a sweat. "It's my house and my land, Slip!" he pleaded suddenly. "It's . . . it's everything. I got a hundred acres. I got a mule I harness up with my horse and plough the bottomland by the creek. I got some cows. I got a white man's chance the first time in my life."

"I told you a year ago that you were a cowpuncher, not a rancher," said Liddell. "You've lost five hundred in a year. You'd lose five hundred more the next year."

The other men leaned forward in their chairs, shifting their glances from face to face, hungry. This was news. This was a story for anybody. Their sympathy was for Pollard; with angry bewilderment they eyed Slip Liddell.

Pollard said: "I had a flock of bad luck. You don't understand. I had three of the fattest steers you ever saw and when that blizzard came in January they drifted against the fence line and there they were in the morning. You don't understand, Slip!"

His voice was hoarse.

"Yeah, I understand," answered Liddell. "Sit down and have a drink."

Pollard sat down, and just then big Henry P. Foster said loudly: "Well, Pollard? It's past noon, you know."

He was smiling a little as he spoke. There was even a sort of smile in his voice and you could tell how glad he was. Pollard only stared at him and then tossed off his drink.

"I'll send my men up in the morning," said Foster. "Just see that nothing is removed."

Pollard jumped up. He shouted out: "You're worse than a coyote! You're worse than a buzzard! You eat rottener meat!"

Foster turned a varnished crimson. He turned from the bar and came at Pollard like a real fighting man, but then his eyes fell on Liddell and he stopped. He kept looking at Liddell as he made a backward step or two and then went suddenly out of the swing-door into the street.

"It's fun for him!" said Pollard. "Putting me out of my house is fun for him. I hope he burns and the money in his pockets. I hope he dies and is damned. I'd like to have the finishing of him."

Liddell said: "You mean some of that for me, don't you?"

Pollard fell wearily into his chair. His head dropped back and he looked sick.

"It was a swell sort of a little dump," he said. "I had a lot of swell times in it. I'd rather hear its windmill clanking and the water going plump into the tank than any other music that I ever heard. I'd rather be buried under those cottonwoods than in a churchyard."

Mark Heath remarked: "There oughta be something done about a buzzard like Henry P. Foster. Somebody oughta take him up in a big way."

That was when Pollard said what everybody remembered afterward. He said: "Yeah, I'm a poor sap. I only talk. I don't *do* anything about it. But I gotta mind. . . ."

Up to about three-thirty you always can get a check cashed in the First National at San Jacinto. The closing hour is three but there is half an hour of leeway and a lot of people are sure to come in at the last minute. It makes them feel that they are being favored. As a matter of fact there were four clients near the cash window at three-twenty that afternoon when a tall man, masked to the eyes, came in with a pair of Colt revolvers and held up the place.

The cashier was a fellow named Clement Stevenson with a big reputation. He was in that Perrytown bank in 1927 when Sam Candy and his gang stuck up the place. Clem Stevenson pulled a gun and fought it out with them. They shot the legs out from under him and he still fought from the floor until Candy and his men had enough and lammed. With a hero like that inside the cage of Foster's bank, you would have thought that no robber could do a thing, single-handed; but as a matter of fact poor Stevenson simply put up his hands and begged the hold-up man not to shoot. Perhaps all the red had run out of his blood back there in Perrytown.

He was not a very experienced robber, or else he was a bit nervous. He could have had what was in the safe, which ran up to more than eighteen thousand dollars; instead, he took only what was in the cashier's cash drawer. Afterward, rumor fixed the loss at only twenty-seven hundred dollars. He took this with the heel of his left hand, without putting up his second gun, and pushed it down into a coat pocket just as Henry P. Foster came out of his office with a double-barreled riot-gun in his hands. The robber beat him to it with a comfortable fifth of a second. He put one bullet under Foster's collarbone and a second one right between his eyes.

Then he ran out and swung onto the back of a gray horse at the curb and galloped away around the first corner. People wandered around in confusion. They talked a considerable bit about outrages and the dilatory law. After a couple of hours somebody remembered the gray mustang that belonged to Frank Pollard, whose place was off on the edge of town.

That was enough to start them off. The sheriff didn't need to ask for volunteers. As a matter of fact the whole town wanted to be in on the show; fifty of the boys went out with Sheriff Chris Tolliver.

Pollard's shack stood on the edge of a deep gully, a big draw where the water ran with a rush in the spring flood time. The boys surrounded the other three sides of the cabin while the sheriff and a couple more went up to the front door. Perhaps Chris Tolliver made a mistake in saying why he had come. At any rate the first thing they knew there was a crash down the side of the gorge through the bushes.

They got there too late.

Frank Pollard had jumped right out through a window. He should have broken his neck, but the bushes broke his fall. He legged it down the windings of the draw into the dusk; and, while the posse scattered and pursued and shouted and fired a lot of shots at shadows, only a few of them saw Pollard gallop away on a gray horse into the willows down by the creek.

They spent two days searching the willows but they never found Frank Pollard. It made a good-sized bit of talking. A lot of people were glad that the banker was no longer with them but on the whole it was considered a slap at the reputation of San Jacinto and a black eye for the old town at the very moment when the fiesta was about to begin.

The bank itself offered a thousand dollars as a reward; and then some of the heartier merchants and ranchers around San Jacinto got together in town and built that reward clear up to five thousand dollars.

About three hundred of the lads went right out on the man-trail. But along came a sandstorm the very next evening and swept the entire crowd back into town with red eyes. And when the next morning came, there was the opening of the fiesta and all that to think about so that hardly a single manhunter remained on the trail that afternoon. Nearly everybody was out on the fiesta grounds when Liddell rode into town with Pollard's gray mustang on a lead and went to the sheriff's office.

That office is in one of the few San Jacinto buildings that is not of 'dobe. It is a small frame shack that started out as a school, turned into a grocery store, and wound up in the hands of the sheriff.

Liddell went up the steps and walked into the big, echoing, single room. It offered merely the imaginary privacy of corners for the clerk and the two deputies. Only the clerk was there with the sheriff on this day, and the sheriff was standing at the window looking out at the street.

This fellow, Sheriff Chris Tolliver, had that winey, sallow, sour Italian look about him, with plenty of end to his nose, bulge to his eyes, and pout to his lips. He had one of the biggest mouths you ever saw and the middle of the lower lip was always cracking to the raw so that it was a painful thing to see him smoke a cigar.

He turned now and said: "I see you found Pollard's horse."

Liddell nodded. He went over to the sheriff's desk. The clerk was standing up looking rather frightened.

Liddell took out a pair of spurs and laid them on the desk. They were expensive spurs, gold-plated except for the rowel that stood out at the end of a long spoon-handle curve.

"Kind of pretty," remarked the sheriff.

"Pollard thought so," stated the clerk.

"Did those belong to Pollard?" asked Sheriff Tolliver.

The clerk answered again, saying: "They sure did! I remember them fine."

Liddell laid an old-fashioned single-action Colt on the desk; then he paused to wink his eyes and dab at them with a fingertip. He must have been through the thick of the sandstorm. The whites of his eyes were pink and he could not see very well.

"Here's the initials carved into the butt," observed the sheriff. "Did this belong to Pollard, too? I thought you were his friend."

"Did you?" asked Liddell.

Some heavy footfalls came up the steps and across the porch where Liddell was squinting the water out of his eyes. The door was nudged open.

"Hey, look!" shouted the clerk.

The golden-bay head of a horse was looking in through the doorway.

"Is that your mare?" asked the sheriff. "Tell her to come on in."

"She's just a young fool," said Liddell, with disgust. "Come on in, Sis, while you're about it."

She came in. The floor was old and had a slant to it. Sis did not trust the creaking of the boards. She studied them with a lowered head, sniffing. She picked her feet up and put them down with intelligent care, like a good mountain-horse.

"And shut the door behind you," said Liddell, still with a face of disgust. "Where were you raised, anyway? In a barn?"

She turned, taking delicate care of her footing, and with a swing of her head she shut the door. Then she came to Liddell. When she reached him, she uttered a little whinny, no louder than a man's chuckle.

"She's spoiled," said Liddell. "No mare has as much sense as a horse, and this is just a young fool that's been spoiled."

"I can see that," said the sheriff.

His clerk made a step or two away from his desk, grinning enormously with joy.

"Back up!" commanded Liddell.

The mare backed up half a step. She stretched out her neck and nibbled at the rim of Liddell's hat.

"Quit it!" said Liddell.

She quit it and tossed her head high in the air as though he had struck at her with his hand.

"She's spoiled a hat or two for me already," said Liddell. "I'm trying to get rid of her but nobody wants her."

"Maybe not," agreed the sheriff. "Not at your price, maybe they don't. If there was an inch more on her legs, she'd be a Thoroughbred."

"She has the inch more on her legs," answered Liddell.

He took a wallet out of his inside coat pocket and laid it on the desk. There was a thick wad of bills in it and through the lower part of the wallet and the bills drove a half-inch hole, or nearly half an inch.

The clerk swore.

He had the seen the blood on one side of the wallet that glued the greenbacks together. There was plenty of the dark stain on the yellow of the pigskin. The sheriff picked up the wallet.

"You aim to say that this is Pollard's wallet?"

Liddell said nothing. The sheriff opened the flap of the wallet and began to count the money inside, flipping the corners of the bills without withdrawing them. "There's twenty-seven hundred and fifteen dollars in here."

"That's what Pollard stole from the bank, isn't it?" asked Liddell.

"That's what the bank was saying yesterday," agreed the sheriff.

He took out a cigar and bit the end off it. He stuck out his tongue and moistened the ragged end of the cigar. Then he lighted his smoke while Liddell watched the crack in the middle of the lower lip.

"Where's the body?"

"In the San Jacinto," said Liddell.

"How come?" asked Tolliver, looking at Liddell with his tired, bulging, sour-wine eyes.

"I came up with him at the mouth of the cañon," answered Liddell. "After he dropped, I thought it was too bad to leave him out there for the coyotes . . . and the flies. The river was jumping and yelling its head off. I just rolled him down the slope."

"It was a fool thing to do."

"Why? He used to be a friend of mine."

The clerk made a face like he had swallowed acid.

"A friend of yours . . . an old friend, wasn't he?" asked the sheriff, studying Liddell. He licked the crack in his lip and waited.

"There's a five thousand dollar reward offered for Pollard," remarked Liddell, without the slightest emotion. "I'll take that along with me."

"Maybe you will," nodded Tolliver, "but just wait till I look the thing over, will you? The people that are putting up the cash will want to be sure that Pollard is dead. The bank will want to be sure, too."

"The bank won't care, so long as it gets its money back," stated Liddell, "and the rest of the people will take your word. Are you going to give it?"

The sheriff said: "Don't get tough with me, Slip!"

Liddell answered, smiling: "I never get tough with anybody."

The sheriff said: "All right. Only don't ever think that you can get tough with me. You can't get away with it."

Liddell was smoking a cigarette. He took a puff of the smoke in his hand and threw it gently toward the sheriff, still smiling. The smoke made a dim streak in the air to mark the gesture.

"Old Tolliver!" said the mild voice of Liddell.

Then he walked out of the office. The mare followed him; she went down the front steps gingerly and on the street below she cut a caper or two as though she were glad to be out of there.

The sheriff shut the door. He took out a handkerchief and scrubbed a sudden sweat from his face. He said to his clerk: "I thought for a minute the hellion was going to be tough with me."

The clerk, who was watching with a sick smile, answered: "Yeah, so did I!"

III "The House of the Silversmith"

Out there in the street, staring at Pollard's gray mustang and looking white around the gills, was young Mark Heath. He looked at Liddell with eyes that kept on seeing trouble.

"Has he come in and given himself up?" asked Heath. "Is he in there?"

"Who, Pollard? He's dead," answered Liddell.

"Dead?" gasped Heath.

He caught hold of a stirrup leather and leaned against the gray old mustang, and the mustang leaned back a little.

"Did you like him a lot?" Liddell wanted to know.

"He was swell to me," said Heath. "He was swell to everybody, but he was fine to me. Did he have the bank's money on him?"

"Yeah. Twenty-seven hundred dollars."

"Twenty-seven hundred. . . ."

"That's just what the bank missed."

"Sure. Sure. That's right," agreed Heath. "Only it seemed like a pile of cash for poor old Frank Pollard to get all at once. He was a kind old boy, all right." He half closed his eyes and took a couple of deep breaths.

Liddell said: "You're a good fellow, Heath. I like you. I believe in you. That's why I'm sorry to tell you that I was the one who killed Frank Pollard."

He went off down the street and left Heath stunned behind him.

The mare followed Liddell. Now and then she pretended to be afraid of the flapping of the pennants and streamers that decorated the street, and breaking into a gallop she went a jump or two beyond her master and then turned and waited for his comments. He said: "You're silly. You're silly, is all you are." But she did not seem to mind these remarks.

From the far side of the town automobile horns honked and there was a rapid muttering of hoofbeats as the people came back from the races; the thirsty ones were traveling the fastest, but everybody was pretty thirsty. And there were ten horses to one automobile.

The way San Jacinto lies with only a bit of flat laid down in a junk heap of mountains, not much of 1938 can leak into the atmosphere.

The only direction you can use an automobile is right up and down the river windings but, if you travel toward any other points to the compass, a horse is better and a mule is best. That is why San Jacinto keeps its flavor like an old story which children love.

When there are two thousand more added to its population one of the big airlines intends to make it a stopping point so that air-tourists can get a glimpse of the old color, but probably San Jacinto never will add the needed two thousand. It goes on living on sheep and goats and cattle and mules and burros and that sort of thing, although the Mexicans raise some good crops on the irrigated flats below the town. So when the population came in from the races at the fair grounds, most of it was aboard mustangs; they were what made the rapid drumming to which Liddell listened as he passed on through the town.

It was hard for him to believe that he was escaping all notice and now, in fact, he discovered a pair of people on saddle mules, following behind him, kicking their short-stepping animals into a trot to keep up with him. One of the two was an old man with a humped-over back and a gray spade of a beard and a long face, pulled out far in front. The other was a raggle-taggle youngster in blue jeans and a cap. It seemed apparent that they had recognized him but he turned out of the main avenue before they could overtake him.

The streets of San Jacinto wind about as though they were laid out by the maundering leisure of grazing cows. They are narrow streets. In some of them two riders hardly can pass without touching stirrups. Liddell turned down one of the darkest of these alleys until he came to the shop of a silversmith that had a window full of silver wheelwork and other intricate spiderwebs of metal; there was even cloth of silver and gold woven by the wife of the smith.

Liddell went into the shop and saw in a corner among the shadows the immobile figure of the silversmith's wife. She was a pyramidal creature, declining upward from large hips to narrower shoulders which supported a head without the column of a visible neck. She wore a mustache of formidable black hairs. Her complexion was that of an old chamois which has been used for years to polish automobiles. Everything about her was gross, heavy, and static except her hands which seemed to have been kept delicate by the nature of her work. Her fingers were aflash with rings and she gestured a great deal when she talked.

Liddell said: "Juanita, I am very tired. Show me where I may sleep."

"Armando!" called Juanita. No emotion could struggle through the fat of her face, but her voice went up a half octave with each word and her shoulders hunched as she repeated: "Armando! Armando!"

Armando Pinelli rushed out of the inner shop. He wore a leather apron and glasses. He was no bigger than a wasp, a dingy wasp that tunnels in the earth. When he saw Liddell, he threw up both hands and cried out: "Saint Anne . . . Saint Mary of God . . . it is the *señor!*"

Juanita said: "Take him to the rear room where he can sleep. His eyes are sick, so call Dolores to put something on them. He is very tired, so hurry!"

Armando Pinelli was all voice and hands as he led Liddell out of the shop through the cramped little courtyard where the paving stones were always as damp as winter, and so into the shed where a mule stood in a dark stall. They put Cicely, the bay mare, in the adjoining stall, and Pinelli took his guest across the court and into the house again. He was about to climb the stairs, but Liddell said: "A downstairs room, Armando. Any place will do. But the idiot mare gets lonely and has to have a look at me from time to time. Otherwise she grows nervous."

Armando was distressed. There was no place on the first floor worthy of a dog's kennel, he said; and in fact he had to show Liddell into a little room whose low, unshaded window opened on the court. There was a washstand in a corner and a ledgeless box-spring laid on the floor against the inner wall. Liddell groaned at the sight of it and fell flat. The springs creaked up and down under his weight.

Armando, at the door, shouted: "Dolores! Dolores!" When he had no answer, he named two or three saints with a good deal of violence and shouted again. But it was not until three or four outbursts and until he had begun to bring in the name of St. Christopher, the patron of travelers, that a casual step came down the stairs. Her hands were still raised to her hair; and at the same time, with a girl's multiplicity of mind, she was arranging a lovely mantilla of black lace.

"Idiot!" said her father. "I haven't asked you to go out on the promenade! Why have you loitered to make yourself fine?"

"Do you think I want to look like an Indian squaw when I see *him?*" she demanded, without being in the least degree perturbed.

"How do you know it is he?" demanded her father with an instant suspicion.

"I heard his voice in the court," she answered. "Besides, for what other person in the world would you be rushing about and shouting?"

"Ha?" said Armando. "Nevertheless, run instantly and get something to wash and comfort his eyes."

"¡Dios!" said Dolores. "Do you mean to say that he can't see me, after all?"

But she ran up the stairs again as lightly as a dancer, and when she came down again she was carrying a bowl of warmed water and cloths. Even with that to bear, she made an important entrance, holding the basin on her fingertips as though it were a precious vase, and crying out: "Señor Jimmy! Welcome to San Jacinto!"

He folded back one arm to lift his head and look at her. "I thought that I came here to sleep, but the fact is that all I needed was to see Dolores."

"The poor eyes . . . the poor eyes!" murmured Dolores. "Can you see me at all?"

"I can," said Liddell, "from your slippers to the beautiful shawl."

"Mother of heaven!" cried Dolores. "It is a mantilla of the sheerest lace . . . you are blind! My poor little old one!"

She sat down beside him on the box-springs and began to wash his eyes with a small daub of cloth, uttering tender murmurings.

Armando Pinelli, who was a man of an intensely practical nature, appeared for an instant at the door to say: "That is good, my sweet. Be kind to him, but not too kind!"

A moment later, Dolores was explaining to Liddell: "My little father has no brains except in his hands and he uses all their wits on his silver. But what a day for me! To see you again when you are more than half blind and when I have on my new fiesta dress!"

"Tell me about it," suggested Liddell. "It's red, isn't it?"

"It is red," she agreed, "with little workings of gold through the pattern so that it shines and shadows in folds as the light runs over it."

"Dolores, it must be as lovely as an altar cloth."

"No, if you are going to open your eyes and stare, stare at me and not at a worthless dress. Now close your poor eyes again, and tell me what you saw. No, don't tell me!"

"Why not?" he asked.

"Because you will tell me the truth. And the truth is a terrible thing for a girl. I don't even dare to look into my mirror without smiling and fixing my eyes a certain way and tipping my silly head to one side or the other."

"I'll sing you a song," said Liddell.

"I'll get the mandolin, then," said Dolores.

"No. Give me your hand instead."

"So!" murmured the girl. "Ah, my crazy heart! It's doing a dance, *Señor* Jimmy."

He sang one of those old Mexican songs which are hard to translate because there is so much idiom in them. He sang it softly, and the words made a sense somehow like this:

> *The waterfall sings night and day*
> *It throws up its white hands, rejoicing;*
> *The currents are like wild horses*
> *But after running a little way they stand still;*
> *Their windy manes fall down;*
> *The waters grow as quiet as ice*
> *Because they wish to take, deeply, an image*
> *Of a tree whose feet are close to the pool.*
> *They take the whole of that slender image to the top*
> *And show also the stars toward which it is pointing.*

When he had ended, the girl still swayed a little with the rhythm of the music. At last she began to bathe the closed eyes once more.

"When you sing . . . ," she said.

"Well?"

"When you sing, it is not a very good voice."

"No. I'm only a campfire howler."

"It is not a very good voice, but it is as though you took my heart in your hands. *Señor* Jimmy!"

"Dolores?"

"If my mother were not so big and fat, would you marry me?"

"Dolores!"

"If it were not for that black, horrible mustache, would you marry me?"

"Sweetheart . . . ," said Liddell.

"No!" said the girl. "Don't answer. But you can feel with the tips of your fingers that *my* lip is smooth."

She leaned so close that he did not need to use the tips of his fingers.

"Dolores," he said, "you are more to me than. . . ."

"Hush!" she broke in. "Everything is so beautiful inside me, just now, that one lie would break my heart. Now . . . let the big yawn come . . . and now you are comforted and ready for sleep. Ah, you men . . . there is not much priest in you."

She put small wet pads over his eyes and arranged a bandage around them.

"When will you be hungry?" she asked

"When I wake up," answered Liddell.

"When will you wake up?"

"When you leave me," said Liddell.

But as a matter of fact he slept on through the end of the day, through the twilight and the night, and into the crisp chill of the dawn.

IV "Meet Skeeter, Folks"

At the end of the day there is a change in the Royal Saloon of San Jacinto. During the sunlight hours there rarely are any except Americans in the place but in the evening Mexicans of the upper classes and even a few *vaqueros* come into the Royal to sit down to a poker game or play the roulette wheel. For the first time during the day, wine appears. Chuck Sladin keeps good French wine in his cellar and he always has a supply of California, red and white; he even can produce champagne for great celebrations. With his grim, tired old eyes, like the eyes of an ancient eagle, he discourages arm-waving and loud noises so that the games at the rear of the saloon will not be too annoyed.

In the evening, also, the bar service is enlarged by Mexican waiters in clean whites who go softly about among the tables. An oddity is the way the Mexicans and the Americans keep apart and aloof even when they are rubbing elbows. The Spanish and the English language gather in separate pools; Spanish and English eyes forget one another and seek only faces of the same blood.

The Royal did a good business on this night, with Mark Heath at a table against the wall talking with Pudge McArthur and Soapy Jones. It was three in the morning, the hour when the tongue begins to stumble and repeat itself as alcohol commences to anæsthetize the brain. It was the time when maudlin good will enlarges the hearts of the drinkers, unbuttons pocketbooks and mouths, and pours mist into every eye. An inward, spiritual struggle was troubling the soul of Heath. At last he had his chin resting in both hands, his face almost covered by the fingers as he said: "This is what eats me: he makes poor old Frank love him, and then he shoots him in the back."

"How do you know he shot Pollard in the back?" asked Pudge, opening his eyes and his mouth to express his astonishment.

"Why else would he have rolled the body down into the river?"

"I don't foller that," said Pudge, shaking his head.

"Listen, dummy," broke in Soapy Jones, who was the brains of the pair, "if he hadn't shot him through the back, why didn't he leave the body lie and let the sheriff go out and identify his dead man?"

"He says it was because he didn't want the coyotes and the buzzards to get at the body," protested Pudge.

"Sure he says," sneered Heath. "Go on, Soapy, and make it straight for Pudge."

"Look, flathead," pursued Soapy. "He comes up to Frank out there by the San Jacinto and he shakes hands and talks to him, and tells Frank about things, and pretty soon Frank turns his back and then this Liddell, this Slip Liddell, he sinks a bullet though the back of Frank's head."

"What a skunk this Liddell turned out to be. And me looking up to him all this time like he was something extra!" complained Pudge. "Sure, if he shot Frank through the back, he wouldn't want people to see it. He'd have that much shame."

"Yeah, he'd have that much," sighed Heath. "But will I ever have shame enough to do anything about it? Frank was swell to me. He took me in. He loaned me money. He set me up when I was flat. But I let him be murdered and then I let the murderer walk around and collect blood money for the dirty job!"

"It ain't your job to butt in," advised Soapy. "Me and Pudge have known Frank three times as long as you. The question is: what should we do about it?"

"Pull a gun and shoot Liddell!" suggested Pudge. The violent idea shocked him, and he showed the shock in his eyes. Their chance to develop this theme was interrupted, however.

The same couple who had followed Liddell down the street—the old fellow with the long, pulled-out face and the ragged youngster who accompanied him—had entered the saloon and gone up to the bar. The old fellow carried an accordion under one arm.

"We don't want no free music in here," said Chuck Sladin, sternly. "And how old are you, kid? I don't serve anyone under eighteen."

This brown-faced youngster, obscured by a cap that looked much too big for his head, turned to the old man and said quietly: "Well, Pop?"

"Go ahead. Show 'em how old you are," directed Pop.

In a moment, coat and trousers of blue jeans were tossed to Pop; the heavy shoes were kicked off the feet and replaced with dancing slippers; and finally the big cap followed the rest of the outfit, and let a bright bob of hair tumble out around her ears. She had on loose blue trousers and a blue silk shirt and around her middle she wore a red sash that took all the boy out of her and left only woman.

"Yeah, and what is it? A circus turn?"

Old Pop unlimbered the accordion at the same moment. He rocked it into a rippling, crazy, swinging jigtime and the girl began a tap dance.

Chuck Sladin leaned over the bar to watch her feet with critical eyes. He was not fool enough to turn a real attraction out of doors but he wanted no cheap panhandling in his place. It took him a long moment to decide; then he leaned back and began to clap his hands softly together to keep the beat of the music.

She really was good. She had no great weight to shift about and she was as supple as a blacksnake; besides, she had imagination in her feet.

In the bar that night there were a couple of lads from the Truxton ranch up in the hills. A radio gave them music on the long winter nights and when the range didn't leave them too tired they used to knock the frost out of their toes by tap-dancing, and when they heard the clatter of the girl's slippers it was too much for them. They came out with a couple of Indian yells and raised a good rattling thunder on each side of her.

"Go it, Skeeter!" yelled Pop. "Hop onto a table where they can see your feet!"

Instead of that, the Truxton lads pitched her up onto the bar and she began to sway and skip and ripple her feet up and down the bar, her slippers seeing their own way among the glasses and the bottles. Chuck Sladin only made sure that that those light slippers failed to scar his varnish and then he let the show go on. A thing like that was good for business. The Truxton boys got out of breath, but Skeeter was as tireless as a hawk on the wing.

She was not beautiful. When her face was still, she looked as grim as any boy but she took care to be smiling and she knew how to let her teeth and her eyes flash. She knew how to put in the old appeal, too, and a hermit would have come right out of his cave to see Skeeter weaving into some of her warmer numbers; but all the while the cool little devil was taking stock of the men in the place and reading the minds of their pocketbooks.

She wound up with a bit that old Pop announced as "Saturday Night." The music for it was only a soft humpty-thumpty on the accordion, but the feet of Skeeter brought a galloping horse right into town, walked a cowpuncher into a drunken party, staggered him through a fight, gave a couple of pistol-shot stamps for his death, and finally followed his body to church the next morning with a demure piety that made even the Mexicans laugh till they cried.

After that, she hopped off the bar and went around with Pop while he passed the hat. When they came to Mark Heath, he put in a ten-dollar bill. The brown claw of Pop tried to close over that tidbit, but the girl's hand flashed in and got the money away. She stuffed it back in Mark's pocket and said: "Thanks, but I don't know you that well."

In spite of that they made a good haul of fourteen or fifteen dollars because the men in the place were heeled for fiesta spending; then they went over to a corner table with a couple of tall beers and Pop undid a package of lunch while Skeeter slid back into blue jeans and tucked the brightness of her hair under the big cap again. Nobody bothered her, either, because she had a way of taking an admiring glance out of the air and handing it back well frosted.

Only Mark Heath came over and tried to sit at her table. Old Pop was thinking of that ten-dollar bill and he pulled back a chair, but the girl said to Mark: "Don't you go and try to get yourself dizzy about me, handsome; because *I* am not getting dizzy about anybody these days."

"Will you have a drink on me, then?"

"I won't have that either," answered Skeeter. "You can't give me anything but love, baby, and I don't want that today."

So Heath went back to his table and people laughed at his lack of success; but the clumsy blue jeans and the cap swallowed her up so completely that she was almost forgotten, as she sat with her back to the crowd, digging her small, white teeth into a tough slice of yesterday's bread with a slab of bologna laid over it. She took big bites and chewed hard, and helped mastication along with a good swallow of beer from time to time.

She was the hardy one for you. She could turn her hand into a fist that meant something. She looked as light and strong as a jockey, and she was still stronger than her looks. Ten minutes before, half the men in that room were giddy and grinning about her, but now she was nobody's business except her own.

Old Pop had his yellow fangs in a sandwich and said through the bread: "Ten dollars! Ten dollars! You keep us in the gutter! You keep us in the dirt!"

"Listen, Pop," she answered, "I'd rather heist the dough than glom it off a kid like that when he's dizzy about me."

"Let them be dizzy, you fool!" directed Pop. "God made you . . . and you make men dizzy . . . and that's that! Use the gifts that God gave you, Skeeter."

He frowned at her.

"If I had a drop of your blood in me," said Skeeter, "I'd cut my throat and hang myself up by the heels to get rid of it. But shut up and listen to the talk that's going around. They're all talking about Slip Liddell. That *was* Slip that we followed today, then."

"Yeah," agreed Pop. "He shot a pal out in the hills and came back to town to grab the blood money. That's what your hero done, and the boys don't seem to like it."

"I don't believe it," said the girl.

"Who cares what you believe?" demanded Pop. "I'm talking about the facts."

"You can't talk facts, poison-face," answered Skeeter. "You hate everything too much to tell the truth about it. Slip Liddell. . . ."

"He shot his partner in the back. The whole town knows about it."

"He never shot a man in the back in his life."

"Yeah. You ought to know. You were raised in the same house with him," sneered Pop.

"I know what I've heard of him," she said. "I've seen the faces of some shacks that he'd worked on. I've heard the line they pull about him all the way from 'Frisco to the Big Noise. Listen, poison, he won't even play a sucker; he saves himself for the professional crooks and beats them at their own stuff."

"He shot Frank Pollard in the back for five grand," said Pop, and grinned till his teeth showed and his eyes disappeared. "What made him Gallahad to you, anyway?"

She replied: "Who do they still talk about up and down the line? He lived where he wanted to and never hit the stem; he never battered privates. He was tramp royal when he wanted to travel. His hand was heavier than the other guy's blackjack. The cops and the shacks had chills and fever when they turned him up. He always had a limit and he always had it while the day was young. He never pulled a job; he never gave a pal the red lights; he shelled out to every sucker that was on the fritz; he never passed up a gal that was on the street without giving her a handout. And now you try to cross him up with me by saying that he shot somebody in the back? Listen, Pop, one of these days when you try to pull the poison on me like this, I'm going to take it on the lam, and then you can try to walk the cash out of the pockets without Skeeter."

"You're dopey about a guy you never saw," commented Pop, totally undisturbed by this outburst.

"I *have* seen him," said the girl. "I saw him today. I knew him by his picture."

"When did you ever see a picture of him?"

"Four, five years back I saw it in a daily rag, somewhere. But I wouldn't've had to see his picture. I would have known him by the way he walked."

"How did he walk?" asked Pop.

"Like he was going somewhere," said Skeeter.

"You're nuts," said Pop.

The voice of Pudge McArthur suddenly dominated the saloon. He was standing on a chair at the bar, ordering a round of drinks and making a speech as the liquor went down.

"We're not gonna take it!" roared Pudge. "We're not gonna lie down and take it!"

"We ain't gonna lie down and take it!" shouted an answering voice from the crowd.

That was Soapy Jones. The girl spotted him at once. Then she glanced over at the wall and saw Mark Heath still at his table with his chin on his fist and his eyes bright with calculation. She studied him with a bright curiosity for an instant.

"Nobody is gonna bamboozle San Jacinto!" bellowed Pudge. "Not even if his name is a big name. Nobody is gonna shoot a friend through the back and come in to get blood money. They can't put it over in San Jacinto. Not while we got so many good ropes in this town!"

"We got trees to hang the ropes on, too," shouted Soapy Jones.

"Who you talking about?" demanded old Chuck Sladin.

"You know who I'm talking about!" answered Pudge. "And I wanta tell you that the dead man was a friend of mine. He was the kind of a man that he would give you his last ten cents, and he smiled when he done it. He was the kind of a man that he couldn't say no to a friend. He was more'n a brother to me. He was more'n a brother to the rat that shot him through the back."

"Name him! Name him!" called two or three voices. The others waited with faces prepared for anger and outrage, and Pudge McArthur roared mightily: "Slip Liddell . . . the crook . . . the gambler . . . the murderer. It's Liddell that I'm talking about. And there ain't guts enough to San Jacinto and there ain't ropes enough and there ain't hands to pull 'em, to take care of a skunk like Liddell. There ain't. . . ."

His voice grew dim in the rising outcry of the mob.

Skeeter said: "Unlimber that accordion, Pop. Play something jolly. Play something that'll get into my feet. We've got to change the mind of these boys."

She was whipping out of the blue jeans as she spoke and tucking her feet into the slippers.

"Leave them be," answered Pop, grinning. "If he's as much man as you think, they'll do nothing but bend their teeth when they bite him. If he's as much man as you think, he'll blow 'em down faster than they can come up."

She said: "Get that accordion off the strap and hop lively or I'll never shake a foot for you again."

He obeyed, gloomily, and muttered: "It's a wrong gag to play twice in the same joint. They get tired of handing out the cash."

"They're not handing out the cash. We are!" she answered.

And a moment later she was at the bar rapping money on the edge of it, and calling for a drink all around. She hardly could make herself heard, for the anger and the resolution of Pudge McArthur had spread to nearly everyone in the room and they were beginning to mill like cattle before a stampede. Once they started spilling through the door into the street, nothing but more men and more guns could stop them.

There was no harm in having another free drink, however; and there was no harm in watching the girl clattering up and down the bar. To see her laughing made you think of every good time you ever had in your life; it made your own toe start tapping and started your head nodding. And it was plain that there was nothing but good nature and merriment in her, for now she was buying another round. When she jumped to the floor, Pop got her by the shoulder and shook her.

"Are you gone clean crazy?" gasped Pop. "Are *you* spendin' money when it's your job to make others spend on *you?*"

"Shut up and make an accompaniment for those two over there who've started singing," directed Skeeter. "Keep on playing. Liven it up. Put a smile on that old leather mug of yours."

"Wait . . . ," said Pop, but she was gone through the side door of the saloon before the others could notice her swift way in a crowd.

V "The Butcher-bird"

It was not the cold of the morning that wakened Liddell, but a young voice that said: "Hi, Slip! Hi! You're overdue. Wake up!"

He pulled away the bandage and found his eyes almost healed from the effects of the sandstorm. Still a haze remained across them, slowly clearing, and through that haze he saw a slim figure seated in his window. A big cap slopped down over the head. The jacket and trousers were faded jeans. He saw a brown face weathered right into the grain of the skin. It was a sleek, slim youngster, almost too handsome, almost too effeminately light of wrist and hand.

"Who are you, brother?" asked Liddell.

"Skeet they call me. Or Skeeter, sometimes. You better be up and vamoose, Slip."

"Yeah?" drawled Liddell, making his head comfortable on the fold of his arm.

"Some old pals of yours are around smoking up trouble."

"What pals?"

"Those two fat-faced hams, Soapy Jones and Pudge McArthur. And who's that smooth guy, called Heath?"

"Mark Heath? He's one of the best fellows in the world," answered Liddell. "He's a straight-shooter and he's worth having for a friend."

"Is he *your* friend?"

"He'll never be my friend, I'm afraid," said Liddell.

"He's making trouble for you now," she told him.

"What trouble?"

"Talk," said Skeeter.

"Where?"

"Up at the Royal all night. They're still there."

"What were *you* doing at the Royal all night?" demanded Liddell.

"I helped the barman washing up and snitched a few beers. I'm not talking about me. I'm talking about you."

"I hear you."

"D'you want to know what they're saying?"

"I can't keep you from telling me."

"You won't be so upstage when I tell you. They're saying that you double-crossed your old partner. They're saying that you did in Frank Pollard. They're saying that you killed him when he wasn't looking . . . for the blood money."

"Did I shoot him in the back?"

"You did."

"Was somebody looking from behind a rock?"

"No. But that's why you rolled the body down into the San Jacinto, so that nobody could see where the bullet went in through the head and came out through the face."

"If I murdered a friend like that . . . they ought to raise a mob and lynch me," commented Liddell.

"That's what Soapy and Pudge are talking up. They almost got a crowd started before I left and came to tell you. They ought to be along in ten minutes. Maybe less."

Liddell yawned. "I'd better be getting along, maybe."

"You better be!" declared Skeeter. "There's a bay mare walking loose in the court here. You borrow her and light out. She looks as fast as a hawk."

"Sis!" called Liddell. "Hi, Cicely!"

The bay mare put her head in through the window. She seemed to be resting her chin on Skeeter's knees.

"Ready for another trip?" asked Liddell.

The mare shook her head.

"Couldn't you take me on just a little, tiny trip?" asked Liddell.

Cicely shook her head with an angry decision.

"Get out of my sight, then!" exclaimed Liddell. "Fine gratitude you've got for all the oats and barley I've poured into you!"

The mare backed away into the courtyard again.

"How'd you do it?" asked Skeeter. "How'd you make her shake her head like that?"

"Why, I asked her a question, and she answered it, that's all," said Liddell. "She's like all women. There's no gratitude in her."

"You're a funny sort of a guy, all right," observed Skeeter. "But maybe you'll feel less funny when they use you to stretch out forty feet of new rope."

"Maybe I will," agreed Liddell.

He began to make a cigarette. His hands, using separate intelligences, found the brown wheat-straw papers, and the little sack of tobacco with the big revenue stamp stuck on it. The fingers turned the paper into a trough, sifted in the tobacco, smoothed it, leveled it off, turned it hard, then engaged one lip under the other and rolled up the smoke. He glued it with the tip of his tongue, turned one end over, and lighted his smoke. But not for an instant did he give this bit of work his attention. He was saying: "How did you know I was down here?"

"There's a good beam end sticking out the stable window," remarked Skeeter, pointing. "That'll be better than the limb of a tree when they come to string you up. Wait a minute! You hear them now?"

In fact there seemed to be a swarming hum from higher up the street.

"They don't know where to find me, brother," Liddell pointed out.

"Everybody in town knows where you are and why you're here," answered Skeeter.

"Why am I here?" asked Liddell.

"Because there's a gal in the house with hips and eyes that work together. Even the kids in the street laugh at her when she goes by; but everybody knows that when it comes to the gals you're a swell horse-trainer."

"You little pint of dishwater," said Liddell, sitting up. "I've got a mind to take you by the nape of the neck and pour you down the sink!"

"You big, four-flushing ham," said Skeeter, "I've a mind to come down in there and knock the dust out of you."

Liddell leaned back on his bed with a sigh. "Breeze along, kid," he said. "Thanks for bringing me the news. Breeze along back where you came from. By the way, where *did* you come from?"

"That's my business," answered Skeeter. "You hear 'em coming now? Slip, get up and out of here! There's thirty, forty of those bums and they're mean."

Liddell rubbed at the dimness of his eyes, but they wouldn't clear. There was something about Skeeter that was very unlike other people.

"How old are you, Skeet?" he asked.

"To hell with me!" snapped Skeeter. "Are you going to lie right there and let 'em grab you?"

"Fourteen . . . fifteen . . . ? said Liddell. "Where you live?"

"Wherever I find the living good."

"Are you on the bum?"

"Are you gonna be sorry for me?" asked Skeeter, with head tipped to one side.

"I'd as soon be sorry for a wasp or a butcher-bird, or any other thing that's small and full of teeth and claws. How long you been on the bum?"

"Listen, mug," said Skeeter, "I'm not one of the punks that batter the back doors and get the dog or a cold hand-out. I come in the front way and sit down to my ham and. . . ."

"You play a sob story and get the women mothering you, eh?" asked Liddell.

"Leave me out," said Skeeter. "There's a mob in this town that's going to have the hanging of you and like it."

"It's after five," answered Liddell. "If whiskey started them, the booze will be stale and cold in 'em. If a man-sized dog barked at 'em, that whole gang would turn and run."

"You don't think you're taking a big chance?" asked Skeeter.

"No," answered Liddell. "A mob is like a mob of town dogs. They only chase the things that'll run from 'em."

"It knocks me for a loop!" murmured Skeeter.

"Thanks for bringing me word," he said. "Wait a minute? Are you broke?"

"I don't want your coin," answered Skeeter.

"Why not?" asked Liddell.

"I ought to be doing the paying. You're putting on the show," said Skeeter.

"You're a queer little mug," yawned Liddell.

"I'll tell you something a lot queerer than me. Some of those thugs in the saloon are going to think you over when they're dirt-dry and stone-sober. And then maybe they'll oil up their guns and come for you. Maybe they're coming now."

"They won't come now," said Liddell.

"That fellow Soapy Jones, has he always hated you?"

"No. Soapy used to be a friend."

"He'd chew poison if he could spit it in your face now. He hates your heart, Slip!"

"Why shouldn't he?" asked Liddell.

"You mean, it don't bother you?"

"It bothers me, all right. Soapy is a bulldog, and he'll hold on."

"But you don't hate him for it?"

"Listen, kid. I killed the guy he loved."

"Everybody seems to've loved this Frank Pollard," remarked Skeeter.

"He was one of the kind that was always trying to help others and the poor sucker couldn't help himself," answered Liddell.

"How come you slipped the lead into him?" asked Skeeter.

"Don't you go through life being surprised by things. I'll give you some advice."

"Shoot," said Skeeter.

"Get off the road . . . settle down. You'll never be more than half a man. You couldn't take care of yourself in a pinch."

"The hell I couldn't," said Skeeter.

"What you use? A knife or a blackjack?"

There was a silence.

"You settle down. You're going to be one of those slim sizes all your life. Learn stenography. Get off the road."

"I'll be darned if I sharpen pencils all my life," declared Skeeter.

"You're a fresh sort of a kid," said Liddell, sleepily. "I don't know why I like you. But you get off the road and settle down. I'm telling you."

"It's okay. It's okay," muttered Skeeter. "But leave me out of this. The point is there's a gang in this town that'll never rest easy till they shoot the wishbone right out of you. Why don't you get out?"

"Maybe I will. Right now, I'm sleeping," answered Liddell. "So long, kid. Thanks for coming."

"Okay," nodded Skeeter. "I've just tried to get some sense into you. When you wake up and find things have happened, remember me. I tried to make you move with common sense."

"I'll remember. Good night," said Liddell, and turned his face to the wall.

*

VI "Ride into the Desert"

After that interruption, Liddell slept on into the warmth of the morning. Then he took a bath and sat down to a breakfast of toast and Mexican chocolate, frothed by Dolores herself, with Dolores to look at as he ate and drank. Her beauty had an extra edge because she was frightened, and she was frightened because she had heard ugly rumors from the street. She followed him to the door, afterward, begging him not to go out through the curious crowd that was gathered in front of the silversmith's.

But Liddell went out. All voices stopped when he appeared. Then murmurs began. They were pointing him out. They were saying that he was the man who had done it. A woman with a broad face and a red nose leaned out of a window and yelled: "He shot his partner in the back! Put the dogs on him! He shot him in the back!"

It was plain that the town of San Jacinto had been hearing plenty about Slip Liddell during the night. When he walked into the sheriff's office, Chris Tolliver was running the tip of his tongue, with a painful slowness, over the crack in his lip. He looked at Liddell as though at a bodiless image of the night before.

"What about that five thousand?" asked Liddell.

"I've forwarded your claim and proofs," said the sheriff, shortly. "I sent it up to the attorney general. Maybe we'll be hearing in a couple of days."

He smiled all on one side of his mouth, as though in that way he would less endanger that splitting lower lip.

"It's funny, is it?" asked Liddell.

"Kind of," agreed the sheriff. He rubbed his bulging eyes, always tired, always reddened.

"A five thousand dollar joke, eh?" asked Liddell.

"Kind of," repeated Chris Tolliver.

The secretary pretended to be busy, but he had stopped typewriting and shuffled many papers softly together, searching for something which he obviously would not find.

"Tell me where the point is. I could use a good joke," observed Liddell.

"The point is . . . will you be here in San Jacinto when the money comes through?" asked Tolliver.

"Why not?" answered Liddell.

"Some of the boys were ready to pay a call on you this morning!"

"They'd've found me in, too. What about it?"

"When they come to call, will you be there?"

"They won't be calling."

"Won't they?"

"No," said Liddell.

"Maybe not. Maybe I don't know my town," remarked Tolliver.

Liddell went back to the silversmith's. The air was full of noise like the Fourth of July. For the custom in San Jacinto during the fiesta season was to keep the day and the night alive. Hurdy-gurdies pushed through the streets; mandolin players strolled and serenaded favored windows; snatches of band music always were growing and disappearing out of the distances; and the children of the town suddenly multiplied by ten and poured chattering and yelling into every crevice of quiet.

In spite of himself, he did not wish to pass down the street in front of Pinelli's. He did not want that fat-faced woman to lean out of the window with her denunciation as she had done before. So he took another way home, though it meant climbing a wall. When he reached the courtyard, he stepped into the stable. The mule stood there with dreaming eyes and a cruelly puckered mouth but Cicely was gone.

When he asked in the house, no one could tell what had happened. Armando rushed off upstairs to Dolores and that left Liddell for a moment alone in the shop with Juanita. She softened her voice in a half audible whisper.

She looked up at Liddell with the most friendly of smiles so that if her husband returned down the inner hall he would observe only that expression on her face, but what she was saying was: "Why don't you go, *Señor* Jimmy? Why don't you go before you have the house pulled down over our heads? The whole town hates you. And Saint Mary of God knows that I've hated you these years!"

She was still smiling.

"It's good for your complexion to do a little hating," answered Liddell. "It takes ten years off that pretty face, Juanita."

Her smile stretched and froze in place; then both her husband and her daughter came with clattering feet and a double outcry down the stairs and into the hall.

Liddell did not wait for them. He knew by the exclamations of dismay that they had no news of how the mare had gone, so he stepped into the street and ran the gantlet this time of silent eyes, which looked at him as at something monstrous.

He went neither north or south through the town with his inquiries because in those directions ran the river roads, where automobiles could overtake even the swiftest of horses. But he went east with inquiry first and then west; and it was near the western rim of the little town that he found a peddler leading a mule that carried two great hampers and the peddler had, in fact, seen just such a golden-bay mare ridden toward the hills by a ragged young lad.

He described the rider.

"Skeeter!" said Liddell softly to himself, and stood still, looking west toward the ragged sides of the range so ineptly named Monte Verde. No horse in San Jacinto could overtake that wise-footed Cicely with such a feather-weight as Skeeter on her back, and an automobile might as well try to run down a shark's throat as through those rocks.

He stood there for a moment with anger overtaking him from behind, as it were, until the weight of it turned his face crimson.

After a while he went down to the station, taking empty byways because he had no wish to be recognized again; but most of the people were away at the fair grounds and the streets were clear enough. He had been looking at his mental map of the country all the way, and he was quite clear as to what he would do. He found out at the station that no passenger train went east for some time but while he was asking questions a long freight came around the bend like thunder out of the west. It came closer, the empties in the string rattling like snaredrums.

Liddell walked away from the station platform until some stacked piles shut him away from the view of San Jacinto. The big engine passed him at that moment, struggling powerfully against the grade, and a moment later he spotted a brakeman, a big man with arms akimbo and a deep-visored cap.

To him Liddell signaled a high sign that every tramp and every brakeman understands. The answer was a favorable wave of the hand and Liddell decided on the next empty flat-car. The train was not doing more than thirty miles an hour. When he sprinted, the procession of cars slowed up perceptibly. Then he turned and jumped for the steel ladder with arms and legs stretched out before him, as a cat jumps when it goes into a fight. Feet and hands struck their chosen rungs of the ladder. He swung violently back to the left, then clambered up the side and sat down at the end of the flat-car.

The high sides kept him from seeing anything except the ridges of Monte Verde and the sun-faded blue of the sky with two or three buzzards adrift in the high light like a few ugly words on a blank page of white. Then the rattling of the flat-car began to shake his wits into a thoughtless jumble for it was a rough bit of roadbed and the heavy flat-car crashed and shook like a vast cargo of tin and iron junk. The vibration set the sky trembling.

It shivered the teeth of Liddell together and set a tingle in his lips and eyelids. No shadow of warning came over him, but he turned his head about suddenly and saw the big brakeman coming up behind him, still with the same smile. This fellow had a pair of small, watchful eyes that had no relation whatever to the smile on his lips. Liddell stood up and held out a dollar bill.

"Okay, chief?" he asked. "I'm dropping off a few miles up the line."

The brakeman took the bill, looked at it a moment, tucked it into a trouser pocket, and struck Liddell violently across the head with a leather-covered blackjack. The blow knocked him back against the end of the car. He teetered far over, out of balance. Part of his brain remained alive to tell him that if he fell the wheels that rushed behind the flat-car would finish him; but his hands had no sense of them.

They would not grip the edge of the car and maintain a secure grip. The heavy jolting was helping to unbalance him. And then he saw the big brakeman coming at him again with the blackjack in the hollow of his hand, the knob of it just inside the tip of his fingers. Still only a small instinct in Liddell told him to fight. The rest of his mind was telling him that this was a dream and that the still-smiling face of the brakeman was that of a friend.

The brakeman took his time. He set his feet wide apart. His smile broadened. Even the little eyes twinkled with pleasure, now. Then he slapped the blackjack at Liddell's head. He was so sure of himself that it was easy to duck the blow. Liddell spilled forward and threw his arms around the fellow's body.

It was like embracing a barrel sheathed with India rubber, the bones were so big, the muscles so hard. He took Liddell by the throat, pushed him off to arm's length and struck at his face with the blackjack.

The car heeled at a curve. That was why he missed that stroke. Otherwise he should have smashed Liddell's face to a pulp. As it was, he not only missed but lost his grip and Liddell hit him twice about the head.

There was no force in the punches. His shoulders were soggy and his elbows were cork. The brakeman kept on smiling. Some of the deliberate surety had left him, however. He freshened his grip on the blackjack. He came in like a boxer, with short, shuffling steps, his long left hand out.

Liddell paid no heed to that. A man with a club strikes hard only with the club hand. Liddell watched the blackjack. The life was coming back to him. The pain in his head was burning away the fog. The top of his skull seemed to be off. But he was glad of the torment. It was whiskey to him.

It made him hot all over with strength. The wits came back into his feet; they made sense as they leaped to the side and let the brakeman's rush go by. Liddell buried his fist in the soft of the body. It went right in deep. It creased the brakeman like a piece of paper and doubled him over.

Liddell crouched. Only the shudder and jouncing of the car unsteadied his target. So he got in two lifting punches that straightened his man. The brakeman was back on his heels making a futile swipe through the air with the blackjack. A thin line of blood, like a stroke of red paint, appeared on his mouth.

Liddell hit for that mark. Then he stepped back and let the brakeman fall on his face. The blackjack, as though there was intelligent malice in it, flew out of the nerveless hand and rapped against Liddell's shin. He picked it up and threw it away; then he sat down to wait.

He was scarcely aware of the weariness in his body because the pain from his head was reaching down through him and touching all his nerves. Each rattling bounce of the car brought him taut with pain.

The head of the brakeman kept jouncing up and down. He had red hair, long and thin. The dust on the floor of the car blew into it and clogged with the blood. For he was still bleeding. A good pool of it gathered around his head. When he tried to sit up, his hand slipped in the blood. He fell on his face again. He lay there for another long moment, his body jouncing loosely. After a while he managed to sit up and his face was bad to see.

He covered it with his hands and sat there with his back bowed as though there were no spine in it. Liddell squatted on the quivering car, leaning on one hand to steady himself, and stared at the man he had beaten. The brakeman was silent and slack, as if he were still unconscious.

He was very big. He must have weighed two hundred and twenty or thirty pounds and Liddell knew that he had never been beaten before. Now the manhood was gone out of him. This shack never would be able to bully a tramp again. Before long he would not be able to look any angry man in the face. It made Liddell sick to think of what was coming. Still the fellow sat there with his hands over his face and the blood leaking out between his fingers and running down over his wrists.

Now the ridges of Monte Verde were diminishing rapidly in height; the country began to smooth out. Off to the left lay a flat land with a reddish-brown mist gathered low down over it. It made the throat of Liddell dry to look at it for he had spent time enough on the desert.

The wheels of the train began to rattle in an increasing staccato, They had passed the long grade, at last, and were heading down. He went over the side of the car, hung on the lowest rung of the ladder, and looked back to see if the brakeman were in sight; but the big man was still hidden from view.

The rough of the tiles beside the track now gave way to a broad, cinder-spread shoulder. Liddell swung back, slanted his body, and let go. By the time he had come to a walk the caboose of the train was going by, with a dirty flag blowing and snapping off the rear of it.

Now that he was on the ground, there was no wind whatever. The sun burned down through his hat. Two hot thumbs pressed against the top of his head as though there were no bone to shelter the brain itself. His right hand was painful, also. He had used it for the last, finishing punch and one of the brakeman's teeth, cutting straight through his lip, had driven into Liddell's middle finger just below the knuckle, cutting to the bone. It still bled. His whole hand was red.

For a hundred yards or so he followed the rails until he came to a faintly traced path. He thought, as he turned into the rough along the side of Monte Verde, that brakemen are a queer lot. Usually they are as tough as shoe leather but this fellow had been too big. All big men are soft, somewhere. They have some small dimension somewhere. Usually it's the neck. Big heads set on small necks are no good. Even he himself was too big. He was three inches too tall. Five feet ten is plenty. Condense a hundred and eighty pounds in five feet ten and you have plenty of man, rubbery with strength, compact, hard all over. If you're closer to the ground, you don't have so far to fall. If you're closer to the ground, you're not apt to break your back when you lift.

He kept thinking of these things in a monotone of the mind, a dreary repetition, pacing out the words of his thinking with the steps he took; and the pain got worse and worse in his head.

He came to a little song of running water. It was a rill that went among the rocks quick as the flash of a fleeing snake. The water was no good for drinking. It was brackish with alkali. But it did pretty well for washing his hand and his head. There was not much of a lump on top of his head but the scalp was cut, and he was perfectly certain that the skull was fractured. At last he made himself take the full strength of his hands and work on each side of the pain. He had a feeling that if there were a fracture he would feel and even hear the bone edges rasp together. When he heard nothing, he felt much better. The sea-sickness left the pit of his belly when he stood up and marched ahead.

When you go west out of San Jacinto, there is only one easy way of climbing Monte Verde. If you take the easy way, it leads you off into a shallow depression that deepens and narrows to a valley and at last the valley cuts down to a gorge which is not twenty feet wide in places. It is cut by water that only runs down that draw during the spring rains. In seasons of light rainfall there is no run of water at all.

The gorge has straight sides. The bottom of it is set with boulders as big as a horse and rider, and there are some shrubs growing, too, because the rain water never runs down the draw long enough to drown a plant. But it's a desolate gorge.

Up the mountain sides there is some smoky green of palo verde, and cactus sticks out catclaws at you and the rocks are hand-polished by the sun so that they hurt your eyes at midday. This was where Liddell sat down on the shady side of the boulder to wait.

VII "The Most Man"

He worked himself up to such a point as he sat there in the airless swelter that it seemed to him the brakeman, whom he'd fought on the freight, had not used the blackjack. It was as though Skeeter had beaten him over the head. Then he began to feel a horrible riot of nerves as he realized how the time was drifting past him because there *were* other ways, of course, by which the mare could have been taken out of San Jacinto and into the west. He had come to a grim certainty that he never would see the silk and shine and beauty of Cicely again, when he heard a horse dog-trotting down the gorge, and of course that was Cicely with blue-jeaned Skeeter on her back.

He got himself back behind the rock and coiled his strength into one big spring. He had made up his mind that he would make Skeeter take all that was possible. There would be no more horse-stealing in that career after he had tied Skeeter's hands to that thorn bush and used the buckle end of a belt thoroughly.

That was the trouble with youngsters. They could not even be disciplined. There was nothing you could close your hands on or sink your teeth into, so to speak. But Cicely's hoofs rapping over the rocks were like beats on a drum, coming closer and closer until the noise was right upon Liddell.

Then he leaped out.

Cicely was a little quicker than a cat, but she was not quick enough to get away from that surprising charge, or perhaps she recognized her master even faster than she felt fear. At any rate, he got in a flying leap, fastened his hand on the nape of Skeeter's neck, and brought that young rider to the ground with a sound like a loud hand clap.

Breath and senses were knocked out of Skeeter at the same instant, and as the body turned inertly from the side to its back, the big cap spilled off the head and allowed the hair to go tumbling down around the ears.

Well, some of the boys, when they feel their blood, can wear hair as long as that, but Liddell was using his eyes all the way, now; and as he looked at the hands and the turn of the throat and the delicate care with which the nose and the lips had been fashioned he felt a strong, new horror come up in him.

His mark was distinctly on this act. It was the little red trickle of blood that formed at the corner of her mouth, exactly like the line of red which had been the target on the brakeman's face not so very long before. Liddell fell into a mighty sweat, for it seemed to him that heads were lifting from the shadows of the rocks and staring at him, and that a whisper ran up and down the gorge.

Once, in his earliest school days, he had seen a boy hit a girl. Her head bobbed right back as though her neck were only a loose spring. She hadn't run away. She hadn't even screamed. She just stood there, bewildered. And then the whole schoolyard descended on that lad and winnowed him small with fists and feet. Once in his life, also, he had seen a man who was known to beat his wife.

Liddell, before the girl was half-conscious, had her up off the ground, not at all worried about her health but only concerned to get the dust brushed from the blue jeans and the blood from her face. When he handled her, the soft of her body sort of slid from his grasp and he kept swearing under his breath and sweating. He felt as though he were losing a frightful race against Public Opinion.

All at once, he saw that although she let her body remain as limp as ever, she was smiling a little. He sat her down rather hard and stood back. He took off his hat. She permitted herself to be conscious.

"I'm seven kinds of a fool," said Liddell, in an uncertain voice, "but this morning I wasn't half awake when you were sitting up there in the window . . . the dust storm had knocked the tar out of my eyes."

He picked up her cap, dusted it conscientiously, and gave it into her hands. She kept on smiling a little, and looking him up and down. He said, huskily: "I'm giving you my word of honor . . . I didn't see you well enough. I thought you were a boy. I beg your pardon," said Liddell.

She pulled out a handkerchief and dabbed at her lip and then looked at the drop of blood on the white cloth. She said nothing.

"If I'd known . . . if I'd guessed . . . if I hadn't been such a stupid fool," said Liddell, his agony increasing with her silence.

He hoped that her smile meant kindness, but he could not be sure. She kept looking at the drop of blood on her handkerchief. Another speck of blood was forming at her lip. "Suppose I'd just been a boy . . . ?" she suggested.

"Why, that would have been different," said Liddell. He started to make himself a cigarette with nervous hands. He offered the makings to her.

"I don't smoke," she said.

"I beg your pardon," said Liddell.

"If I'd been a boy, you'd have torn the hide right off my back, wouldn't you?" she asked, still with that smile. It was like the smile of the brakeman. It could mean anything in the world.

"I didn't guess," stammered Liddell. The cigarette went to pieces in those sure fingers of his.

"Man or woman, I'd still be a horse thief, wouldn't I?" she asked.

"I wouldn't dream . . . ," said Liddell. "Of course everybody likes a joke."

"How'd you get here, anyway?" she asked.

"I hopped a freight," he answered. "When I found out that you'd ridden west, I hopped a westbound freight, because I remembered how this trail came to a narrow. . . ."

"Tell me," asked Skeeter, "why I grabbed that Cicely mare of yours?"

"You had to get somewhere and you didn't have time . . . ," he began, politely.

She put her chin on her fist and studied him curiously. The wind kept knocking her hair to one side. Sometimes a flicking of it came across her face. Even the stillness was gone from the air, since she arrived.

"I stole that horse because I knew you'd follow," she said. "And if you stayed in San Jacinto, I knew that those apes would do you in sooner or later. So I thought that I'd lead you a paper chase. Because I knew that you wouldn't give up Cicely without a fight. Believe me?"

"Certainly," said Liddell. "Of course I believe you."

"What's the matter with you?" asked the girl.

She stood up, suddenly. She put her fists on her hips—what a fool he had been not to see at a glance the woman in her—and said: "I see what it is. You're afraid that I'll go back and tell people that you beat me up. Afraid I'll say that you manhandled a girl, eh? Listen, Slip, what sort of a hound would that make you?"

He was pale with the thought of it. His face was the color of grease.

"Go on and tell me," insisted the girl. "If I went back and said that, and showed 'em the place on my mouth, what would they think of you?"

"You wouldn't do it," said Liddell. "Of course it's a joke."

He tried a laugh that was a poor, staggering excuse for mirth.

"I'll tell you what," she answered, "if you try to turn back into San Jacinto now, I'll spill the news all over the place."

He made a two-handed gesture of appeal clumsily, because he was not used to making gestures of appeal.

"But I've got to go back," he said.

"You gotta go back, why?" she demanded. "You gotta go back and be lynched, why? Mind you, those fellows Pudge and Soapy and that bright young Mark Heath, they won't stop till they've started a lynching mob after you!"

"Were any of the three of them spending a lot of money last night?" he asked.

"No. But what's that got to do with it?" she asked. "I'm saying: how'll you have it? Do you keep away from San Jacinto or do you have me spill the beans about how the big guy slammed the girl around?"

He fought through a real agony. He sat down on his heels and took one of her hands in his.

"There'll be nothing hard for me in San Jacinto," he said. "And I've got to get back there and stay until. . . ."

"What's all this?" she asked. She took her hand away from him. "Some crazy matter of honor . . . or is it a bet?"

"It's more than honor."

"You're going back?"

"I have to go," he told her.

"Then I spill the beans about you all over town."

He held himself so hard that he trembled. After a while he said: "Get up on the mare, then, and I'll take you back to town."

"You've got to go back and take it, do you?" she asked. "Slip, what's come over you? What's the matter with you, anyway? Do you think I don't know what those mugs can do and will do? What is it that pulls you back to San Jacinto?"

"Business," he said.

"Five thousand dollars in blood money?"

He made no answer.

"Listen," she said. "Tell me one thing. If you hadn't grabbed me with Cicely right here, would you have gone on trekking farther west to trail me?"

"No," he said.

"Then it doesn't matter," she sighed. "I would have lost anyway."

He said: "If I hadn't caught up with you here . . . you would have come back to San Jacinto?"

"Of course I would," she said. "Hi, quit it, Slip! Don't be polite and doubting. I'm for you. Can't you see that?"

"Are you?" he asked, bewildered more than ever, and still very nervous.

"What do you make of that?" she murmured to herself. And then aloud and with anger she demanded: "You don't think I'm a *horse* thief, do you, Slip?"

"No," he said, following a sudden light. "You're not a thief, Skeeter!"

"No?" she echoed. She began to laugh. "When I hit the stem, you watch my smoke. And when I'm on the road with Pop, who finds the chickens in the dark and wishes them off the roost so soft they keep right on sleeping till they find themselves in the mulligan? Oh, Slip, I could swipe eyelashes and never make the eyes blink, but I'm a regular sort of guy, at that. Do you think I could be?"

"I think you could be," said Liddell. "I think you are!"

He swung into the saddle on Cicely. "Hop on behind," he said.

She stepped on his stirrup and was suddenly seated behind the cantle with an arm lightly around him.

"You're breathing deep and feeling better," she observed. "Did you think I'd really go to town and pull a phony on you?"

"I wasn't thinking straight," he answered, as the mare picked her way among the boulders.

"They're talking in the streets about you," she said. "Those people will never rest easy till they've done something about you and, when they start, they'll have ropes in their hands. You know that?"

"I know that," he said.

"And still you're not scared of death?"

"I suppose I'm scared," he answered.

"But you've got to go back?"

"I've got to go back."

"All right," she answered, chiefly to herself. "Will you let me see a lot of you while you last?"

"All you can stand."

"D'you ever suppose things?"

"Yeah, once in a while."

"Well, suppose that I was dolled up in fluff and zingo and perfume, would you like me a lot better?"

"I like you fine the way you are."

"Fine?" she repeated.

"Yeah, fine."

"Once I was at a masquerade and I swiped a dress and made up like a girl," said Skeeter. "I tell you what I did. I went and combed out my hair and brushed it up, and a million waves and curls came into it, and it shone like nobody's business."

"It shines plenty right now."

"Yeah, but you got no idea," said Skeeter. "And I got myself into a red dress with a yellow kind of a whatnot around the neck. It had a lot of zingo, is what that old dress had, and believe you me."

"I believe you, all right," said Liddell.

"And there was red slippers that squeezed my toes," said Skeeter, "because from going barefoot my feet are kind of spread. But they're not very big feet, at that? Would you say?"

She stuck out a foot.

"They're okay feet, I'd say," replied Liddell.

"But those slippers went with the dress and when you start getting fashionable the pain don't count," she observed. "I had on a lot of things underneath too, so it was kind of hard to breathe. But the point I make is what I did to the men at that party. I knocked 'em right out of their chairs."

"I'll bet you did," agreed Liddell.

"If I was to take and lean forward and look at you, I'd see a smile on your pan, right now," she declared.

"No, you wouldn't," he replied. "Except enjoying what you're saying. That's the only smile you'd see."

"Honest?" she answered.

"Honest."

"Well," she said, "they certainly were a dizzy lot; but the slippers wore me out and I pretty near died before the last dance was over. And I walked home barefoot, and I'll tell you what, Slip, I kind of felt sorry for men, the way a skirt and a dish of perfume knock 'em for a row of loops. What kind of perfume do you like, Slip?"

"Soap," he answered.

"What?" she demanded.

"Just a kind of a clean smell," he told her.

"Geez, you're a funny kind of a guy," she remarked after thinking this over. "But take you by and large, you're the most man that I ever bumped into."

"Thanks," said Liddell, "and you're the most. . . ."

"Wait a minute," she interrupted. "You don't half know about me, yet. You haven't even read the headlines. You wait and see."

"All right. I'll wait," said Liddell.

VIII "Gun-Gambit Refused"

It was dusk when they came to the edge of San Jacinto. "You get off here," he told her. "I've got to get to an appointment and I'm nearly late now."

"Is it a blonde?" she asked. She stood by the mare with her arms akimbo, looking up.

"It's not a blonde," he told her, smiling down.

"I know," said Skeeter. "It's old lipstick . . . old powder-her-nose . . . that Dolores, the poor dummy that couldn't get past the third grade."

"She's not a bad sort of a girl. You ought to know her," said Liddell. "Where do you stay, Skeeter?"

"You know the second bridge, and a string of little white shacks down south of it? I live in one of those."

"Thanks," said Liddell. "I'll be seeing you."

"Thanks for asking," said the girl. And then as he cantered the mare away she was adding: "Thanks for nothing . . . thanks for being a saphead . . . I never saw such a cockeyed bozo in my life! Can't he see I'm eating my heart like bread, because of him?"

But suddenly she broke into a run, following behind him when she saw him turn the mare onto the river road.

It would have done you good to see her run. You know how most girls scamper, leaning forward as though they were about to fall on their faces, and their feet stuttering along behind them and their hands catching at the air? Well, Skeeter ran with a good knee-lift and her legs blowing out behind her the way a champion runs when he means business. She slid along through the shadows as easy as you please, keeping close to the side of the lane so that the willows would cover her, because she wanted to know what Liddell had to do down the river road, that time of the day.

The road took a good dip from the town level down to the waterside and the big San Jacinto went drifting along and, through the gaps in the tulles, she could see the last golden, rusting, tarnishing stain of the sunset afloat on the water. Then there was nothing but tulles, and the dust raised by the galloping mare burned the lungs of Skeeter because the wind had fallen away to nothing as it generally does out there at sundown and the dust hung where the heels of the mare kicked it.

The light grew dull, also, but she was able to see her man turn off the road and go into the tulles. They were tall enough to cover him to the neck. Just his head moved along above the feathery tips of the tulles. And Skeeter dropped down on a bank and watched, and panted, and listened.

She could hear the plopping of the feet of the mare as Cicely entered the muck out of which the tulles grew; and far back of her out of the town floated the voice of the fiesta, made up of the bawling of cattle—they had been doing some roping that day—and the pattering hoofs of horses, and the barking of dogs that made no sense at all, and the shrill of children calling out as they played, and the trembling of musical strings.

That sharp, accurate ear of hers dissolved the cloud of sound into these thin elements but still she could hear the mare working her way out into the marsh land. It took nerve to ride the mare out there into the dark, where a quicksand might grab her legs any moment.

Then she heard something else that stopped her heart, for some reason. It was a whistle composed of three notes—one long and two short. It was repeated, on a high pitch. In that musical brain of hers she recorded the pitch and the rhythm faultlessly.

Three or four times the whistle was repeated. Then a silence set in and out of the silence grew the faint noise of oars groaning in their locks. This noise also ended, and the silence closed in, and the damp coolness of the night covered her body and rose to her lips. She was listening so hard that she almost forgot to breathe.

Minutes of this followed. At last the noise of hoofs plumping through the marsh came back again toward the river bank. The black silhouette of a horseman lurched out of the tulles and turned up the road.

Skeeter, lying flat behind the trunk of a tree, peered out, and she knew against the stars the outline of the rider. She could tell him by the angle of his hat and the cant of his head. The mare wanted to gallop hard but he reined her in. She heard his voice saying gently: "Easy, Sis! Easy does it, honey! Easy, girl!"

The words did something to her. She smiled all the way down the line to the shack where old Pop was waiting. They had two ground-floor rooms, to the back, where they could hear the swish-swash of the river currents all night long. When Pop heard her, he did not turn his head at once. He was sewing up a second-hand pair of trousers. Because when you buy second-hand stuff, it's always better to go over the seams, first, and tighten up the bad places, and all the buttons can do with a stitch or two. That way, they last twice as long. So when he heard her come in, he stopped sewing but he did not turn his head. Neither of them spoke.

There was a little, round, rusted iron stove in a corner with an iron pot simmering on top of it and filling the room with a greasy smell. She took a granite cooking spoon off the table, went over to the pot, and stirred the contents. She lifted a spoonful and let it slop back. There were carrots, beans, some sort of greens, tomatoes, and strings and fragments of meat all mushed up from long cooking. She piled a good heap of the mulligan stew on a paper plate and sat on the table with the plate in her lap. She used the graniteware spoon to eat with and a big chunk of bread as a pusher. When the end of the bread was well-smeared with gravy, she bit off the wet part. Otherwise the bread was too stale and hard to bite into.

Pop said: "I been knowing all the time that you'd turn soft. And today's the time. I been trying for years and years to keep you clean and straight. But the dirt that's under the skin has gotta come out. So you went and run off with somebody, did you? He gives you a whistle and you go right off with him. I been seeing it come over you."

She looked calmly upon him, working hard over a mouthful. Time had put its hands on him, and twisted. Time had taken him by the nape of the neck and pushed his head forward and bent a crook in his back. A shag of greasy gray hair stuck down over the collar of his shirt.

He was old. He was like a man going downhill, a long step every day. So she merely said: "What's been happening in town?"

He answered: "You don't wanta talk about where you been?"

"What's been happening in town?" she repeated.

"Money. That's what's been happening. Everybody's had his hand in his pocket all day long, shelling out cash. If you'd been here to do the dance, we'd've taken in a hundred bucks. Even me alone doing jigs on the accordion with my hat on the sidewalk, even me, I took in more'n eight dollars."

"That's good," she nodded.

"Not that you get any share nor hide nor hair of it!" he shouted. "You didn't take a step to help in the making of it."

"Okay," said the girl. "Nothing else important?"

"Nothing except what they're all talking about. This bozo that you went to warn this morning . . . this Slip Liddell . . . he's yella. He took a run-out powder. He blew out of town. He'll never be seen in San Jacinto again. He's got no more name than a Chinaman, right now. The people are laughing at him."

"Maybe I made a mistake," she said, as she finished her meal.

She got down from the table, filled a tin bucket with water from the tap, and went into the next room. "Whatcha gonna do?" demanded Pop.

"I'm taking a bath," she said.

"Why you gonna take a bath?" he asked. "You ain't done any dancing today or sweated yourself up any."

For answer, the key turned into the lock. Drowsily he heard the swishing of water in the next room. Before his mind turned two more gloomy corners, she was back again, still toweling her hair.

"That perfume is over there in the second drawer . . . ," he said.

"I got a new kind of perfume."

"Whatcha mean?" asked Pop.

"Soap," she said.

"You gone and lost your mind?" cried Pop. "A good, sweet smell on you is what you need, particular after you been dancing hard. It'll turn dimes into quarters when the boys come to chuck money into the hat."

"A good clean smell is good enough for me," said Skeeter. "How come they all say that Liddell is yella? Because they didn't find him around town?"

"I'll tell you what it's come to," answered Pop. "There's a young feller by the name of Heath . . . remember him?"

"I remember him," she nodded.

"He's been telling the world that if it can find Liddell, he'll be waiting for him up in the Royal Saloon."

"He's been telling what?" exclaimed Skeeter.

"Telling the whole world . . . that he's waiting there in the Royal for Liddell, if Slip has the nerve to come and have a showdown with him," said Pop. "He's daring Liddell to show his face inside the Royal Saloon, and he'll change his looks for him. Because he says that the longer he thinks, the surer he is that he can't leave in the world the sort of rat that took and murdered poor Frank Pollard. And if. . . ."

He started up from his chair, shouting: "Hi, Skeeter! Where are you . . . ?"

But Skeeter was gone through the door and up the street. She ran the entire way and her knees were gone under her when she reached the Royal Saloon. She cut right in across the vacant lot beside it to save time, and in this way came to the open window. Something was very odd about the place. She realized, as she hurried up, that not a sound was coming from the Royal at what should have been one of its busiest moments of the day. When she looked through the window, she saw the reason at a glance and the heart went out of her.

For everything inside the Royal was as still as paint. It looked, in fact, as though an artist had snapshot the scene. Some of the men at the tables, half-risen, rested their weight on the arms of their chairs as though still in the act of rising. Instead of the long line at the bar, a dozen or so had stepped back to leave it clear for two people, and these were Liddell and young Mark Heath.

The pause must have lasted for some time.

Heath was green-white but his eyes were fixed and dangerous. He said now in a strained, high-pitched voice: "I'm telling you again. You've got a gun. Fill your hand and we start!"

It was like something out of a ghost of an old barroom in the West. He must have remembered it out of stories of the past, that phrase about filling the hand with a gun. His own hand was back behind his hip and he was leaning forward a little as though to balance the weight of the draw.

She saw Pudge McArthur and Soapy Jones, too. They were at a table near the bar. Pudge had his hand under his coat; Soapy's gun was out in plain view and it pointed steadily toward Liddell. It looked too big—a caricature of a weapon, a funny-paper revolver.

She wanted to yell out something as a warning to Liddell but she had become a part of that frozen scene inside the Royal, and no voice would issue from her lips.

Then she heard Liddell saying: "I've got something better than a gun to fill my hand. I've got a drink here, Heath. Here's to you and here's to everybody."

He lifted the whiskey, waved it left and right to the crowd, and poured it down his throat.

"Keep the change, Chuck," he said, and walked out of the place with a deliberate step. The swing-door was still oscillating when Pudge McArthur jumped out of his chair and shouted: "I told you he was yella, Mark! I told you he'd lost his guts! Foller him up! Give him hell!"

But whatever Mark Heath was prepared to do in the future, he was at this moment wiping the sweat from his face and reaching an uncertain hand for his own drink.

*

IX "Liddell Is Dead"

Skeeter felt very sick. Twice as she went down the street she paused to rest her hand against a wall and regain breath and strength. There was a great bustling everywhere and the voices of girls giggling and laughing, for almost the gayest moment of the fiesta came this night with the open-air dance on the platform under the cypresses by the river. This stir of expectancy and happiness sickened her more than ever. For her, this was a funeral moment; she walked wretchedly in procession after the death of a man's reputation.

She was at the mouth of the narrow street on which the silversmith had his shop when two men went by, stepping large and fast, and she heard them saying: "Did you see the kind of a fool smile he wore when he picked up his drink?"

"Yeah, like a punch-drunk bum in the ring . . . grinning . . . pretending he's not hurt! This here Slip, he's had the whole world buffaloed with a big bluff. Say, maybe that's why they call him *Señor Coyote*. . . ."

"You'd think he'd rather of died."

That was it. That was what one would think.

She went down the alley into the little cramped courtyard of Pinelli, with the sense of winter dampness underfoot and in the air. When she leaned through the window, she could see the length of big Liddell stretched on the bed. He did not have a lamp lighted. Enough illumination came from the hall to show her he was face down. She slid through the window and dropped to the floor.

"Who's that?" asked Liddell.

"Nobody," said Skeeter, as she closed the hall door.

She was glad of the darkness. It would be easier to talk in the black of the night. It would have been better if no stars looked in through the window, showing the narrow roof of the next building and letting the thought of the exterior world come to them. In the murk she found the bed and sat on her heels beside it.

"Listen, Slip," she said. "I know how you feel. Once I went to school and having the girls look at me and my funny rig, it made me terrible sick. I used to be so happy when Friday night came, that I cried. Yeah. Me. I really cried. And I used to nearly cry again when Monday morning came. I know what I felt when I had to hop my first freight, too. That was five years back, when Pop still had some spring in his legs."

"Is he your father?" asked Liddell.

"That old . . . what do you think?"

"No, I don't think he is."

"Thanks, Slip. But he's been pretty good to me in a lot of ways; and I'm going to take care of him when he gets too old and mean to make his way. I didn't come to talk about him and me. Slip . . . I was at the window of the Royal and I saw. And the whole town is saying that you took water."

She heard his body turn but she said nothing. After a moment she reached through the darkness and by a sure instinct found his hand. It closed hard and suddenly over hers.

She said: "Sometimes it looks to me like we only have so much stuff in us. Just so much and no more. You've been all over. I know where you've been. All up and down the line I've met shacks and tramps and straight people that told me things you've done. Now the nerve is gone out of you. Courage, that's like strength. It can't last forever. It's like some people live fast and die young; and some people live slow, and last a long time. But each of them do the same amount of living. Isn't that true?"

"Perhaps it is," said Liddell.

She could feel a tension in him, and knew he was listening as no one ever had listened to her before. "Look at you," said the girl. "The way you've lived is half a dozen lives. That's why it doesn't matter so much if you should have to stop living."

"D'you think I have to die, now?" asked Liddell.

A sob came up in her throat and almost strangled her. She choked it back. The effort knocked her voice to pieces when she spoke. "You've gotta go out and meet Heath, and McArthur, and Soapy Jones," she said.

He was silent.

"There's thousands and thousands of folks that know about you, Slip. They've heard about you and they wouldn't want to hear that you'd shown the white feather. Right now there's something alive that belongs to you. It's part of your name. Young fellas that get into a pinch ask themselves what Slip Liddell would do at a time like that. But if they were to hear what happened tonight . . . ."

"It's already happened. I'm dead to the world."

"The dead could up and rise again!" panted the girl. "You could go and laugh in Heath's face, even with Pudge and Soapy behind him. You *gotta* go and laugh in his face. What's three men to the real Slip Liddell? To *Señor* Coyote? What did he do to the three shacks down in the yards at Phoenix? But unless you stand up to 'em, everything good that's ever been said about you is gonna die in the throats that said it. It's better for *you* to die, Slip! Don't turn your name into cheapness, Slip. A coyote would run away, Slip. . . ."

"I wonder," said Liddell.

"Listen to me," remarked the girl, "if I could have my way, I'd follow you around the world like a squaw and I wouldn't care. I know what you've been, and that would be good enough for me. And I'd take you off somewheres up in the mountains where you'd never have to bump into tough mugs any more. I'd fix you up fine, Slip. If you wanted to marry me, that would be swell. If you didn't want to marry me, I wouldn't care. I'd cook for you, and make the house shine, and keep your clothes right; and you'd always have a slick horse to ride and money in your pocket and me and Pop would go out once in a while and just rake in the dough. We'd play the big joints and just rake it in."

"It sounds good to me," said Liddell, softly. "But can't we do that anyway?"

"We can't, Slip," said the girl.

She got up and stood at the window, drinking in deeper breaths of the air. The silence drew out long between them.

"Come back to me a minute, Skeeter, will you?" he asked.

"If I touch you again, I'll be crying like a fool," she said.

"You want me to go back to the Royal now?" said Liddell.

"You mean that you *would* go?" gasped Skeeter.

"I'd try to," said Liddell.

"Did me coming and talking, did that help?"

"It put a different kind of a heart in me," he told her.

"Then thank God that I came. Dying isn't hard, Slip. You'll find out that it isn't hard. . . ."

"Are you sure?" asked Liddell.

"I know it isn't. Once I nearly drowned. I got under the ice and I couldn't break through. I was nine or ten or something. And it wasn't so bad. A funny thing was the way the world looked through the ice. The naked trees sort of blurred over, like there was leaves and things on them. And somehow it seemed to me that the whole world was full of summer, outside of the ice. But it wasn't bad. Just kind of choking a good deal."

"Come here," said Liddell. She came to the edge of the bed. "Sit down by me," said Liddell.

"One way or another, I've been telling you that I like you a lot," said Skeeter. "That wouldn't make you be foolish with me, would it?"

"I hope not," said Liddell.

"Because that wouldn't be a very good last thing for you to do in the world," said Skeeter.

"No, it wouldn't," he agreed.

She sat down beside him. He put a big arm around her, turning on his side.

"How did you get out from under the ice?" asked Liddell.

"Don't say anything," whispered Skeeter. "It's sort of wonderful, just being here close. I mean, it's wonderful for me."

He said nothing, obediently. One of her hands found his face and remained touching it, the fingertips moving softly as though it were a blind hand, reading.

After a long time she said: "Suppose that sky pilots and the preachers and the teachers were right? Suppose that praying did any good? Wouldn't that make a fool out of me? Suppose that praying would jam the gun of Soapy Jones and make Pudge McArthur miss and leave only Heath for you to face. Just supposing that prayer was worth a damn and that I could somehow save you . . . ?"

"You ever come close to praying, Skeeter?" asked Liddell.

"What's the good?" she answered. "In the jungle or on the main stem or on the rattlers, or wherever you are, a fast hand and a quick lam are what get away with the goods, so far as I can see . . . there wouldn't be time for praying except afterward. Whatta *you* think, Slip? Is there a God tucked away somewhere?"

After a bit of consideration he said: "Not the kind that will stop a roulette wheel at the right place."

"Or make your old shoes last," she suggested.

"Or give you another stake," said Liddell.

"Or take the frost out of a midnight ride on the rods," she added. "But I don't want to talk about Him. I want to talk about you. What chance would you have, if you went down there to the dance, this evening? If you went down and faced them?"

Instead of answering he countered with rather a queer question. "Up there at the Royal you saw Heath and Pudge and Soapy, all three?"

"Yes," she answered, "and Soapy with his rod out ready to shoot."

"Were any of them spending a lot of money?" he asked.

"Not that I saw. I only saw you, at the last minute, taking the drink."

She buried her face in her hands, shuddering. The big hand of Liddell patted her back.

She broke out: "Am I wrong, Slip? Had you better get out of here and run for it? If you take it on the lam, I'd go with you."

"No, you wouldn't," answered Liddell. "You'd rather run away with a ghost than with me after my name's dead."

"Maybe that's right. I wonder," said the girl. "You get a name by just playing around and doing the things that are fun when you want to do them. And the name gets bigger and bigger. And after a while, it's so big that you've got to die for it. That's a funny thing, Slip, isn't it?"

He was silent till she exclaimed: "You wouldn't go and change your mind back to the other side again, would you?"

"No," said Liddell.

"That's having the old nerve again!" said the girl. "I can hear what they're gonna say. They're gonna say: 'We thought there was only this kid. We thought there was McArthur and Soapy Jones on the side all the time, with their guns ready. And that was why Slip hesitated a little. But finally he crashed through. He went down with his guns smoking. He never did a finer thing than the day he died.' They'll talk about you like that. Everybody that ever speaks about you is gonna look up, is what they're gonna do."

Her voice broke into bits again. "I'll be going along," she said.

She stood up. Liddell rose with her.

"If I had clothes or something, I could be down there at the finish," said Skeeter.

"Take this money and get clothes," said Liddell.

"All the stores are closed up tight."

"Take this money and see if you can't pry a store open, Skeeter."

"Yeah. Maybe I could."

Her hand closed feebly over a wad of bills.

"You want me there?" she asked.

"I sure want you there," said Liddell. "But so far as I'm concerned, these clothes of yours are plenty good."

"Everybody'd laugh at me," she answered. "Slip, it's kind of funny. This morning I was thinking that we had years and years and years laid out ahead when we'd be seeing each other now and then, and you'd be laid up in the back of my mind like a bit of summer weather, and all that. And now here it is the end, already. It makes me feel queer. It makes me feel kind of sick in the stomach. . . . And good bye!"

She was out the window in a flash, but in the open air she turned again.

"Should I come back? Would you kiss me good bye?" she asked.

"You don't have to come back for that," he said. And he picked up her hand and leaned over and kissed it with a long, light pressure of his lips.

Afterward she lifted the hand to her cheek. She began to laugh, but the laughter staggered and went out suddenly.

"Slip!" she whispered. "I'm not going to live long after you."

"Stop talking rot!" he commanded.

"I never could be another man's," said Skeeter.

"Wait, Skeeter . . . ," he called, leaning across the window sill.

But she already was gone into the night.

After that he paused for a moment, lighted the lamp in his room, and then smoked half of a cigarette before his brain cleared. He went up to the second floor and tapped on a door.

"Hello?" called Dolores.

"Come to the dance with me," invited Liddell.

She pulled the door open. She was only partly dressed. Some of her makeup had not been put on so that she seemed to stand half in light and half in shadow.

"Did you ask me to go with you, *Señor* Jimmy?" she repeated

Her face had no expression.

"That's right. We haven't stepped out for a long time," said Liddell.

"Ah, but I'm not the right size, am I?" she asked.

"You'd do fine for me," said Liddell.

"Ah, but I wouldn't, I wouldn't!" cried Dolores. "I'm not nearly big enough for you to hide behind my skirts, am I, *Señor* Coyote?" There was shrill irony in her voice as she said it.

She pinched and flashed her eyes with malice as she delivered the insult, and a hearty, husky roar of laughter came from the corner of the room. That was mama, waddling into view with her fat arms folded over her fat stomach, shaking herself with mirth and contempt. Liddell closed the door softly and went back down the stairs.

X "Fate Dances at the Fiesta"

Skeeter, under the first street lamp, counted the money in her hand and found a hundred and sixty-five dollars. It stopped her brain. It took the reality out of the night and set the stars spinning. She had dreamed of a man like that, who handed out a whole fistful of money without counting; and here was the money in her grasp.

Then she went on. It was queer to feel that stab, that upthrusting of joy, and know that it came from a dead man.

Once she went to a funeral home in southern California to do a little honor to a famous hobo's death. They got a church funeral for him, some way. And the church was filled with flowers and organ music and she almost had fainted. Now the air of San Jacinto was sweetened with flowers at every window and music was never still in the air from one side of the town to the other. So that sense of death remained with her constantly. Nevertheless, her mind was grimly determined to see the end even if to give testimony later on against the numbers which were sure to combine against him.

Besides, there was some sort of a ghost of a hope remaining in her that help would come in the final moment. Yet as she remembered how quiet he had been in the dark of his room, listening to her, she knew that she was wrong. He had submitted his will to hers, his judgment to hers, almost like a child. At this thought, the tears went suddenly down her face; she did not know they were there and let them dry in the warm air of the night.

She had in mind a Mexican shop well out of the polite center of town. It could be opened by a little extra money if any store in the town could be unbarred at this time of the night. But she found it securely closed. Even this place obeyed the custom on the nights of the fiesta.

This brought her to a pause. She stood gloomily on a corner, her head hanging, as an open automobile swung past filled with laughter and color. It turned the next corner toward the river and the laughter was shut out instantly, as though a velvet-edged door had closed be-

tween them. But other automobiles followed, and now a long, low, luxurious limousine with two men in front in uniform and a hint of ladies and gentry pointed out by street lamps as the car went by. They
came, no doubt, from one of the houses on San Jacinto Hill.

It was not much of a hill. Probably it did not rise a hundred feet above the river, but the swells and rich people who had their houses on it were fond of speaking of the superior stir of air, and the purity of the wind that blew through their precincts. For there were plenty of rich people in San Jacinto—Mexicans, most of them.

When she thought of that, Skeeter moved straight into that superior section of the town. This was a region of iron grilles and barred lattices across windows and over balconies so that modesty could take the air and see the world at the same time. The same devices offered very perfect ladders and Skeeter, after walking a few swift blocks to pick the best prize, selected her mansion and was up a second story balcony in no time at all. The balcony window was not even locked. In a moment she was in a boudoir that fairly loosened her knees and made her sit down to take stock. But she could not sit down.

The *señorita*, on this evening, had not been able to suit her fancy at once. Across the bed lay a cloud of green, a shimmer of white, a mist of rose, and then a dashing design of all colors that she could think of. Skeeter made up her own mind while she was locking the door, with her head turned over her shoulder. She would take the green and use the scarf of the rose.

The overalls came off with a few pulls and kicks. The rest of her clothes followed. Sometimes her face was a bit of a trial to her but the whole of herself was a great satisfaction, always. She stood for half of a priceless moment within the angle of a great triple mirror made of three expensive pier glasses, and with her arms folded behind her head she admired every slightness and every curve; for, as though gifted with new eyes, the mirror showed her more than she ever had seen before.

But time counted. It might be desperately important.

Her hands found their way to spider-webbing of lingerie, and to stockings that could be felt, but hardly seen, a mere overlaying of pink mist on the gold brown which she had picked up at a thousand swimming holes. Then the dress. Then the makeup. But who could choose with ease among ten colors of lipstick?

She made a choice, however, cursing the flight of time a little as she did so. And then she could darken those pale eyebrows with such effect that she hardly knew her own face! She worked on with frantic hands until the picture was such that she trembled a little at sight of it while she brushed out the tangle and left the curl of her hair. Over all, a black cloak. And she was ready.

For what? To climb again down that irregular ladder of lattice and bars? She thought the thing over while she bundled up the overalls that were her stock in trade. After all, that descent should not be a big problem to one who could climb a rope like a sailor. She tied the bundle of clothing to her shoulder, scanned the street, blessed its emptiness, and in a moment had swung down to the pavement.

What those clothes were worth she could not guess, but she had left a full hundred dollars on the dressing table of the room above. For she felt, somehow, that it would not do to go as a thief in a thief's apparel on this night, when she was to witness what seemed to Skeeter a sacred thing that only a church should house.

Her feet found their way across the town. Her mind was not on the streets and the turnings, but raced forward to deal with great images of struggle and death. So she found herself almost by surprise at the coolness of the river air.

She had come down onto the river road and now she was passing a familiar place. She stopped. For she remembered that this was exactly the spot at which earlier in the evening Liddell had ridden into the tulles.

She tried to walk on but some imp of the perverse made her step to the edge of the tulles. The infinitesimal waves that worked through the growth whispered against the shore; the faint night breeze went with shiverings through the tulles. And silently sounding the pitch in the back of her mind, she whistled a high, long note, followed by two short ones. When she waited, there was only the whispering sound of the little waves again and the hushing sound of the wind.

She had to get on to the dance under the cypresses and to the last scene of big Slip Liddell; and yet something held her there at the verge of the river, as fire is said to hold horses enchanted until they burn. Once more she whistled and listened.

And now she heard the dim noise of oars in their oarlocks; she heard something pushing through the tall reeds. Again she whistled, more softly, and almost at once the tulles were parted. A light skiff was barely distinguishable, and the loom of a man's figure against the paler rushes. He was standing in the boat.

"Hi . . . Slip?" he called softly.

That name, out of the dimness, did strange things to her. She said: "Are you a friend of Slip Liddell?"

The boatman thrust his skiff back into instant invisibility among the reeds. "Come back! There's no danger!" she called, careful of the pitch of her voice.

The boat returned, very slowly. "What you got? Money or just news?" asked the boatman.

"What's Slip to you?" asked Skeeter.

"He's okay to me," he answered.

"Would you lift a hand to help him?"

"Maybe I would, at that. Is he in a pinch?"

She found her voice altered, breathless, rapid with excitement as she said: "He's going to die. They've ganged up on him . . . because they say he killed Frank Pollard. He's going to the dance and they're going to gang up on him!"

"That's easy," said the boatman. "Stop that fool from going to the dance. Why not?"

"Who can stop him when he's made up his mind?" she demanded. "But he's going to need his friends tonight!"

"Did he send you to tell me that?" asked the man from the river.

She pretended not to hear and, waving her hand, turned and hurried down the bank.

"Why'd he send you?" called the boatman after her, but still she went on, hurrying, until she saw before her the cloudy heads of the cypress trees and heard the singing of the strings of the orchestra.

The big dance floor under the cypresses was swarming with people. They had hung the lights from the outstretching branches of the trees and placed some of them high in the foliage where they twinkled like stars; and each of those immense trees might have been called a separate heaven, a particular little firmament. Crowds of little tables surrounded the dance floor and off at one side had been erected an open-air bar draped with gaudy bunting where a long line of bartenders served a crowd that never diminished.

Everyone in San Jacinto seemed to be there, but in fact everyone was not, for there was a two-dollar admission and a good many were ruled out. They stood in compacted lines outside of the barrier that had been built shoulder-high around the place of festival. They were free to see and they were enjoying the sight to the full. This was no occasion for babies to be put to bed early. They were carried around on the shoulders of their mothers so that they could enjoy the color and the noise and their squealing and shouting made a background of sound that gave a certain unexpected privacy to the conversations at the tables inside the barrier.

Beyond all, certain lighted, decorated floats stood out into the river, like stages in a green meadow, the water lilies grew so thickly in the still shadows of the San Jacinto. She saw all this at once but her anxious eye had to wander a bit before it located Liddell. He sat at a table well back toward the barrier, looking very much like any of the other cowpunchers who were there except that, to her eye at least, something about the carriage of his head made him different from every other man in the world.

And now, as she passed the entrance toward the dance floor, she saw three figures take a place at a table not two away from Liddell. She knew them almost before her eyes could distinguish their faces clearly. They were Pudge McArthur, Soapy Jones, and Mark Heath; and they had not gone so near to Liddell except that they looked for trouble. She had come in time for the execution, then, and there were the three executioners.

A big cowhand, all silk and silver and jingle, plunged up to her and said: "Don't leave yourself without a man. Leave me try to fill in till your regular man comes around."

She did what the proud ones do in the movies. She walked ahead looking at nothing but her future, and she could feel the big fellow wilt behind her. She walked the way some of them do in the movies, too. That is to say, she put her feet down one exactly in front of the other. She could feel that make her body go forward on a level line. Somehow, she despised herself for doing this. A girl looked at her, looked down at her feet—smiled. She stopped walking with one foot placed exactly in front of the other.

Somewhere in the crowd was undoubtedly the girl from whom she had taken the green dress. Perhaps when she unveiled that dress it would be like exhibiting a face, well-known to all its friends. There might be an outcry of: "Thief! Thief!"

She slid off the black cloak and waited for the yell to begin. It did not begin.

She could see that Heath, McArthur and Soapy Jones were seated on one side of their table so that they could face, not the dance floor, but Liddell. Other people, in nearby places, were moving hastily to distant tables; an open desert was forming around Liddell and his three enemies as she came up with the cloak fluttering over her arm and stood by Slip's table, saying: "I'm sorry, Slip, that I'm late!"

His bewildered glance ran from her face to her feet and from her feet to her face again. Then he was up, taking her hand.

"How did you do it, Skeeter?" he asked. "Are you sitting or dancing?"

"Dancing," she said, slumping the cloak over a chair; and then they were out on the floor and swinging into the rhythm. He danced pretty well. He was not like one of those hobo specialists who have feathers on their heels and interpret the music better with their feet than a conductor can with his baton, but he danced well enough.

"Are you all right?" she asked.

"I'm all right."

"You look fine," she declared, with wonder. "You look steady and fine."

"Where did you find that much Paris in San Jacinto?" he asked.

"I bought it," she answered. "It doesn't matter where."

"You didn't get enough money from me to pay for it," he told her.

"A hundred bucks . . . everything from the skin out," said Skeeter.

"How many horses did you throw in to boot?" demanded Liddell.

"Slip, tell me what you've planned!"

"I haven't planned, except I want to watch what the people spend. If you see anybody breaking loose with a lot of easy money, let me know, will you?"

"What has the spending of money to do with you, Slip? It's not money that *you* are going to spend tonight, is it?"

"I'm going to hand you something when we get into the thick of that bunch. Get that bag of yours open. And now take it."

He pushed a sheaf of bills into the bag.

"There's several hundred," said Liddell. "Use it to get back to civilization. And then stay civilized. Promise me that you'll stay off the road."

"I might have known that it would be this way," said Skeeter, bitterly. "I might have known that you'd be clean, and right, and generous, and everything that I want in the world."

"Quit talking about me," said Liddell. "Watch the faces as they sail by you. See the men put on the brakes. Look at them lifting their heads. They're seeing a new country, with gold in them hills, Skeeter. You grew two inches on your legs and let yourself out and pulled yourself in all over."

"I mugged myself up with makeup," said Skeeter. "And the rest is all clothes."

She saw Mark Heath dancing, but staring earnestly at her. On a sudden impulse, she gave Mark Heath her sweetest smile. A good Hollywood director would have known the star from whom that smile was copied, the slowness of it, and the melancholy.

When she looked again, someone had tagged Mark's girl and he was waiting on the edge of the dance floor.

"What did you say again about a cabin off in the mountains somewhere?" asked Liddell. "Say it again, will you?"

"I'll say it if you want," she answered. "I'll say it now and mean it all my life."

She looked up at his face and saw that he was smiling a little. He looked old. He looked the way a man in front of guns might have looked.

"I don't want you to say it," answered Liddell. He looked like a man at whom guns had pointed for a long time. If she could gain for him even an added hour of life, it seemed to Skeeter the most important objective in the world.

She had almost forgotten Mark Heath, but suddenly Liddell was stepping back and Heath was there, taking her in his arms to finish the dance.

"Get away and keep away," said Heath, not too softly.

And he took her away, and she could see the insult strike the face of Liddell like a fist as he turned and went off.

"Was I wrong?" asked Mark Heath. "Did you give me the eye, or was I wrong?"

"You weren't wrong," she said.

"I thought you were glad to see him, but maybe that was my mistake," said Heath. "You know what kind of an *hombre* that one is? He shoots 'em in the back. He's murdered his partner for the blood money. He killed Frank Pollard! Why, that's"—he laughed—"*Señor* Coyote."

She saw big Liddell walking from the edge of the dance floor to his table. He was not waiting to cut in again. How much nerve was left to him, she wondered, if he accepted an insult in front of her? But that must not be the topic of her thought. Her one effort must be to stay close to Mark Heath. He could not pull guns, surely, when she was with him. And the other two, would they matter at all if Heath were not there to lead them?

XI "Stars in the Sky"

It wasn't a long dance because San Jacinto had an artist up from Mexico City, a girl who was all smile and eyes and a few ounces of fluff to protect her from the weather, and now they turned out the lights and flashed the spot for her and the orchestra started up some shudderingly fast rhythms. She had the footwork to go with it. Skeeter, taken from the floor as the regular dance ended, had been guided back not to Liddell's table, but to that of Heath and the other two. Soapy Jones was on one side of her, Mark on the other, and Pudge farther away watched the dance over his shoulder and made a sour face.

"It makes me kind of sick," confided Soapy Jones. "I mean the way they strip, nowadays. You'd think off here at the end of no place that they'd try to be a little decent."

"Legs like that . . . wouldn't it be a crime not to show 'em?" asked Skeeter.

"Legs like them? Scrawny things!" said Soapy Jones confidentially. "When the knee sticks out like that, it don't mean anything to me."

"I know what you mean. You like 'em overstuffed," said Skeeter. "Well, I've got a pair of shanks like those out there, and I'm proud of 'em."

"Why, you know what I mean . . . ," commenced Soapy.

"Shut up, Soapy. You don't know how to talk to her," declared Mark Heath. He explained to the girl: "Soapy's all right, but he don't understand."

She hated the complacency of Mark Heath with all her heart; and from the corner of her eye she watched Liddell seated alone at his table. He was trying to catch the eye of a waiter to order a drink, but they walked past him with a deliberate insolence. They did not want him there. Even his money seemed to be no good.

Then the dance ended. The flashlight went out. The regular lights came on.

"But *you* understand!" she heard her voice saying to Heath, as she kept herself smiling. "You know how to dance. You know how to talk. What else do you know?"

"You ask me questions," said Heath.

"Will you know the answers?" she asked.

"Ah, I get by most of the examinations," answered Heath, with a grin, and his eyes began to take possession of her. "What are we drinking?"

"It ought to be a good drink," said Skeeter. "Because I'm meeting a fellow who knows all the answers, it ought to be the best. What about champagne?"

She waited for them to laugh, all three. She was ready to laugh herself. She never had tasted the stuff.

Pudge, in fact, said: "Aw, take it easy. That stuff puts a tingle up your nose and makes you sneeze, and it costs. . . ."

"Who cares what it costs?" asked Heath. "We're going over to the bar where they got it good and cold. Come on over to the bar with me where we can get it cold. You come, Pudge; and you come along, Soapy. I'm going to show you what it's like."

They were all trailing across the dance floor; and the orchestra was swinging into its beat again; and they were off the dance floor and at the long bar, with its gaudy drapings of bunting, and the crowd lined up three deep, and the cool damp of the river air kept drifting in and pinching at the bare shoulders of Skeeter with small, chilly fingers. But nobody else seemed to think that she was cold. It was very wonderful to see what clothes would do. It was she who made a place for them all at the bar, in fact. A dumpy fellow with enormous shoulders spread out his arms, when he saw her coming, and backed up, jostling many people behind him.

"Clear the track," he said. "Can't you bozos see the green light and give it the right of way?"

" . . . and stick a couple more bottles into the ice," Mark Heath was saying. "We've gotta drink three times to get the taste. And fetch down those big glasses. Here's to you, sweetheart!"

The bubbles came racing up and bursting at the brim, but there were not as many bubbles as there are in ginger ale and the water didn't squirt up with the bursting of them in the same way. But the bubbles kept on rising from the bottom of the glass in the exact center, as though there were a magic source of life at that point.

The stuff had a funny taste. It tasted sour and it tasted sweet. It tasted sharp and brittle, and it tasted smooth and long-drawn out, like molasses. Then, while she was savoring it, Skeeter remembered that she was supposed to be having a good time with young Mark Heath and Pudge McArthur and Soapy Jones. So she finished off her glass and flourished the emptiness over her head. And she sang out: "Mark, Mark, here's to all the good fellows, all over the world; and down with the rats and the shacks wherever they are!"

She turned her glass upside down and the last drops trickled away to the fate that should overtake all rats and shacks wherever they may be.

This gesture enchanted Mark Heath. He stood up on a chair so that he could make his eyes felt as well as his voice heard, and he shouted: "Open 'em up down the line, there. Everybody's gotta have a drink with me. Open 'em up right down the line of the bar, there. Crack out a dozen bottles!" shouted Mark Heath.

The bartenders looked at him for a moment, wildly. He laughed in their faces.

"A dozen of 'em!" he shouted.

The dozen bottles popped open with a lively cannonade. Then Mark Heath took a small billfold out of his hip pocket and tossed on the bar, carelessly, a hundred dollar bill. It was the first bill of that denomination that Skeeter had ever seen. She snatched it up with a swift motion, like a bird picking up a seed. She looked at it on both sides and then laid it down again, with a sigh. It was rather strange, but there was no doubt about it that the possession of money made a man into a new thing. Mark Heath might be an enemy of Slip Liddell, but nevertheless a certain aura, a certain dignity attached to any man who could throw hundred-dollar bills around, in this fashion.

The head bartender came down the line, picked up that bill, glanced at both sides of it, and then stuck it into the cash register, calling out: "Sixty . . . out of a *hundred!*"

It was magnificent. Sixty dollars out, and still forty dollars left in that single little piece of paper; and a whole handful of crinkling change being brought to Mark Heath. Now the glasses were filled and lifted, and expectant, broad grins were turning to Heath. He held the drinkers from their wine for a moment.

"Nobody would wanta be any place but San Jacinto," he said, "but when there's a rat in the house, why don't you poison it? And there's a rat over there at that table. There's Slip Liddell! There's the gent that pats his partner on the back with one hand and shoots him through the head with the other. D'you want *him* in San Jacinto? There ain't even any man in him. He's a yella, yella, yella hound."

Skeeter tasted those words far deeper than champagne; and a black agony rose like a mist across her eye. She stared at the table where Liddell was sitting, and now in fact she saw that he was rising and advancing straight toward the bar.

"He's coming right on over," someone said.

"He knows there's free drinks. And he feels a tickling in his ears, we been talking about him so much. His ears is real hot so he's coming to join the good time!"

Skeeter, who knew that this moment would be the most dreadful of her life, reached out desperately in her mind to find some way in which she could intervene, but a man who can be saved by a woman's strength is not a man at all.

She had a strange way of phrasing this moment to herself. She was hoping, bitterly, that there would be enough power in Liddell for him to reach his destiny like a man—just enough strength for him to die as one hero beaten down by many hands.

She heard a man say, near her: "Jimmy, get that rope over there. We're gonna need a rope before we get through with Liddell."

Then Liddell came in on the crowd along the bar. Faces half cold and half smiling received him. Everyone turned to watch; and even the orchestra felt the nerve-strain that was tensing the air and stammered and began to die out in the midst of a piece. It was strange, but every person inside the enclosure and perhaps most of those outside it seemed to know exactly what was happening and the dangers that lay ahead of Liddell as he walked down the length of the bar.

He walked straight on toward Skeeter herself. Her heart cringed in her with pity and with shame and with love.

Then she saw him step past her and take Mark Heath by the right wrist.

She recognized the cleverness of that move. You take a man by one wrist and he's helpless. If he tried to make a vital move, he draws you with him. All his physical efforts are muffled. Then she looked up at Liddell's face and realized that it was not a trick. Some mist of ennui or indifference was blown away from him. She thought she was seeing him for the first time.

He was saying: "Where did you get the money, Mark? Where did you get the big money? You were flat broke a couple of days ago."

Someone behind was saying quietly: "Give me the rope. I'll handle it!"

But if Liddell heard that and knew what it meant, he gave no sign. He seemed unaware of the way the crowd was pooling around him, thick as lodgepole pines where one of the old forest giants has fallen and left an opening.

Mark Heath shouted out: "I got that money from roulette . . . and what made you a chum of mine all at once? Get your hand off me, you damned. . . ."

Liddell flicked his free hand across the face of Heath. The blow made a loud, popping sound. It struck the mind of Skeeter with a stunning force. It seemed to lift the hair on her head, and it knocked the closely thronging faces agape. It froze the lips of Mark Heath over the next few words he was about to utter. Everyone could hear Liddell, though he was not lifting his voice, when he said: "They don't pay you off with hundred dollar bills at roulette. But you can get 'em from a bank. You can rob a bank and get 'em! If you reach for a gun, I'll break your back, Mark."

Mark Heath cried out: "Soapy . . . Pudge . . . are you gonna just stand there . . . ?"

But Soapy and Pudge just stood there, and everybody else was just standing until an outcry from the side split that crowd apart as water splits under the forefoot of a boat, for the outcry said: "It's Pollard . . . that tall guy . . . that's Pollard or the ghost of him!"

He came slumping along with an awkward, shambling step and a foolish grin on his face, making gestures that might be construed as apologies. With him came Sheriff Chris Tolliver, tenderly licking his cracked lip with the tip of his tongue, with more of the sour wine in his face than ever before.

Mark Heath saw that tall figure coming and groaned half audibly.

Liddell said: "Frank, you're all kinds of a fool to show your face. It's too early."

This dead man who had returned to life put his hand on the shoulder of Liddell and said: "And leave them string you up to a cypress tree, Slip?"

"Gimme that hundred dollar bill," said the sheriff, and when it was brought to him from the register, he spread it out flat on the bar and said: "There's the ink mark, all right. That's what the bank teller said that I'd find."

He put the bill in his pocket and, drawing out a bright little pair of handcuffs, fitted them over the wrists of Mark Heath with a click.

Pudge McArthur and Soapy Jones were pawing at Frank Pollard, vainly trying to get attention from him.

Liddell said: "Did you know right along, Chris? Did you know I was faking right along?"

"It was a slick trick of yours," said the sheriff. "That bullet hole in the wallet, and the blood, and everything was pretty slick. But the fact was that the first word the bank give out about the money it lost was wrong. They found a whole thousand bucks that the thief had overlooked. So when I counted twenty-seven hundred in the wallet, I knew that you put that money there. I knew Frank, here, never had a hand in the dirty deal. I knew you had his horse, but you hadn't put bullets into him. I knew you and him was framing it to lie low till we got the real crook. But who would've thought that a bank robber would be fool enough to stay right in the town and start spending what he'd stole?"

Liddell said to Heath: "When I met you outside the sheriff's office and you looking at Pollard's horse and kind of white and sick, you were afraid that he'd come in and given himself up. Wasn't that it?"

But Heath could not answer. He kept moistening his lips and swallowing. For his brain was a cold blank, but the taste of the champagne was still in his mouth.

Skeeter, in the meantime, slid through that crowd, and got away from them; and, when she reached the river road, she ran through the darkness and the cool of the air. For she was burning with grief and with shame, and yet there was a triumphant joy in her, also. She ran down the road past the place where she had whistled the man out of the tulles. That man had been Frank Pollard, of course.

A horse at a swinging gallop came up behind her, so she drew over to the side of the road and reduced her run to a dog-trot. She was not far from the shack in which old Pop would be waiting. She was panting; it had been hard to run in the clinging fluff of that green dress.

The rider pulled up beside her.

"Hi, Skeeter," said the voice of Liddell.

"Yeah. All right. Go on and guy me," said Skeeter. "I thought you were scared, and you showed me up. You showed everybody up. I was a fool. Go on and yap at me, and then get out of my sight!"

Liddell dropped to the ground beside her. "Are you through talking?"

"Yeah, I'm through talking. Go on and say your piece."

"What's the good of talking?" asked Liddell. "You know me almost better than Sis does; so I suppose you know I love you, Skeeter?"

"Wait a minute," said Skeeter. "What are you trying to put over on me, Slip? Are you trying to make me cry or something? Because I won't!"

"Are you old enough to marry me?" asked Liddell. "How old are you, Skeeter?"

"None of your business," said Skeeter.

"I told you it was no good talking," remarked Liddell.

"Yeah, but I'm terribly old, really," said Skeeter.

"Sure you are. Sure. You're as old as the hills," said Liddell.

They walked on down the road. He found her hand and drew it inside his arm. They passed the tulles. They did not speak. They could see the stars in the sky and in the flat of the river at the same time. Still they walked on, more and more slowly with Cicely following wearily behind.

A Matter of Honor

"A Matter of Honor" was published under the title "'Jerico's' Garrison Finish" by John Frederick in *Western Story Magazine* (5/21/21). Frank Black-
well, editor of *Western Story Magazine*, changed the title because he evidently
wanted to suggest that the focus of the story was on horse racing, on an ac-
tivity and not on a state of mind.

Yet "A Matter of Honor" is ultimately not about horse racing but about
generosity. In 1932 at the depth of the Great Depression Faust wrote 1,600,000
words for the magazine market and earned about $80,000. He wrote that much
and he earned that much and Carl Brandt, his agent, still had had to lend him
money and go to the bank for a loan to pay his agency staff. Where did all
Faust's money go? He did not live lavishly, ever. The villa he rented outside Florence may seem glamorous, but it was relatively inexpensive to live in Italy at
the time. Maintenance of the villa cost only a small portion of his great earnings
in any given year. No, Faust was a man generous to a fault. Carl Brandt was
charged with sending money to numerous struggling writers Faust had met and
believed would be great authors someday if they only had the chance to write
without having to work at anything else. Surely Jim Orchard in this story is cut
from the same cloth as his creator.

I "The Promise"

When Sue Hampton looked down to the pale, lithe hands which were folded in her lap, Jim Orchard had his first opportunity to examine her face. He thought her whiter than ever, and thinner, and he disliked the heavy shadows around her eyes. But when she looked up to him, the thick lashes lifting slowly, he forgot the pallor.

That slow trick with the eyes had first won him—that, and a certain wistfulness in her smile. There was nothing direct and commanding about Sue. Most girls a tithe as pretty as she were in the habit of demanding things. They accepted applause and admiration, as a barbarian king accepts tribute from the conquered. It was no more than their due. But it seemed to Jim that Sue Hampton was never quite sure of herself.

She turned her engagement ring absently and waited for Jim to go on.

"Let's see," he said, going back with difficulty to the thread of his story. "I left off where . . . ?"

"You and Chalmers had started for the claim."

"Sue, you don't seem half glad to see me."

He went to her, half angry and half impatient, and took her hands. They were limp under his touch, and the limpness baffled him. The absence of resistance in her was always the stone wall which stopped him. Sometimes he grew furious. Sometimes it made him feel like a brute.

"I am glad to see you," she said in her gentle voice.

"But . . . confound it . . . pardon me, Sue! Look up . . . smile, can't you?"

She obeyed to the letter; and he at once felt that he had struck a child. He went gloomily back to his chair. "All right," he said, "go ahead and talk."

"If you wish me to, Jim."

"Confound it, Sue, are you ever going to stop being so . . . so. . . ."

"Well?"

"Oh, I don't know! Well, I'll tell you why I came back ahead of time."

"Ahead of time?"

"In a way. Someone drifted up where I was and told me that Garry Munn was hanging around and getting pretty thick with you."

There was no answer. That was one of the maddening things about her. She never went out of her way to show her innocence of blame, or to win over the hostile.

"Well," went on Jim Orchard, growing less and less sure of himself and more and more inclined to bully his way out of the scene, in spite of the fact that he loved her, "well, Sue, is it straight? Has Garry Munn been around a lot?"

"Yes."

He had come some two hundred miles for the pleasure of seeing her, but chiefly for the joy of a denial of this tale.

"You mean to say that Garry is getting sort of . . . sort of . . . ?"

She did not help him out either by an indignant denial or laughter. Accordingly his sentence stumbled away to obscurity. "Well," he said finally, "what do you think of him?"

"I like him a great deal."

He became seriously alarmed. "You don't mean to say that he's turned your head with his fine riding and all that?"

Tomorrow would be the last day of the great rodeo which had packed the little town of Martinville with visitors, and in that rodeo the spectacular name, from first to last, had been that of Garry Munn. In the bucking and roping and shooting contests he had carried away the first prize. The concern of Jim Orchard had some foundation. When he reached Martinville that day, the first thing of which he was told had been the exploits of Garry.

"Sue," he said suddenly, "what they told me is true!"

She merely watched him in her unemotional way. In her gentleness there was a force that tied his hands. It had always been so. In another moment he was on his knees beside her chair, leaning close to her.

"Honey, have you stopped loving me?"

"No."

The beat of his heart returned to the normal.

"Then say it."

"I love you, Jim." She turned on him those calm eyes which never winced, and which from the first had always looked straight into his heart.

"Just for a minute . . . ," he said, stammering, and then finished by touching her hands with his lips and returning to his chair. Another girl would have gloried in her triumph, but in the smile of Sue Hampton he saw no pride. How she did it he was never able to learn, but she was continually holding him at arm's length and wooing him toward her.

"I know you're the straightest of the straight," confessed Jim Orchard. "If you changed your mind about me, I'd be the first one to hear of it. Well . . . where was I?"

"You were telling me about the trip to the mines."

"Chalmers had the main idea. I staked the party, and we hit it rich!"

He paused. The slight brightening of her face meant more to him than tears or laughter in another woman.

"I didn't want to see how things would pan out. The second day after we'd made the strike I asked Chalmers if he'd buy my share for five thousand. I didn't care much about having more than that. Five thousand was the figure you named, wasn't it? Five thousand before we could safely get married?"

"Yes."

"Chalmers jumped at the chance, and I beat it with the coin. Five thousand iron boys!"

"That was nearly five months ago?"

His jubilation departed. "You see, honey, on the way back I ran into McGuire. You know Mac?"

"I've heard you talk about him."

"Well, Mac was down and out. Doctor told him he'd have to take a long rest, and he needed a thousand to rest on. Lung trouble, you see? So, what could I do? There was a dying man, you might say, and I had five thousand in my wallet. What would you have done?"

"You gave him the money?" she countered, adroitly enough.

"I had to. And then, instead of going away for his rest, he blew it in one big drunk! Can you beat that, Sue?"

She was looking down at her hands again, and Jim began to show signs of distress.

"Well, I looked at my coin and saw that I was a thousand short. Four thousand was short of the mark, anyway, so I thought I might as well spend a little of it getting over my disappointment about Mac. I started out on a quiet little party. Well, when I woke up the next day, what do you think?"

"The money was gone, I think," said the girl.

"All except about a hundred," replied Jim. "But I took that hundred and started to play with it. I'm a pretty good hand at the cards, you know. For three months I played steadily, stopping when I'd won my percentage. The hundred grew like a weed. When I landed six thousand, I thought it was safe to quit. Just about then I met Ferguson. Fergie had a fine claim going. Just finished timbering the shaft and laying in a bunch of machinery. Mortgaged his soul to get the stuff sometime before, and they were pinching in on him. He needed four thousand to save forty. There wasn't any doubt that he was right. What could I do? What would you have done?"

"You gave him the money?" murmured Sue Hampton.

"I sure did. And then what do you think?"

"He lost it?"

"The mine burned, the shafts caved, and there was Ferguson flat busted, and my four thousand gone. But I took what I had left . . . and here I am with two thousand, Sue. I would have tried to get a bigger stake, and I would have made it, sure, but this news about Garry had me bothered a lot. I came back to find out how things stood and . . . Sue . . . I want you to take the chance. It's a small start, but with you to manage things we'll get on fine. Isn't two thousand enough in a pinch for a marriage?"

He had grown enthusiastic as he talked, but when she did not raise her eyes again the flush went out of his face.

"Jim, how old are you?"

"Thirty-two . . . thirty-three . . . never did know exactly which."

"Twelve years ago you had a whole ranch."

"Loaded to the head with debts."

"Not your debts. You came into the ranch without a cent against it. They were your brother's debts, and you took them over."

"What would you have done, Sue? Good heavens, there's such a thing as the family honor, you know! Billy didn't have any money; I did. What could I do? I had to make his word good, didn't I?"

"And the debts kept piling up until finally the ranch had to be sold."

"Ah," sighed Jim Orchard, remembering.

"For eight years you fought against it. Finally you were beaten. Then you became a manager for another rancher. You had a big salary and a part interest, but the rancher had a younger brother who couldn't fit into life. You stepped out and let the younger brother buy your interest for a song."

"What would you have done? It was his own brother. I couldn't very well break up a family, could I?"

"After that," went on the gentle voice, "you did a number of things. Among others, you asked me to marry you. How long ago was that?"

"Three years ago last April fifth."

She smiled at this instant accuracy—the small, wistful smile that always made the heart of Jim Orchard ache.

"And for three years we've been waiting to be married. Three years is a long time, Jim."

This brought him out of his chair. "Yes," he admitted huskily, "it's a long time."

"Don't stand there like . . . like a man about to be shot, Jim," she whispered.

He attempted to laugh. "Go on."

"I've kept on teaching school . . . and waiting."

"It's been hard, and you're a trump, Sue!"

"But I think it's no use. You'll never have enough money. Not that I want money. But, if we marry, I want children . . . right away . . . and that means money."

"You know I'd slave for you and them!"

"I know you would, and after you'd made a lot of money, somebody would come along who needed it more than we did."

"Never in the world, Sue!"

"You can't help it."

"You'd keep me from being a fool."

"I couldn't, because I believe in every gift you've ever made. What could I do?"

"Then . . . I'm simply a failure?"

"A glorious failure . . . yes."

"And that means?"

"That I'd better give back your ring."

"Is that final, Sue?"

"Yes."

"Then I was right. Mind you, I don't blame you a bit. I know you're tired out waiting and hoping. And finally, you've stopped loving me."

She went to him with a smile that he was never to forget. "Don't you see," she said, "that every failure, which has made it a little more impossible for me to marry you, has made me love you a little more? But when we marry, we put our lives in trust for the children."

"And you couldn't trust me like that, of course."

"No."

She held out the ring.

"Sue," he cried in agony, "when a man's sentenced to die he isn't killed right away. Give me a chance . . . a time limit . . . a week . . . two days. I'll get that five thousand."

"If you wish it, Jim."

"First . . . put back that ring!"

"Yes."

He caught her in his arms in an anguish of love, of despair.

"I'll get it somehow."

"But no violence, Jim?" All at once she clung to him. "Promise!"

In the past of Jim Orchard there had been certain scenes of violence never dwelt upon by his friends. There was a battered look about his face which time alone did not account for, or mere mental strain. In cold weather he limped a little with his right leg; and on his body there was a telltale story of scars.

Not that his worst enemies would accuse him of cruelty or malignancy, but when Jim was wronged a fiendish temper possessed him. Some of those tales of Jim Orchard in action with fist, knife, or gun came back to the girl, and now she pleaded with him.

"All right," he said at length. "I promise! It's two days, Sue?"

"Yes."

"One last thing . . . if any man. . . ."

"Jim!"

"All right. I've promised . . . and I won't harm him."

II "A Trick for a Trick"

He went out and stood with his hat in his hand, heedless of the blinding sunshine. In the distance, from the field of the rodeo, there was a chorus of shouting, and Jim Orchard glared in that direction. In all the ups and downs of his life, this was the first time that the happiness of others had roused in him something akin to hatred.

"They've given me a rotten deal—they've stacked the cards!" thought Jim. And certainly he was right. The history of his hard work, all undone by fits of blind generosity which Susan Hampton had outlined to him, was only a small portion of the truth.

They said of Jim Orchard: "He's got a heart too big for his own good!" And again: "An easy mark!"

There was just a touch of contempt in these judgments. Generosity is a virtue admired nowhere more ardently than in the West; but reckless generosity never wins respect. Because of the speed of his hand and the accuracy of his eye, no one was apt to taunt Jim with his failings in this respect, but there was a good deal of talk behind his back. He knew it and despised the talkers.

But now his weakness had been driven home as never before. Jim felt that the world owed him something. He could be even more exact. He needed five thousand, and he had two thousand. In terms of cold cash he felt that the world owed him exactly three thousand dollars, and he was determined to get it. Sue had not judged him wrongly. For a moment a grim determination, to take by force what he needed, had formed in his mind, but now his hands were tied, and that possibility was closed to him.

However, there were always the gaming tables, and his luck was proverbial. He turned in that direction to see a little procession coming slowly up the street. Four men were carrying another on a stretcher, and a small crowd was following them. They stopped near Jim Orchard to rest a moment.

"Jerico's got another man," he was told briefly.

He went to the side of the litter. It was Bud Castor, his face white with pain, the freckles standing out on his forehead. The heavy splints and bandages around his right leg and the swathing of his body were eloquent. Jerico had done a "brown" job of Bud. He had never seen the horse, but everyone had heard of Sam Jordan's great black stallion. As a rule he pitched off those who attempted to ride him. Again he might submit with scarcely a struggle, only to bide his time and attack his would-be master at an opportune moment with tigerish ferocity.

"Jim," pleaded the injured man, "do me a favor. Get your gat and plug that black devil, will you?"

But Jim Orchard turned and went on his way. After all he felt a poetic justice in the deviltry of Jerico. They had run that black mustang for a whole season and, when they could not wear him down, had captured him by a trick. This was part of his revenge—a trick for a trick. Who could blame him?

Savagery of any kind was easily understandable by Jim Orchard on this day. In the meantime he headed straight for the big gaming house of Fitzpatrick. He entered and walked straight to that last resort of the desperate—the roulette wheel. Fitzpatrick welcomed him with both a sigh and a smile; if he was a royal spender, he was also a lucky winner.

But the little buzz of pleasure and recognition which met Jim Orchard was not music to his ears today. He nodded to the greetings and took his place in the crowded semicircle before the wheel. He began playing tentatively, a five here, a ten there, losing steadily. And then, as all gamblers who play on sheer chance will do, he got his hunch and began betting in chunks of fifty and a hundred on the odd.

"Orchard has started a run," the rumor ran through the room, and the little crowd began to grow.

As he played, wholly intent on the work before him, he heard someone say: "Who'd he get?"

"Bud Castor. Nice for Bud, eh?"

"But who'll take care of Bud's family? Sam Jordan?"

"Bah! Sam Jordan wouldn't take care of a dog."

"They'll take up a collection, maybe."

"They's been too many collections at this here rodeo, I say, for one."

"And you're right, too."

Again the odd won, and Jim, raking in his money, prepared to switch his bets. His momentary withdrawal was taken advantage of by a squat-built, powerful fellow who touched his arm.

"How are you, Jim?"

"Hello, Harry. What you want?"

"How'd you know I was busted?"

"Are you flat, Harry?"

"I'll tell a man!"

"What'll fix you up?"

"Sure hate to touch you, Jim, but if you can let a hundred go for a couple of days . . . ?"

"Sure."

His hand was on his wallet when he remembered—remembered about Sue Hampton, his grudge against the world, and that debt which he felt society owed him.

He hesitated. "Haven't you got a cent, Harry?"

"Not a red, partner."

Orchard set his jaw in the face of the ingratiating grin. From a corner of his eye he had noted the passing of a wink and a wise smile between a couple of bystanders. There followed a sudden scuffle, without warning, without words. At the end of it, Harry, with one arm crooked into the small of his back, had been jammed into the bar in a position of absolute helplessness, and the deft hands of Jim Orchard went swiftly through the pockets of his victim. Presently he found what he wanted. He drew forth the chamois bag, shook it, and a little shower of gold pieces fell to the floor.

He released Harry with a jerk that sent him spinning across the floor.

"A cold hundred if you got a cent," he declared. "Is that what you call flat broke? You skunk!"

The crowd split away and drew back, like a wave receding from two high rocks. There was a very good possibility of gun play, and no one wanted to be within the direct course of the bullets. It required a very steady nerve to face Jim Orchard, but Harry Jarvis was by no means a coward. He was half turned away from Jim, with his face fully toward him; the hidden arm was crooked and tensed, with the hand near the holster of his gun. The weight of a hair might turn the balance and substitute bullets for words. Jim Orchard was talking softly and coldly.

"You come to me like a drowned rat," he said, "and you beg for a hundred. Where's the hundred I gave you six months ago? There was another hundred before that, and a fifty and a couple of twenties still further back. You've used me like a sponge and squeezed me dry. And there's a lot of the rest of you that've done the same thing. Where's the gent in this room that's ever heard of me begging or borrowing a cent from anybody? Let him step out and say his little piece. But the next four-flushing hound dog that tries a bluff with me like Harry's is going to get paid in lead on the spot. Gents, I'm tired . . . I'm considerable tired of the way things have been going. There's going to be a change. I'm here to announce it."

Then he deliberately turned his back on Harry Jarvis and stepped to the bar. Harry Jarvis, great though the temptation of that turned back was, knew perfectly well by the sternness of the faces around him that his gun would be better off in its leather than exposed to the air. Jarvis, also, turned and disappeared through the door.

"Well, Jim," said the bartender, "there's a hundred saved."

"There's more than a hundred spent," answered Jim gloomily. "He's busted up my run."

For the gamester's superstition had hold on Jim Orchard. Nothing could have persuaded him to tempt fortune again on that day, once his happy streak of winning had been interrupted from the outside. He counted his winnings as he left the gaming hall. He was some five hundred and fifty dollars ahead, as the result of the few moments he had spent in the place. At least it was a comfortable beginning toward the goal which had been set for him by Susan Hampton. When he reached the dust of the street, he had so far relaxed his grim humor that he was humming softly to himself. The result of his contentment was that he nearly ran over a barefooted urchin who was scuffing his way moodily through the dust.

"Hey!" yelled the youngster, "whatcha doing?" He changed to a surly grin. "Hello, Jim."

"Hello," said Jim Orchard. "You're Bud Castor's boy, I figure."

"Sure."

"What's the news? What's the doctor say?"

"He says pa won't never be able to ride ag'in."

Fate made the fingers of Jim Orchard at that moment close over the money which he had just won at the gaming hall. Before the impulse left him he had counted out five hundred and fifty dollars into the hand of the youngster.

"You take that to your mother, you hear? Tell her to put it away for the rainy day. Or, maybe she can use it to help get Bud fixed up."

"Gee," exclaimed the boy, "you're white. I'll tell a man you're white. I . . . I'd about die for you, Jim Orchard!"

"Hm," mused the spendthrift. "Now, you cotton on to this: if you ever tell your ma or your pa where you got the money, I'll come and skin you alive. Don't forget!"

He accompanied this warning with a scowl so terrible that the child changed color. Jim Orchard left him agape and went on down the street, smiling faintly. When he reached the hotel, his smile went out suddenly.

"Good glory," said Jim, "I've done it ag'in! I've done it ag'in!" But he instantly consoled himself in his usual manner. "What else was they for me to do? Bud needs it more'n I do, I guess!"

III "With the Mask Off"

He was beginning to feel a certain leaden helplessness, as men will when they think that destiny is against them. He had had half of the five thousand in his pocket, but now he was back to the two thousand again. He went with a heavy step into the bar of the hotel and leaned against the wall. Here the heroes of that day's events at the rodeo were holding forth on their luck. With immense grins and crimson blushes they accepted the congratulations of the less daring or the less lucky. He was picked out by one or two and invited to drink, but he shook his head. The invitations were not pressed home, for Jim Orchard was obviously in one of his moods. At such times those who knew him best avoided him the most.

Only the hotel proprietor ventured to pause for an exchange of words. "How's things?"

"Rotten! I'd staked every cent I have on Jerico, and now he's out of the running for the race tomorrow."

"How come?"

"Ain't Bud Castor all mashed up? Who'll ride Jerico?"

"That's right. I forgot. Maybe you'd try a fling at him, Jim?"

"I'm not that tired of living, partner."

"Then they's no hope unless Garry Munn takes on the job."

Jim Orchard pricked his ears. "Yep, there's Garry. Handy on a horse, too."

"Not the man you are in the saddle," said the flattering host.

"I'm past my day," said Jim Orchard. "I've seen the time . . . but let that go. By the way, where's Garry?"

"Gone up to his room."

"I want to see him," replied Jim. Having learned the room number, he straightway climbed the stairs.

What were the emotions that made it so necessary to see Garry Munn, he did not know until he had entered the room and shaken hands with the man. Then he understood. A strong premonition told him that this was the man who would eventually marry Susan Hampton. Here, again, there was a feeling of fate. Indeed, Garry Munn had so often secured the things he wished that it was hard to imagine him failing with the woman he wanted to make his wife. He was a fine, handsome fellow with a clear-blue eye and decidedly blond hair—the Scandinavian type. He was as tall as Jim Orchard, and far more heavily set. Altogether he was a fine physical specimen, and his brain did not lag behind his body. He had been born with the proverbial silver spoon in his mouth, and it was well known that he had improved his opportunities from the first. The ranch, which his father left him as a prosperous property, had been flourishing ever since, as Munn bought adjacent land. He was well on his way, indeed, to becoming a true cattle king. No wonder that Jim Orchard had to swallow a lump of envy that rose in his throat as he looked at his companion.

"I hear you been tearing things up at the rodeo," he began, "and walking off with the prizes, Garry."

"Because you weren't around to give me a run for my money," answered the diplomatic Garry. "How's things, Jim? How's mining coming on?"

"Rotten."

For all of his diplomacy, Garry could not keep a little twinkle of gratification out of his eye, and Jim felt an overwhelming desire to drive his bony fist into the smirk on the other's lips. He wanted trouble, and only his promise to Sue Hampton kept him from plunging into a fight on the spur of the moment.

"Mining's always a hard gamble," went on Garry.

"But the luck still stays good with you, Garry?"

"Tolerable."

"Sue has been telling me a lot about you."

"Oh."

The diplomatic Garry became instantly wary.

"You been seeing a good deal of her lately, I guess?"

"Sure," said Garry Munn. "I tried to keep her company while you were out of town. No harm done, I guess?"

"Sure not. Mighty thoughtful of you, Garry."

Down in his heart he had always felt that Garry was a good deal of a clever sneak, and now he gave his voice a proper edge of irony. Yet the younger man was continually surprising him by unexpected bursts of frankness. One of these bursts came now.

"You see, Jim," he declared, "I always aim to let Sue know that, while I ain't running any competition with you, I'd rather be second best with her than first with any other girl around these parts."

"That's kind of consoling for Sue, I figure."

"Oh, she don't take me no ways serious. I'm just a sort of handy man for her. I take her around to the parties when you ain't here to do it. She treats me like an old shoe. Nothing showy, but sort of comfortable to have around." He chuckled at his statement of the case.

"Sort of queer," murmured Jim Orchard. "Here you are with mostly everything that I lack and still I got something, it appears, that you want for yourself."

"You don't mean that serious, Jim?"

"Mean what?"

"You don't think I'm trying to cut in between you and Sue Hampton?"

"Garry, all I think would near fill a book."

It was plain that Garry Munn did not desire trouble. He even cast one of those wandering glances around the room which proclaim the man who knows he is cornered. Then he looked steadily at his guest.

"Let's hear a couple of chapters."

"You been running a pretty good man-sized bluff, Garry. You been playing rough and ready all your life. Underneath I figure you for a fox!"

"Kind of looks as though you're aiming at trouble, Jim."

"Take it anyway you want."

Garry shrugged his shoulders. He saw the twin devils gleaming in the eyes of Orchard and knew what they meant. He had seen Orchard at work in more than one brawl, and the memories were not pleasant.

"You can't insult me, Jim."

"Seems that way," returned Jim Orchard. "Somehow, I never had a hunch that you was as low as this, Garry."

"What have I got to gain by fighting you up here? You're a shifter, a wastrel . . . pretty close to a tramp. Why should I risk myself in a mix-up with you? Where's the audience?"

"I'll try you in a crowd, Garry."

The other became deadly serious. "Don't do it, Jim. Between you and me, I know you're a bad man in a fight. So am I. But in private I'm going to dodge trouble. If you cut loose in public, I'll fight back, and it'll be the hottest fight of your life."

"I think it would be," admitted Jim with candid interest, as he ran his glance over the powerful body of the other.

"Now that we've got down to facts," ran on Munn, "I don't mind saying that I'm out for you, Orchard. I'm out to get Sue Hampton, and I'm going to get her. In the first place she's waited long enough for you. In the second place there never was a time when you been worthy of looking twice at her."

"You get more and more interesting," said Orchard, smiling. He appeared to grow cooler as the other increased in heat. "But you never took no notice of Sue until I began to call on her."

"A good reason, Orchard. We started out with an even break. We both had ranches, and about the same layout of stock, and things like that. I made up my mind I was going to beat you out . . . and I did it. Who started by lending you money? I did! Who kept on lending? I did! And who finally bought the whole shebang? I did! I got your ranch, I got your cows, I got your horses. I put you right off the cow map."

"And you decided to keep right on?" queried Jim Orchard pleasantly.

"Why not? I started you downhill and I'm going to keep you going. And the job ain't complete if I don't get your girl away from you. I'm going to get her. You can lay to that!"

Orchard's face flushed crimson, as his hand instinctively reached out. Then he remembered his promise. With difficulty he controlled himself and moved toward the door. There he paused and looked back over his shoulder.

"It does me a pile of good to have the mask off your good-lookin' face, Garry. I've had one look at the skunk you are inside and I won't forget!"

"Fair means or foul," replied Garry calmly, settling back into his chair. "I was always out for your scalp, Orchard, and now I'm sure I'm going to get it."

There was a tensing of the gaunt figure at the door, and for a moment Garry thought he had gone too far. But instead of making the fatal move toward his gun, Jim Orchard allowed his long face to wrinkle into a smile. He swept his hat in mock politeness toward the floor and then disappeared with his usual slow, stalking walk.

IV "The Gambler's Instinct"

Among the unnamed good things which Sue Hampton had done in her life, a prevented homicide was now to be numbered, and Jim Orchard was well aware of it as he closed the door and went down the groaning stairs. His muscles were still hard set, and he was struggling to keep himself in hand. When he reached the verandah, he stopped to breathe deeply, waiting for the red mist to clear away. But in spite of the passing of moments, the tips of the fingers of his right hand still itched for the feel of the handle of his revolver.

Into his mind cut the sharp, small voice of Sam Jordan. He turned and saw the man coming with difficulty toward him. His legs trailed behind him or wobbled awkwardly to the sides, as he dragged himself on with the crutches. For many a month, now, every waking moment of Sam Jordan's life had been a torture. His face was old and gray with pain, and his smile was a ghastly caricature. Yet he never complained; he never surrendered to whining.

He had been a sound and hale man when he attempted to ride Jerico. The former owner of that fierce mustang had a standing offer of the gift of the beast and five hundred dollars besides, to any man who could stay on his back for five minutes. Sam Jordan had made the attempt—and he stayed on for the prescribed length of time.

Sam's riding of Jerico was something of which even strong men still talked with a shudder. For Jerico had been posed by his captor as an "outlaw" and had already gone to a finishing school of bucking. There have been fables of men who could ride anything "on four feet and with hair on its back," but these are truly fables. Jerico was a king among outlaws. He leaped like a bouncing spring, and with equal uncertainty of direction, and his endurance was a bottomless pit.

He was full of freaky humors, however. Sometimes he pitched like a fiend, while on other occasions he demonstrated for only a moment or so and waited for another day, when he was more in the humor of deviltry. With Sam Jordan he began mildly with straight bucking as he ran. Then he turned and came back fence rowing, and then, getting warmed to his work, he commenced to weave. And still Sam Jordan stayed to his work, until, at the end of the fourth minute, the great black stallion began to sunfish.

Of all forms of bucking this is the most dreaded, and Jerico "fished for the sun" almost literally. In other words, he leaped a prodigious height and then came down on stiffened forelegs. The result was a shock that stunned the brain and nearly wrenched the head from the shoulders of Sam Jordan.

With only one minute remaining for him to fulfill his contract, Jordan was doing well enough when Jerico began his master work. The third of these grim shocks sent the blood bursting from the nose and mouth of the unfortunate Jordan. But Jerico was only beginning. He added a consummate touch. Instead of landing on both stiff forelegs, he struck on only one. The result was a heavy impact, and then a swift lurch to one side—a snap-the-whip effect. With glazing eye and awful face Sam Jordan stayed in the saddle, rapidly being jarred into unconsciousness.

But the minute slipped past, and exactly at the end of the scheduled five minutes, Jerico reared and pitched back. His whole weight crushed upon the body of Sam Jordan and, when the latter was raised from the ground, he was an unspeakable wreck with hardly six inches of sound bone in either of his legs. He was now the proud possessor of the fiend who had wrecked his body and his life.

One might have expected Sam Jordan to spend the rest of his days tormenting the wild mustang. He did quite the reverse. He managed to secure an old Negro, named Tom, who was the first and only human being whom the stallion could endure around him, and he made Tom care for the mustang as if for a great race horse. Nothing was too good for Jerico, as far as the fortune of Sam Jordan extended.

One by one Sam hired or tempted famous riders to back his horse. The results were usually disastrous. Sometimes it was merely a broken arm or leg; sometimes it was much worse. Sometimes, to be sure, a lucky fellow got off with merely a stunning fall. But the great danger from Jerico lay not in the fall, but in what was apt to happen afterward—for Jerico would whirl on the fallen man like a tiger and do his best with teeth and hoofs to end his life. Sooner or later, of course, he would succeed and kill his rider—and then it would be necessary to kill Jerico. In fact, why Sam Jordan allowed the beast to live was more than anyone could tell. Yet he professed a great affection for Jerico, and the mustang continued to live on the fat of the land.

Of late, an ugly rumor had sprung up to the effect that Sam Jordan, crippled for life and in constant torment, had come to hate the world, and he kept Jerico merely for the pleasure of seeing the great horse do to others as he had already done to Sam Jordan. But the whisper was so ugly that it was not generally believed. Indeed, it seemed that Bud Castor, the last hero to attempt the subjugation of Jerico, had almost succeeded. The horse had even begun to evince signs of affection for his rider and had never been known to buck his hardest when Bud was in the saddle. Today, however, had ended the reign of Bud Castor in a horrible manner. Jerico was once more free, and the thought of entering him in the race, which was to end the festivities of the rodeo, had become a complete illusion and a dream.

Something of all this went through the mind of Jim Orchard, as he watched Sam drag his body across the verandah. He picked up a chair and met the cripple halfway with it and forced him to sit down. Sam accepted it with a grunt. Lowering himself cautiously into it, he remained speechless for a moment, leaning on his crutches, with his eyes closed and his face covered with perspiration. The agony of moving that deformed body on the crutches would have brought groans from the most stoical, but after a while Sam recovered his self-possession and actually looked up to Jim with a smile. They were unpleasant things to see, those smiles of Jordan's. Still he did not speak until his breathing became regular and easy and Jim Orchard, looking down at the other in horror and pity, did not offer to begin the talk.

"So you're back, Jim?" began the cripple.

"You see me. Back from the mines, Sam."

"And what luck?"

"My usual luck."

"That's been pretty bad, lately. Eh?"

"Worst in the world."

"Hm."

Jordan changed the conversation suddenly. "Did you ever see Jerico run?"

"Never."

"Don't know how fast he is?"

"Sure. I have an idea. I've heard them tell how they ran him for a whole season with relays of fresh horses and never could get nearer than the smell of his dust. He used to just loaf along and play with the fastest horseflesh they could bring out."

"Play with 'em . . . that's it!" Sam chuckled. "He's a playful horse, is Jerico . . . playful all the way through, he is!"

The thought convulsed him with silent mirth, which he checked to look slyly up at Jim Orchard, as though in fear the other might have understood too much. It was sickening to the cowpuncher.

He had known Sam in the old days, free and easy, good-looking, strong, recklessly brave, open of heart as a child. But now there was an indescribable malice in that face. He did not talk, but he purred with caressing tones, and under the purr Orchard was horribly conscious of the malignant heart. The fellow had suffered so much and so long that he seemed to be living on hatred.

"Fast!" went on Sam. "Why, you ain't got no idea how fast he is! Why, Jerico could run a circle around the fastest horse that's entered for the race tomorrow. That's how fast he is. Sort of a shame he ain't going to have the chance at it, eh?"

"Too bad. No way of getting him ridden?"

"Not a chance, unless you'd try, Jim. That'd be a thing to see . . . a man that's never been throwed, and a hoss that's never been rode! That'd be a thing to see!"

All at once Orchard saw the whole point to the talk. Sam Jordan was up to his old tricks, and this time he had picked on Orchard to be the victim of this trained devil in the hide of a horse.

"Who told you I'd never been thrown?" demanded Jim. "I've been thrown, and often, too."

"Not that nobody knows about," put in Jordan eagerly. "Not that anybody around here remembers! Just this morning I heard a couple of the boys talking. 'Who's the best rider around these parts?' they say. 'Hawkins,' says one. 'Lorrimer,' says another. 'Garry Munn,' says another. 'You're fools, all of you,' says the first gent. 'They ain't one of 'em that can touch Jim Orchard. Why he's never been throwed!' That's the way they talk about you around these parts, Jim, and if you was to ride Jerico, everybody'd believe it!"

The malice of the man was patent, now. He kept smiling and nodding so that it would be unnecessary for him to meet the eye of Jim Orchard. But why should he hate such an old friend and companion? Simply because he, Sam Jordan, was a shapeless wreck, and Jim Orchard was as tall and straight and agile as ever.

"It's no good, Sam. I won't try Jerico. My pride isn't that kind. I don't pretend to be the best rider in the world. Maybe I'm not half as good as the fellows Jerico has pretty near killed in the past."

Sam Jordan sighed. "I thought maybe I'd find you kind of down in the pocket. I figured on paying quite a bit if you could ride Jerico in the race."

Temptation surged up in the mind of Jim Orchard, but he shook his head. The memory of Bud Castor came back upon his mind. "I'm not your man, Sam."

"It ain't so easy to pick up a hundred every day."

"I'll take my money the harder ways, then."

"Or two hundred, say. I'd like to see my hoss entered, Jim."

"Not any hope of it, as far as I'm concerned."

The face of Sam Jordan went black and he bowed his head for a moment. "Five hundred," he whispered suddenly, and Jim winced as though he had been struck.

"What makes you so sure that I've got a price today?" he asked fiercely.

"I can tell it by the hungry look you got in your eye. How about it? Five hundred, Jim, payable the minute that horse finishes the race."

"No. No use in talking, Sam."

"You're a hard gent to do business with. Well, here's my rock-bottom offer: one thousand cold iron men for you, if you ride Jerico in the race, Orchard!"

"It's a lot of money," said Jim, "but it's not as much as I need."

"Besides, you can bet. The minute they know that Jerico is in the race the odds will drop. They won't give you even money, but for every three bucks you bet you can win two."

He paused, for the face of Jim Orchard had become troubled, and he wisely allowed the temptation to work. It was the way the proposition came pat that appealed to the gambling instinct in Orchard. He had two thousand; then a thousand from Jordan would make three thousand; and the amount won would add two thousand, making up the total of five thousand which he needed. It was almost as if Jordan knew the amount of money in his pocket and the need he had for exactly three thousand more.

"Sam," he said, "I take you."

"Good boy! I knew I'd fetch you!" He was rubbing his hands together in glee. "When do you want to try out Jerico?"

"Now's as good a time as any. Go down and have him taken out into the corral. Do I have to rope him and saddle him, or do you give me a flying start?"

"Give you every sort of a start. All you have to do is climb into the saddle, and off you go!"

But Jim Orchard turned away with a sick smile. He had not the slightest of hopes; only his gambler's instinct had ruled him, and the crushed body of Bud Castor came back into his mind with a premonition of death.

But if he were crippled, who would be the donor of five hundred dollars to "give him a chance?" Or would he live a cripple with a mind poisoned like that of Sam Jordan? He did one of those foolish things which the oldest and strongest men are apt to do now and then in a pinch. He took out a little leather folder from his pocket, opened a picture of Sue Hampton, and touched it covertly with his lips.

V "Overtures to Jerico"

There was no need to spread the tidings through the village with messengers. It was late afternoon by this time and, the events of the rodeo having been entirely completed and the crowd packed back into the town to wait for the crowning glory of the race of the next day, rumor took up the tale of what Jim intended to attempt.

Most people were incredulous, but not only did rumor say he was to attempt the riding, but that he would make the first experiment with Jerico on that very day. It was remembered that he had passed the broken body of Bud Castor earlier in the day. The romantic took up the story and embroidered it. Jim Orchard, being an old friend of Bud's, had sworn to him to ride the stallion into submission, or else die in the attempt. The conversation between Bud and Jim was even invented and elaborated.

All this took place within some thirty minutes. At the end of that time Sue Hampton came to the hotel asking for Jim Orchard. She was shown to his room.

"Shucks," said the disgusted public, "she'll keep Jim from going through with it."

"You don't know Jim," answered the fat proprietor of the hotel. "Nothing'll stop him."

Jim Orchard had just finished dressing. He knew that he was about to take the center of the stage in a public manner and, whether it ended tragically or happily, he wanted to fit the great occasion. A rap at his door interrupted him, and he opened it to Sue Hampton.

He was so astonished by her appearance that he retreated before her into the center of the room as though she had presented a loaded revolver to his head. She closed the door behind her without taking her resolute eyes from him, and then she followed him a little ways.

"What's the matter, Sue?" he kept repeating helplessly.

For he was completely at sea. How had the dim, quiet Sue Hampton he knew been transformed into this creature with eyes of fire and trembling lips and flaring color?

"You coward!" cried Sue Hampton. "You coward, Jim Orchard!"

Orchard stood agape. "What's wrong, Sue?"

"You promised me that you'd play square . . . and now . . . you're going to ride Jerico . . . and get killed like Bud . . . oh, is it fair, Jim?"

"Bud wasn't killed. He. . . ."

"What happened to him was worse. I know. I talked to the doctor. Lucky for Bud that you gave him five hundred dollars!"

So that was known! Jim set his teeth. If he ever found that worthless boy, he would skin him alive and throw the skin away! On this day of all days to have such a thing brought to the ear of Sue!

She went running on in a storm of protest. "It isn't the money. You know it isn't. All that I want you to prove is that you can make it and keep it long enough. And now you're throwing yourself away . . . do you think I could ever raise my head again if anything happened? I want you to promise that you'll not try to ride Jerico."

He took her by the arm and led her to the window.

"Look down there!"

A crowd of a hundred or more persons had gathered, and more people were constantly arriving.

"They're getting ready to go along with me when I start for Jerico. That's why they're there. Everybody in town knows that I've told Sam Jordan I'm going to ride the brute. Do you think I can back down, now?"

"You value your pride more than you do me, Jim!"

He lost a good deal of color at her reply, but he answered gravely: "It's more than pride. It's a matter of honor."

All at once she had slipped into his arms, and her hands were locked behind his head.

"Dear Jim! Dear old Jim! Tell me you won't?"

It was another revelation to Jim. Something in him started toward her like iron toward a magnet.

"We won't wait for the money. We'll marry now . . . today . . . this minute. But promise me to give up Jerico! Oh, I've seen that horse fight!"

"No!"

He managed to say the word after a bitter effort. And the girl slipped away and looked at him, bewildered.

"Is that the last word, Jim?"

With despair he saw her returning to her habitual placidity. The fire died away and left her more colorless than ever. Her eyes went down to her folded hands.

"It's a matter of honor, Sue."

At that she went toward the door, and Jim, sick at heart, tried to stop her. Something about her lowered head, however, warned him not to touch her. She went out, the door closed, and he heard her light, quick step fade away down the hall. It was to Jim as if she had stepped out of his life.

It was a long minute later that the growing murmur of the crowd below gave him the courage to put on his hat and go down. When he came onto the verandah, there was a murmur, and then followed an actual shout of greeting. He saw the weaving faces in a haze. Particularly, as he remembered later, there was the handsome face of Garry Munn at the outskirts of the crowd, and Garry was indubitably worried.

The crowd trailed out behind Jim, as he went down the street, like the tail streaming behind a comet; and so he came to the shack where Sam Jordan was staying until the rodeo ended. Sam himself was seated in a wheel chair in front of the door, and he began waving and nodding a greeting to the crowd. He seemed in amazing good humor. But Jim Orchard had only a casual glance for the owner. His attention was for the horse. The great black stood in the corral where he had been roped, thrown, blindfolded, and saddled. He was still blindfolded, but as one who senses danger, he stood with his head thrown high and his ears flat against his neck.

Orchard had never seen such a horse. He must have stood a full sixteen hands. Every ounce of him was made for speed and strength in the best combination. There was the long forehead, which meant the rider's ease in controlling him; there was the long back of the racer, but not too long for weight-carrying purposes; the great breast spoke of the generous heart beneath; the head was poised with exquisite nicety. All this strength was superimposed upon legs slender and strong as hammered iron. There was not a mar in the black, except an irregular white splotch between the eyes, and a single white fetlock.

Such was Jerico. And at sight of him the crowd murmured in fear and admiration. He was like one of those rarely beautiful women who are always new.

At the murmur Jim Orchard looked back across the crowd. In his heart of hearts he despised them. They had come with divided will to see one of the two beaten—either the horse or the man—and he knew that they hardly cared which. To see the horse beaten into submission would be gratifying; to see the rider thrown and broken would be infinitely more exciting. What right had they to come like spectators to a gladiatorial combat?

His heart went out with a sudden sympathy to the beautiful mustang. The saddle on his back and the heavily curbed bridle were a travesty. He should be shaking that glorious mane in the wind, at the head of a band of his mates. What right had they to imprison and torture him? With speed against speed, which was all that he was supposed to know, he had beaten them. Only by a trick they had taken him. The lesson of cunning and cruelty which they had taught him he now used against his captors. And Jim Orchard silently approved. Strangely he felt a kinship with this imprisoned beast. He was imprisoned, also—blindfolded by a promise to a man—the love of a woman.

He climbed the high fence and dropped into the corral. "We'll have an even break," he said to the old Negro who stood near the head of the stallion. "Take the blindfold off Jerico. Take it off, I say," he repeated, as the other merely gaped at him.

The white-haired old fellow groaned. "Does this heah man knows what all he's talking about, Glory?" He bowed his head and addressed a fat-bodied, sleepy-eyed bull terrier beside him, and the dog twitched the stump of his tail.

"Don't act crazy, Orchard!" called someone from the mob. "You'll never get on that horse unless he's blindfolded!"

"Let him alone. Jim'll work it out his own way. He's going to teach us something new about horse-breaking!"

That was Garry Munn's voice. Jim deliberately turned and smiled over the heads of the crowd into the face of Garry. This was another thing to be remembered.

He turned back and, at his repeated order, the Negro finally climbed up on the side of the fence and, leaning cautiously, jerked away the bandage from Jerico's eyes. The latter tossed his head to the light and at the same instant left the ground, bucked in midair, and came down with stiffly braced legs, before he seemed to realize that there was no rider in the saddle. Then he stood quivering with excitement and anger in the center of the corral, until he caught sight of Jim Orchard standing alone, unprotected by the fence which kept Jerico from that hated mass of faces.

He snorted once in amazement and suspicion—then lunged straight at the solitary stranger. From the crowd there went up a yell of horror—a familiar music to the ear of Jerico—he had heard it many a time when the would-be rider was flung like a stone from the saddle and crushed against the ground. So let it be with this man!

But Jim Orchard did not stir. All in a split part of a second he reviewed his life, knew he was a fool, and cursed his luck, because there was no escape from this tigerish devil of a horse. And then he stood his ground without lifting a hand and watched death come at him.

It came—and swerved aside. Jerico leaped away and stood beside the bars once more, snorting, stamping, flaunting his tail. Things which did not stir when he charged them were usually lifeless, like the post of a fence. And, if one rashly collided with such things, there was only a stunning repulse for a reward. Certainly, said the brute mind, that is a man, and yet he did not stir. A doubt came to Jerico. This was a man, and yet no man had ever approached him before on foot, unarmed with even the stinging whip. Besides, the others, who had screamed a moment ago and stood so hushed, so terribly silent now, were protected by the fence. This creature must be different from the others.

He made a step toward Jim Orchard, paused, made another step, and then sprang away. The man had slowly raised his hand and now held it out in the immemorial sign of friendship and conciliation which even brute beasts learn sooner than any other human gesture. Jerico cocked his head and watched in amazement.

Then a voice began over the silence of the hundreds, a smooth, steady voice. It was an oddly fascinating voice, and it instantly convinced him that this was a new species—not a man at all. Other men yelled and made harsh sounds of fury, while they beat him with quirts and tore his tender sides with spurs. Yes, this creature was not a man at all. The sound of his voice took hold of the nerves of Jerico and soothed them and gave him queer reassurance.

But what was this? The creature was walking straight toward him. Jerico flung himself away into the farthest corner like a flash and waited again, very curious. Behold, the man came toward him again, always speaking steadily, softly, his hand extended.

It was not altogether new. One other human being had seemed not dangerous to Jerico, and that was old Tom, the Negro. He had learned from Tom that it is not unpleasant to have a hand run down one's neck, or across the velvet of the nose. And the approach of this stranger bore with it infinite promises of pleasure, safety, protection from that horde of white, mute faces beyond the fence.

He began to tremble, more in curiosity than fear or, rather, with a mixture of both emotions. And now the man was close, closer! The hand moved out. Should he tear it with his strong teeth? No, there was no danger. There was no dreaded rope in those fingers. He waited, blinked, and then, as he had almost known, the finger tips trailed across his nose. A miracle!

A miracle, indeed, it seemed to the waiting throng when, after some breathless moments, they beheld the black stallion actually drop his nose on the shoulder of Jim Orchard and stare defiantly at the faces beyond the fence.

There was only one sound. It was the voice of old Tom, the Negro, saying in a sort of chant: "Glory be! Glory be!"

And still the crowd was incredulous. They would not believe their eyes as they saw Jim Orchard work his way to the side of the animal, test the stirrup, and put weight upon it with his hand. The stallion winced and turned his head with the ears flattened. His great teeth closed on the arm of Jim and crushed the flesh against the bone but, in spite of the torture, Orchard did not vary the tone of his voice a jot. Presently the teeth relaxed their hold. There was a groan of relief from the crowd—a groan full of horror and tense excitement. In a way this was the most horrible horse-breaking that had ever been seen.

Finally the foot of Jim Orchard was in that stirrup, his weight grew heavier, and at length he raised himself slowly up, and up, swung his leg over, and settled into the stirrups. That familiar burden for one moment drove the stallion mad with fear and rage. He hurtled in the air and gave for ten seconds a hair-raising exhibition of bucking.

And then, with the shrieking of the delighted spectators in his ears, he stopped abruptly.

He was right. This was some other creature and not a man at all. In spite of his frantic efforts, no tearing steel points had been driven into his sides, no stinging whip had cut his flanks, no hoarse voice had bellowed curses at him.

Instead, the smooth, even voice had begun again—steadying, steadying, steadying. The sound of that voice fell like sleep upon the ragged nerves of Jerico. Someone near the fence yelled and waved a hat. Jerico tossed up his head and crouched for a leap.

"Gents!" rang the voice of Jim Orchard. "Another stunt like that and I out with my gun and start spraying lead. I mean it! You're going to give me and Jerico a fair chance to get acquainted. Show's over for the day!"

But before he dismounted, he glanced across to the door of the shack and saw the face of Sam Jordan convulsed with wonder and ugly malice!

VI "Crooked Rivals"

Until the very last act of that little drama Garry Munn had not stirred. For five minutes he had been praying silently. If Jerico had been susceptible to the influence of mental telepathy, he would certainly have smashed Jim Orchard to small bits. Instead, the miracle had happened, and Garry turned away and hurried back to the hotel. There he swung into his saddle, trotted to the outskirts of the town, and then rode at full speed out the road, deep in the dust which the unaccustomed traffic had churned up around the town.

Two miles of hard galloping, and he swung from the road down a cattle trail which brought him, almost at once, to a right-angled bend, and then to a full view of a little shack. There was a broad, perfectly level meadowland stretching away to the left, and across this smooth ground a midget of a man was galloping a long-legged bay. Garry Munn drew his own horse down to a walk and watched with a brightening eye. Yet the bay was not a horse to win the admiration of the ordinary cowpuncher. He was too long in the back, too thin of legs, too gaunt of neck, too meager of shoulders and hips to please men who look at a horse with an eye for his usefulness on long journeys and the heart-breaking labors of the roundup.

The bay was a horse which, it could be seen at a glance, needed the proverbial "forty-acre lot" to turn around in. Neither was his action imposing. He stood awkwardly; his trot was a spiritless shamble, his canter a loose-jointed, shuffling gait. But, when he began to run, there was a distinct difference. He thrust out his long neck, and the Roman-nosed head at the end of it. His little thin ear flagged back along his neck, the lengthy legs flung out in amazing strides, and the ground whirled under him with deceptive speed. He ran not with the jerky labor of a cowpony, but with jack-rabbit bounds, and he was far faster than he looked. Garry Munn eyed him with distinct favor. When the midget rider saw him, he brought the bay to a jolting trot that landed him in front of the shack.

"He's coming into shape," said Garry, joining the other.

The only reply was a brief grunt. The little man industriously set about removing the saddle and then began to rub the bay. He continued his ministrations with a sort of grim energy for a full twenty minutes; then, having tethered the horse in the lean-to beside the shack, he gave some attention to Garry.

"He ain't in shape. Not by a lot," he declared. "How d'you expect me to get him in shape, running on plowed ground?"

"Plowed ground?" asked Garry Munn. "Why, Tim, I picked this place out because it's the smoothest ground around the town. You can't beat it anywhere."

"Smooth, eh?" demanded little Tim. "It's so rough that I ain't dared to let him out. I ain't been able to give Exeter his head, once."

"Wasn't he going full tilt a minute ago?" asked Garry, admiringly.

"Him? Nothing like it! Now when Exeter. . . ."

"Cut out that name. He's in this race as Long Tom. You'll spoil everything if you let that name drop."

"He's long enough, and the rules will find him a bit too long when he gets going. Only I wish I was down to weight."

"What's your weight now?"

"Clothes and all, maybe I tip the old beam around a hundred and fifteen."

He was well under five feet tall, with a withered skull face, a pinched neck, and diminutive legs. All his strength lay in the abnormally long arms and the sturdy shoulders.

"Why, Hogan," said Garry Munn, "that's a good thirty pounds lighter than any other rider."

"Maybe it is, maybe it isn't. But Exeter . . . Long Tom, I mean . . . is cut out for flyweight racing. Put him in with ninety pounds, and he's a whirlwind. Stick more'n a hundred on him, and he don't like it. He ain't got the underpinning for weight."

"It's only a mile," said Garry eagerly. "He'll surely last that?"

"Easy, if I don't have to stretch him out. How's the black? What come of that Castor fellow?"

"He's smashed. One arm and both legs busted up."

The little man sighed.

"You owe me a lot for that little piece of work," he said gloomily.

"You'll find I'll pay," said Garry. "How'd you fix it?"

"I just sneaked around until I found out what saddle they were going to use on the black. Then I fixed the saddle."

He grinned briefly with malicious pleasure, and then his expression sobered.

"What happened?"

"Jerico went mad. That's all. He smashed Bud to pieces. I never saw such a devil when it comes to bucking."

"Well, now that we got the black out of the race, I ain't worrying. I've timed the others, and they're a cinch."

Garry delivered his bad news.

"Tim, Jerico is in the race again."

Tim Hogan blinked.

"A dare-devil named Orchard rode Jerico just a while ago and got on with him, as if Jerico were an old pack horse. We're in for it. How fast can the black go?"

"How fast? Too fast!"

"How far did you see him run?"

"It ain't what the clock told me. It's what my eyes told me. That Jerico has a racing heart. You'll find him doing about twice better in a race than he does in practice. Well, put Exeter on a good fast track with ninety pounds up, a little racing luck, and he'd trim all the Jericos that ever stepped on plates. But Exeter had to pack thirty pounds more'n he likes, and I don't know what he'll do. He may quit on me. Chief, you got to get Jerico out of the way, if you want to win that race!"

Garry Munn cursed softly and fluently.

"It can't be done, now. You don't know this fellow Orchard. He has an eye like a hawk's and, if he finds anyone around tampering with a bridle, or saddle, he'll fill the man full of lead. That's Orchard's way. He shoots first, and asks his questions of the coroner. But there's one thing to help us, Tim. That's the weight. Orchard is a big fellow. He must weigh a hundred and eighty . . . thirty pounds more than Castor."

"A hundred and eighty?" asked Tim Hogan cheerfully. "Why that'd anchor another Salvator!"

"It'll beat Jerico, then?"

But Tim had grown thoughtful. "You can't always tell about a horse," he declared. "No way of figuring whether a horse will be a hog for carrying the weight or not. And Jerico looks like an iron horse. Never saw such legs. He could carry a ton, from his looks. A hundred and eighty would break Exeter's back; but Jerico might dance with it. It ain't likely . . . but then you never can tell. You got to fix that horse so's he can't run if you want to be sure of the race."

"I've got to win," declared Munn. "They'll give me odds of three to one against Long Tom, and I've raked together thousands for the plunge. They don't like the looks of Tom. They think he'll break to pieces when he starts running. I can get any odds I want against him."

"What'd happen if they knew Exeter was off a race track, with a record of wins as long as my arm? What'd happen if they knew I was a jockey, that I don't own the horse, and that you brought me on for this clean-up? I've been sizing up the boys around here, guns and all, and I just been wondering what would happen to us both, Mr. Munn, if they had a hunch about what's happening."

"They'd string us up to the nearest tree and fill us full of lead," said Garry quickly. "That's their way."

Tim Hogan shook himself. "It don't bother me none," he declared. "I was in the ring before I started riding a string. I won't get cold feet. But say, Mr. Munn, why don't you fix this rider . . . this Orchard . . . as long as you can't fix the horse."

"Fix him? How?"

"Get him to pull Jerico in the race."

Garry started, but then shook his head. "You don't know Jim Orchard. Besides, I couldn't approach him."

"You don't have to. I'll do it. I've done it before. They all got a price, if you can go high enough."

"I wonder," said Garry, sweating with anxiety. "Nine chances out of ten he'd throw you out the window."

"I don't pack much weight . . . I'd light easy."

"It can't be done."

"It can be done. They all got a price. How high could I go with him?"

His confidence was contagious.

"You could go to the sky," said Garry Munn. "Why, if Jerico's in the race, the men around here will bet everything down to their socks. I know half a dozen ranchers who'd go ten thousand apiece on Jerico if they could find anyone to cover their money. There's an idea around these parts that Jerico can't be beaten by anything in the shape of horseflesh." He became excited. "If Jerico runs, there'll be a hundred thousand . . . maybe more . . . in sight to bet on him."

"Then cop it. Cop it, Mr. Munn. But where do I come in?"

"If you work the deal, Tim, it means a thousand flat to you, and ten percent of everything I make!"

"And how'd I be sure you'd come through?"

"I've never gone back on a promise in my life."

The little man watched him with a peculiar glance of scorn. "I guess you ain't," he admitted at last. "Besides, you don't dare go back on me. How high with this Jim Orchard?"

"A thousand, five thousand, ten thousand . . . anything you want. There's a better way. Get him to bet his money on Exeter."

"Chief," declared the jockey with a grin, "you learn fast."

VII "Orchard's Bargain"

As for Jim Orchard, when he swung down gently from the saddle on Jerico, there was a relieved groan of appreciation and wonder, but he paid no further attention to the crowd.

"He's just putting off your little party," one of the men called warningly to Orchard.

And perhaps he was, but something told Orchard that for the first time a man had stepped into the confidence of the black stallion. After all, had not many a stranger thing than this episode been told of horses? And was it not possible that Jerico, having battled and hated his would-be masters for so long, had finally decided that one, at least, might be accepted on trust? Jim Orchard decided to take the chance.

All his life he had done nothing but play some such chance— whether he were gambling on the turn of a card, or the dependable qualities in a man. Deliberately he raised the stirrup and stirrup flap and put them across the saddle. Then he commenced to work at the knots of the cinches. The moment he had brought them loose and drew on the cinch straps to free them, the head of Jerico swung on him again. But this time the stallion merely bared his teeth without touching Orchard. The ears, which were flattened against the horse's neck, pricked a little as he watched Orchard loose the cinches and remove the saddle.

It was the first time that Jerico had seen this done. Hitherto he had been roped and blinded for saddling or unsaddling, to keep his murderous, striking hoofs still. Now he discovered that no matter what hateful agency put the saddle upon him, this man, this stranger of the gentle voice, could remove it. Jerico was not quite sure of any of this, but his misty animal brain was moving faintly toward the conviction that the man was at least not harmful. At the first suspicious move he was ready to scatter the brains of Jim Orchard in the dust of the corral; in the meantime his would be a policy of watchful waiting.

Orchard was keen enough to sense what went on behind the suspicious eyes of the horse. No matter how well he had succeeded so far, he took care to make every motion slow, gentle, and kept up a steady stream of talk. Then with the saddle over the crook of his arm, he walked calmly out of the corral, his back actually turned upon the man-killer! His hand was wrung on every side the moment the gate closed behind him.

It was: "Good old Jim, I sure was saying good bye to you for a minute or two!"

"That's the nerve, Jim!"

"You win, old boy."

"Tame the lions, Orchard."

But Jim Orchard wondered if everyone of them was not just a trifle disappointed. It would have been sufficiently thrilling to see either man or horse beaten, but this compromise, which left dignity and physical soundness to both man and beast, was a wretched compromise. Jim hung the saddle on its peg in the barn. The crowd had already scattered, now that the crisis had passed. There was only the grinning old

Negro, Tom, and the fat bull terrier which trailed at his heels, almost bumping his nose against them. No matter where Tom turned, the dog made it an earnest practice to keep directly behind him.

"I knowed it all the time, Mistah Orchard," averred Tom. "Trouble with all them others was they was sure dead set on breaking Jerico's heart. For why? Had poor ol' Jerico done 'em any harm? No, suh, that he hadn't! But I take off my hat to you, suh. It took a brave man to find out that Jerico weren't no murderer, but jus' an honest hoss that had been taught all wrong."

"I hear you've got on pretty well with Jerico yourself," said Jim Orchard.

"Couldn't be better, suh. When I first come, Jerico he takes a couple of swipes at ol' Tom's head. But he missed, praise the Lawd, and pretty soon he find out that Tom ain't doin' him no harm, jus' foolin' aroun' and feedin' him and bringin' him out to water. He's been mighty afraid, that's all that's been wrong with ol' Jerico, Mistah Orchard."

"You broke the ice for me," said Jim. "If it hadn't been for what you'd taught him, he'd've busted me into little bits. I'm going to saddle him up myself later on, when there isn't a crowd to watch, and we'll try a canter down the road together."

"He's a wise hoss, Mistah Orchard. He'll know you same's if you raised him from a colt, by morning. All Jerico needs is just to make up his mind about something. Look at ol' Glory, now. Jerico wouldn't have my dog aroun' for a long time. And now they're jus' plumb friendly. Go talk to Jerico, Glory!"

Old Glory, hearing this order, cast a skulking glance at Jim Orchard and then slunk toward the corral. Once outside the barn he seemed to gather courage. He trotted straight for the stallion and, rising on his hind legs under the nose of the horse, barked at him softly. Jerico in answer deliberately and gently tipped old Glory over with a push of his nose. But Glory came up again and danced, with all the agility his fat allowed, around the great horse. Jerico followed, pretending anger, striking gently with his forefeet, wide of the mark.

"Look there, now," exclaimed Tom delighted. "I ask you, Mistah Orchard, is that the way a man-killin' hoss ought to act? Why, Jerico's plumb gentle, once he gets to know you! It's the cussin' and the whips that he's been fighting, not the men."

"You're right," agreed Jim Orchard, amazed at that dumb show in the corral. "You're right from the first. But what's the matter with that dog, Tom? Has somebody been beating him?"

"They's a long story about ol' Glory, Mistah Orchard. You see him sneakin' aroun' like he didn't have no soul of his own? Well, suh, I seen him the best fighting dog that ever was. Plumb wild, ol' Glory was. His master used to keep him half starved to have him wild, and then he'd bet on Glory to his last nickel . . . and always Glory won, chewin' up the other dog sump'n terrible to talk of. But one time Mistah Simpson . . . that was him that owned Glory . . . done le' him go without no food for a long time. Po' white trash, that man was, suh! An' he put ol' Glory all weak and tremblin' into the ring. Shucks, Glory would've made jus' two mouthfuls of the other dog, if he'd been strong. But he was like a little puppy afraid of the cold, that day . . . he was so weak.

"He got chewed up scandalous, suh, Glory did that day. They got the other dog off'n him just in time, and after that Glory ain't been no good. They fatted him up and got him strong and put him back ag'in another dog, suh, but Glory jus' got down in the corner an' wouldn't come out. His heart had been broke, suh, you see? An' ever since he's been like this. Jus' draggin' around dodgin' eyes when folks look at him. Even ol' Tom can't get Glory to look him in the eye, but he keeps skulkin' and draggin' and bumpin' his nose ag'in my heels, suh."

"But why do you keep him, Tom?"

"You git sorter fond of a dog, suh. But always I keep dreamin' and thinkin' of the dog that ol' Glory used to be and the dog he might've been . . . if the heart hadn't been plumb busted in him, suh!"

"Tom," said Jim Orchard, much moved, "you're a good sort. And you're right, I figure. I've known horses the same way. Particular the wild ones. Beat 'em once and they're no good ever after. I'll wager that Jerico might be that sort of a horse. What do you think?"

"They ain't no doubt. Beat him once and he'll go aroun' hangin' his head . . . an' any boy could git on him and thump him with his bare heels."

Orchard sighed. "Kind of a responsibility, a horse like that. How much do you think Sam Jordan would be wanting for Jerico?"

The Negro shrugged his shoulders and peered up into the face of Orchard with a timid smile.

"I don't think no man has got money to buy him from Mistah Jordan, suh."

"Why not? Sam isn't rich."

"Well, suh. . . ." Tom paused.

"I won't repeat what you say. Go ahead, Tom."

"Ever get stung by wasps, Mistah Orchard, and go back to the rest of the boys and say nothin' about it and get 'em to come and walk over the same hole in the ground to see what'd happen to 'em?"

There was a pause during which the whole meaning of this sunk into the brain of Jim Orchard. He had had the ugly suspicion concerning Sam Jordan before, and he could not forget the singular expression on the face of the cripple at the moment when Jerico stopped bucking. It was a bad affair from the beginning to end.

He glanced out the barn door and saw old Glory trotting back to his master. At that moment a cowpuncher sauntered past. The terrier crouched till his belly touched the ground, skidded deftly around the stranger, and then raced for dear life until he was safe behind the shoes of Tom.

Jim Orchard had seen enough. He was filled with an insane desire to find that former master of the fighting bull terrier and beat the brutal fellow to a pulp, until he became as cringing a coward as he had made his dog.

In the meantime he walked to the front of the shack and stopped beside Sam Jordan. There was no hint of friendliness in the glance which the cripple cast at him. There was a smile, to be sure, but it was so forced and bespoke so much hidden malice, that it chilled the tall 'puncher's blood.

"That was a pretty clever trick," said Sam Jordan, still smiling. "What'd you do? Dope Jerico first? Get old Tom to mix something in his feed before you tried him out?"

"Did I have a chance to get at Tom before I tried to ride Jerico?"

Sam Jordan thought a moment. "I dunno," he admitted grudgingly. "It don't seem no ways possible."

"How about selling Jerico, Sam?"

"Selling him? Not in a thousand years!"

"But what's he worth to you, man?"

The grin of Sam Jordan became a horrible caricature of mirth. "He's worth . . . this!" With a slow, inclusive gesture, he indicated the crippled legs. "I've paid for him with my legs. D'you think you could raise that price, maybe, Jim?"

"But what use is he to you, man?"

"I dunno. I'm just sort of used to having him around. You planning on turning him into a family pet, Jim? Just keep watching your step, partner. Jerico ain't through by no means!"

"But I've thought of this, Sam. By the time I have him tame enough to ride in the race tomorrow he'll be pretty well broken. Besides, I don't think the thousand is worth the chance I'm taking."

"You ain't calling the bargain off, Jim?" asked the cripple, growing suddenly conciliatory. His expression made Orchard think of the spider that sees the fly creeping off beyond his reach. He decided to see what bluffing would do.

"I'll stick to the bargain, if you'll let me make another deal with you. Suppose I take all the chances, and I'm able to ride Jerico in the race? Well, then, name a reasonable price and let me buy him when the race is over."

"No chance, Jim!"

"Then I'm through. Try out somebody else for your jockey!"

"Wait!"

"You've heard me, Sam. I mean it."

"Take a price after the race is finished?" argued Sam Jordan, evidently turning the proposition in his mind and deciding that there was very little chance of Jim Orchard or any other man staying on the back of the stallion through the excitement which was bound to seize the mustang during a contest with other horses.

"Name a good round figure, Sam."

"One thousand for Jerico, then, if you stick on him through the whole race."

"A thousand it is!"

They shook hands, and the fingers of Sam Jordan were bloodless and cold to the touch.

VIII "Hogan Exposes His Cards"

Turning his back on Jordan, Jim Orchard strode off down the street. He had taken on a new obligation. To the original five thousand which had been his goal, and which he now had an excellent chance of winning, provided Jerico was first in the race, there was added the purchase price of the stallion. The total he needed was six thousand dollars.

Again he was glad that the girl could not know. He had already placed his chance of happiness under the danger of a mortgage. What would she think if she knew that he had admitted a brute beast—a horse—on the same plane with her?

He turned on his heel. Jerico was still visible. He had pressed forward against the fence of the corral, and he was watching his late rider disappear. He even tossed up his head and whinnied when he saw Jim turn. The latter remained for a moment staring, a lump growing in his throat. Then he resumed his walk.

"I've got to have that horse," said Orchard conclusively. Then his mind turned happily to Sue Hampton. Of course, she would not have had the courage to come to see the riding and, though she must have learned of the outcome of his daring by this time, no doubt she would be glad to see him and be reassured that all was well. He went to her house.

She was on the little verandah with a heap of silky stuff in her lap and a basket beside her. She raised her head and watched him coming up the path. When she saw him, she laid aside the sewing and folded her hands, and Jim Orchard knew that he was distinctly out of favor. Another girl in such a mood would have pretended not to see him. But it was one of Sue's peculiarities that she made no pretenses. She was as inexorable with herself as she was with others. He had known her to go out of her way to make quaint confessions of wrong thoughts that had been in her mind, after she had been proved wrong. But the terrible part of this was that she more or less expected others to treat her as she treated them. Unfortunately she expected the qualities of a saint in an ordinary cowpuncher.

It was one of the things that made Orchard love her; it was also one of the things that kept him at arm's length and gave him occasionally a little touch of dread. Today it made him a little more swaggering. He tried to bluff his way through.

"Well," he greeted her, "you see everything's all right?"

It was always wonderful to see her brighten. "Then you're not going to ride Jerico?"

"But, Sue, I've already ridden him!"

"I mean in the race tomorrow?"

"But he's safe enough. Haven't I just finished trying him out?"

"I heard about it," said the girl. "They told me how you . . . almost tempted him to kill you!"

"It was the only thing to do," said Jim, growing sullen as he saw what position she was going to take. "Other fellows have fought Jerico . . . plenty of them . . . and I thought I'd try persuasion."

"I think I know," she answered with that deadly softness. "There was such a crowd . . . you had to do something to thrill them. So you forgot about your own safety . . . you forgot about me . . . you gave the crowd a show!"

The injustice of it rankled in him. "Do you think, sure enough, that I'm low enough for that?"

It was her turn to flush with anger. "You shouldn't have said that, Jim. But if we start out with misunderstanding. . . ."

"You're going to threaten to give that ring back to me again?" he asked coldly.

"I think it would be better."

Jim Orchard for the moment almost forgot that he was talking to a woman—the woman he loved. He put his boot on the edge of the verandah, dropped his elbow on his knee, and lectured her with a raised forefinger.

"You'll keep that ring till the end of tomorrow," he said fiercely. "It makes me tired, Sue, the way you women act. A gent might think that honor didn't have nothing to do with women. It's just for men only. I give you a promise and I got to stick to it to the bitter end. You give me a promise that you're going to stick by me until tomorrow night. Now you welch and try to get out of your promise, but it don't work with me. You're going to keep that ring, Sue. And, if I've got the money by tomorrow night, you're going to marry me. Don't you forget it in the meanwhile!"

Then he turned his back on her and strode away without further adieu, rage straightening his shoulders. Sue Hampton gazed after him as though a new star had swum into her heaven—a blazing comet dazzling her. She sat for a long time with her sewing unheeded, while the day faded, and the darkness came. Before the end she was smiling tenderly to herself.

"There's something about Jim," she decided, "something different."

The "something different" made Jim stamp his way up the stairs of the hotel to his room and fling himself on his cot. In the nick of time he recalled a comforting remark which a friend of his had once made.

"No man that's worth his salt ever understands his womenfolk, really. The point is women are like mules . . . they go by opposites."

This reflection cheered Jim Orchard vastly, and he was about to go downstairs for his dinner when a knock came at the door, and a little man with a fleshless face of excessive ugliness stood before him.

"You're Jim Orchard?"

"Yes."

"You're interested in the race?"

"I'm riding Jerico."

"Can you give me half an hour, Mr. Orchard?"

"Why, sure."

He was putting his hat on as he spoke. Of course it might be some sort of a trap, but the little man was reckless, indeed, if he were trying to bait a trap for Jim Orchard. He followed down the stairs and stepped into a buckboard beside the other.

"I'm Tim Hogan," said the small man, and not once did he open his lips after that, but sent his span of horses at full speed across the town and over the dusty road. They turned to the left after a time and bumped over a cattle trail, the driver skillfully picking his way in spite of the dimness of the moonlight. When they reached a little shack, before which a tall bay horse stood saddled, they stopped and climbed down.

"Now," said Tim Hogan, "have you got a stop watch?"

"Nope."

"I have. Here it is. You take it. It works like this." He explained deftly. He went on: "It's four hundred yards from the stump yonder to that white rock. Want to pace it?"

"I'll take your word," said Jim Orchard, wondering if he had fallen into the hands of a maniac.

"Here goes."

Tim Hogan climbed up the lofty side of the bay and dropped into the saddle. He rode to the stump.

"Now raise your left arm."

Jim obeyed.

"When you drop that arm, I'm going to start the bay for the rock; when I start the bay, you start the watch."

At last Orchard understood. "Good."

He raised his arm, and as he did so the rider raised himself a little in his short stirrups and threw his weight well over the withers of the horse. He was bowed so that his body was straightened out at right angles to the perpendicular.

"Go!" exclaimed Jim, dropping his arm, and with the word the long bay gathered himself and flung out.

He was going at full speed in half a dozen jumps—and such jumps! The flying legs well-nigh disappeared in that dim light. It seemed that the rakish body and the long, snaky neck were shooting through space with no visible means of support. The dark outline whipped past the white rock, and Jim stopped the watch.

He raised it high to read the hand in the dim light, and in this position he remained as one turned to stone. So Tim Hogan found him when he jogged back on Exeter, alias Long Tom. He dismounted, grinning broadly, but the dimness concealed his exultation.

"What do you think?" he asked.

Without a word Jim Orchard returned the stop watch to the jockey. "A quarter of a mile is not a mile," he said.

"Never anything truer that I've heard say," returned Tim. "And the longer the distance the better for the horse with the lightest weight up. I guess that's straight, Mr. Orchard."

"Hm," said Jim.

"Jerico never saw the day he could step a quarter as fast as that one . . . and he never will!"

"What's the main idea behind all this?" asked Jim suspiciously.

"The main idea is that Long Tom is going to win tomorrow."

"Why bring me out in the night to show that to me? Why not win my money and tell me after the race is run?"

"Look here," said Tim, "I'm laying my cards on the table."

"That's the way to talk to me. Now come out with it."

"Well, sir, I've put up a lot of hard cash on this race, and tomorrow I'm going to get down a lot more."

"Well?"

"What do you think of the chances of the rest of the ponies against Long Tom . . . eh?"

"Jerico. . . ."

"Leave out Jerico."

"Leave out Jerico and there's no race. They'll be too far back of Long Tom . . . the rest of 'em . . . to eat his dust."

"You've said a mouthful, general. With Jerico out it'd be just an exercise gallop for Long Tom. But the rest of the boys around here don't know it. They ain't seen what Ex . . . Long Tom can do. They haven't any idea. They figure his long legs will get all tied up in knots, and he'll break down inside a hundred yards. But he ain't going to get tied up. He's going to win."

"You've said that plenty of times, partner. What's the point?"

"The point is the rest of the gents around here are going to plunge on Jerico. They got an idea that nothing can beat that horse. They're going to give me big odds on Long Tom, and I'm going to cover every cent they'll put up. Besides, I've got backing. I've got a backer who's investing every cent he can rake together . . . going into this up to his eyes. Now you can figure for yourself that he wants to make this a safe race, eh?"

"That's easy to follow."

"And there's only one danger . . . that's Jerico. You see, I'm putting the cards on the table."

"I see."

"What we want to be sure of is that no matter what happens to the rest of the horses, and no matter how fast Long Tom has to run to beat 'em, he won't have to worry about Jerico."

"But you've already tried to show me, partner, that you ain't a bit afraid of Jerico."

"Have I? Well, we are afraid, a little. At least he's what keeps our game from being a sure thing. Nobody knows just how fast Jerico can run if he's put to it, or how far he can carry the weight. Now, our proposition is to make sure that Jerico finishes behind Long Tom. That is, if Tom's leading. Mind you, if one of the other ponies gets out in front, then you're free to let go with Jerico and win if you can. But as long as Tom's in front you're to keep back with the black. Is that clear?"

"I hear you talk," said Jim Orchard, "but I don't get you. It ain't no ways possible that you figure I'd pull Jerico? That I'd keep him from doing his best?"

"Look here," replied Tim Hogan, "I ask you man to man: do you think Jerico can beat Long Tom?"

"Man to man, I don't think he can. But I don't know."

"You don't think so; neither do I. But I simply want to make it a sure thing. I'm putting up too much coin to take a chance, no matter how small the chance is. Orchard, I am asking you to pull Jerico!"

Something came into the face of Orchard that made the other spring away.

"Easy!" he cried. "Easy, Orchard! Jerico hasn't a chance in a hundred. I'm just asking you to wipe out even that hundredth chance. And I'm talking business. I'm talking money."

"Get into that buckboard," said Jim Orchard hoarsely, "and drive me back to town."

"D'you mean that? But I say, I'm talking money. I'm talking a thousand dollars, man, if you'll pull Jerico on the hundredth chance!"

"Climb into that buckboard and drive me back. If you had a gun, Hogan, I'd do more than talk to you!"

"I'm talking two thousand . . . three thousand dollars, Orchard. Are you deaf?"

"Deaf as a stone!"

"Four thousand. I'll do better. Give me what money you have, and I'll get it down for you on Long Tom at three to one. How does that sound to you?"

"Hogan, for the last time, will you drive me back, or do I drive back alone?"

Tim Hogan climbed obediently into the buckboard. Not once on the return trip did he speak, feeling the silent loathing and scorn of the big man. But when Jim Orchard climbed down near the hotel, the jockey leaned far out across the wheel and whispered: "Think it over, Orchard. I'll expect an answer. Think it over. Easy money, man. Easy money! Three dollars for one!" He put the whip to the mustangs, and the buckboard jumped away from the curse of Jim Orchard.

IX "The Root of All Evil"

The cowpuncher felt that the matter was closed the moment the wagon whirled out of sight around the corner but, oddly enough, the silence that followed was more tempting than the voice of the jockey. It was the first time in his life that anyone had ever attempted to bribe him. Ordinarily he would have made his revolver reply to such an offer, but one could not draw a weapon on an unarmed man, and it was impossible to use fists on a fellow of the size of Tim Hogan.

The heart of Jim Orchard was heavy. He pushed through a crowd on the verandah—a crowd that wanted to tell him one by one how much they thought of the nerve he had shown in the riding of Jerico that day. He broke through them and entered the hotel.

To those men on the verandah the race was already run and won. They would bet their last dollars on Jerico, for had they not heard how he had been run? Were there not men at the rodeo who had actually taken part in the chase of the wild mustang, and who had seen him wear out horse after horse in the relay that followed Jerico?

But Jerico was beaten. He was as sure of it as if he had actually seen the gallant black pounding down the home stretch, behind the flaunting tail of the long-legged bay. Nothing equine that he had ever seen had moved with the speed of Long Tom. Of course there were unknown possibilities in Jerico. And in a longer race—five or six miles, say—in spite of the greater weight he had to carry, he would undoubtedly break the heart of Long Tom and win as he pleased. But for a single flash of speed—a single mile of sprinting—what chance had Jerico against the long legs and the flyweight rider of the bay?

Jim Orchard dragged a chair up to the window of his room and looked gloomily into the night. He looked forward to the beating of Jerico as to a personal shame and mortification. There was something wrong about it. It should not be allowed. Take Long Tom in the open desert with a day's ride ahead, and what use would he be? And, therefore, was it not bitterer than words could tell that he should be allowed to win fame and name by outstepping the staunch Jerico over a single mile?

There was a sudden outburst of noise, a chorus of voices, shouts, laughter, mocking yells, spilling across the verandah.

What was it?

"On what? On Long Tom?"

"What horse is that?"

"Never seen him."

"I have, it's a bay with legs almost as long as I'm tall."

Then, as the hubbub died away, he made out a clear, strong voice: "All right, boys, have your laugh. But I think those long legs can carry the horse over the ground. What's more, I'll back up what I say with money."

It was the voice of Garry Munn.

"But you're nutty, Munn. Jerico's in the race! And he's like a lamb with Jim Orchard in the saddle. Didn't you see Jim ride the black today?"

"I saw it. Still I have some faith in Long Tom. What odds will you give me, chief?"

"Anything you want."

"Five to one."

"Five to one what?"

"Five thousand to one thousand!"

"Take you, Garry!"

The hubbub roared again. It became a blur, blotting the mind of Jim Orchard.

Garry Munn was the backer of Tim Hogan and the bay horse? Garry Munn was the man who was prepared to plunge "up to the eyes?" Jim bowed his head, for this was more than he could bear. The very day which was to see him fail to make good in making six thousand, which he had set his heart on possessing, this was to be the day of all days for Garry Munn. The very day which saw him fail to win either Sue Hampton or the black stallion, this was the day which was to give Garry Munn a real fortune—and Sue Hampton as well. About the girl, Jim was perfectly certain. She had waited too long. When she finally left him, she would go to the man who could offer her all that Jim lacked.

Then, into the confusion of his mind, came the voice of the little man with the withered face as he leaned out across the wheel of the buckboard. What was it he had said with so much confidence?

"You'll think it over. Easy money, man. Easy money. Three dollars for one."

Of course it was easy money. It was more than easy. It was picking the gold out of the street. What difference did it make? Garry Munn would never bet on a rash chance, and yet he was apparently backing Long Tom with thousands. And whether Jerico were "pulled" or not in the race, he had not a chance in ten of winning. Why not get in on the clean-up? Why not wager his two thousand at odds of three or four to one? Then, even if Jerico were beaten, he would win both the girl and the horse. Was it double-crossing those men who were wagering their very boots on Jerico?

"Forget them!" said Jim Orchard savagely to himself, as this thought came home to him. "The world owes me something!"

On that thought he stuck. The world did, indeed, owe him something. Tomorrow should be his collection day. There might be some pangs of conscience afterward, but in the end Sue Hampton and

Jerico would certainly salve those wounds. The babble had increased on the verandah.

"Wait a minute! One at a time!"

Garry Munn was fighting them off. They were wild with joy at the thought of putting a bet on Jerico. They were offering any odds he would take. Five, seven, ten to one.

It was too much for Jim Orchard.

He counted out the two thousand which made up his worldly fortune, scribbled a brief note which he stuffed into the mouth of the bag and, going down to the back of the hotel, found and saddled his horse and galloped to the shack of Tim Hogan. He kicked open the door without dismounting.

"Hogan!"

The little man with the withered face sauntered out to meet him.

"I knew . . . ," he began.

"Take this and be hanged!" said Orchard. Flinging down the bag, he wheeled his horse and spurred away.

As for Tim Hogan, he picked up the bag and opened it gingerly. His face lighted at the sight of the contents, and then he drew out the paper. He stood for a long time looking down at it. Finally he crumpled it again and dropped it into its former place.

"I didn't think he'd come around," said Tim. "Didn't really think it."

He added joyously after a time: "But I guess they all got their price. Every one of 'em's got the tag on if you can only hit the right figure!"

He was not half an hour alone before a second horseman galloped to his door. "He's changed his mind!" said Tim Hogan, almost happily.

But it was Garry Munn. He came in pale with excitement.

"What's happened?" he asked. "Anything happened?"

"That," said Tim dryly, and pointed to the little sack of money.

"From Orchard? He's come through?"

"He has."

"We're to bet this on Long Tom?"

"We are."

Garry Munn shouted with relief and joy.

"I knew it'd work!"

"What you done?"

"When you told me that Orchard had turned you down, I made up my mind to try a little bluff. I went to the verandah of the hotel and started betting on Long Tom to win."

"Before you knew Orchard would pull Jerico?"

"Sure! I was playing for Jim. I knew he'd hear me and get to thinking that Tom was sure to win no matter what he does."

"And Tom will win."

"Aye, but we can't take chances. They went mad when they heard that there was actually money out against Jerico. They gave me any odds I could ask. I didn't get much down. I let them waste time talking and making a noise to reach the ears of Orchard. All I bet was a few hundred . . . at anything from five to one to ten to one! Think of that! And it hooked him?"

"He came riding up a half hour ago and threw down that."

"Why, you fool, aren't you pleased?"

"I s'pose so. But it means one more good man gone to the bad. You won't hear me cheer. I've seen too much of it."

"But suppose something happens to Long Tom? Suppose he don't win? I'm ruined, Tim, because I'm going to plunge in this up to the eyes. I'm going to soak every cent I can get my hands on into this race." He broke off as he drew out the paper which was in the mouth of the money bag.

"What's here?" He read aloud:

Here you are, Hogan. Bet this on Long Tom for me.

He repeated that message, a smile slowly growing on his face.

"Well?" asked Tim Hogan. "Anything mysterious about that?"

But Garry Munn slowly spread and closed into a fist the fingers of one hand, as though he were strangling a creature of thin air.

"I've got him," he said.

"Got what?"

"He'll get paid the money he wins . . . and long odds at that, as pat as I can get for him. But he loses everything else."

"What?"

"His honor, Tim, and his girl!"

X "Friend to Friend"

Fortunately for his own self-esteem, Garry Munn did not see the cynical smile with which Tim Hogan greeted his last speech. Tim had long since buried the last of his own scruples and could not even remember the long-distant day when he had decided to get along in the world minus the burden of a sense of honor. In his palmy times on the track he had done everything, from artistically "roughing" the most dangerous of his competitors to cleverly "pocketing" or "pulling" his own mount.

He had made a great deal of money in this manner and had always been clever enough to keep away from suspicion. But for the very reason that he had decided to do without moral scruples in his own life, Tim was the keener critic of the morals of others. There was something highly repulsive to him in the apparent good nature of Garry Munn and the real, cold unscrupulousness which underlay the surface appearances.

Unaware of the scorn which was sneering behind his back, Garry went out from the shack singing gaily, and he took his way straight back to the town and then to the house of Susan Hampton. In the old days he had never paid much attention to Sue. Indeed, it was not until Jim Orchard took her up that Garry wakened to her possibilities. But he had long since formed such a habit of trying to get the same things that Jim Orchard wanted that, when Jim seriously courted a woman, it seemed perfectly natural for Garry to desire the same girl.

He never pretended to understand Sue. But, next to his own fortunes, he loved her as much as he was able to love anything. And the pleasure of beating out Jim Orchard in this most important of competitions would suffice to sweeten an entire married life, he felt.

Before he knocked at her door he composed himself. In his hand he carried that sack of Orchard's money with which he was to destroy forever Jim's chances with the girl. In his mind he carried a convincing story. When he had arranged the details, he tapped. The lamp was picked up in the sitting room. He saw the light slant across the window and fade. Then the crack around the front door became an edging of light. The door was opened by Sue herself, who stood back, shading the lamp to keep the glare out of her eyes. It seemed to Garry Munn that the fingers of that hand were transparent.

"Is there anyone with you?" he asked.

"No one."

"Then come out on the verandah, Sue. I've got something to tell you. You don't mind me calling as late as this?"

"Of course not."

She disappeared and joined him at once in the semi-darkness. He was glad to have that sheltering dark, for from the first he had never been entirely at ease, so long as the grave, quiet eyes of the girl could probe his face. The lamplight, he felt, would have been an ally for Jim Orchard. The darkness, on the other hand, would be an ally for Garry Munn. He struck at once into the heart of his subject, because he knew that she was too clever to be fooled by his diplomacy.

"Sue," he said, "I've got a mighty ugly job, tonight. Before I get through talking you'll know I'm the best friend you've got in the world, or else you'll think I'm a hound. Shall I go ahead?"

"I don't know," answered the smooth voice of Sue Hampton. "Of course I won't know till I hear."

That was a characteristic speech, he felt. It would also be characteristic for Sue to suspend judgment to the very end of his story. He felt that he must prepare her.

"Well, we'll start supposing. Suppose you had a friend you thought a lot of . . . and that friend had another friend he thought a lot of. . . ."

"I'm getting the friends all mixed up, Garry."

He blurted out impatiently: "It's about Jim Orchard!"

There was a long pause. He was not so sure that he was glad to have darkness. He would have given a good deal to be able to make out more than the blur of her features.

"Well?" she said at length.

"I've never bluffed with you, Sue," he went on. "I guess you know where I stand?"

"Just what do you mean?"

This coolness was always a dash of water in his face.

"I mean you know my attitude toward you."

She hesitated just a trifle: "I think you've acted as if . . . as if you're a firm friend of mine, Garry. Is that what you mean?"

"Nothing more than a friend?"

"Yes," she admitted willingly enough, "more than a friend."

"And it hasn't bothered you to have me around so much?"

"I don't know just what all this leads to, Garry."

"Nothing that'll embarrass you, Sue. I'll give you my word."

"Then . . . of course, it hasn't bothered me. I like you a lot, Garry. Partly for reasons that aren't reasons. Partly because you're so clean."

He winced.

"That's fine to hear. It gives me courage to go ahead and take chances with what's to come. But in the first place you admit that I've never tried to force myself on you, Sue. I've just gone on being fond of you for quite a time now, and never asking any return, never expecting anything? Is that true?"

"I think it is, Garry."

"Because I've taken it for granted that you belong to Jim Orchard."

She paused again. And he was glad of it. "No woman belongs to a man, until they're married."

"Not even then, really, Sue."

"Oh, yes. After a marriage . . . that means a giving without any reservation . . . a giving of the whole heart, Garry. But I don't think a man can understand."

"The point is this. You know that I've never made any pretenses about you. I've never asked any return. I've never had any hopes. Do you know why? Because I've always thought Jim was worthy of you."

"Go on," said a faint voice.

"Tonight it's different!"

He had ventured everything on the blunt statement; he half expected that she would order him to leave. But she made no murmur of a reply.

"I'm going to tell you why. It may seem like coming behind Jim's back. I'm sorry, but I don't see any other way out of it. You can be the judge. Sue, you know that he's going to ride Jerico tomorrow?"

"Of course."

"Which isn't a very peaceful thing for a man about to be married to do. Anyway, he's going to ride Jerico. But do you know what horse he's betting on?"

"No."

"On Long Tom!"

"But . . . I don't understand. He's riding Jerico!"

"He is."

"And surely no horse can beat Jerico. Everyone says no horse around here can beat Jerico."

"And maybe they're right."

"Then why should Jim bet on another horse?"

"Because he's riding Jerico."

"My brain is whirling, Garry. What does it mean?"

"You understand that everyone who bets against Jerico will get long odds . . . five dollars for one?"

"I've heard that."

"Doesn't Jim need money?"

"I think so."

"Then don't you see? He's betting on Long Tom because he's going to see to it that Jerico won't win the race."

"You mean he won't give Jerico an honest ride?"

"Just that."

He thought that the silence which followed would never end. Then: "It isn't possible."

"I've brought you the proof."

He placed the sack of money on her knees, lighted a match, and by that light spread out Jim Orchard's note for her to read. Of course she would know the handwriting. And she did know it. She suddenly sank back into the chair, and Garry Munn removed both money and paper.

"I'm sorry, Sue," he said, after a proper interval.

No answer.

"It isn't a pleasant thing to do, but you see the boat I'm in? I ask you, friend to friend, could I let you go on with a man like Jim Orchard . . . a man who would even cheat a horse?"

"I understand."

"You don't hold it against me?"

"No."

For some reason he would have preferred it if she had broken into tears. This thin whisper spoke of a heart withering with pain.

"Once more I'm sorry, Sue . . . and good night."

"Good night, Garry."

And that was all.

But Garry knew well enough that no matter how honestly Jim Orchard rode the next day, if Jerico lost the race Jim had lost Sue Hampton.

XI "In the Thick of the Race"

It should have been a very quiet and unimportant affair, that race of the next day, because there was a horse entered whose appearance seemed to remove all hope of competition. In spite of the fact that Jerico was entered, several of the cattlemen had decided to let their horses run, but that was merely because they were good sports, and not because they had any hope of beating the black stallion. Garrison had put in his Foxy; Oldham had entered Snorter; Lewis had Trix; and Noonan was backing Mame; to say nothing of Long Tom, the stranger. But it was felt that these horses were merely a background against which Jerico would appear the more glorious.

There were two elements, however, which gave the race a touch of the spectacular. In the first place one could never tell if the mustang would run quietly from the beginning to the end, There seemed every possibility that Jim Orchard had mastered the strange horse, but that remained to be seen. He was as apt as not to stop in the middle of the race and buck like a devil. The second exciting element was that a head as cool as that of Garry Munn had actually chosen to bet against Jerico.

A little money would not have made a great deal of difference, but Garry was apparently willing to stake his entire fortune. It became known that he had stretched his credit at the bank to the uttermost limit to supply the cash and, when that cash was gone, he was willing to give his note for any amount. At first the cattlemen held back, suspecting a trick. After they had gone down to see Jerico out for an exercise canter with Jim Orchard in the saddle, acting like a docile old family pet under the hand of the cowpuncher; and when, again, they had seen Tim Hogan trotting Long Tom at a shuffling, far-stepping gait, they decided that a temporary insanity had taken possession of the young rancher, and they began to cover his money in great chunks. Bets began to be registered in sums of a thousand up. Under the hammering of Garry Munn's fortune the odds dropped slowly from ten to one to two to one.

The cattlemen were as sure that Jerico would win as they were that they walked and breathed, but the confidence of Garry, backed by money, made them more conservative, as the hour for the race approached. Yet two to one was "fat" enough, when a man was betting on a sure thing; and Garry Munn kept pouring out his fortune in money and notes, until the very value of his ranch itself was almost represented in his outstanding promises.

In spite of that it was the happiest morning of Munn's life. He went to the race track as if he were stepping into a gold mine.

A full mile around, the track had been hastily constructed and roughly leveled. A flimsy fence on either side of the roadway directed the horses and riders. There was no pretense at a stand to hold the crowd. Both inside and outside the oval track the throng stood along the fences, or sat in their buckboards, or in the saddle to look over the heads of the early comers. But the noise of wagering was confined to one moving spot, and that was where Garry Munn walked. He paused near Sue Hampton. She stood close to the fence, both hands resting on the top of the post, as though she needed that support. When he spoke to her, she returned no answer. Indeed, her face was that of a sleepwalker. It troubled even the cold nerve of Garry Munn as he turned away.

"But, after all," he argued to himself, "Jim's as big a crook as I am . . . almost. What's to choose between us except that he's a beggar, and I'll be rich before tonight?"

His smile returned, and his voice rang as gaily as ever, shouting: "My last thousand, gentlemen. Who'll cover it? One to two on Long Tom. There he goes. How d'you like his looks? I'm betting on those long legs. Two jumps and he'll be around the track. Who takes me up?"

The ring of that familiar voice struck across to Jim Orchard as he stood beside the head of Jerico. Tom, the old Negro, was close by.

"You see them others?" he said, pointing to the cattle ponies which were being trotted up and down to make sure they would be warm and loose-muscled for the race. "Them boys thinks they's on hosses, but they ain't. There's only one hoss here, and that's Jerico. Oh, Jerry'll show 'em what's what today!"

Jim Orchard returned no answer. He had seen close to the fence the white face of Sue Hampton, and the ugly thought had come to him: how was it possible for him to win the woman he most loved and honored in the world by a piece of mean chicanery? How would it be possible for him to face her level eyes after this race?

He turned for consolation to Jerico himself. The great stallion kept always behind his new rider, as though he wanted protection from the crowd, which he hated. If a man passed too close to him, his ears flattened instantly, and his nostrils expanded and quivered; but, as soon as the shadow of fear had passed, he would touch the shoulder of Jim Orchard with his nose and then meet the glance of the rider with pricking ears. It was as though he said in mute language: "I understand. You look the same, but you're different."

Every time Jim Orchard saw that noble head his heart sank.

Long Tom came onto the track and was greeted by a murmur of mingled interest and amusement. They were not used to seeing such horses as this, these cattlemen. They could not understand how those gaunt muscles, flattening and sinking at shoulders and thighs, might mean elastic striding power and astonishing speed. To them he was more a freak than a horse for riding.

But Jim Orchard had seen the bay in action, and he understood. It comforted him to see Long Tom. No matter how he rode, what chance had Jerico against this speed machine?

Now they were summoning the horses to the post. He mounted Jerico and jogged slowly to the position. Opposite Sue Hampton, in spite of Jerico's plunging, as they approached the fence and the crowd, he cut far in and leaned to speak to her.

"Give Jerico luck, Sue!" he called.

She raised her white face and murmured an answer. It was not until he had passed on that he straightened out the meaning of the words.

"Oh, Jim, I'm praying for you!"

Why for him?

He had no time to get to the meaning of the riddle. He was coming past the main section of the crowd, where they were packed around the line which was both start and finish. What a roar went up to greet the black! Jerico crouched and quivered before it; then, as though he understood that this was a welcome and not a threat, he tossed up his head proudly and looked across the mass of faces.

The places were tossed for. Foxy got the inside; Snorter was number two; then came Jerico with an ample space on either side for fear of his heels; then Trix, then Mame, and last of all, on the outside, was Long Tom.

"There's your luck. There's the end of your freak horse, Garry!" shouted someone in the crowd.

The voice was hissed. It was thought a shameful thing to laugh at a man who had wagered the very home over his head on a horse race. Betting on such a scale was a thing to be almost reverenced.

Jerico behaved at the post as though he had raced a hundred times, standing perfectly still, with the steady voice of Jim Orchard to steady him. Jim looked across the line of horses and saw little Tim Hogan bouncing up and down, as Long Tom pranced awkwardly, eager to be away.

A voice came to him from a distance. It was Judge McCreavy giving the riders their instructions and telling them not to swing wide at the turns, for fear of cutting off horses behind them. He added other instructions. There was a pause; the crowd became deadly silent, and then the crack of the pistol.

The others were off their marks in a flash, but Jim Orchard purposely allowed Jerico to twist his head around at the last moment. When he twitched the head around and straightened Jerico to run after the pack, there was a groan from the crowd—the rest of the horses were lengths and lengths away! Jim Orchard, calmly, bitterly, cast his eye over that straining line of horseflesh ahead, with the riders bending low over their necks. Each was laboring to the full speed—each except Long Tom. The gaunt bay galloped clumsily, slowly, slowly, on the outside of the string—and yet, somehow, he floated along abreast of the best of the others, and a yell of wonder came from the crowd.

Jim Orchard understood and swallowed a smile. Tim Hogan must have been instructed to make this seem as much like a race as possible, He would race Long Tom along with the rest of the pack, until they straightened away around the last turn with the finish in sight.

Suddenly all things were blotted from the mind of Jim except the one miraculous fact that the horses, which raced ahead of him, were coming back to Jerico as if they were walking, and he running at full speed. Running, indeed!

The evening before, for a hundred yards or so, he had loosed Jerico down the open road and had thought the gait of the stallion breathtaking, but that was nothing compared to the way the black was running now. His body seemed to settle more and more to the ground as his stride lengthened. His ears were blown back flat against his neck. He poured himself over the track. Run? Jim Orchard had never dreamed that horseflesh could race with such smooth, machine-like strides, never a jolt up and down, but driving always straight ahead with dizzy speed.

There was no question that Jerico understood that this was a race, and that he loved it. As for the riders on the other horses, he did not appear to think of them. All that he knew was that here was an old custom of the free days, when the wild band of horses had raced for the water hole. And in the old days his place had always been in the front, leading the rest. He hated this rear running. Snorting the dust out of his nostrils, he sprang on at a harder pace.

Each furlong was marked by a white post and, as the signal for the first eighth flashed by him, Orchard found himself on the very heels of the pack. He drew back on the reins with an iron hand. There was not the slightest response. Jerico had the bit securely in his teeth.

Would the black devil run away and make him break that contract with Tim Hogan? He leaned desperately and called gently to Jerico, and suddenly the head was raised, the ears pricked, and from his running gait the stallion broke into a great rocking gallop. Yet even that pace held him up with the others.

In the distance Jim heard the crowd yelling its delight. That first burst of Jerico's speed meant everything to them. They would expect him to go on now, and leave the others trailing behind them.

He swung Jerico to the right and drove him straight into a pocket! Trix and Mame ran to left and right of him, and Long Tom and Foxy were in front. The crowd shouted: "Dirty work! They're boxing Jerico! Let him through!"

They called to each of the other riders in turn, berating them, but the wedge-like formation held, and Jerico galloped easily, easily in the rear.

XII "For You and for Me"

He could only pray that that pocket formation would hold. They were yelling advice to him to draw back and ride around the others, but he stuck doggedly in his place. To Jerico it was a manifest torment. Again and again he came up against the bit, and then tossed his head impatiently as he heard the steady voice of the master calling him back. Plainly the heart of the stallion was breaking. His place was in front, with the sweet, clean air in his nostrils, not back there breathing the dust of all these horses.

Jim Orchard heard a shrill, cracked cry above the rest. He looked across the track and saw old Tom standing beside the track with old Glory, terrified by the noise, trying to wedge his way to a place of safety between the legs of the Negro.

When they reached the turn at the first quarter, the pocket opened as the horses swung wide around the turn, and a clear way opened before Jerico. He would have sprung through like a greyhound, but the voice of the rider called him back. Then Jim Orchard heard a cry of dismay from the crowd and, looking ahead, he saw the reason for it.

Tim Hogan had apparently decided that he had waited long enough and now he was out to show the "rubes" what real speed in horseflesh meant.

Long Tom had thrust out his long neck, and now he was driving away from the rest. In vain they flogged and yelled at their mounts— Long Tom still drew away, and the crowd groaned.

For one thing Jim was glad; it was no longer necessary to disguise the speed of Jerico. There went Long Tom full tilt; he could loose the black and let him do his best with his sixty-pound handicap. The gap was still opened before him and now, touching the flank of the stallion with his open hand, he sent Jerico through it. It was a marvelous thing, that response from the black. Foxy and Trix drifted back to him and then disappeared behind his shoulders, their heads jerking foolishly up and down as they strove in vain to meet that terrific pace.

But Jerico had slipped through, and there was only Long Tom racing ahead. The three-furlong pole whipped past in a flash of white.

"Oh, Jerry, boy," said Orchard. "You ain't got a chance. If we had that skinny bay in the open country, we'd make a fool of him inside half an hour. Go it, boy, but there's not a chance."

He dropped his head and waited—waited for Jerico to slacken and fall back under that grilling strain. But there was no slackening. Instead there was a perceptible increase in the rush of wind that beat down the brim of his sombrero.

The groaning of the crowd had ceased, followed by a prolonged series of wild, cowboy yells. Jim looked up again and to his astonishment he saw that Long Tom had not increased his lead. Was Tim Hogan keeping the bay back?

No, Tim Hogan rode with his tiny body flattened along Tom's neck, giving his mount his head, and Long Tom was doing his noble best. But that best was not good enough!

The stunning truth came home to Jim Orchard. In spite of the cruel handicap of weight, in spite of the poor start, Jerico was slowly, surely, methodically cutting down the lead. Indeed, it might be that the very slowness of the start and the delay while he was held in the pocket were helping him now. It might be that early handicap and restraint had allowed the great stallion to come slowly into his pace, warming him for the greater test, sharpening his nerves and rousing his mighty heart.

All that heart, beyond a doubt, was going into the race for supremacy. By the quiver of the strong body beneath him, Jim knew that the stallion was giving his best. He spoke again, and slowly, unwillingly, tossing his head as though to ask for an explanation, Jerico answered the call and slackened his pace.

But Tim Hogan had been frightened. Jim saw the little fellow glance back and then draw his whip! Long Tom shot into a great lead at once, and there was the long, despairing murmur from the crowd.

The half-mile post gleamed and was gone behind them.

But, oddly enough, a picture came into the mind of Jim Orchard, of old Glory, the bull terrier, crowding close to the Negro for protection. Once that dog might have been among other dogs what Jerico was among other horses. One beating had robbed him of his spirit. One beating had made him what he was today, broken, skulking, a creature that made even the spirit of a man cringe with shame to see. And might not one beating do the same for Jerico? To be conquered by one of his kind, under the handicap which men had imposed on him, might well break his heart. And what would Jerico be then? A stumbling, worthless, shameful caricature of the horse he was today. Whose work? The work of Jim Orchard!

Still keeping the rein taut, he looked ahead. Long Tom had opened up a great gap, and the five-furlong post darted like a ghost behind them! Seeking for courage, Jim Orchard looked back where the crowd was packed at the finish. It was a white blur of faces, and somewhere among them was the face of the girl praying for him—for Jim Orchard. Underneath him Jerico was straining to be free from the restraint, praying, if ever a horse could pray, to follow Long Tom with every ounce of energy in his glorious body.

It was already hopeless to overtake Tim Hogan, surely. And, besides, there was the girl—but logic had no hold on Jim Orchard. Suddenly he had dashed the hat from his head with a yell that went pealing across the track and thrilled the crowd. It caught the ear of Tim Hogan and made him turn again in the saddle to look back. It caught Jerico as if with a new force and shot him forward at full speed.

Jim was riding for victory—victory for Jerico, and wretched defeat for himself. But the latter seemed nothing. His fortune—Sue Hampton—nothing mattered except that Jerico should have an honest chance to win his race. A weight fell from his heart as he made that resolve; and it seemed as though a literal weight fell from the back of Jerico, as lightly he sprang forward.

Tim Hogan had taken warning. His whip was out again, and he turned the last corner and drove the tall bay frantically into the home-stretch. Jim Orchard swung forward in the stirrups, throwing his weight across the withers, where weight least burdens a racing horse.

"Jerico," he whispered, "give all you've got. It may be enough. It's got to be enough. Go after 'em! Go after 'em.'"

It had seemed impossible for the stallion to gain another particle of speed, and yet there was a perceptible response now. He streaked around the turn. The three-quarters post gleamed and fled behind them, and the shout of the crowd at the finish crashed up the track and thundered in the ears of Orchard.

The bit was no longer in the teeth of Jerico. He had loosed his grip as though he felt that there could be no danger in the guidance of this rider. He had surrendered himself to the will of a master as though he knew that will would lift him on to overtake the flying bay.

The eager eye of Jim Orchard saw the distance between them diminish. Long Tom was still running nobly, but he was not ready for such a test as this. His strength was failing and Jerico, like a creature possessed with a devil, seemed to gain with every stride he made. Well did the rider know the secret of that strength! It was the strength which men use in lost causes and forlorn hopes; it was the generous last effort of the fighter.

Now he heard Tim Hogan cursing—a shrill voice that piped back at him, the words cut short and blown away by the wind of the mad gallop. And then the yelling of the crowd drowned all other sound.

One name on all those lips. It roared and beat into the very soul of Orchard. One name all those frantic hands were imploring: "Jerico! Jerico! Jerico!"

Tim Hogan glanced back for the third time, and Jim Orchard caught a glimpse of a white, convulsed face. Then the jockey whirled and was back at his work, lifting Long Tom ahead with savage slashes of the whip.

The seven-furlong post shot past; the finish lay straight ahead. Two breaths and the race would be over!

The cry of the mob became Orchard's cry in the ear of the straining stallion: "Jerico! Jerico!" Every time there was a quiver of the thin ears which flattened against the stallion's neck.

Now they were on the hip of Long Tom, and the tail, flying straight back with the wind of the gallop, was blowing beside Jim Orchard's stirrup.

"Jerico! Jerico!"

For every call there was an effort like the efforts which answered the whip of Tim Hogan! Orchard felt that his voice had become a power. It was pouring an electric energy out of his body, and out of his soul into the body and soul of his horse. It lifted him past the hip of Long Tom; it brought the black nose to the flank of the bay—the flank so gaunt and hollow with the strain of the gallop. It carried him to the saddle girth.

Too late, for the massed faces at the finish line were straight before them. "Jerico!"

Oh, great heart, what an answer! The scream of Tim Hogan and the sting of his whip brought no such response as this. Foam spattered the breast of Long Tom, and still he labored, still he winced under the whip, but his speed was slackening, his head was going up, up—the head of a beaten horse. Beaten he was in spirit, whether he won or lost.

Would he win? There was Judge McCreavy standing at the finish post with his arm extended, as though to point out to them that this was the end.

"Jerico!"

Past the girth and to the shoulder with one lunge.

"Jerico!"

And now only the snaky head of the bay is in the lead.

"Jerico!"

They are over the finish. The shout of the mob was a scream and a sob in one.

But who had conquered? There stood Long Tom, with dropped head, and here was Jerico, dancing beneath him, as he drew to a halt and then turned and faced the crowd with his glorious head raised. He waited like a gladiator for their judgment, and with what a voice they gave it, all in a chorus, thundering in waves around Jim Orchard.

"Jerico!"

Jerico had won! After that, all things grew hazy before the staring eyes of Jim Orchard. He was searching in that crowd for one face.

He saw Tim Hogan slowly dismounting. He saw Garry Munn standing like one who has been stunned. And then she came to him through the mob! For all their excitement, they gave way before her as though they knew it was her right.

Here was old Tom with the terrible head of Jerico in his fearless arms, weeping like a child.

Here was Sue Hampton holding up both her hands to him, with a face that opened heaven to Jim Orchard.

"Jerico's won," he said miserably, "but I've lost . . . everything!"

"But nothing matters . . . don't you see? . . . except. . . ."

She was sobbing, in her excitement, so that she could scarcely speak.

"Except what, Sue?"

"Except that Jerico has won, Jim . . . for you and for me!"

Acknowledgments

"The Ghost Wagon" was first published under the title "The Cure of Silver Cañon" by John Frederick in *Western Story Magazine* (1/15/21). Copyright © 1920 by Street & Smith Publications, Inc. Copyright © renewed 1948 by Dorothy Faust. Copyright © 1996 for restored material by Jane Faust Easton and Adriana Faust Bianchi. Acknowledgment is made to Condé Nast Publications, Inc., for their cooperation. Reprinted by arrangement with Golden West Literary Agency. All rights reserved.

"Rodeo Ranch" by Max Brand was first published in *Western Story Magazine* (9/1/23). Copyright © 1923 by Street & Smith Publications, Inc. Copyright © renewed 1951 by Dorothy Faust. Copyright © 1996 for restored material by Jane Faust Easton and Adriana Faust Bianchi. Acknowledgment is made to Condé Nast Publications, Inc., for their cooperation. Reprinted by arrangement with Golden West Literary Agency. All rights reserved.

"Slip Liddell" was first published under the title "Señor Coyote" by Max Brand in two installments in *Argosy* (6/18/38–6/25/38). Copyright © 1938 by Frank A. Munsey Company. Copyright © renewed 1966 by Jane Faust Easton, John Frederick Faust, and Judith Faust. Copyright © 1996 for restored material by Jane Faust Easton and Adriana Faust Bianchi. Reprinted by arrangement with Golden West Literary Agency. All rights reserved.

"A Matter of Honor" was first published under the title "Jerico's 'Garrison Finish'" by John Frederick in *Western Story Magazine* (5/21/21). Copy-

244